continued . . .

SWEET SURRENDER

"This story ran my heart through the wringer more than once."
—*CK2S Kwips and Kritiques*

"From page one, I was drawn into the story and literally could not stop reading until the last page." —*The Romance Studio*

"Maya Banks's story lines are always full of situations that captivate readers, but it's the emotional pull you experience which brings the story to life." —*Romance Junkies*

FOR HER PLEASURE

"[It] is the ultimate in pleasurable reading. Enticing, enchanting and sinfully sensual, I couldn't have asked for a better anthology."
—*Joyfully Reviewed*

"Full of emotional situations, lovable characters and kick-butt story lines that will leave you desperate for more . . . For readers who like spicy romances with a suspenseful element—it's definitely a must-read!" —*Romance Junkies*

"Totally intoxicating, *For Her Pleasure* is one of those reads you won't be forgetting anytime soon." —*The Road to Romance*

COLTERS' GIFT

MAYA BANKS

BERKLEY BOOKS, NEW YORK

THE BERKLEY PUBLISHING GROUP
Published by the Penguin Group
Penguin Group (USA) LLC
375 Hudson Street, New York, New York 10014

USA • Canada • UK • Ireland • Australia • New Zealand • India • South Africa • China

penguin.com

A Penguin Random House Company

This book is an original publication of The Berkley Publishing Group.

Library of Congress Cataloging-in-Publication Data

Banks, Maya.
Colters' gift / Maya Banks.—Berkley trade paperback edition.
pages cm
ISBN 978-0-425-25603-9 (pbk.)
1. Abused women—Fiction.   2. Triangles (Interpersonal relations)—Fiction.
3. Bodyguards—Fiction.   4. Colorado—Fiction.   I. Title.
PS3602.A643C65 2013
813'.6—dc23   2013029910

PUBLISHING HISTORY
Berkley trade paperback edition / November 2013

PRINTED IN THE UNITED STATES OF AMERICA

10 9 8 7 6 5 4 3 2 1

Cover art photo composition by S. Miroque. Cover photos of couple © Edw/Shutterstock;
guy © CURAphotography/Shutterstock; Colorado Mountains © Sharon Day/Shutterstock.
Cover design by Rita Frangie.

For every reader who loved and supported Colters' Woman
and didn't want their story to end there.
This final installment in the Colters' Legacy series is for you,
and I hope you enjoy one last visit with the Colter family.
Love always, Maya xoxo

COLTERS'
GIFT

CHAPTER 1

❧

LAUREN Wilder descended the steps from her second-story apartment above the Main Street Medical Clinic and breathed in the crisp spring mountain air.

The wind kicked up and a few tendrils of hair escaped the hastily done ponytail. She pulled her light sweater tighter around her and looked for traffic before crossing the street to the diner where she worked.

Not that there was ever much traffic in Clyde, and certainly not this early in the morning, but later, the sleepy town would come alive and a host of regulars would filter into the diner for their morning coffee, breakfast and, more importantly, the day's gossip.

The bell jangled when she entered the front door. It was a sound she never heard when the small diner was filled with customers, but in the morning, it seemed jarringly loud and it always startled the quiet peace that blanketed the tiny mountain town.

Her town.

It had taken her months to settle in and truly feel as though she belonged here. It was a far cry from the hustle and bustle of New York City, and a year ago, if someone had told her that she'd end up taking refuge here, in a place that still hadn't caught up to the rest of the world, she would have laughed and said never.

She was, or at least she had been, a total city girl. She loved the conveniences of living in one of the world's largest cities. Everything was at her fingertips. A walk, or a subway ride away. Sometimes a cab ride if she was in a hurry.

Max, her older brother, had found his way to Clyde when he'd fallen in love with Callie. Her family had lived here for decades. They were as much a part of this small town as the fixtures and buildings themselves.

Lauren had always assumed she'd stay in the city. Settle down with a businessman who shared the same interests as she. Have two children, a boy and a girl, and complete the American dream.

The problem with that fantasy was that she'd chosen the wrong man, and now she could never return to her old life. She didn't *want* to return to her old life.

She'd found more than just sanctuary in Clyde. She'd found the family she'd always longed for in the Colters. She understood well why Max had been willing to give up his wanderlust and settle in these mountains, surrounded by the family who'd pulled him—and Lauren—into their arms.

For the first time in months, she was starting to regain some of her old confidence. More importantly, she was learning to forgive herself for the choices she'd made. She could now go to sleep at night without cringing over her naïveté. Or at least most nights.

The first step for her had been moving out of Max and Callie's home and into her own apartment in town. It hadn't been easy to convince her protective older brother—or the Colters for that matter—that she was ready to be out on her own. They'd grown used to having her close and watching over her, and while she adored them for their unconditional love and protection, she'd been thrilled to take that step.

She had a place of her own, and she had a job. So it wasn't the career she'd planned, nor was it a job worthy of her college degree, but it was a job that paid well. She made enough to get by on, and she wasn't depending on her brother's fortune to support her.

She went into the kitchen, where she found Clark warming up the fryers and the grill and Evie brewing the coffee. She reached for one of the aprons and quickly tied it around her waist.

After smiling and offering her good morning to Clark and Evie, she headed out front to make sure the tables were in order and that the sugar and spice containers were filled.

It was a routine she followed daily. Same schedule. Same time. In her previous life, she would have been bored and ready to go stir-crazy. Now she found the routine predictable and soothing.

It was safe.

There was no constant fear that she'd do or say the wrong thing. No worrying endlessly over what kind of mood Joel was in. No blaming herself when he took his temper out on her.

She hadn't realized just how far she'd been beaten down by the man she was involved with, until she'd been away for months and was able to objectively look back at just how stupid she'd been.

She sucked in a deep breath and chastised herself for going back. She couldn't undo the past, but she could sure as hell make certain she didn't make the same mistakes again.

New life. New chance. New opportunity to be a different person. Or at least to find the person she'd been before she'd allowed Joel to change her.

At six A.M. sharp, she flipped the switch to the neon Open sign and made sure she had an order pad and a pen in her apron pocket.

She and Evie worked the morning shift with Clark manning the grill. The diner closed at two because Dillon Colter's pub opened at lunch and the pub usually attracted the evening crowd.

Lauren liked the hours because it left her with the entire afternoon off, and her workday was behind her. She often spent the afternoons with Callie and Max or when they were gone, she'd visit with Holly and Lily Colter.

They tended to stop in to visit Lauren more often now that she'd moved into town. Lauren knew they still worried about her and that none of them had been thrilled with the idea of her moving out on her own so soon.

Except Holly.

Of all of them, Holly understood Lauren the best, and Lauren loved the older woman for her willingness to give Lauren room to breathe.

She needed to regain her confidence and reassert herself. Make her own decisions and live her own life. She may not be ready to take on the entire world yet, but she could safely say she was ready to take on the town of Clyde.

She smiled when the bell jangled, signaling the first customer of the day. She turned, already having a good idea of who it would be, and she was right.

Seth Colter, the sheriff, strode into the diner and took his usual seat by the window.

"Morning, Seth," she said as she approached his table.

Seth looked up, giving her a warm smile that made her insides squeeze. All of the Colters had been so good to her.

"Morning, Lauren. Everything okay today?"

It was the same question he asked her everyday.

"Yep. How is Lily doing? You want your usual?"

Seth's entire face softened at the mention of his wife.

"She's doing great. More tired than usual, but we're taking good care of her. And yeah, my usual will be great. Keep the coffee coming if you don't mind. Had a late call last night and I'm operating on three hours' sleep."

Lauren winced. "Ouch. Anything major?"

Seth laughed. "As major as it ever gets here. Lost hiker. His girlfriend got worried when he didn't show up for dinner. Turns out he was over in the next town with another woman."

Lauren shook her head and then turned in the direction of the kitchen. "I'll be right back with your coffee."

She grabbed the freshly brewed pot of coffee and poured a cup, adding two sugars and one cream. She quickly scribbled Seth's order, tore off the paper and then slid it across the divider to Clark.

Then she went back to Seth's table with his cup of coffee.

"You're a goddess," Seth said, grabbing for the cup before it left her hand. "Hey, before I forget, I'm supposed to tell you that Callie is coming over to visit Lily this afternoon and Lily wanted me to tell you that you should stop over after your shift."

"Thanks. I just might do that," Lauren said.

"How are you liking the new place?" Seth asked, peering at her intently over his coffee. "You having any problems?"

She smiled at the concern in his eyes. It was nice to have people who cared about her.

"The place is great. Just perfect for me. It's cozy and it's right here in town. I know Max worries, but—"

"We *all* worry," Seth corrected gently.

"Yes, I know, but you shouldn't. I'm fine. The apartment is great. I love the job. It's nice to be around people again without . . ."

She trailed off, embarrassed by where she'd nearly gone with the conversation.

"Without?" Seth prompted.

"Worrying that they'll hurt me," she said softly.

Seth reached over and squeezed her hand. "Now that you don't have to worry about here. You have me and Max plus the dads and

Dillon and Michael to watch out for you. Not to mention Callie,
Lily and my mother, and between you and me, someone would be
a damn fool to ever cross my mother. She's pretty scary when it
comes to protecting her babies, even if her babies are grown damn
men and women."

Lauren chuckled. "She's the best."

Seth nodded. "That she is. She's currently on a tear about the
arrival of her first grandchild. Dillon, Michael and I just try to stay
out of her way."

"Thank you, Seth," she said solemnly, when he lifted his hand
away. "I appreciate your kindness more than you know. I don't
know what I would have done without all of you and especially
your mom."

His expression was serious. "You're family now, Lauren. We
take family very serious. You can come to us for anything, anytime.
We want you to be happy here."

She raised her head when another customer came in. "Let me
go get this customer. Your food should be up in just a sec and I'll
get it out to you."

Seth smiled and nodded and then called out a greeting to the
person who'd walked in. Lauren was still learning the people of the
town, but she prided herself on knowing most of their faces, even
if she hadn't put names to everyone yet.

Small-town life wasn't ever anything that had appealed to her
in the past, but she'd grown to love Clyde and all its inhabitants.
They'd embraced her. Made her feel welcome. She'd only been here
since just before Christmas and already it was like she'd lived here
all her life.

She sighed a little as she walked away from Seth and warmly
greeted the man at the next table. Seth was a good man. As were
both his brothers Dillon and Michael.

The Colters were . . . Well, they were different. There were no two ways about it. Seth's parents, or "the dads" as he called them, were not that standard set of parental figures. Holly Colter was married to three brothers and in turn their three sons were married to one woman. Lily.

Callie, the baby of the bunch, was the only one who had what could be deemed a traditional relationship. She was married to Lauren's brother, Max.

The hell of it was that Lauren envied all three women with all her heart. Holly, Lily and Callie. Maybe even especially Holly and Lily.

Each woman had three men completely and utterly devoted to their happiness and well-being. They loved Holly and Lily, and their devotion ran so deep that sometimes it hurt Lauren to look at them.

What would it be like to be cherished and adored by three men? To have that kind of relationship where she would be the heart and foundation, the very core of it all. She couldn't even fathom being so loved, but she wanted it with all her heart.

Old feelings of insecurity crept to the surface. And with it, accompanying shame and humiliation. She'd been so desperate to find love that she'd found herself in a relationship she never should have been involved in. Worse, she'd remained in it when it had been clear that she didn't belong.

She had only herself to blame for remaining. She couldn't be blamed for his actions, but she sure as hell could take responsibility for not standing up for herself sooner.

Shaking off the cloud of sadness that hovered over her, she busied herself with the rapidly filling diner. For the next few hours, she barely had time to breathe, much less dwell on her past mistakes.

Besides, she was beyond that now. The future was what she made it. Here in this tiny Colorado mountain town, she'd found her niche. A new life. A brand new beginning where the mistakes of the past wouldn't continue to haunt her.

CHAPTER 2

NEW YORK CITY

"WE'VE been at this for months and still don't have a single goddamn lead," Liam Prescott bit out.

His partner, Noah Sullivan, grimaced. "You aren't telling me anything I don't know. But here's the thing. We didn't imagine those bruises on Lauren. And we damn sure didn't imagine how terrified and ashamed she was. Still gets my gut all into a knot every time I think of how she looked the first day we met her."

Liam's lips drew back into a snarl as he pulled the SUV into a tight parking spot outside of a brownstone divided into apartments. He sat for a long moment, his big hands curled around the steering wheel as he stared up at the number above the archway to the front door of the building.

"This better turn up something," he said. "We've exhausted all our options. It's like this guy doesn't exist."

Noah got out and Liam followed. They walked up the steps and

Noah buzzed the apartment. They waited a long moment and Noah buzzed again.

"Doesn't look like she's home," Liam muttered.

Noah blew out his breath. "Okay, let's go wait in the car. We'll hang out for a while and see if she shows."

The men retreated, climbing back into the SUV. Noah propped his elbow against the window and frowned. Then he glanced in Liam's direction.

"Do you think she was straight with us? With her brother?"

Liam's brow creased and he turned, angling his body so he leaned against the driver's side door. "You think she lied? You saw her, Noah. She sure as hell didn't make that shit up."

Noah held up his hand. "Don't get all pissed off. I know she didn't lie about what the bastard did to her."

"Then what the hell do you think she lied about?"

Noah hesitated. "I'm not sure, but I don't think we got the full story. This guy is a ghost. No one knows a damn thing about him. No prints in the system, and I doubt Lauren was the first woman he beat up. Assholes like him usually have a few run-ins with the law."

"You think she's protecting him?" Liam asked incredulously.

There was a hint of anger to his voice and his scowl deepened.

"No," Noah said quietly. "I think she's scared out of her mind."

Liam's expression darkened even further and he gripped the steering wheel until his knuckles went white. "I want that bastard."

Noah nodded because he felt the same way. When they'd taken the job from Max Wilder, they'd expected a stereotypical rich-girl scenario. An overprotective brother who wanted a babysitter for the sister he didn't have time for.

Nothing could have been further from the truth.

Lauren Wilder was a shy, sweet woman who'd been badly abused by a man she'd trusted. From the moment Noah had laid eyes on her, he'd ached to hold her. To wipe away all the hurt and show her that all men weren't abusive assholes.

Liam had reacted even more strongly than Noah had. He'd taken one look at Lauren and had been so furious that he'd ended up scaring the holy hell out of her.

The two men had worked together for a hell of a long time. They'd seen and done it all. But they'd never fallen for the same woman, and Noah still wasn't sure what the hell they were supposed to do about it.

For now, they existed in denial, and they only discussed her in a professional context. Anytime it started to get personal, Liam clammed up and got that look in his eyes that meant the subject was closed.

Noah sighed. "I want him too, but I'm starting to think we're barking up the wrong tree."

Liam's eyes narrowed. "What the hell does that mean?"

Suddenly Noah straightened, his gaze fixed on a tall blond woman walking down the sidewalk.

"I think that's her," he said.

Liam's hand went to the door handle, but he waited, tense and silent.

Both men watched as she turned up the walkway to the apartment. A moment later, she took her keys out and unlocked the door.

"Let's go," Noah said.

He and Liam got out of the car and hurried up the walkway just as the woman swung open the door and stepped inside the foyer.

"Ms. Jennings?" Noah called.

The woman whirled around, fear immediate in her eyes.

Noah held out a placating hand. "My apologies for startling you. My name is Noah Sullivan and this is my partner, Liam Prescott. I was hoping for a moment of your time. We're looking for someone, and it's very important that we find him. We'd just like to ask you a few questions if that's all right."

She stared suspiciously at them, her hand still gripping the edge of the door.

"Are you cops?"

Noah shook his head. "No, ma'am. We're not cops. I guess you could say we're investigators of sorts."

"Like a P.I.? I always thought those weren't real. Just stuff you see on cop shows and in the movies."

"We're not private investigators," Liam said gruffly. "We were employed to keep a woman safe from the jerk who beat on her. We want to find this asshole so we can put him away. We need your help to do that."

She blinked at Liam's bluntness but her stance relaxed and she was clearly conflicted about whether to allow them into her building. Finally she took a step back, opening the door wider.

"Come in," she murmured. "My name is Susan, but my friends call me Suki. Long story, but you can call me Suki."

Noah could tell the woman was as nervous as a cat backed into an alley. He didn't want to frighten her, but he had Liam with him and Liam was . . . Well, he was Liam. Blunt. Overwhelming. And growly.

Especially when it came to Lauren.

Once they walked up to her second floor apartment and were seated in the living room, Noah pulled out a photo of Lauren and slid it across the coffee table toward Suki.

"Can you tell me if you've ever seen this woman?"

Suki went completely still. Noah wasn't even sure she was breathing. Her hands shook as she reached for the photo and fear crowded her eyes.

Then she turned with a fake, too-bright smile and said, "No, sorry I haven't. Did something happen to her? Is she . . . dead?"

The last was asked fearfully and Liam frowned, leaning forward.

"Now why would you assume she's dead or that something's happened to her?"

Panic flared on her face. "I just assumed. I mean something had to have happened to her if you're looking for her, right?"

"We aren't looking for her," Noah said calmly. "We just asked if you've ever seen her."

Suki shook her head. "No. Sorry. Don't know her."

"Why are you lying?" Liam asked bluntly.

The woman vibrated with fear. Most people would have been pissed at blatantly being called a liar. Not this woman. She looked like she was going to be ill.

"Let's try another question," Noah said. "Do you know who this woman was seeing? Know his name? What he looks like?"

"I wish I could help you," she croaked. "But he'd kill me."

Liam and Noah exchanged quick glances. Noah's pulse sped up and he leaned forward, scooting to the edge of his seat in anticipation. Finally, they were getting somewhere.

"Who, Suki? Who would kill you?"

When she looked up, tears shone in her eyes. "He hurt her. We all knew it. He always kept her on a very short leash. He told her how to dress, how to act, where to be and if she didn't fall into step accordingly, she always wore bruises the next day."

A low growl emanated from Liam's throat. Noah shot him a warning look. The last thing they needed was to terrify Suki further and have her shut down and refuse to talk.

"Who did this to her?" Noah asked softly. "I need your help, Suki. I want to nail his ass to the wall and make damn sure he never does this to another woman."

"Just give us his name," Liam urged. "You don't have to tell us anything else. Just give us enough to find him."

She laughed, a raw, hysterical sound that was abrasive to Noah's ears.

"You can't stop him. He has cops on his payroll. He won't ever be punished."

"There are other ways of getting justice that don't necessarily involve cops," Liam bit out.

At that she went quiet and stared intently back at Liam. For a long moment she looked between the two men as if grappling with her decision to confide in them.

Finally she drew in a deep breath. "His name is Joel Knight. It's all I'll say, and I won't testify. I won't give a statement. I'll deny ever seeing you, talking to you or even that I know who the hell you are."

Liam's eyes narrowed to slits. "Joel Knight? Are you sure?"

Noah shook his head. He'd known that Lauren was holding out on them. What he hadn't realized was that she'd blatantly lied. She'd made up some other name of some fictitious guy and they'd spent the last four months wasting their fucking time searching out non-existent leads.

"Of course I'm sure," Suki said, an edge to her voice. "I'm one of his girls."

Noah lifted an eyebrow. "What does that mean exactly?"

She pressed her lips together. "It's time for you to go. I have an appointment in an hour and I have to get ready. I'd like you to leave. I've said all I'm going to say."

Liam opened his mouth to argue, but she'd already risen, her agitation evident as she stalked to the door to open it. Her hand gripped the edge of the door, and she was pale as they walked past. She looked like she was going to be ill at any moment.

As soon as they were over the threshold, the door slammed behind them. Noah winced. "Damn, you get the idea we aren't welcome any longer?"

Liam made a noise that sounded like a snort, and the two men returned to the parked SUV.

It was quiet in the vehicle as Liam drove away. Noah wasn't

entirely certain where he was going. He hadn't gone back in the direction of their offices.

After a moment, Noah pulled out his cell and started to put in a call to his buddy who worked for the NYPD. He hesitated, Suki's words floating back to his mind. Then he cursed and put the phone back.

She was making him paranoid. For all he knew she was talking out her ass.

"Problem?" Liam asked.

"I was going to call Johnny. See what he could dig up on this Joel Knight dude."

"And? Why didn't you?"

Noah grimaced, already feeling a little stupid. "Because Suki said he had cops on his payroll."

He thought Liam would tell him what an idiot he was being. Out of the hundreds of cops in the city, what were the odds that it would involve their contact?

But Liam merely nodded. "Better to be safe. We can do some digging on our own, but I'd rather go straight to the source."

Noah's brows drew together. Liam pulled into a parking place that was half a block down from a pub they frequented.

"What do you mean by that?" Noah asked.

"I'll tell you over a drink," Liam said.

If Liam was actually going to hit a pub so they could sit and talk, this had to be serious. Liam was more of an act-now-think-later kind of guy. Elaborate planning wasn't one of his stronger points. That was Noah's job. Noah thought out issues. Liam carried out the plan. It was a combination that had worked well for them over the years.

They ambled in and instead of sitting at the bar, they took a seat at one of the tables in the far corner, and Liam held up two fingers to the waitress.

Nodding, she offered a hello in greeting and then hurried off to get their order. They were here regularly enough that the staff was well acquainted with their preferences.

"So what's going on in that head of yours?" Noah pressed.

"I think we should go see Lauren," Liam said in a low voice.

Noah frowned. "That's not what we were hired to do."

"Fuck what we were hired for. We can't do the job unless we have all the information from Lauren. And we don't have it. We've been chasing our tails because Lauren was too afraid to tell us or her brother the truth about who abused her. If we confront her, we're less likely to get the brush-off. If we call her up, she's not going to just offer us this information over the phone."

Noah sighed because . . . shit. This was going to open a whole damn can of worms.

"You know this isn't a good idea," Noah said bluntly. "We both obviously have feelings for her. We can't do our job if we're too busy fighting over who gets the girl."

The waitress appeared, and Liam clammed up while she plopped the cold bottles down on the table. Once she left, Liam took a sip before carefully setting it back down. Noah waited. There was definitely something on Liam's mind.

Liam stared directly at Noah, his gaze intent, jaw tight. "You ever wonder why I just let Lauren go so easily?"

Noah's brow crinkled. "Max came to get her and brought her home with him. What could you have possibly done?"

Liam simmered with impatience. "Come on, Noah. Are you telling me you didn't care when she left? That it didn't bother you that we had to trust in the fact that her brother could keep her safe? That you didn't want to tell him he was making a huge fucking mistake so that we could keep her close to us at all times so we'd make sure no one ever hurt her again? Quit pretending you don't care. This is me you're talking to. I know better."

"So what?" Noah snapped. "What the fuck was I supposed to do? I couldn't damn well make a move on her. Not after that shit-head did what he did to her. We were strangers to her, and we scared her shitless."

"It brings me back to my original question."

"No, I don't damn well know why you let her go so easily," Noah said impatiently. "Do enlighten me."

"The few times we got her to actually talk to us, she spoke about the family her brother married into. That her sister-in-law had three fathers—all married to the same woman—and that her brothers were also hooked up with the same woman."

Noah nodded. "Yeah, I remember it. Sounded a little bizarre, but whatever."

Liam's eyes gleamed. "I wanted her to go back with Max because I wanted her to be around that kind of relationship. See how it worked. Become comfortable with it. Maybe even be able to view it as not so unorthodox."

Realization crept into Noah's mind, grabbed hold and shook him until he was staring at Liam in astonishment.

"You aren't saying what I think you're saying are you?"

Liam cocked one eyebrow.

"At what point were you going to ask *me* how I felt about it?" Noah demanded.

"Are you saying you're against it? Are you saying you'll back off if I tell you I want Lauren?"

Anger nipped at Noah's heel. It prickled his nape until he was gripping his beer bottle so tight, he feared it would break.

"Think about it, Noah," Liam said softly. "Think real hard about it. We'll get on a plane and go talk to Lauren about the guy who beat her up. After you see her again, you tell me what you want to do. Because I'm not backing off. I'm going to wait for as long as it takes, but when she's ready, I'm going to be there."

CHAPTER 3

LAUREN finished tidying the tiny living room of her efficiency apartment and stared around in satisfaction. It was small, but it was filled with furniture and knickknacks, and was decorated to look homey and cozy.

Max had been so helpful in her getting back on her feet, but she owed the most to Holly, Lily and Callie. The three women had dragged her shopping and they'd spent a tireless amount of time making sure Lauren's apartment was one she was comfortable and happy in.

It was her day off from the diner, and while she had standing invitations to drop in on her brother and sister-in-law or any of the Colters, today she just wanted a quiet day in her apartment reading.

Later she'd take a walk down Main Street and do some window-shopping. It amused her that window-shopping in Clyde consisted of looking into the one women's boutique that sold everything from lingerie to accessories and everything in between.

There was a small, used bookstore at the end, and she always looked forward to scanning the new stock to see what struck her fancy. Callie had been after her to buy an e-reader so she could just download books from the online retailers without ever leaving her house, but there was something about the trip to the bookstore and returning home with a bag of books she couldn't wait to dig into.

And there was the simple fact that she couldn't afford the e-reader right now. It had taken every penny to move in and buy what was needed for the apartment. If she splurged and bought the reading device, she'd be uncontrollable with buying e-books.

For now, she'd have to stick with gently used and savor every book. Besides, she couldn't trade in a digital book when she was finished.

She perused her bookshelf and finally selected the newest Jaci Burton book she'd purchased. Just as she settled down to indulge, there was a knock at her door

Frowning, she pushed herself up from the couch and went to the front door. It was probably one of the Colter women. It could even be Max, but he was usually better about calling to let her know he was stopping by, whereas the Colter women—especially Holly—just dropped by whenever they got the urge.

But when she opened the door and saw who was standing there, her jaw went completely slack as she gaped at Noah Sullivan and Liam Prescott.

They didn't belong here. They represented a part of her past she wanted to forget. They were a world away, in a city she'd fled.

"Lauren," Noah acknowledged with a tight nod. "You're looking good."

"You look great," Liam amended softly.

She still couldn't find her tongue. What were they doing here?

"Can we come in?" Noah asked. "We need to talk to you."

"A-about w-what?"

She clutched the door tighter and pulled it so it narrowed the gap.

Liam frowned. "Lauren, we aren't going to hurt you. We just need to talk to you. It's important."

Her pulse was racing fast enough to make her light-headed. She knew Noah and Liam posed no danger to her. Or at least she thought she knew. It wasn't them she feared as much as why they were here.

"Open the door, Lauren," Noah said in a quiet tone.

Realizing how much attention they were likely attracting, she finally opened the door and let them walk into the living room.

If it had seemed small to her before, now it was tiny with the two big men filling it.

She had a love seat and an armchair, and she quickly took the armchair so the two men would be left with the love seat.

Perched on the edge, she waited while they made themselves comfortable. Or at least as much as they could, trying to fit their large frames on her small piece of furniture.

She balled up her fingers together and stuck her hands between her knees to prevent them from shaking. Their presence unnerved her for too many reasons to list.

And yet she drank in the sight of them, unable to tear her gaze from the two men who'd once been hired to protect her.

They were the complete antithesis of Joel, and maybe that was why she'd allowed herself to relax around them and trust them. In the beginning she'd thrown up every barrier she could, anything to prevent them from getting close.

But they'd broken every wall she'd placed between them. They'd bullied her mercilessly, making sure she ate, that she took care of herself. They couldn't possibly know just how much she'd softened toward them, because she'd been too intent on shutting them out and treating them indifferently.

When Max had arrived at her apartment, determined to take

her home with him and Callie, part of her was hugely relieved while the other part of her was reluctant to let go of the two men she'd come to rely on.

Having them near her just made her feel safe in a world where she was anything but. If they knew what she'd done and all she'd kept from them, they'd be pissed as hell.

She'd made some horrifically stupid choices. She could admit that now. But at the time, she'd been a scared-out-of-her-mind woman who desperately wanted a way out of her situation. She hadn't been thinking straight. But who could blame her?

She blamed herself enough without anyone else knowing the extent of her stupidity.

"Lauren?"

She looked up quickly at the sound of Liam's voice. She realized that one or both men had been talking to her, and she had no idea what they'd been saying.

"I'm sorry," she blurted. "You should have called. You caught me completely off guard."

Noah's eyes narrowed. "And would you have been here if we'd called? Or would you have been conveniently somewhere else?"

Heat scorched her cheeks. He couldn't possibly know that's what she would have done. And yet he'd called her out on it as if he'd reached right into her head and plucked out her thoughts. Was she so easily read?

Liam cleared his throat. "We're here to discuss Joel Knight."

The blood rushed from her face. Her stomach knotted into a tight ball. She swayed precariously in her seat before making a grab for the arms with each hand so she didn't humiliate herself.

"I want you to leave," she blurted out.

Liam leaned forward, those vivid blue eyes pinning her in place. His hair hung to his shoulders, in varying lengths, as if he didn't worry too much over how it was cut. It had a slight curl, making it look unruly. The ends flipped up this way and that. She could remember her fingers itching to reach out and smooth it.

It suddenly occurred to her why she'd eventually grown to trust these two men. Why she'd relaxed her guard toward the end of their business relationship.

They were nothing like Joel, and while she'd always recognized this, it really hit home with her now.

Joel was polished. Never a hair out of place. Expensive clothing. Only the best suits. A tie. Perfectly shined shoes. Fake tan. He never walked out of his home unless he looked his best. He'd never be caught dead with men like Liam and Noah.

Liam and Noah were . . . . Well, they didn't give a shit. With them it was either take it or leave it, and your loss if you left it.

They both had dark hair, though Liam's was more of a true, midnight black and Noah's was such a dark brown that it was nearly black. Alone one might think his hair was black, but standing next to Liam, it was obvious that Noah's hair was lighter.

Liam's eyes were a shock of blue. Startling and vibrant. He was a man that drew stares from women and men alike. Noah's eyes were dark, like Lauren's own, only he had flecks of green and gold mixed in with the brown. In the right light, the different colors shone, lightening his eyes and making them mesmerizing to look at.

Both sported tattoos. Noah had what looked to be a Japanese symbol on his right arm and then a bracelet tattoo on his right wrist. Liam had intricately, colorfully rendered sleeves on both arms. Lauren had often stared when he wasn't looking, studying the designs. There was so much detail that she couldn't imagine how long it had taken the artist to complete the tattoos or how patient Liam had to have been through the process.

Separately, the men were forces to be reckoned with. But together? Complete badasses. No one in their right mind would cross them.

Except, she had. Crossed them. Or at least lied to them. And now they *knew* she'd lied.

Liam was still staring holes through her. She wanted to crawl underneath her chair and stay there until they were gone. Until she forgot why they'd come. She just wanted to put it all behind her. Them, Joel, everything.

"We're not going anywhere," Liam said grimly. "You've got a hell of a lot of explaining to do."

She didn't want to be the weak, pathetic woman she'd been such a short time ago. But them being here made her want to run for cover. She wanted to barricade herself in her bedroom and shut the world out.

But isn't that what she'd done for so very long? She'd existed in a haze of denial, too stupid, too cowardly to face the truth, and to act.

"Damn it, Lauren, we're not going to hurt you," Noah said. "Stop looking at us like we're that bastard who abused you."

She swallowed and then lowered her head to put her hands over her face.

It was automatic to flinch away when she felt the hand on her shoulder. She heard a soft curse, but the hand was quickly removed.

"Lauren, look at me."

It was Liam, his voice as soft and warm as the first rays of spring sunshine. She was compelled to do as he said, even before she realized she had raised her head.

He took a deep breath, letting it blow out long and slow. It was a sigh that expressed a lot. Exasperation. Pity. She *hated* the pity. People who were truly victims deserved pity and kindness. She was someone who'd allowed bad things to happen to her because she was too much of a coward—and an idiot—to get herself out of it. And on top of it all, she'd lied to her brother, the one person who loved her in this world. She'd lied to the Colters, not overtly. She'd never voiced the lie, but it had been one of omission, which made it just as bad.

And she'd lied to the two men who'd vowed to protect her. She hadn't given them the information they'd needed in order to do their job, because she'd been afraid of what might happen to them.

None of the reasons made sense now. She was honest enough with herself to admit that. She hadn't known what she was doing or saying all those months ago. She'd just reacted.

Now those lies were coming back to haunt her. Just when she'd finally made peace with the choices she'd made.

"We know about Joel Knight," Liam said quietly. "The question is why didn't you tell us about him? Why weren't you honest about who hurt you? Were you protecting him?"

There was a note of fury that accompanied his last question, one she was forced to respond to.

"No!" she said fiercely. "I wasn't protecting him. I *hate* him."

"Then why?" Noah demanded. "Why send us on a wild-goose chase trying to find a man who didn't exist? Do you have any idea how much time we've wasted looking for the son of a bitch who beat you up? We had the local police involved. We pulled so many goddamn strings trying to find this man so he could be arrested, so he'd never hurt another woman. And the entire time, we were looking for a ghost."

She closed her eyes. "I can understand why you're angry. I'm sorry I wasted your time."

Her eyes popped open again when Liam let out an expletive that singed her ears.

"You have no idea why we're angry," Liam snapped.

Her hands were shaking again. Hell, her knees were too. Suddenly both men were close. Way too close. They'd vacated the love seat and were on either side of her armchair. Big and hulking. She should be terrified, but she'd never been afraid of them. They'd always made her feel safe, from the moment they'd accompanied Max to the apartment he'd moved her to.

"Ask us why we're angry, Lauren," Liam continued. "If you want the truth, then ask us."

"W-why are you angry?" she stammered out.

"Because we care about what happens to you," Noah said. "And while we were off looking for the wrong guy, Joel Knight could have gotten to you. He could have hurt you and we would have never seen it coming. We're pissed because we were put in a position where we couldn't do our job. And our job is to make sure nothing happens to you."

Liam shook his head impatiently. "You aren't just a damn job to us, Lauren. Use your head. You have to see that we're attracted to you. That it makes us fucking insane knowing what this asshole did to you and when we think of what could have happened because you didn't tell us the truth, it makes me crazy. What if he'd come after you? Did you ever think about that?"

She glanced rapidly between the two men, her mind in such turmoil that she couldn't even comprehend the meaning of what Liam had just blasted her with.

It was crazy. All of it. But even crazier? She'd thought that she was alone in her fascination with these two men. She'd been bewildered by the fact that she could even look at Noah and Liam and entertain the thoughts she'd had.

He was wrong. She hadn't seen it. She hadn't even entertained the notion that they were attracted to her. All she'd seen in their eyes was pity and rage, two things she would have thought they would feel for any woman in her situation. They were honorable men. Their job was to protect people. Whoever hired them. Why on earth would they feel anything more for her than anyone else they were assigned to protect?

She shook her head, denying it even as they sat in front of her, bluntly laying it out. She'd allowed a man to walk all over her. She'd allowed Joel to manipulate her, dictate to her. How could anyone look at that woman she'd been and feel anything more than disgust?

She was an intelligent woman with a college degree. She had common sense, had always prided herself on being able to stand on her own two feet. And it had only taken Joel a few weeks before he'd completely taken over her life.

What shamed her most was that she'd so easily fallen into the life that Joel had built for her. Before, she would have laughed at anyone who would have told her she would fall into a relationship with someone who controlled her every movement down to what she wore and what she ate.

Everyone around her had been able to see the truth of her relationship with Joel, but she'd been so rooted in denial that she convinced herself they were wrong. She didn't think she'd ever be able to forget the humiliation of having that veil lifted away and finally being able to see herself for what she was.

Gullible. Naïve. *Stupid*.

It pricked her pride. It gutted her and made her feel the kind of worthlessness she never wished on anyone else.

"What the hell are you thinking?" Noah asked in exasperation. "What kind of hell are you putting yourself through right now? I can see the shame in your eyes. It's in your body language and written clearly on your face."

"You can't *possibly* understand what I'm thinking or feeling," she said.

"Then make us understand," Liam challenged. "What could possibly motivate you to lie about the man who did this to you? If you weren't protecting him, then who the hell were you protecting?"

She surged to her feet, her fingers fisted into tight balls. She honest to God wanted to hit someone, something. Anything to vent the rage building inside her. But that made her no better than the monster who'd done the same to her.

"I wasn't afraid for me!" she yelled. "I was afraid for Max. I was afraid for *you*!"

CHAPTER 4

LIAM exchanged glances with Noah before rising to stand in front of Lauren. She wasn't angry, as her tone might indicate. She was terrified. It was evident in her body language and in her eyes.

He took a chance and reached out to her, his hands sliding gently down her arms and then back up again to cup her shoulders. Finding no resistance, he tightened his grip, and then he simply pulled her into his arms.

For a moment she was as stiff as a board. He couldn't even feel her breathe. But she didn't fight him or try to push him away. And then she finally relaxed, melting into him all soft and sweet.

He wrapped both his arms around her, enjoying the feel of her so close. He could smell her, could feel the warmth of her skin right through his clothing.

"Tell me why you were afraid for us, Lauren," he said gently. "Who is this man you think you need to protect us from?"

She pulled away and glanced warily at him, and then in Noah's direction. Noah was scowling, and Liam didn't know if it was because Lauren was in his arms or if he was still pissed over the idea that she was trying to protect them from Joel Knight.

She looked as though she was still waging the battle with herself over whether to divulge the information they needed.

"If you want to protect us, then tell us what we're dealing with," Noah cut in.

She sank back into the chair, slumping in defeat. She looked miserable, and Liam hated that look. Lauren had a beautiful smile. Full of warmth and vibrancy that just made others stop and stare when she laughed. Liam wanted her to smile again, and he'd do anything it took to make that happen.

"Joel is a pimp," she said with a visible shudder. "He'd never call himself that. He'd likely kill anyone for insulting him that way. But it's what he is. No matter how he sugarcoats it, he's a glorified *pimp*."

Liam frowned, dread skating up his spine. His stomach went immediately sour and the meal he'd had hours before churned.

"Did he force you to . . ." He couldn't even choke the words out but Lauren immediately understood what he was trying to ask.

Lauren looked up, horrified. "No! I didn't work for him. God no. But others did. He called them his girls."

Liam immediately looked over at Noah. "Suki," he muttered.

Suki had said she was one of his girls, but at the time they hadn't known what it meant.

Noah settled back on the love seat and gazed over at Lauren. "Why don't you start from the beginning, honey. Tell us everything you know. How you got involved with him. How you know about what he does."

For a moment, Liam thought she'd refuse. Her cheeks tightened and her eyes went dull with shame. He reached for her hand, determined that she not feel that way with him and Noah.

"We aren't judging you, Lauren. We just need the facts. Tell us what you know, okay?"

Whether she intended to or not, she curled her fingers tightly around his, gripping as she glanced back at Noah.

"I won't bore you with the details of my relationship with Joel. Let's just say that I was forced out of denial when I saw him rough up one of his 'girls' one night. I had no idea he was involved in anything like prostitution. I assumed he was the businessman he professed to be. Legitimate business."

Noah frowned. "You said you saw him rough up a girl. How rough are we talking? Did he kill her?"

Lauren paled and shook her head. "No. But he beat her. I mean he was so cold about it. He accused her of pocketing money and holding back on him. He reminded her that she worked for him and that she was nothing without him. He kept going on and on about all he'd done for her and *all* the girls, and he was pissed that this was the way she repaid him."

She closed her eyes for a long moment and swallowed visibly. Her hand shook in Liam's, and this time he was the one to squeeze her fingers, offering her reassurance.

"Her nose was bleeding. Her lip was split. And Joel was pissed because he'd lost his temper. Her face was a valuable asset. She wouldn't be on her back doing her job if a man had to put a paper bag over her head. His words, not mine," she added hastily.

Noah nodded. "Go on. You're doing fine."

"When he calmed down and realized what he'd done, he had Ron, the person I thought was his business partner, break three of her fingers. On her left hand, so she could still give a man a hand job. Oh God," she sobbed. "He broke fingers on her left hand so it wouldn't interfere with her pleasuring a man."

Liam raised her hand and folded his other one over the back so it was completely encased between his palms. He rubbed gently, silently urging her on.

"I was so sickened by what I saw, but what hit me the hardest was that I realized that *I* was that woman. That I'd just been watching a cold-blooded man ruthlessly hurt another woman, and that I'd allowed that and *more* behind closed doors. No, I didn't 'work' for him, but I was as solidly under his control as those women were. If I was so outraged on her behalf, then why the hell wasn't I upset over what I'd allowed him to do to me? I was heartsick. Scared. Angry. So many things. It was like flipping a light switch."

"What happened next?" Liam asked quietly.

"I confronted him." She broke off laughing a dry, hoarse laugh that made Liam's chest tight. "Like an idiot, I confronted him. What I should have done was gotten out of there as fast as I could and never look back. But I was so pissed and so ashamed, that I was compelled to confront him. It was as if I had to let him know that I wasn't that stupid, cowardly woman he'd been pushing around for so long. It was so dumb of me, but I wasn't thinking logically. I wasn't smart."

"Is that how you got the bruises you had when Max hired us?" Noah asked with a growl.

She lowered her eyes in shame. "No, that didn't come until later. I was so stupid," she said with a sob. "He told me that I was nothing but a dumb bitch and that I'd better keep my mouth shut and forget what I saw. I was so afraid of what he might do if I pushed him that I kept silent. And I stayed with him. Even after that. How foolish was that? I lived in constant fear of him, but I didn't know what to do. So I stayed. At least for a little while. It wasn't until a short time after that episode that I finally wised up and got out."

"Jesus," Noah muttered. "And you wouldn't tell us about him, why?"

Liam didn't like the darkness in Lauren's eyes or the knowledge that whatever pushed her to that final decision must have been bad. He wanted to ask her what the hell the bastard had done to make her finally snap, but now wasn't the time. She was tortured enough relating what she was. But Liam wouldn't forget. He'd find out exactly what had happened to push her over the edge. And he knew he damn well wasn't going to like her answer.

She sucked in a deep breath, almost as if she were trying to hold on to the last thread of her control. Liam sent Noah a dark look, silently telling him to back off, but Noah's lips were set into a fine line. He was well and truly pissed off now. Not at Lauren, but at Joel Knight.

"I heard the things he said to the woman he hurt and to Ron, his enforcer. What I never realized is that Ron is sent in to fix situations so that Joel doesn't have to get his hands dirty. Except Joel wanted to set an example of this woman. He wanted to scare her, and so he handled it himself. He has cops on his payroll. He didn't say who. But he taunted the woman with the fact that if she went to the cops, nothing would happen because she was just a whore nobody cared about and he had enough people on his payroll to make *any* problem go away."

Her voice had lowered to a whisper, and a tear slid down her soft cheek. Liam reached up to wipe it away and she flinched away from him. Not in fear, but in shame. It bothered her that she'd cry in front of them.

Rage made his hand shake and he pulled it away so it wouldn't upset her more.

"He talked about 'others' he'd had taken care of. So I knew when I finally got the courage to call Max for help that I couldn't tell him the truth. And then he called in you two, and it got so complicated. Max wanted to swear out a warrant. He wanted to punish whoever hurt me."

"Understandably so," Noah said tightly.

"And let Joel murder my brother?" she asked in horror. "Or you and Liam? How is that supposed to make anything better? How would I be able to live with myself knowing that I got one of you killed? I've made stupid decisions, but wanting to keep my brother and you two alive isn't one of them."

Liam sighed. There was no way for him and Noah to win this argument or sway her from the belief that she'd done the right thing. He wanted to shake her, but that didn't solve anything.

He wanted to ask her why the hell she ever got involved with Knight anyway. What on earth could she possibly have seen in the smarmy asshole?

Before leaving New York City, they'd pulled Knight's record. Squeaky-clean. Not even a parking ticket. Which would certainly lend credence to Lauren's assertion that he had influential people on his payroll.

He made frequent donations to charity. Hosted political fundraisers, though he never officially allied himself with either the Democratic or Republican Parties. He was more into causes. Causes that elevated his own profile and made him look like the all-American good guy. Hell, looking at his merits, he had all the traits of someone looking to get into politics himself.

And wouldn't Lauren be one hell of a skeleton in the man's closet come election time?

That scared the hell out of Liam. If politics were in this guy's future, it would give him even more motivation to silence Lauren so she was never a thorn in his side.

"Lauren—"

Before he could get out what he was going to say, there was a loud knock on the door. Followed by a guy's bellow.

"Lauren! Open up. It's Seth. Are you okay? If you don't answer in thirty seconds, I'm coming in."

Lauren scrambled to her feet. Noah and Liam were instantly on guard. Noah was already reaching for his gun while Lauren made a mad dash for the door.

She threw it open and before she could say a word, she was yanked out the door and shoved behind a man wearing a policeman's uniform.

Gun up in one hand, the other pushing Lauren farther behind him, the cop advanced into the room.

"Put your weapons down and your hands up where I can see them," the cop snarled. "Don't give me any reason to shoot."

"Seth, listen to me," Lauren pleaded. "They aren't here to hurt me."

Seth held up a hand to silence Lauren.

"Who the hell are you and what are you doing in Lauren's apartment? And you better damn well have a permit to carry those guns, otherwise you'll be spending the night in my jail. If you so much as laid one finger on Lauren, I'll make sure I lose the damn key."

"Whoa, dude, you need to chill out and listen to what Lauren's trying to tell you," Noah said, even as he carefully set the gun down on the coffee table.

"Hands up," Seth barked.

Noah complied and Liam tossed his weapon onto the floor, then carefully raised his hands up and laced his fingers behind his head.

Seth slowly advanced, his gun never lowering and his gaze never moving from Liam and Noah. When he was close enough to get to the weapons Liam and Noah had discarded, he bent carefully and retrieved them. Then he motioned for Liam to move to the couch where Noah stood.

"Sit down. Both of you."

Liam blew out an exasperated breath. Damn it, they didn't have time for this shit.

Seth backed toward the door where Lauren still stood, wide-eyed, taking it all in.

"Are you all right?" Seth asked in a low voice.

She nodded vigorously. "Seth, they aren't here to hurt me. Max hired them. I mean before, when I was in New York. He hired them to protect me after what happened. They've been investigating and they came because they needed to ask me some questions."

Seth glanced back and forth between the two men on the couch and Lauren, almost as if trying to gauge whether Lauren was acting and speaking of her own free will.

Evidently satisfied that she was, he slowly lowered his weapon and holstered it. He turned back to Lauren. "One of my deputies reported seeing two badass-looking guys forcing their way into your apartment. He hightailed it into the office to report to me. I told him to call Max, and then I got over here as fast as I could."

Lauren groaned. "Did you have to call Max, Seth? You could have waited to see what was going on before you got him all worked up."

Seth's eyebrow went up. "We all look out for you, Lauren. Max would kick my ass if I didn't let him know about this. Besides, if he hired them, then he ought to be happy they're doing their job."

Then he turned to Noah and Liam and held out his hand. "Seth Colter. I'm sheriff here. Lauren is family, and we take family very seriously. We watch out for her."

Liam stood and shook Seth's hand, and then Noah did the same.

"No hard feelings," Noah said mildly. "I'm glad she has plenty of people watching out for her safety. She needs it since she wasn't exactly truthful about what danger she's in."

Seth frowned and looked back at Lauren. "What does that mean?"

Lauren's face went red and her eyes gleamed with a murderous light.

"Don't think you're getting off scot-free," Noah warned. "Max has to know. Seth sure as hell needs to know. He's the sheriff here and he has responsibility for far too many lives to be kept in the dark."

Seth scowled. "Somebody mind telling me what the hell is going on here?"

Lauren glanced behind her through the still-open door, and when she turned back, her lips were pulled down into an expression of unhappiness

"You may as well hold off on any explanation," she said, displeasure evident in her tone. "Max is here, and he's going to want to hear everything."

CHAPTER 5

HOW had everything so quickly spiraled out of control? Lauren wanted to do nothing more than order everyone out of her apartment and bar the door. But she knew that wasn't going to solve anything.

It was bad enough she was going to have to explain to her brother that she'd lied to him. But now Noah and Liam were here. In the flesh. In her tiny living room. And she was going to have to confess everything in front of Seth, and while he was family, she was uncomfortable with so many people knowing just how badly she'd screwed up.

"Lauren? Seth?" Max called.

She could hear the anxiety in his voice, and she squeezed her eyes shut.

"It's okay, Max. Come on up," Seth called down. "Lauren is fine."

A few moments later, Max burst into the room, his gaze immediately seeking Lauren out. He went to her and pulled her into his arms. She sighed and absorbed the hug, resting her head against his chest. She was just waiting for the bubble to burst and for reality—and her past—to rudely intrude.

Max pulled her away, palming her shoulders. Then he glanced beyond her to where Noah and Liam now stood just a few feet away.

"What's going on? Why are you two here? Is Lauren in danger?"

Liam shot her a look of sympathy. Noah had less mercy, however.

"Lauren lied to us about who hurt her," Noah said bluntly. "When we found out, we came here immediately to question her."

Max frowned, and Lauren could see the wheels turning in his head as he grappled with what Noah had just thrown at him. His jaw went tight, a sure sign of anger, and he started forward, but she put her hand on his arm.

"Don't, Max," she said in a low voice. "I did lie."

He jerked his gaze from Noah and Liam, his eyes wide with astonishment. "Why on earth would you lie? I don't understand. I saw what you looked like, Lauren. You can't tell me that son of a bitch didn't put those bruises on you."

Her lips turned down again, and she glanced away, tears stinging the lids of her eyes. But she gulped them back. She wasn't going to use a dirty trick to get out of this. It was time to own up to what she'd done.

"She made up a name and description of someone else," Liam said.

He took a step toward Lauren until he was close enough that she could feel the warmth emanating from him. His hand slid up her back and remained between her shoulder blades. No one could see where his hand rested, but she appreciated the show of support more than she could possibly verbalize.

"Why?" Max demanded.

Seth frowned and leaned against the doorway that separated the living room from the small kitchen area. "I'm lost."

"She was afraid," Liam said quietly. "Joel Knight is the asshole's name and he's involved in prostitution. According to Lauren, he has quite a few people on his payroll, including several members of law enforcement." He sighed hard and glanced sideways at Lauren. "She was trying to protect you . . . and us."

Max stared at Liam for a long moment as if he thought Liam had lost his mind. Then he turned his gaze to Lauren. "Is this true?"

"Yes," she whispered.

"What else did you lie about?" Max asked bluntly. "What did he do to you, Lauren? You said he hit you. That he slapped and punched you. What else did that son of a bitch do to you? What else haven't you told me?"

The blood drained out of her face, and she could no longer meet her brother's gaze. Liam slid his arm around her, uncaring that Max was mere feet away, and Liam squeezed her shoulders, pulling her underneath his arm until she was flat against him, one shoulder lodged solidly underneath his.

"There's no need to have this discussion in front of so many people," Liam said in a low voice. "Lauren's embarrassed and scared enough as it is."

She wanted to hug him and never let go. But at the same time, she was ashamed of the fact she was still hiding, only this time she was hiding behind Liam.

Max blew out a deep breath and then scrubbed a hand through his hair. "I just want to know what the hell is going on. First question. Is Lauren in any immediate danger? Is this asshole coming after her?"

Noah held up his hand. "We have no reason to believe he has any idea where she is. We sure as hell haven't told anyone. We came because we needed to confirm what our source told us so that we can do some more digging on this guy."

Max's lips tightened. "You should have contacted me first. You work for me."

Liam nodded. "Yeah, we do. But we weren't going to you with the possibility that Lauren had held back information unless we knew that to be true. And the only way to find that out was to ask her."

Max looked long and hard at Lauren, and then his gaze softened. "Are you all right? I wish to hell I knew what you were thinking or why you just wouldn't tell me the truth."

"I'm fine," she croaked, and cringed at how easily she lied to her brother now. The truth was she wanted to crawl into a hole and die. But she couldn't very well *say* that.

"What do we need to do?" Max directed at Noah and Liam. "Are there any precautions that Lauren needs to take? How likely is this guy to come after her?"

"It's hard to say," Noah said grimly. "We need to find out everything we can about him."

Lauren trembled against Liam and his grip tightened on her.

"We aren't going to let anything happen to you, Lauren," Liam murmured.

"I don't want her left alone," Max said sharply. "Is this the sort of thing you can have others do for you?" Then he shook his head. "I think you should move back in with me and Callie, Lauren."

"Max, no," Lauren pleaded. "I like it here. I just got moved in. My job's just across the street. Clyde is a world away from New York City. You heard Noah. They haven't told anyone where I am. How on earth would he find me, and who says he even cares what I'm doing now?"

Max looked torn. Seth was frowning.

"I hate to upset you, Lauren, but I'm in agreement with Max on this one," Seth said. "You shouldn't be alone. Especially until we've had time to investigate this guy. I'm assuming from your tone that you have no desire to press charges?"

She shook her head emphatically. "He'd be out of jail in an hour. He'd never do time. I just want to forget he ever existed. I don't want to give him any reason to care about me one way or another."

Seth didn't look happy, but he didn't try to talk her into it.

"She won't be alone," Noah said. "Liam and I would stick to her until we are absolutely certain this guy poses no threat."

"What do you want to do, Lauren?" Max asked.

He was staring hard at Liam's arm wrapped protectively around her. His gaze swept up and down the bigger man as if trying to figure out what it was he was missing in the big picture.

Lauren sucked in a breath and then glanced at each of the occupants of the room.

If she swore off any protection, A) she'd be the world's biggest dumbass; and B) Max would have her moved back in with him and Callie in an hour flat. So much for asserting any sort of independence.

"I want to stay here. In my apartment," she finally said.

"And you're okay with Noah and Liam shadowing you twenty-four hours a day?" Max asked.

She snuck a quick glance at Noah. Liam, she was relatively sure of. His hold on her spoke volumes. Noah . . . well, she didn't know if he was still pissed or if he would be even more so once he got stuck babysitting her on a full-time basis again.

"Why are you looking at me that way?" Noah asked, his eyes narrowing.

"Because I'm not sure it's fair to ask you to take on the job of babysitting me again," she said bluntly. "I lied to you. I made your job more difficult. I wouldn't blame you if you couldn't wait to see the back of me."

"How about you let me worry about what I consider difficult,"

Noah said softly. "Whether you move in with your brother or you stay here in this apartment, you're stuck with me."

"And me," Liam interjected.

"And Liam," Noah agreed. "So you better just get used to it. Until we know exactly who and what we're dealing with, you're going to be tripping over us on a daily basis."

"I don't want any trouble," Seth said, straightening his stance. "I need to be kept in the loop on everything. If there's a problem in my town, it's my problem. Plus, Lauren is family. My entire family looks out for her. I need to know whatever threat there is because you can damn well bet my wife, mother and sister will be in the thick of it."

"Understood," Liam said, his hold never loosening on Lauren. "We'll give you whatever information we uncover as soon as we get it. We'll get some of our people digging immediately and we'll let everybody know what we come up with."

Max looked reluctantly toward the door and then back at Lauren. "Are you sure you don't want to come home with me?"

She broke loose from Liam and went to her brother. She hugged him tightly and then leaned up on tiptoe to kiss his cheek. "Thank you for worrying about me, and I'm sorry I lied to you, Max. I didn't know what else to do at the time. I was just scared. But I'm fine now. Promise."

He didn't look a hundred percent certain, but he nodded anyway. "Okay. I'll go back home." Then to Noah and Liam, he said, "I expect a report the minute you find out anything further."

"I'll get on out of here too," Seth said. "Keep me posted. Holler if you sense anything out of the ordinary. Things stay pretty much the same around here. People pay attention when they see new faces in town. Get me a description of Knight. A photo. Any pertinent information on people who work close with him. I'll distribute it to my deputies so we can all be on the lookout."

Liam extended his hand to shake Seth's. "Thanks. We'll definitely keep you posted."

Seth shook Liam's hand and then nodded at Lauren. "Take care, Lauren."

"Thank you," she managed to get out.

Max leaned forward, kissed Lauren on the forehead and then trailed behind Seth out her front door.

She damn near wilted on the spot as soon as the door closed behind Max. But the look in Noah's eyes halted her in her tracks.

Her brow furrowed, she glanced at him in question.

"Now that they're gone, we have a hell of a lot else to discuss," Noah said in a determined voice. "Starting with me. You. And Liam."

CHAPTER 6

N OAH stared at Lauren's pale face and for a moment considered backing off. Giving her time and space to deal with the fallout of their arrival. It was obvious she was on shaky ground.

But fuck it all. This whole situation was burning a hole in his brain. Liam had already made his move. And if Noah didn't do some serious catching up, he was going to get left in the dust.

Liam had said for Noah to come back and see Lauren and then make up his mind. Hell. As soon as he'd laid eyes on her again and saw the shame and vulnerability in her gaze, he knew there was no goddamn way he was walking away from her. And Liam, the bastard, probably knew it.

"I don't understand," Lauren said in a faltering tone.

When Noah looked at Liam, his friend's gaze was mocking. Challenging. It made Noah want to wipe the smug smile right off his face.

"Come sit down," Liam said, gently herding Lauren to the love seat.

He settled her down beside him and then glanced expectantly back up at Noah. Noah had no choice but to take the armchair Lauren had sat in earlier.

Once he was settled and staring at Lauren, who was looking at him, expecting him to say what was on his mind, he struggled to find the words. How the hell was he going to explain this one when he didn't fully understand it himself?

Son of a bitch, but he hated this uncertainty. He was a decisive person. He didn't second-guess himself or his decisions, but he was paralyzed by the enormity of the situation. He and Liam hadn't even fully come to terms with this . . . whatever the hell it was. How could he be expected to make Lauren understand what he wanted? What Liam obviously wanted.

"Lauren, will you excuse us for a moment?" Noah said bluntly.

Liam's brows drew together, and then Lauren's brow furrowed in confusion.

Noah stood and motioned for Liam. "We're just going to go across the street."

"And leave her?" Liam demanded.

Noah blew out his breath in frustration. "Come on, Lauren. You're going with us. We'll take her into the sheriff's station."

"What on earth is going on?" Lauren asked in bewilderment.

Her brown eyes were cloudy with confusion, and her mouth opened and shut as she glanced between the two men.

Liam put his hand over hers. "Noah and I need to work out a few things . . . privately. It won't take long."

"But why do I need to leave?"

Liam touched her cheek. "Remember everything that was just said when your brother was here? That wasn't just talk, Lauren. For the next while, where we go, you go, and vice versa."

She looked as though she wanted to argue, but then she closed her mouth and gave a resigned sigh. "Okay. Let's go then. Let me get my book so I'll have something to do. I'm going to feel pretty stupid just sitting in the sheriff's station."

As she walked to her bedroom, Noah leveled a stare at Liam. He was itching to say something. To break the building tension. He was ready to explode, but he didn't want to have this conversation in front of Lauren. Not until he and Liam hashed this out between them. There were so many ways to fuck this up before they even had a chance with her. And that was assuming that Lauren wouldn't run screaming in the opposite direction as soon as they leveled with her.

When Lauren returned, Noah abruptly got up and strode for her front door. Liam brought up the rear, placing Lauren in between the both of them. But then wasn't this what it was all about? Lauren in between them?

He was going to need something stronger than the diner served for this occasion.

Traffic had increased on Main Street. Old pickups making stops at the feed store. Cars pulling into the grocery store at the corner.

Most noticeably was the crowd at the diner.

There was no way in hell he was going to have a conversation about Lauren in the middle of a crowded diner.

He glanced back at Liam and then headed for the sheriff's station. When he pushed in, there was a woman manning the front desk with the phone surgically attached to her ear. She held up one finger and mouthed *I'll be with you in a second.*

Noah waited patiently for her to finish her call, and then she looked up, a bright smile on her face.

"How can I help you?"

"I need to see Seth Colter," Noah said.

He reached behind him, took Lauren's hand and pulled her up to stand beside him.

"I need to leave her with the sheriff."

The woman blinked, and then her eyes widened. "What's she done, sir?"

Noah stared at her in confusion. "She hasn't done anything. Can you get the sheriff for me?"

When he glanced sideways at Lauren, he saw her face was beet red, and she looked as though she wanted the floor to swallow her up.

Hell.

The awkward moment was saved from growing even more awkward when Seth walked out of his office. He frowned when he saw them and came to a full stop.

"Is something wrong?" Seth asked. "Noah, isn't it?"

Noah nodded and then shook his head. "Nothing's wrong. We need to leave Lauren with you until we get a few things straightened out."

Seth blinked. "Here?"

Lauren made a strangled sound. "This is so ridiculous. Let me go to Lily's. You can drop me off there. I'll spend the afternoon with her."

Seth frowned. "No, it's fine. Just caught me off guard. You can sit in my office if you like. If I'm called out, there will be plenty of other people here to keep an eye on you."

"I feel like a damn criminal," Lauren muttered.

Liam leaned over, kissed her temple and then pushed her in Seth's direction. "We'll be back for you in just a bit. Sit tight, okay?"

She sent an unhappy look in Liam and Noah's direction before she walked toward Seth. Seth put his hand on her shoulder and guided her back toward his office.

"Come on," Noah muttered, heading back out the door.

Instead of walking toward the diner, he crossed the street back to Lauren's apartment, leaving Liam to follow. He jogged up the steps and went in, pacing around the living room while Liam closed the door and went to sit on the love seat.

"I'm guessing you've made your decision," Liam drawled.

Noah stopped pacing and spun around, pinning his friend with a glare. "No, the hell I haven't. How am I supposed to make that kind of decision in a split second? Have you even considered the difficulties in what you're proposing? Have you thought past the fact that you want her?"

"Why are you so pissed off?" Liam asked mildly. "You didn't want to talk about it when we could have in New York, when Lauren wasn't anywhere around. You wanted to wait. Well here we are. So talk."

Noah gripped the back of his neck and took in several deep breaths. Then he hunched down in the armchair, shaking his head.

"This is some kind of goddamn joke to you, isn't it?"

At that, Liam surged forward, his eyes darkening with anger. His jaw bulged and Noah realized he'd gone too far. His friend was close to ripping Noah's head off.

"Lauren isn't a *joke* to me," Liam said through tightly clenched teeth. "You're the one with your head up your ass. I was trying to do the right thing. I knew you had feelings for her and you're my friend. I also know that we can protect and take care of Lauren. Together. I don't want her to come between us. We've been through too much and we have history. Your friendship means a lot, but I'm not going to let you fuck things up for me with Lauren. With or without you, I'm here for the long haul. What you decide is up to you. I shot you straight. I leveled with you. I gave you time to think it over."

Noah stared at him in astonishment. "All bullshit aside, you really think this can work? You really think that just because people she knows are in a nontraditional relationship that she'll be all okay with it for herself?"

"If we can't decide between us that it'll work, we'll never convince her that it will," Liam said quietly. "Maybe it won't. But how will we know unless we try? She does it for me, man. I can't explain it. I've heard all kinds of stories about how when a man sees a woman he just knows she's it. But I've never experienced it until now. I've met plenty of women that I was interested in. That I was attracted to. Women I enjoyed spending time with and having sex with. But I've never met a woman who I've had a more powerful reaction to than Lauren. I can't even describe to you what I felt when I saw her the first time. I wanted to go find the asshole who hurt her and take him apart. And then I wanted to take her in my arms and swear to her that nothing bad would ever touch her again, and that I'd spend the rest of my life making sure she was happy. Now if that sounds stupid to you, so be it, but it was like that for me."

"It's not stupid," Noah murmured. "It's not stupid because it's the same way I felt. Even when I told myself I was being ridiculous."

Liam nodded. "Now you tell me this. With you having that strong of a reaction, are you really contemplating stepping aside?" Then his eyes narrowed and he stared hard at Noah. "Unless you're expecting me to."

He leaned forward on the couch, his expression suddenly dark and formidable.

"Not this one, Noah," he said tersely. "I've stepped aside before when I knew you were interested in the same woman I had my eye on. But I didn't feel this way about them. I've never felt so strongly about a woman that I'd risk our friendship over, but I'm telling you right now, I'm not bowing out, and if you can't or won't accept what I'm proposing, that's fine. But don't expect me to sit back and watch you and Lauren together."

Noah knew he had to find a way to defuse a potentially explosive situation. Liam was getting worked up, and if he wasn't careful, the entire thing would blow up in Noah's face.

"Just tell me this, Liam. Do you really think this can work? Forget the bullshit about not wanting to step aside. Put away your emotional reaction and think about this logically. Do you honestly think we can share the same woman without getting jealous or too demanding or getting pissed when things don't go our way?"

Liam pursed his lips and then slowly nodded. "Yeah, I do. I can only speak for me, but I'm willing to do whatever it takes to make it work. Can you say the same? I'm not going into this with a hidden agenda. I've put my cards on the table. I can't be any more blunt than I've been. But so far I've been the one doing all the talking."

If anyone else were questioning him the way Liam was, the fight would already be on. But Liam knew him. Liam was the closest thing Noah had to a family. Hell, Liam's family had all but adopted Noah when he was just a teenager.

He'd spent more time in the Prescott household than he had his own, and by the time he was sixteen, he'd moved in and the Prescotts had pursued legal custody through the courts. Noah's mother hadn't even bothered to show up.

The two boys had graduated from high school together. They'd joined the military together, and even though the Army had taken them in separate directions, they'd always stayed in touch. Noah had spent his leave time with the Prescotts, and one Christmas, he'd spent with them when Liam hadn't gotten leave.

"What about your folks?" Noah asked grimly. "How are they going to take this?"

Liam shrugged. "I'm sure they'll wonder if we've lost our minds. But they'll love Lauren. Mom will love her and so will Dad. I think, as with anything, they'll just need time to adjust. When the time comes, we'll take her to meet them and we'll explain the situation. They aren't going to disown us over it, Noah. You know them better than that."

"I just don't want to hurt them," Noah said. "They've done too much for me."

"I understand that. But you're not giving them enough credit. They just want us to be happy. If Lauren makes us happy and you and I are at peace with it, then everything else will fall into place."

Noah shook his head. "You're disgustingly levelheaded about this whole thing. I'm usually the one having to talk you around on things."

Liam shrugged. "I know what I want, and I'm willing to do whatever is necessary to get it."

"Okay then we give it a try. I don't even know where the hell to start."

Liam laid his forearms across his knees and stared intently at Noah. "We start by being honest with Lauren about what we want, and then we ask her what *she* wants."

CHAPTER 7

❧

AFTER reading the same paragraph five times, Lauren gave up on trying to enjoy the book she'd taken with her into Seth's office. Seth was in and out and thankfully hadn't tried to engage her in conversation. He was kept busy with various calls, but it was one from his wife, Lily, that made Lauren's heart melt.

It was so obvious how adored Lily Colter was. By all three of the men she called husband. Seth's entire face lit up when he realized it was her on the phone, and his eyes had grown so soft with love that Lauren found it hard to watch.

They'd spoken about the baby and how Lily was feeling. Evidently Dillon was home with Lily and it was also obvious that Seth would rather be there instead of stuck in his office. Babysitting Lauren.

It had made Lauren uncomfortable because she felt as though she was intruding on something private and deeply emotional.

She turned away to stare out the window, wondering when Noah and Liam would return and what was so important that they'd had to dump her so they could speak privately. Noah had acted strangely ever since the two had arrived while Liam had acted . . . like he cared about her. Or maybe it was wishful thinking on her part.

She'd never wished for anything as much as she wished she could go back and redo the past year. So much of her time had been spent lamenting the choices she'd made, but she'd compounded bad decision making with yet more bad decisions. Would it ever end for her?

There was more she hadn't told Noah and Liam. Or Max. Or anyone else. But she knew the moment she gave up her secret that she'd be forced to act on it, and she wasn't ready to face her past. Maybe she'd never be ready.

She was a coward. She readily admitted that. But in no way did she ever want to see Joel again, and were she to confess to anyone what she'd taken away when she ran from Joel and begged her brother for help, there would be no way around having to face him.

Just the thought was enough to strike fear in her heart and send a chill down her spine. She shivered and rubbed her arms.

"Are you cold?"

Seth's question jerked her from her thoughts. She yanked her head up to see that he'd returned to his office again and was staring at her.

She stilled her hands so they rested on her arms, and shook her head. "No, I'm fine."

He took a seat behind his desk and riffled through a stack of papers, evidently finding what he was looking for. He sat back, studying it for a long moment, and then he glanced her way again.

Then he put the paper down and leaned forward so his forearms rested on his desk.

"You know if you ever need help, with anything, that you only have to ask."

She nodded.

Seth hesitated a moment, fiddled with a pen on his desk and then looked back at her again, as if he was trying to figure out the best way to broach the subject he wanted to discuss.

"Noah and Liam . . . are these guys you're comfortable with? I can talk to Max. We can work out something else if you'd rather they go back to New York."

She surged forward. "No! I mean no, it's okay, they're fine, I mean. It's just that I was caught off guard. But really, they've been great. They were so sweet to me right after . . . you know, when what happened happened. Thank you, though. I appreciate what you and all your family have done for me."

"You're family, Lauren. And the Colters always look after family."

She smiled. "I know. It's one of the things I love the most about all of you. Max and I didn't have that. I mean, we did, but it was just us and Mom for so long, and then we lost her. I was in awe of all of you when I first came here. To have such a large, close-knit family is pretty special."

"You're a part of that now," Seth said. "Don't forget that."

Warmth filled her heart. It felt good to be a part of something as loving and wonderful as the Colter family.

Seth glanced toward the door and then turned back to her. "Looks like Noah and Liam are back for you. They're out front. Come on, I'll walk you up."

She stood. "No need. Thanks for letting me stay and I'm sorry to be such a bother. Please give Lily my love and tell her I'll see her when I can. I'm not sure how much freedom I'm going to have going forward," she added ruefully.

"We'll make it happen. She enjoys spending time with you and Callie. She won't be able to go that long without getting together with you."

"Thanks again. See you later," she said as she exited his office.

Down the hall she saw Noah and Liam standing in the small reception area. They looked relieved when they saw her. Where did they think she'd go?

Noah reached for her hand as soon as she got close enough. To her surprise, he laced his fingers through hers, squeezed and then pulled her toward the door.

Liam followed them across the street, and Noah never let loose as they climbed the steps to her apartment. When he pushed inside, he kept ahold of her hand and led her to the love seat.

He seemed nervous. Ill at ease. Even Liam looked a little . . . unsure.

"Is something wrong?" she blurted. "You both look worried. Is it Joel?"

Liam got up, shoved her coffee table out of the way and dropped down onto one knee in front of her.

"No, baby. I don't want you to worry about Joel, okay? We're going to do everything in our power to make sure you never have to see him again."

"We wanted to talk to you about something personal," Noah said.

Her gaze swung to him and her heart began to race. She licked her lips nervously because she knew that whatever they wanted to discuss was going to be . . . huge. It was there to read in their expressions. They were focused intently. On her. Like she was the most important person in the world.

"O-okay," she breathed out.

Liam slid his big hand over hers, warm and soothing. Noah took her other hand and turned it palm up, his finger tracing the lines to her fingers.

"The thing is . . ." He trailed off then ran his free hand over his head. "Hell, I'm making a total mess of this."

"What is it, Noah?" she asked softly.

"Do you have feelings for us?" Liam asked bluntly. "Or are we way off base here."

Heat seeped into her cheeks and she was mortified. Had she been so transparent? She'd tried her best to be indifferent toward them. She hadn't even truly sorted out what she felt for them. They intrigued her. She'd allowed herself to fall into the fantasy that she wasn't just a job to them, that their protection came not from their job description, but from a need that sprang from their attraction to her.

She'd gone back and forth with herself over whether she was genuinely attracted to two men or whether it was just a product of going from a man who abused her to men who treated her like she was . . . special. Like she meant something to them, and that they genuinely cared about her. Wouldn't any woman fall for a man in the same situation? But did it make her feelings real?

Noah reached up to softly caress her cheek. "Please don't be embarrassed by the question. We wanted—*needed*—to know because we have feelings for you, Lauren. And before we can proceed, we need to know if those feelings are returned."

She swallowed hard, her pulse thundering in her temples. "You *both* have feelings for me?"

"Yes, we do," Liam said in that same matter-of-fact tone.

She licked her lips, and suddenly Liam was there, his mouth covering hers in a heated rush. For a moment she had no idea what to do, but then she found herself responding, returning his kiss, opening her mouth to the thrust of his tongue.

There was nothing perfunctory about the kiss. She loved the roughness, how unsteady and eager he seemed. Almost like he was doing everything he could to hold himself in check. Joel had rarely kissed her, and when he had, it felt more like a punishment than a gesture of affection.

When he pulled away, his breath hiccupped over his lips and his eyes glowed warm and dark. He smoothed a thumb over the fullness of her bottom lip, now swollen from his kiss.

"I could so easily fall in love with you," he said in a near whisper.

Her heart clenched and she soaked in the words like a parched desert soaking up rain.

Noah made a sound and she jerked toward him, suddenly numb with guilt. He immediately shook his head.

"Don't look at me like that, sweetheart. You have nothing to feel guilty over. This is what we want to talk to you about. The thing is, we both care about you. We both want to see where our relationship will take us. But we have to make sure you're on board for something like that. Plus, this isn't the most ideal time to embark on any relationship, much less one with our particular elements. Our first priority has to be keeping you safe."

"You want to have the sort of relationship that the Colters have," she said, her mind whirling with the implications.

She'd known of the "different" marriage that Holly and Lily Colter had with each of their three husbands even before she'd ever met them. She'd learned of it from Max. She'd known what to expect, so when she'd witnessed firsthand the bond between the women and their husbands, she hadn't been taken aback.

No, she wasn't shocked. She'd been curious and more than a little envious because it was so obvious that the Colter men adored their wives. She'd often wondered what it would be like to be the center of such a relationship, the very heart and the core in which the arrangement was centered on.

Never in a million years would she have dreamed that such a relationship would find her.

Noah nodded. Liam squeezed her hand.

"Would you even consider such an arrangement?" Liam asked. "I know we're asking for a lot. We're nowhere near the permanent commitment stage. We haven't even had what qualifies as a date.

All we want is a chance. We want to open your mind to the possibility and see where it takes us."

"This is a lot to take in," she murmured. "I had no idea. I mean that you returned my interest."

Noah's eyes gleamed in sudden triumph. "So you are attracted to us."

Her cheeks flamed, but she nodded. They'd given her the truth, and while she'd certainly started their acquaintance with lies, she didn't want to continue that path.

Liam leaned in and kissed her again. Long and sweet until she was breathless. This time she slid her hand around the back of his neck and buried her fingers in his long hair. He groaned against her mouth and then pulled back, his eyes blazing.

"If I had my way, we'd bypass the dating stage altogether and I'd have you in my bed every damn night."

She gaped at his bluntness and nearly glanced in Noah's direction, but remembering his admonishment the last time she'd looked his way to gauge his reaction, she forced herself not to peek at him.

"We'll take things slow," Noah said. "We'll go whatever pace you need, Lauren. You'll take the lead and we'll do whatever we need to for you to be comfortable. We want this to work."

"Okay," she said in a shaky voice.

Noah touched his finger to her cheekbone and ran it down to her jaw and then over to trace a line around her mouth.

"I want very much to kiss you," he said huskily.

"Then kiss me," she whispered.

He leaned in, slowly, angling his head so their mouths aligned. And then he pressed his lips to hers. Lightly at first. Then he deepened the kiss, tentatively seeking entrance with his tongue.

It was sweet and slow, like the first kiss between lovers. A kiss to be remembered for the way it made her feel when things were all shiny and new and emotions were still running high.

His hand fell to the side of her neck and then, as she'd done to Liam, his hand crept upward, into her hair.

He broke away but rested his forehead against hers, his chest heaving as he rested there a moment, their mouths so very close.

"I want this," he whispered. "I didn't think I did, but God, I want this, Lauren. I want you, and I'll make any sacrifice for this to work."

His words opened a part of her soul that hadn't been previously opened. He and Liam had reached a part of her she'd closed off, a protective measure so that Joel couldn't reach the very core of her and damage it.

It was scary and exhilarating all at the same time to open up and allow herself to trust again. But mostly it terrified her because she knew she hadn't made good decisions in the past. How was she supposed to know if she was making the right ones now?

CHAPTER 8

❧

LAUREN sat between Noah and Liam at her small dinette set that accommodated four people. Four normal-sized people. Noah and Liam weren't exactly normal sized. They made her apartment seem overstuffed and crowded, where before she'd relished the warm, cozy feel of it.

They'd ordered dinner from Dillon Colter's pub, and Liam had gone out to get it, leaving Lauren and Noah alone for a time in the apartment.

Lauren still wasn't sure of herself in this strange, new environment she existed in, so she'd excused herself to take a shower and get into more comfortable clothing for lounging. By the time she'd returned, Liam was back with the food, and she'd sighed in relief.

"I meant what I said before," Noah said around a bite of steak.

Lauren raised her eyebrows. "Oh?"

"About not letting our relationship interfere with our primary objective, which is keeping you safe and finding out any and all information we can uncover on Joel Knight. As discreetly as possible."

She lowered her head and picked at her food.

"Don't do that, honey," Noah said softly. "Stop beating yourself up over him. Put the bastard in the past where he belongs. It's time to move forward. With me and Liam. And we're damn sure never going to give you reason to believe that we're anything like that asshole. Don't give him that kind of power over you."

She sighed. "I know. Logically I do. I'm smart enough to know that he can't control me anymore. But it's hard to shake that off, you know? When I think of what I allowed him to turn me into, I'm so ashamed, I can barely stand it. I'm supposed to be smarter than that, and I never saw him for what he was until it was nearly too late."

The phone rang, interrupting the conversation. Lauren walked over to where her cell phone was charging and quickly unplugged it.

"Hey Max," she greeted.

"How are things with you?" he asked.

"Fine. We're just enjoying a quiet dinner in the apartment."

"That's good. I wanted to make sure you were still comfortable with the arrangements. I can always do something different."

"You're too good to me, Max. But I'm fine. I promise. I'm going to be okay this time. I've learned from my past mistakes. I don't want to make them again."

"You're too hard on yourself," he said quietly. "We all make mistakes, Lauren. I fucked up royally with Callie. Not once, but twice."

She smiled. "You sure did. It's a wonder she took you back."

"I was lucky," he said in a somber tone. "I didn't deserve the second chances she gave me."

"She loves you."

"And I love her. And speaking of Callie and her family. Holly wants you to come to dinner tomorrow and bring Noah and Liam with you. You know Mama C. She gets all nervous about her chicks, and you are definitely one of them now. She wants to eyeball these two men herself before she signs her approval to the whole plan."

Lauren chuckled. "That sounds exactly like her. I'd love to come. It's been a few days since I've seen her, and right now I could use her company." And her wisdom and insight. There was nothing more that Lauren wanted to do than run to her with the situation she'd found herself in. Of all people, Holly would understand. She'd been a rock during the time that Lily was finding her way with Holly's three sons. Always offering wisdom and advice. Maybe she could help Lauren sort out how she was going to make a relationship with two very demanding alpha men work.

After all, she was married to three of the most demanding alpha men on earth. Adam, Ethan and Ryan Colter. It had certainly been passed onto their three sons and to an extent their only daughter, Callie.

Callie was strong-willed, independent and had been raised by a houseful of overprotective men who thought nothing of spoiling the women they loved completely rotten.

Just thinking of the Colters made Lauren wistful.

Hope crowded in as she peeked up at Liam and Noah, who were enjoying the takeout from the Mountain Pass Bar and Grill.

Here was her shot at a relationship that mimicked the ones the Colters had. She had two very protective badass men determined to keep her safe from anything that threatened her. And they wanted a chance to make a relationship work between the three of them.

"Then we'll see you tomorrow?" Max asked.

"Hang on just a moment. Let me ask Liam and Noah what they think."

She had pulled the phone away from her ear and had started to ask permission, of all things, when it dawned on her what she was doing. She was acting as though she were with Joel. Always needing his approval for everything she did. She no longer had to do that. She made her own decisions. If she wanted to go visit with the Colters, then Noah and Liam could either come or stay behind. But she wanted to go.

With a quick frown, she pulled the phone up to her ear again, ignoring the raised eyebrows of Noah and Liam.

"We'll be there. I'll text Holly to let her know to expect us."

She ended the call, angry with herself for being such a damn wuss.

"Any particular reason you look mad at the world?" Noah asked mildly when she returned to the table.

"I'm disgusted with myself," she muttered.

"Why?" Liam demanded.

"Because I told my brother I was going to ask you if I could go, like I need your permission or something. It's absolutely what I would have done when I was with Joel. I did nothing without his say so. I didn't even go to the bathroom without telling him what I was doing."

"I see," Noah said carefully. "But Lauren, you do see the difference here, don't you? We care about what happens to you. We care that there's a threat out there that's as of yet unresolved. We'd never stop you from doing something you wanted to do. Unless it was determined that the risk was too great. I need you to understand that now so that if the time ever comes that we shut you down, it won't be because we're controlling dickheads. It'll be because your safety comes first, and we'd much rather have you alive and pissed off than dead and appeased."

"I understand. I do. Just give me time, Noah. This is all very new to me. I wish I could just let go of the past and resolve to not let it affect me so much now. But it's not that easy. God, I wish it were. I'd give anything to be able to wipe him from my memory and go on like he never existed. But it's like he's there, a shadow in my mind, and he pops out at the most inopportune times. He makes me doubt myself, and I hate that most of all."

Liam's eyes softened and he reached over to squeeze her hand. "I get it, baby. I do. Cut yourself some slack. You'll get there, and Noah and I will be helping you every step of the way."

She smiled tremulously. "Thank you."

"So I take it we're going out tomorrow?" Noah said. "I just need to know details so I can plan accordingly."

She nodded. "Yes, up the mountain to where the older Colters live. Seth's parents. Callie and Max live just across the meadow from them. Seth and his brothers and their wife, Lily, live closer to town, but their home is still out of the way and secluded. It's very beautiful."

"*You're* very beautiful," Liam said, his voice gruff and husky.

Befuddled by the abrupt change in direction, she went silent, not knowing how to respond.

"You're not used to compliments, are you?" Noah asked. "Did the bastard never tell you that you were beautiful? Wait. Don't answer that. I'm sorry I brought him up."

Lauren slowly shook her head. "In the beginning he did. I mean he said and did all the right things when we first met. But they were just . . . words. He didn't mean them. It was all very perfunctory. The way he kissed me. The way he touched me. Looking back, I have no idea why he even bothered. It was obvious he wasn't attracted to me. Physically I mean. Or emotionally for that matter. It was like I was a thing to him."

A low growl emanated from Liam's throat.

"For men like him it's about control. Not how attracted he is to you. It's about having someone he can control. It's a high. It makes him feel powerful," Noah said grimly.

"And I was such an easy mark," Lauren said sadly.

Liam ran his hand over her face, brushing his thumb in a gentle caress over her cheekbone. "He played you, Lauren. He sold you something you wanted by pretending he cared. It's not a crime to want someone to love you or to be in love or to want a relationship. Isn't it what we all want at the end of the day?"

She reached for his hand and leaned her head further into his hold. For a moment she closed her eyes, savoring the contact. There was nothing threatening in Liam's touch. He was so very careful with her.

She brushed her cheek along his palm as she raised her gaze to meet his. "And why do you want *me*?" she whispered.

He frowned, his eyes darkening. He looked . . . angry.

She withdrew immediately, wary of his body language. It was automatic for her to stiffen her posture and put her hands down in her lap, averting her gaze.

Beside her she heard Noah curse, and she flinched, closing her eyes as she waited for the impending outburst.

When she felt the hand on her skin, it was instinctive to shrink away and make herself a smaller target. It shocked her. Logically, she was denying that either of these men would hurt her, but it was as if her mind was paying no heed to what she knew. It only knew that she had to protect herself.

But the hand slid soothingly over her shoulder, up and down, the touch so light it could only be his fingertips.

"Lauren, look at me please," Liam said hoarsely.

Slowly she raised her head until she met his tortured gaze. There was *pain* in his eyes and so much regret.

Noah scooted his chair over and carefully reached into her lap where her fingers were tightly laced. He gently pried them apart and lifted her hand, pulling it to his mouth. She was visibly shaking, and she hated having such weakness so evident.

"Baby," Liam said softly. "Listen to me, okay? I have so much

to say right now and I'm fighting a hell of a lot of conflicting emotions, so be patient with me. The first thing you need to know is that I will never hurt you. Do you understand that? I don't expect you to believe it right away, but I want you to file it away in your mind and I want you to pull it out every time you get afraid. I will never, *ever*, hurt you physically. I can't promise that I won't fuck up and hurt you emotionally. Believe me when I say it's the very last thing I want to do, but I'm a guy, and we do stupid shit. We say stupid shit. I don't always think before I speak. That's going to happen, okay? But you have nothing to fear from me physically."
She gave a jerky nod.

"The second thing you need to know is that I don't have a grand explanation for why you do it for me. But I knew from the moment I met you that I was gone in a pretty serious way. You were different from the other women I've been involved with. Not different in a bad way, but in a very, very good way. You filled the void that was left by my other relationships. I can only explain it by saying that it was like finding a missing piece to a puzzle. You fit. I hope to hell *we* fit. I hope this isn't one-sided, and I'm willing to play a little dirty and try my best to convince you that I'm someone you need. I want you to depend on me, and not in a fucked-up way like Joel wanted you to depend on him. This isn't about control. I just want you to know that you can count on me. For anything. And that good or bad, I'm in it for the long haul. I can't be any more blunt than that."

Noah remained silent, but his hold on her hand never loosened. He continued to press tiny kisses to her fingers, and he gradually opened her palm and pressed his mouth to her open hand.

"You reacted to my anger," Liam continued. "I can't promise never to get angry. It was like a kick in the balls to watch you with those big brown eyes look at me and ask why on earth I would want you, as if you were somehow unworthy. God, Lauren. *Unworthy?*

Noah and I are just hoping like hell to prove ourselves worthy of *you*. I'm not mad at you, baby. I'm mad at the son of a bitch who has made you question yourself as a woman."

Tears stung her eyelids, and she turned her head but found herself staring into Noah's eyes. There was no escape from them.

Noah leaned forward and tenderly kissed the corner of her eye where a tear had escaped.

"Don't cry, sweetheart. Liam's usually not so damn eloquent, but in this case, I couldn't have said it better myself. We want you to relax. It's not going to be easy as we fumble and feel our way around a very delicate relationship. I have no experience in this kind of arrangement. Neither does Liam. We just both want to make you happy, and we want you to eventually be able to trust us. Everything else will work itself out. We'll take it one step at a time and figure it out as we go."

She nodded and then impulsively wrapped her arms around Noah's neck, hugging him tightly.

Noah felt her go tense against him. She went so still, he was sure she was holding her breath. Waiting. For what? Did she expect a reprimand? Fuck that.

He wrapped his arms around her and hauled her into his lap, hugging her fiercely. He kissed the top of her silky hair and she gradually relaxed in his arms, melting sweetly against him.

"He never was affectionate with me," she whispered. "I hated that. I hated what I became. I've always been a demonstrative person, and he took that away. He hated for me to touch him."

Noah's lips tightened as he met Liam's surly gaze across the table. God, he wanted to kick Joel Knight's ass. Men like him didn't deserve to breathe.

Carefully he pulled Lauren away and pushed the hair from her face.

"You can touch me anytime you feel like it, sweetheart. I guarantee I won't complain. And you can bet that I'm going to want to touch you often. I won't be able to resist."

"Come here, Lauren," Liam said.

Noah kissed her temple and then helped her to her feet so she could walk around the table to Liam.

Liam opened his arms and she went willingly, and soon Liam had her nestled on his lap, his arms snugly around her. She cuddled into his embrace like a kitten seeking warmth, and Noah realized that what she needed most was comfort. She was starved for the things that most people took for granted. Affection. Tenderness.

Love.

"Anytime you want a hug, you come to me," Liam said gruffly. "I'd happily spend all damn night holding you."

"I'll make mistakes," Lauren said painfully. "I don't know how to have a normal relationship, but I want to learn."

"We're going to make mistakes too, Lauren. We'll just be patient with each other," Noah said.

She straightened in Liam's lap and looked directly into Noah's eyes, her expression fierce and determined.

"I want this," she said in a rush, almost as if she'd been afraid to admit it before. "I want it more than I can say. I'm just so afraid of screwing up."

Noah's heart melted. If there had been any lingering doubt on his part about the viability of entering a relationship that involved sharing a woman with his best friend, it was swiftly removed as he stared into Lauren's eyes.

She was starkly vulnerable. She was afraid and she was still beaten down by a man whose hold on her had yet to be fully broken. But he saw hope in her eyes. He saw fierce determination to make things work between the three of them.

If she could take such a huge step and put her trust in him and Liam, then he could certainly do the same.

It was time to stop overthinking all the what-ifs and maybes and focus on the only thing he could control. His contribution.

"I want this too," Noah said honestly.

There was relief in Liam's eyes, and his hold tightened around Lauren.

Liam's gaze met and held with Noah's as silent understanding passed between them.

For better or worse, they were in this together.

CHAPTER 9

WHEN Noah and Liam had inserted themselves into Lauren's life—and apartment—they obviously hadn't given a lot of thought to sleeping arrangements. The one bedroom was tiny, and Lauren had a daybed instead of a regular bed. There was barely room for the small chest of drawers she'd crammed into the room so she'd have a place for her clothing.

The men certainly weren't going to fit on the love seat, so after much discussion, Liam went down the street to buy sleeping bags at the sporting goods store.

It was decided that one of them would sleep in the living room, and since there wasn't room for two sleeping bags unless they moved furniture out, the other would roll out his sleeping bag on the floor directly below where Lauren slept on the daybed.

She felt guilty until she remembered that she hadn't asked for this, and yes, they were helping her. They were protecting her. She was extremely grateful. But there was no definite timeline on how long they would need to shadow her every movement. If she knew it was only for a few days or even a week or so, she would be willing to move to a hotel or consider other accommodations, but it could be much longer. She had a job. It was a job she liked and one she couldn't afford to lose.

Sure, Max would help her. She wouldn't even have to ask. But it was important to her that she stand on her own two feet and stop relying on her big brother to bail her out of trouble.

He was married now. He had Callie. It wasn't fair to saddle him with the responsibility of his younger sister when he should be focused on his new family.

The men decided to alternate nights in her bedroom, and Liam claimed the first night. Lauren felt ridiculously nervous about having him in her bedroom, but he acted as though it was an ordinary occurrence.

He paid her no attention when she went into the bathroom to change into pajamas, brush her teeth and brush her hair. She spent longer than necessary and then realized he or Noah would likely need to use the bathroom before they went to bed.

But when she reentered her bedroom, Liam was already in his sleeping bag, one of the cushions from the couch tucked underneath his head.

At first she thought he was already asleep, but when she turned off the light and began to make her way toward the bed, he said, "Be careful. Don't fall."

She stepped over him and then crawled onto the bed. He'd pulled back the covers for her. The sweetness of the gesture made her want to hug him. It was a simple thing, but it showed his thoughtfulness and his determination to make her comfortable.

She settled underneath the covers and turned on her side, edging closer to the outside so she could peer over at Liam on the floor.

"Liam?" she called softly. "You still awake?"

"Yes, baby. You okay?"

She smiled at the soft endearment and the concern in his voice. It was nice having someone other than family care about her. It filled a void that had long been empty.

"Yeah, I'm fine. I just wanted to say thank you."

There was a rustle and movement and suddenly Liam was staring her in the eye. He'd pushed up and leaned in close until their faces were just inches apart.

"Don't thank me for protecting someone I care about. I don't give a damn about your brother hiring us. That's not why we're here. He could fire us tomorrow and we'd still be right here. With you. We aren't going anywhere."

She lifted her head, shifting so she could rest it in her palm, her elbow dug into the mattress.

"I wasn't going to thank you for protecting me, though I am grateful."

"Then what were you thanking me for?"

"For being so patient and understanding. For knowing all the right things to say to ease my fears. I know they're irrational, but you never got annoyed. I'm still taking it all in. That you and Noah both care about me when I was already struggling to understand the feelings I had for both of you."

Liam got to his knees and propped his arms on the mattress just in front of her. He rested his chin so their noses were nearly touching, and then he pushed forward, the barest of inches, and brushed his lips across hers.

She could barely make out in the dim light that shone from the streetlights through her window that Liam was shirtless. She wished there were more light, because she wanted to see if he had more tattoos or how far up his arms the sleeves extended.

Who was she kidding? She just wanted to see his body. Wanted to touch him. He stirred feelings of desire that she'd sworn she'd never feel for a man again.

He kissed her again and smoothed a hand over her face.

"I love the feel of your skin," he said. "I could keep touching you forever. I don't think I'll ever grow tired of it."

She gathered her courage and held it tightly to her. Joel had taught her that rejection was pain. It was humiliation. It meant feeling completely alone. He'd rejected her advances at every turn until she'd numbly fallen into the robotic routine of only doing what pleased him and never acting spontaneously. Did she dare risk being rejected by Liam?

She closed her eyes, her pulse accelerating. It was such a simple thing and yet she was terrified that he'd back away.

"Hey, are you okay?" Liam asked. "You just went incredibly tense. You know I'm not going to hurt you, don't you?"

"I know," she whispered. "I was going to . . ." She swallowed hard. "I was going to ask you . . ."

He trailed a finger down her cheek and then back up again. "What do you want to ask me, baby?"

Bracing herself for crushing disappointment, she held her breath and voiced her request.

"I was going to ask if you'd hold me. There's enough room," she hastily added before he could respond. "And I understand if you'd rather stay where you are. I know the bed is small—"

He hushed her with a deep, hungry kiss. His mouth covered hers and for a long moment, there was complete silence. Only the light sounds of his tongue, moving hot over hers. The harsh exhalation of breaths. And then he pulled away, his chest heaving audibly.

He didn't issue a response. Didn't say a single thing. He simply rose and then lifted her into his arms. Then he maneuvered his way onto the bed and settled her in the crook of his arm between him and the wall. They were both on their sides, pressed tight against each other. She wondered if he had any room or if he was on the very edge of the bed.

And then she realized she didn't care. She was in his arms.

Nothing had ever felt so right. So perfect.

Peace settled over her as he cuddled her closer, fitting their bodies together. He reached down to pull the covers over the both of them, and then he hooked one leg over hers.

He was just wearing boxers. And she could feel his erection against her leg. She should feel trapped. He was wrapped completely around her. But what she felt was safe.

"Better?" he asked.

"Better," she agreed, nuzzling closer still.

She could smell him, loved the sensation of his chest against her chin and lips. She inserted her hand between them and smoothed from his belly upward to his chest and then upward over his shoulder.

His muscles quivered and jumped beneath her touch. She just wanted to soak him in. Savor this moment and the closeness between them.

He rubbed his hand up and down her back, and then he slipped his hand underneath the hem of her pajama top and slid his palm over her bare back.

She shivered in reaction and closed her eyes. She was very nearly lulled to sleep when his chest rumbled and his words broke the silence.

"Lauren, how badly did he hurt you?" he asked softly.

She stiffened but he kept rubbing her back and pressed a kiss to her temple.

"He can't hurt you, baby. You're here with me, in my arms. I'm wrapped around you, and to get to you, someone has to go through me. I'm a mean son of a bitch when I'm riled. No one's going to fuck with me."

"Why is it important to know?" she asked, her throat closing in as she remembered that last night when her world had been shattered. Her faith. Her belief in Joel. He'd become real to her then. No longer a fantasy she'd created in her denial. He'd hurt her. But sometimes she wondered if he hadn't done her a favor by losing control. If he hadn't would she still be under his thumb? Would she still be trying to please him by losing more of herself every single day?

"Because you've never told anyone. Or at least you didn't tell Max and you didn't tell me or Noah. You were vague and let the bruises do most of the talking for you. You let us draw our own conclusions about what happened, but you've never talked about it."

"H-he snapped," she said falteringly. "To this day I can't remember what made him lose his temper. He came home in a mood. I knew it and I tried my best to fade into the background. Become invisible. I knew he wouldn't want me in the way. I remember going into the kitchen. I was nervous and scared and I kept thinking, this is wrong. This is so wrong. Why am I with a man who terrifies me? Why am I tiptoeing around? I dropped a glass and I panicked. Had he heard it? I got the broom and a dustpan but when I turned around to clean it up, he was there."

She was shaking against Liam. Cold. She no longer felt warm and safe. She was back in that cold, sterile environment that had suddenly erupted in violence.

"He dragged me into the bedroom, shoved me face down on the bed. I remember his hand in my hair and his knee in my back and the sound of his zipper."

"Oh God, baby," Liam said as he hugged her tighter to him.

"I always wore dresses or skirts. He liked thin, feminine material. He liked easy access. He shoved up my dress, yanked my underwear down, and then he was on top of me. I-inside me. Oh God, I hated it, Liam. I hated him."

Liam rocked her back and forth, his body so rigid that there was absolutely no give in him.

"That son of a bitch."

Lauren yanked away from Liam and scrambled up as she heard Noah's explosive outburst from the doorway of the bedroom.

"Goddamn it, Noah!" Liam bit out. "You scared her to death. What the fuck, man?"

"Is it all right if I turn on the bathroom light, Lauren?" Noah asked, his voice still tight.

"Y-yes," she stammered out.

A moment later, light poured into the bedroom, illuminating the bed where Liam lay and she sat, her knees hunched to her chest and her back against the wall.

She glanced warily at Noah, who stood at the end of the bed. Her bedroom was getting crowded with three people. It was hard to breathe. Her chest felt tight and constricted.

Liam pushed himself upward into a sitting position, and it was then she saw the tattoos that swirled over his shoulders and to his chest. She'd been right. He had more than just the ones on his arms.

"Lauren?" Noah asked softly.

She glanced back up at him.

He sat on the very end of the bed, and she wondered if the bed would bear up under the weight of all three of them.

"Come here, sweetheart."

She flew into his arms and wrapped hers around his neck. He held her tightly for what seemed like forever. Just holding her. He buried his face in her hair and smoothed his hand up and down her back much like Liam had done.

"I'm sorry if I startled you," he said against her hair. "I wasn't trying to eavesdrop. I got up to come to the bathroom and I heard you and Liam talking. I heard what that bastard did to you. I couldn't just walk away and pretend I hadn't heard."

"I didn't fight him," Lauren said in a small voice. "I was in shock. He wasn't that rough. He was punishing me. But I wasn't ready. I mean how could I have been? It hurt. A lot. But more than the physical pain was how violated I felt."

"Did you want him to do that to you?" Liam asked.

"No!" she said, shocked by the question.

"Did you say no?" Liam prodded further.

"Yes," she whispered. "I said no. I sobbed it. I begged him to stop."

"Then goddamn it, he raped you. He forced himself on you," Noah said fiercely. "If you said no. If you even *thought* no. If you had no power to make him stop, then how could it be anything else? You sure as hell didn't give him your consent."

"No one else would see it that way," she said, tears welling in her eyes.

"I don't give a fuck how anyone else sees it," Noah bit out. "He took the choice from you, Lauren. He had absolute power over you. He held you down and forced you to have sex with him. How can that be anything but rape? And worse, he made you believe you deserved it."

"I don't like it that way," she said, her voice cracking.

"What way, baby?" Liam asked gently.

"It was the way he always had sex with me. He held me face-down and he took me from behind. I hate it. I feel so helpless."

Noah found her lips and kissed her. It wasn't an overwhelming kiss meant to dazzle her senses or overcome her with passion. It was a tender, sweet kiss that she felt all the way to her soul.

He framed her face in his hands and pulled away so she was forced to look into his eyes.

"When the time comes that you're ready to make love to us, we will do nothing that frightens you or makes you uncomfortable. We're not to that point yet. Yes, we want to hold you. Touch you.

Kiss you as many times as we can get away with it. But making love is a big step and it's not one we need to take before you have absolute trust in the fact that we're not going to hurt you. But you know what? It'll come. Maybe not next week or next month. But we'll get there and I'm willing to wait for as long as it takes you to heal from what that bastard did to your confidence and your heart and your mind."

"I could so easily fall in love with you both," she whispered, mimicking Liam's earlier words.

"That makes us very happy to hear, sweetheart," Noah murmured. "Now why don't you try to get some rest. Today's been one hell of a day for you. I'm sure you're exhausted mentally and physically."

She glanced up at him, touched his cheek. "Does it bother you . . . I mean, are you okay with . . ."

"Just spit it out, honey. You don't have to pull your punches with me," Noah said gently.

"Will it make you angry that I'm sleeping next to Liam? That I asked him to hold me?" she asked hesitantly.

Noah smiled. "Not at all. Because you know what? Tomorrow night it'll be me in here, holding you and sleeping next to you."

CHAPTER 10

LAUREN had always been a little overwhelmed by the Colter family. Not in a bad way. They'd been nothing but loving and accepting of her from the very start.

But they were just so . . .

Everything. They were everything she'd imagine in the perfect American family. What most people dreamed of. Closeness. Tight-knit. Fiercely loyal.

Except that they hardly fit the picture of the typical American family.

When Max had first begun to tell her of Callie's family, Lauren had thought he was playing a joke on her. How ironic that now Lauren found herself in a similar situation, and moreover, it was one she wanted to be in.

The Colters had opened her eyes to a whole new world. One that was filled with love and acceptance. It was a world she much preferred over her old one.

As she and Liam and Noah got out of the rental they'd driven from Denver to Clyde, Lauren grew nervous. Would it be evident to everyone that Liam and Noah were more than just bodyguards hired by her brother?

Liam whistled. "Nice place they have here. It looks like a postcard."

And indeed it did.

The log cabin was nestled against the mountain, surrounded by aspens and pine and afforded a beautiful view in every direction.

She pointed to the meadow in the distance where a stream cut through the land. Spring had come, bringing with it bountiful flowers and lush greenery. It was a place that calmed the senses and signaled peace. She took a deep breath, sucking in the pine scented cool air.

"That's where Max and Callie live. Across the meadow in the house Max built for Callie. It's not a long walk and there's a worn trail that leads to their property. Callie's property," she amended.

The land had been a bone of contention between Max and Callie. It had once belonged to Lauren's stepfather, the man who'd raised her and Max, and after he passed, her mother had sold it to the Colters. Max had believed the elder Colter brothers had taken advantage of her mom and had fully intended to do whatever necessary to get the land back. Even if it meant deceiving Callie in the process.

She shook her head. Her brother had very nearly screwed up the best thing that had ever happened to him. He was at peace now. Maybe it was what the land and the Colters had done for him. Maybe it was what would do the same for her.

The front door opened, and Ethan Colter stepped out, a smile broadening his features.

"Hello, Lauren! Come on in."

Lauren relaxed, smiling back at the older man. She hurried

toward the door, eager to be back in the bosom of the Colter family. She always looked forward to her visits here, no matter how frequently she came.

Liam and Noah followed closely behind, and when she got to the porch, Ethan enfolded her in a huge hug.

In the beginning she'd been hesitant around the loving, demonstrative family, even though it was in her nature to be just as affectionate. But Joel had taught her reserve and it was a hard lesson to forget.

"It's good to see you, honey," Ethan said.

She squeezed back. "And you."

She turned to Noah and Liam standing a few steps back. "Ethan, this is Noah Sullivan and Liam Prescott. Noah and Liam, this is Ethan Colter."

Ethan immediately extended his hand to Noah and then to Liam.

"It's a pleasure to meet you, sir," Noah said.

"Come on in, all of you. Holly is dying to get her hands on you. I'll warn you now. Just take whatever comes. My wife is used to getting her own way. She'll likely interrogate you and then smother you with hugs."

He smiled indulgently, his love for his wife softening his eyes and expression.

Lauren pushed by Ethan, eager to be inside. As soon as she stepped into the living room, it was like coming home. Memories of the previous Christmas when she'd been so unsure of her place in the world, and in this family came to mind.

Warmth, love and peace washed over her, cradling her in their soothing embrace.

"Lauren!"

Holly Colter surged up from her place on the couch between Adam and Ryan Colter, and she rushed over, pulling Lauren into a fierce hug that was even bigger than the one Ethan had given her.

Behind her, Adam and Ryan rose, their gazes drawn to Noah and Liam. There was wary reserve and sharp appraisal in their stares. Lauren smiled as the force that was Holly Colter surrounded her, making her feel love and concern that had extended to one who wasn't Holly's own. Not that Holly would ever draw that distinction. She'd made it clear from the day she'd come to see Lauren, when Lauren had still been in seclusion at Max and Callie's home, that she considered Lauren one of her children.

"It's so good to see you, baby," Holly whispered. "How are you? Are you okay?"

Lauren pulled away. "I'm fine. Truly. You don't need to worry about me. Noah and Liam have promised to take care of me."

Holly frowned a little as she looked past Lauren to the two men behind her. Then she pushed past Lauren, and Lauren turned to see what was in store for Noah and Liam.

"I'm Holly Colter," she said. "Max told me about you, but I wanted to set eyes on you myself and make sure that you were the kind of men I can trust to take care of my baby."

Liam's lips twitched into a smile while Noah looked a little more wary.

"I'm very pleased to meet you, ma'am," Liam said solemnly. "And I promise to take very good care of Lauren. Noah and I are going to make sure that no one ever hurts Lauren again."

There was a flicker of response in the Colter brothers' eyes. Adam's eyebrows went up a notch while Ryan's eyes narrowed.

Holly stared at them for a long time, and then she smiled broadly. Then she pulled the much larger Liam into a huge hug and patted him on the back.

"I think I like you, Liam."

Then she turned to Noah as if she hadn't yet made up her mind about him.

"And what have you got to say, young man?"

At that Ethan chuckled while Adam and Ryan smothered their smiles of amusement. Noah looked befuddled as the much smaller woman took him to task.

He looked like he'd rather take on a group of terrorists than answer to her.

"I care very much about Lauren's safety," Noah finally said. "And as Liam said, we're here to protect her. You can trust us with her safety. Someone will have to go through us to get close to her."

Holly gave him the same frank appraisal she'd given Liam and then she smiled.

"You'll do."

Then she hugged him just as enthusiastically as she had Liam and then promptly ordered him and Liam to have a seat.

Once satisfied that Noah and Liam were taken care of, she turned back to Lauren.

"Lily and the boys are on their way over now, and I expect Max and Callie at any moment. I prepared lunch today," she said proudly.

Adam gave her an indulgent smile.

Ryan took his seat on the couch across from where Liam and Noah had taken their seats. And sent them both a look of amusement.

"After more than thirty years, our wife has taken it upon herself to learn how to cook. She made Christmas dinner for us all without burning the kitchen down, so we've agreed to turn her loose on occasion. What's she's prepared is anyone's guess, so I hope you brought the antacid."

Holly sent a glare in Ryan's direction. "Oh hush. You're going to scare them and have them thinking I'm going to poison them."

Ethan ruffled her hair affectionately. "Not too long ago, that would have been the truth. I have the fire extinguishers on standby."

Noah and Liam both wore peculiar expressions, as if they weren't sure how seriously to take the bantering. Lauren just laughed and hugged Holly again.

"I think you're a wonderful cook, Mama C. I'll be happy to eat whatever you fix."

Holly beamed and patted Lauren's arm. "I always knew you were my favorite child. Come into the kitchen with me. We can talk while I finish up and we'll leave the men out here to do whatever it is men do when they're together."

Then she sent another glare in her husbands' direction. "You don't say another word about my cooking. You've liked what I've cooked just fine."

Ethan put his arm around her. "Sweetheart, you've only cooked twice more since Christmas. Give us time to adjust. We're too used to having the fire department on standby when you venture into the kitchen."

Holly shook her head then reached for Lauren's hand. "Come on. I've got nothing left to say to these men."

Lauren allowed herself to be dragged into the kitchen, though she felt a brief moment of guilt for pitching Noah and Liam to the wolves. They'd probably get grilled by the Colter men. Hopefully the others would arrive soon. At least Noah and Liam knew Max and Seth already.

But on the other hand . . . If she was truly going to entertain having a relationship with Noah and Liam, the Colter family was going to be something they would have to get used to, because the Colters were too important to Lauren.

They were her family.

"Sit and keep me company," Holly said, steering her toward the L-shaped bar that curved from the kitchen counters.

Lauren slid onto one of the leather stools and propped her elbows on the counter.

"So what are you cooking today?" Lauren asked.

Holly grinned, her eyes twinkling mischievously. "I'm totally cheating. Lily brought me three pans of lasagna yesterday, premade. All I have to do is pop them in the oven and voila, a mouthwatering Italian dinner. I have bakery rolls from town and bag salad from the store."

Lauren laughed. "I won't breathe a word."

Holly took the lasagna from the fridge and slid them into the double-wall oven, set the timer and then came back to the bar and peered across it at Lauren.

"So tell me about Noah and Liam. I sense there's more to this whole thing than their being some random strangers Max hired to protect you."

Heat crept into Lauren's cheeks and she fidgeted nervously on the stool.

"Why do you say that?" Lauren asked curiously.

Holly smiled. "Baby, the way those men look at you tells its own story. And the way Liam talked about people going through him and Noah to get to you? If you were just a job, they would have had some polished spiel they regurgitated for every client. There was passion in his voice and I absolutely believed him when he said he wouldn't let anyone hurt you."

Lauren sighed. "I wanted to talk to you about them." She dug her fingertips into her temples and rubbed.

Holly's look turned to one of concern. "What is it, Lauren? You know you can talk to me about anything."

"They want a relationship with me. Like the one you have with your . . . husbands."

Holly's eyes widened a bit and then her brow furrowed. "Isn't it a bit soon? Didn't they just arrive?" Then she broke into a wry smile. "Like I can talk. Adam, Ethan and Ryan took one look at me and decided I was the one. They never looked back. It was the same when Seth first laid eyes on Lily. People laugh at the idea of love at first sight, but I've certainly witnessed it firsthand. Over thirty years later, here I am, still just as much in love with those old fools as I was as a starry-eyed naïve girl in my twenties."

"I love hearing about you and the dads," Lauren said wistfully.

Holly leaned across the bar and took Lauren's hands in hers. "Back to Noah and Liam. You've talked about this? Already I mean?"

Lauren shook her head. "Yes, we've talked, but it's not like I just met them. Max hired them when I was still in New York City. Before he and Callie came to bring me here. They started out a giant pain in my butt."

Holly laughed. "Sounds like a typical start to a relationship to me."

"According to them, the attraction was there from the beginning."

"And what about you?" Holly asked softly.

"I noticed them," Lauren hedged.

Holly laughed again. "Kind of hard not to notice those two. They tend to stand out in a crowd. I figure Dillon's going to get along with them just fine. They'll be comparing tattoos and earrings. I swear I don't know where that child of mine got his tastes."

"How hard is it, really?" Lauren asked in a quiet voice. "I'm scared of messing up. I'm drawn to both of them. I love the idea of having these two wonderful men both devoted to me. But I'm using your husbands and Lily's husbands as measuring sticks. I don't want to go in with unrealistic expectations. Am I crazy for wanting this? To agreeing to try it with them?"

"Oh, sweetie, you're overthinking this. There's really one question to ask. Do you love them?"

Lauren dropped her gaze. "I don't know. It's so soon after Joel. What if I'm just latching on to the first opportunity after a really bad relationship? I don't want to use them."

"Okay, let me rephrase the question. Could you see yourself eventually falling in love with them?"

"Oh yes," Lauren breathed.

Holly squeezed her hands. "Do they love you?"

"I think they could. Maybe they do. I'm not sure. But they act like I'm the most important person in the world to them. They're so loving and patient and gentle. They aren't trying to rush me."

"Then that's all that's important. If you can see yourself falling in love with both men and they both care about you, everything else will work itself out."

"You make it sound so easy," Lauren said. "I just keep thinking of everything that can go wrong. What if one of them gets jealous? What if I don't spend exactly the same amount of time with both of them?" Her face went beet red with heat. "What if I have sex more with one than the other? It all makes my head hurt."

Holly walked around the bar and slid onto the stool next to Lauren.

"You're taking far too much on your shoulders, baby. Listen to me. You can only control what you do. You can't be responsible for how they react or what they do. In a lot of ways, the relationship is much harder on the men than it is the woman, and in some aspects it's more difficult for the woman."

"You're confusing me," Lauren said in amusement.

"The men have to form a bond. I know it sounds silly. In my case, the men were brothers. Trust was already there. Trust is very important between the men so they're working on the same page. When you have a case like with Noah and Liam, that friendship and trust has to be there so that jealousy doesn't become an issue or they're not always wondering if the other is trying to get you to agree to kick one out of the relationship."

"That makes sense," Lauren agreed.

"And the way it's more difficult for a woman, is that she has multiple personalities to learn and work around. The men are working with one woman. She's their focus. But the woman's focus is split between two, or in my case, three men. She has to know what makes each of them tick. And sometimes it's a delicate balance juggling those different personalities because each man has his own set of desires, and what he wants from the relationship. One might need one thing from you while the other needs something entirely different. It can be exhausting, especially in the beginning when you're learning."

Lauren nodded again. "I knew I could count on you to make perfect sense, Mama C. But you know, it's kind of exciting when everything is all shiny and new and when the mere thought of a relationship makes you breathless. They give me . . . hope. I'm almost afraid to believe, because I don't know what I'll do if it doesn't work out."

Holly cupped Lauren's face in her hands. "Just take it one day at a time, baby. It's all you can do. But let me tell you. Those two men are the luckiest guys on earth to have you and they don't need to forget it. You are a beautiful, intelligent, loving young woman and one I'm very proud to call my daughter. And you are, you know. You may not bear the Colter last name, but that's the only thing that sets you apart from one of my own."

"Hey, Mom!"

Lauren whirled around to see Callie burst into the kitchen, a sunny smile on her face.

Holly's expression softened, and she hopped off the stool to go hug her youngest child. Except that according to Holly, Lauren was one of her brood, which actually made Lauren the youngest.

It did heart-stopping things to Lauren to fully comprehend that she had a place in this wonderful family. God, it made her want to tear all up, and if that wasn't just stupid after so many months, she didn't know what it was.

As Callie was hugging her mom, Lily Colter walked in behind them. Seven months pregnant, Lily still moved gracefully despite the bulge on her small frame. She was a petite woman with delicate features.

As Lauren glanced around at the women gathered in the Colter kitchen, she realized that this was a room full of women who'd survived unimaginable tragedies, dangerous situations and heartbreak. It was one thing they all had in common.

Lily had been married before she'd met Holly's sons, and she'd suffered a terrible loss when her newborn baby had died of sudden infant death syndrome. Her husband had blamed her and divorced Lily. Devastated and grief stricken, Lily had walked away, living on the streets, homeless, until Seth, who'd then worked as a police office in Denver, had spotted her at a soup kitchen where he volunteered.

He'd taken her home and when his brothers had met her, they'd had the same instant recognition that Seth himself had felt. They all knew that she was the one.

Lauren firmly believed that Max had also known instantly that Callie was the one, but he'd been a lot more hardheaded than the Colter men, and the result had been nearly losing Callie forever.

It had never really occurred to Lauren how drastically her own life would have changed if Max and Callie hadn't been able to work things out. Lauren would have never come to know the Colters. Never would have been a part of the family she now considered her own.

After Holly hugged and fussed over Lily, Lily broke away and came to give Lauren a quick hug. Concern darkened her blue eyes as she struggled to get onto the bar stool next to Lauren.

"Seth told me a little of what happened. Are you okay?" Lily asked anxiously.

Lauren smiled and nodded. "I'm fine. Noah and Liam won't let anything happen to me."

Lily's eyes lightened but then gleamed, and she pursed her lips. "And speaking of Noah and Liam, you've got to give me the dirt on those two gorgeous hunks. God, they remind me of Dillon. Well him and Michael both. It's like taking Dillon and Michael and producing their offspring."

"Oh God, Lily. Really? I so don't need that image branded into my brain," Callie said with a groan as she took the stool on the other side of Lauren.

"All that long dark hair and tattoos on Liam?" Lily said. "That man is gorgeous and so dangerous looking."

Lauren grinned and preened under the praise from the other woman. And she could even see how Lily made the comparison. Dillon Colter was the wild child. The one that seemingly broke the mold in the Colter family. He looked like a total badass but he had a heart of gold. He sported tattoos and an earring, but his hair was cut short and spiked on top. Michael was certainly more conservative, but his one rebellion seemed to be his hair, which he wore shoulder length. Liam seemed a good combination of both men.

"And Noah isn't bad to look at either," Callie broke in. "I'd certainly lick those arms of his. They're huge! You can't tell me those two don't lift weights to have biceps that big. His tats are cool too. Definitely more subtle than Liam's, but it just works for him. He has that quiet badass look to him."

Holly chuckled as she walked back to the fridge. She pulled out the bag of lettuce, two tomatoes, a cucumber and a packet of shredded carrots.

"Better not let Max hear you talking about licking another man's anything, Callie."

Callie made a face. "It's not like I really would. But it's certainly tempting."

"So what's the story on those two?" Lily asked. "Am I the only one in the dark here? Seth said very little. Just that they were here to protect you. He nearly gave me a heart attack and then he had to spend the next half hour assuring me that someone wasn't trying to kill you or something."

Lauren put her hand over Lily's. "I'm sorry he worried you. It's really nothing. I'm more than a little embarrassed over it all. I kept important information from Max and from Noah and Liam. Max hired them months ago. Before I came here at Christmas. It was when I got the nerve to leave . . . Joel . . . and finally called Max for help. But I didn't tell them the truth about who I was involved in."

Callie wrinkled her nose. "Why?"

Lauren sighed. "I know it sounds stupid."

"No, no," Lily rushed to say. "We don't think you're stupid at all, Lauren. I'm so proud of you for having the guts to walk away from that jerk. But why would you protect him?"

Lauren shook her head emphatically. "I was never protecting him. I was trying to protect Max. And Noah and Liam. I knew if Max knew the truth, he'd go after Joel. He was furious at the time. And Joel was—is—involved in illegal activities. I doubt I even know the extent of it. He has many people on his payroll, including cops. If Max or Noah and Liam were to threaten him in any way, who's to say he wouldn't have them killed? It sounds dramatic and over the top, but you have to understand the kind of man Joel is. I honestly just wanted as far away from him as possible and I want to forget he exists."

Callie wrapped her arm protectively around Lauren and squeezed fiercely. "Of course you do and I don't blame you a bit. Besides, who wouldn't want to be protected by two hunks like Noah and Liam?" she added cheekily.

Lily laughed and Lauren relaxed. She was surrounded by dear friends. Family. Women she cared deeply about and who loved her in return. This was what she loved most about being with the Colters. The freedom to be herself. To confide, discuss, laugh and joke.

No one told her how to act. Hugs were given as freely as breathing. Someone was always touching, showing affection. No one blinked an eye over it.

The ache inside her grew until she rubbed her chest to alleviate the discomfort.

How wonderful would it be if she and Noah and Liam could live right here in these mountains, surrounded by the family who'd made Lauren one of their own?

CHAPTER 11

O N the drive home, Lauren stared out the window as dusk
settled over the mountains. She'd enjoyed herself. She always
did. Any time she was feeling down, she could count on a visit with
the Colters to pick her up.

They made her believe that things would get better. They
always did.

But one thought that had passed through her mind, sitting in
Holly's kitchen, haunted her.

She'd wished for a happily ever after with Noah and Liam, right
here in these mountains, surrounded by her family and the people
she loved.

How realistic was that?

The stark truth was that it wasn't at all realistic. Noah's and
Liam's lives were in New York. Their business was in New York.
And when they had ascertained that there was no longer a threat
to her, whether they remained in a relationship with her or not,

they'd move on to another job, guarding other people. Providing personal security. In New York City.

The mere thought of being in the same city as Joel Knight, no matter how huge the city was or how unlikely it was that they'd ever cross paths, sent her into complete panic.

What if he knew, even now, what she'd done? She hadn't been that careful. She didn't know enough about computers to know if what she'd done could be discovered. He might have known that she'd been through his files the moment she disappeared.

As much as she'd tried not to focus on him, as much as she'd tried to shove him from her mind and move on with her life, how did she know that he wasn't looking for her?

She'd made a big deal to the other women that she'd wanted to protect Max and Noah and Liam, and that was true, but she also feared coming into contact with him again in case he knew what she'd stolen.

It was laughable that she'd even done such a stupid thing. Especially when she had no plans to do anything with the information she'd copied from his computer. At the time, in her fragile mind, it had been an insurance policy. So that if he did ever come after her, she could threaten him.

Which made her the biggest idiot in the world. Threaten a man like Joel Knight? He could squash her like a bug and never blink an eye. She was nobody. Certainly not someone strong enough to stand up to him and back him into a corner.

She'd vowed to herself that she'd stop beating herself up over her past mistakes, but it was hard sometimes when she thought back on just how brainwashed she'd been; and then when she'd finally been gutsy enough to get out, she'd all but ensured that if he discovered what she'd taken, he'd never simply let her go and forget about her.

It was something she needed to confide in Noah and Liam. She knew she needed to tell them, but the words simply wouldn't come. Maybe they were right in that she didn't fully trust them yet. Maybe in time she'd feel at ease with confessing her stupidity. She just knew that right now wasn't the time. She had to be more sure of them— of her and them.

"You're quiet, baby," Liam said from the backseat.

She started, suddenly aware of just how zoned out she'd been, immersed deeply in her thoughts and recriminations.

Noah reached over from the driver's seat to take her hand, and he laced their fingers together.

"Everything okay?" Noah asked. "Did you enjoy your visit?"

Lauren smiled. No question there. "I love the Colters. Being with them always makes me happy."

"I'll admit, I wasn't sure what to expect," Liam said. "It sounds pretty incredible when someone explains the kind of relationship the Colter men have with their wives. But then when you see them together, you don't even question it. It's so obvious they belong together and that it works for them."

He broke off for a long moment, and then he leaned forward, resting his elbows on the edges of Lauren's and Noah's seats.

"I want that for us, Lauren. That sense of rightness. The closeness. I want for people to look at us and say the same things we say about the Colters."

Lauren turned as much in her seat as the seat belt allowed. Noah was focused on the road, but it was apparent that he was tuned in completely to the conversation.

She sighed, allowing her earlier unhappiness to escape. It was impossible to keep her mouth from turning down.

"Hey, what's wrong?" Liam asked, concern in his voice. "Are you having second thoughts? Did someone say anything to you today to change your mind?"

She slowly shook her head. "No. Holly was extremely supportive. I didn't talk to Callie or Lily about you. Not for any other reason than this is still new and I'm not one to air my private life to everyone."

"Then what's made you unhappy?" Noah asked. "You've been in another world ever since we left, and it's obvious you have something on your mind you're not telling us about."

She glanced nervously between them, not because she feared a physical response. She feared the confirmation of her realization and the bursting of her created fantasy. The intrusion of reality was not always welcome. The problem was, she'd lived outside the realm of reality for too long.

Denial didn't change the outcome of anything.

"I was sitting at the bar with the other women, and we were all talking and I was reminded, as I always am, how much I love the Colters. And then I was struck by the thought of how wonderful it would be to live here . . . with you . . . to be with both of you and be so close to my family."

She sucked in another breath while Liam and Noah both waited expectantly for her to continue.

"And as we drove away, I realized how impossible that is. Your lives are in New York. I realize you have feelings for me that go above and beyond me being a job to you, but once whatever threat is determined and eliminated, you'll go on to another job. In New York. And whatever relationship we attempt would also have to be in New York. I realized how afraid I still am to be in the same city, no matter how vast, that Joel's in. This has become home to me, and I hate the thought of having to leave it."

There, she'd said it. She held her breath, not wanting to hear what they would say. She hated having reality intrude when things were new and exciting and hope had sprung.

"I don't know that we've even given that a thought," Noah said honestly.

"It's certainly something we would need to discuss and work out between us," Liam said in a careful tone. "My primary focus was you. And somehow getting you to accept what we proposed. Beyond that hurdle, I've given little thought to anything else, except to realize that we have to take it as it comes, one day at a time."

She nodded her understanding, but the issue was still there, like a giant roadblock, and it was one she didn't see a way around.

She couldn't expect them to sacrifice everything they'd worked to achieve for her. What did she have to offer them here anyway? She was a waitress. In a diner. She made barely enough to pay her rent and get by on. And there wasn't a high demand for personal protection in Clyde.

For that matter what could she offer them in New York? She'd quit her job at Joel's demand. He'd wanted her available to him at all times and he wanted nothing to interfere in his schedule.

Stupidly—God, she used that word a lot to describe her actions—she'd thought it romantic that he'd wanted her to quit so he could take care of her. She'd been too naïve to realize it was the first step in putting her squarely under his complete control.

A year without work didn't do wonders for the resume. When asked by employers to explain the gap in employment, what could she say? Oh, I was a naïve twit who quit my job to allow a man to take over my life, but hey, I've got my crap together now so you should feel absolutely comfortable in giving me a job.

Yeah. Not happening.

Her degree was useless in Clyde. There was about as much need for someone with marketing experience as there was for personal protection.

"Lauren?" Liam called softly.

She turned in the direction of his voice and met the vivid blue of his gaze.

"We'll work it out, okay?"

She nodded again, not trusting herself to speak.

Noah pulled her hand onto his lap, almost as if he were sending her the message that he wasn't letting go and he wasn't giving up.

Maybe she was being too fatalistic. It wasn't as if their only two choices were Clyde or New York. While she'd grown very attached to where she lived and to the Colters, there was nothing to say that she couldn't be happy somewhere else.

She hadn't planned to live here forever before, had she?

Or maybe that's precisely what she'd planned. To spend the rest of her life hiding, never really living. Just existing.

Noah and Liam were giving her the opportunity to live a full, rich life filled with love. They wanted to make her happy, had sworn to do everything in their power to make her happy.

Maybe they could even live out of the city and they could commute. She doubted they'd ever travel in the same circles that Joel did. They'd probably never encounter him in their lifetime.

You have the power to put him away.

The insidious whisper stole through her mind.

With the information she'd copied from Joel's computer, she had the power to make Joel a nonissue for a very long time. But in order to do that, she had to have courage she didn't currently possess.

And more importantly, she'd have to be willing to face Joel Knight again.

CHAPTER 12

⮺

LAUREN dressed for bed in the tiny bathroom and took longer than normal to brush out her hair and clean her teeth. Noah was in her bedroom, also undressing for bed, while Liam was settling into the living room.

There was no way this arrangement could last long term. Not that she'd minded sleeping in Liam's arms last night, but he couldn't have been comfortable on the bed. They'd been forced to remain on their sides, locked together the entire night. Even she'd woken up stiff and with a crick in her neck. She couldn't imagine how Liam must have felt.

Should she extend the same invitation to Noah to sleep with her? She'd needed comfort the evening before. The day had exhausted her and left her feeling uncertain. Or at least that was the excuse she'd used to whisper the shy request to Liam.

But if she didn't, would Noah think she preferred Liam over him?

Pain throbbed at her temples and she reached up to massage them, closing her eyes as she took deep, steadying breaths.

To her surprise the bathroom door opened. Her eyes flew open to see Noah standing in the doorway, worry reflected in his gaze.

Before she could speak, he moved in, carefully lowering her wrists so that her fingers no longer dug into her temples.

"Head hurt?" he asked.

She was still trying to find words. His sudden appearance had taken her completely off guard.

"Sorry to barge in on you like that, but you had me worried. I called your name three times and I couldn't hear a damn thing going on behind the door. I was worried you'd fallen or passed out."

She grimaced. "Sorry. I was just lost in thoughts. So much going on and it's still kind of hard to take in."

He gently pulled her into his arms, pressing his lips to her forehead.

"Come to bed. Want me to get you something for the headache?"

"No. I'll be fine. Really."

He laced his fingers with hers and pulled her into the bedroom. His bedroll was carefully made on the floor, but he directed her to the bed.

To her surprise, he crawled onto the mattress, positioned himself so his back rested against the rail at the head of the bed, and then he spread his legs and patted the space between them.

"Come here and I'll rub your head and neck."

Relieved that she didn't have to tackle the issue of whether she should invite him to the bed or not, she put her knee up on the bed and scooted toward him.

When she turned, he immediately wrapped his arms around her and pulled her back against him so she was flush against his chest.

For a moment she let her head fall back against his shoulder and turned her face into his neck, savoring the intimacy of the position.

His hands glided up her bare arms and then over the thin spaghetti straps of her cami pajama top. Then he slid his fingers into her hair from her nape, traveling upward to the top of her head. He was careful not to pull her hair, and he worked his fingers gently over her scalp, exerting subtle pressure at various intervals.

"That's nice," she breathed.

He let one hand fall briefly and leaned down to press his lips against the side of her neck just below her ear. It sent a cascade of chills over her bare arms until she shivered in reaction.

Her breasts tingled and swelled, her nipples tightening against the thin material. It was instinctive to raise her arms to shield the obvious reaction her body had to the simple kiss.

"Don't hide from me, sweetheart," Noah whispered.

He reached around and took her arms, lowering them back to her lap.

"I like seeing how you react to me, that you want me. It's nothing to be ashamed of."

He kissed her again, grazing his teeth lightly over her skin, and then he let his mouth wander lower to the curve of her neck.

Then he went back to rubbing her head, massaging her temples and then down to her shoulders, those big hands working their magic. Tension leaked from her, leaving her limp in his arms.

"Can I ask you something?" she said in a low voice.

"Of course."

She shifted and attempted to turn around so she could face him. After awkwardly maneuvering her legs and body, she knelt between his legs, sitting back on her heels so she was at eye level with him.

Maybe it would have been better to ask him when she was facing away, because now as he stared intently back at her, courage fled and her tongue felt tied in a dozen knots.

He reached up, tracing her mouth with his thumb. "What's on your mind, sweetheart?"

"This is kind of awkward," she mumbled.

He didn't say anything. He simply waited, patient, as she gathered her thoughts.

"Will you and Liam want . . ."

Heat suffused her cheeks and she couldn't get the words past her lips. She felt like a complete moron. How on earth were they going to be able to have an honest and open relationship between the three of them if she couldn't even broach the subject of sex without breaking out into hives?

"Will Liam and I want what?" he prompted.

"To have sex with me . . . at the same time," she finally blurted out. "You know, like a threesome."

Noah blinked in surprise, but then his eyes went dark, smoldering with enough heat to cause an odd flutter deep in her chest.

He leaned forward, wrapping his arms around her, crushing her to his chest until their noses touched and she could feel the warmth of his breath on her chin.

"To be perfectly honest, it's not something we've discussed. You're what's important to us. Not sex. Don't get me wrong, honey. I want you in my bed, you wrapped around me so tight and me deep inside you. But I want to give you the time you need to adjust to the idea. As for a threesome, I've never had one, but the idea is hot as hell and I'd love to try it. But first? I want you. Just you. Not an audience. Not someone else in the picture. Just your mouth wrapped around my dick. My tongue between your legs. I want to taste you so badly that I ache. I want to touch you, learn you. I want to discover what excites you and how to please you. But yeah, a threesome would be pretty damn cool."

"Oh," she breathed out, her entire body tingling and hyperaware as he whispered the blunt words.

"Does that excite you?" he murmured. "The idea of me and Liam taking you at the same time? Do you like the idea of us both touching you and filling you, kissing you, making you mindless with pleasure?"

She nodded, not trusting herself to speak.

Then she swallowed and asked the other question burning a hole in her brain.

"Will you make love to me? Tonight?"

His entire body tightened against her. His breathing changed and his eyes darkened, making him so damn dangerous looking. And sexy as hell.

"Are you ready for that?" he asked, his tone wary. "I don't want to rush this, Lauren. The very last thing I want to do is to hurry into something that we'll regret. I'm willing to wait for as long as it takes for you to trust that I'm never going to hurt you."

She slid her fingers over his jaw until her palms cradled his face so very close to hers.

"I want to try," she said honestly. And she did. She wanted it more than she could explain. "I do trust you. My heart trusts you. My mind is a little more cautious, but my heart tells me that I want this."

He let out a groan and briefly closed his eyes.

"Noah?"

The hesitancy in Lauren's voice made Noah open his eyes. It was obvious she was nervous about something. Her teeth were dug into her full bottom lip, and her eyes were shadowed where just moments ago, they'd been alight with desire.

"What is it, honey?"

She glanced over her shoulder to where the bedroom door was closed, a barrier between them and Liam. He knew what her worry was before she even voiced it.

"If I make love with you tonight . . . What about Liam? Will it hurt him that we had sex first? He slept here with me last night. He held me. But we didn't make love. And it's not that I trust you more than him. It's just that I was still too nervous."

He kissed her to stop the flow of anxious chatter. So sweet and soft. He hated the worry and anxiety in her voice. He wanted to sweep her away, take her in his arms and make her forget everything but this moment.

This was a huge step in their newly forming relationship, one he hadn't anticipated taking so soon. He'd been fully prepared to wait weeks, if not months, if that was what it took for her to give him such a precious gift.

"Baby, listen to me," he said when he pulled away so he could look her in the eye. "Don't make yourself crazy keeping score. I swear to you that Liam and I aren't keeping up and don't expect you to divide your time fifty-fifty with us. If Liam had made love to you last night, it would have been okay with me because I know that eventually it will be me. Just like if you and I take that step tonight, when you're ready you'll take that step with Liam.

"Am I glad it's me? Hell yes. I'm not going to lie. I'm sure if Liam were the one sitting here with you between his legs looking at him with those beautiful brown eyes, he wouldn't give one damn about what I thought. He'd be on his knees grateful that you trusted him enough to give him that same gift."

"I just don't want to ever hurt either of you," she said in a somber voice.

He touched her face, stroking his fingers down her cheek. He couldn't get enough of simply touching her. The idea that she was here, so close, asking him to make love to her. It was more than he could stand.

He'd been so very right. He could fall in love with her so easily. Maybe he'd already fallen. Maybe this is what it felt like, sort of like plunging over the side of a cliff in a free fall. Exhilarating. Magnificent. Scary as hell.

"Can I ask *you* something now?" he said.

She nodded.

He took a breath, not believing he was about to do this when all his instincts screamed to take the gift she offered and make love to her as tenderly and gently as she deserved.

He'd just told her moments earlier that he wanted the first time with her to be just the two of them, just like he was sure that Liam would feel the same and want his first time with her to be without company.

But it was evident that she was worried—a lot—about the ramifications of making love to one before the other and how the other would feel.

He shoved aside his preference, because more than anything he wanted for the first time to be all about her. All for her. And he'd do anything at all she wanted.

"Would you prefer that Liam and I make love to you together the first time? Would it make you more comfortable and remove any fear of showing favoritism?"

Her cheeks went pink and he could see the wheels turning in her head. Her blush grew darker and her breathing shallowed and became more rapid.

Then slowly, almost in slow motion, she nodded.

"I'd like Liam here, yes," she said softly. "I'm not sure it'll ever feel right no matter which of you I made love with first. And maybe it'll never be an issue for you or for Liam. But *I* don't want these doubts."

He cupped her cheek, wanting to ease any concern she had about the way they embarked on the physical side of their relationship.

"Then maybe we should call Liam in here and see what he has to say on the matter."

CHAPTER 13

❧

LAUREN tried to calm her racing pulse as Noah got up and went to the door. She rocked back on her heels in the middle of the daybed and then glanced around in mortification.

How on earth were they going to pull this off in her bedroom?

She had little time to contemplate the matter before Noah returned with Liam behind him.

Liam's hair was unkempt, in a sexy, bed-rumpled kind of way. His eyes were alert, though, as if he hadn't yet been to sleep. His gaze immediately homed in on Lauren, warming her as it glided up her body to her face.

Noah climbed onto the bed, pulled one knee up and let his other leg hang off so his foot was planted on the floor. Liam took a seat at the opposite end and turned in a nearly identical position as Noah so he could look at Lauren.

"Noah said you wanted to talk to us about something," Liam said, his deep voice rumbling out of his chest.

Her gaze swung to Noah in panic. She hadn't expected that she'd have to repeat it all.

Noah reached for her hand and squeezed. Then he turned to Liam.

"Lauren is afraid that if she makes love to me tonight that it will hurt you. Or if she were to make love to you first, that I'd be hurt."

Liam frowned as he glanced between her and Noah. Maybe she'd been right to worry.

"Let me back up to an earlier point in our conversation," Noah said. "Before this was brought up, Lauren asked if you and I would want to have sex with her at the same time."

At that Liam's eyebrows went up and his eyes widened. Before Noah could continue, Liam's expression became serious and he turned to take Lauren's other hand.

"I only want what you're comfortable with, baby."

Noah cleared his throat. "When she brought up her fear of making love with me before you, I asked her if she would be more comfortable if we made love to her . . . together . . . the first time."

Understanding registered in Liam's eyes. His eyes went smoky blue and he reached his hand up to cup her cheek, stroking his thumb lightly over her skin.

"Is that what you want?" he asked softly.

She nodded, nuzzling her cheek further into his palm.

"It's not that I don't trust you and Noah not to get angry or jealous. But I don't like the way it makes *me* feel to leave one of you out. I think it bothers me more than it does either of you. I want to start things . . . right. I don't want to worry that I've hurt you or worry about what you're thinking. I just want to be with you both."

Liam leaned forward to kiss her forehead. "You have to know I'd do anything in the damn world for you, baby."

"I don't know how to do this," she admitted. "I'm a little scared."

Liam smiled. "I have zero experience in threesomes. I guess we'll learn together won't we? I'll tell you right now, I'm not down with another guy seeing me naked, but if it's going to be, at least it's a guy I've known almost my entire life."

Noah snorted. "I'll be looking at Lauren, thank you very much."

The lighthearted banter did a lot to ease Lauren's nerves. Her shoulders relaxed. But she still peeked at both of them because now that they'd had the discussion, how on earth did they proceed? Surely sex wasn't usually this orchestrated.

"Come here, Lauren," Liam said, extending his hand.

Apparently he had no such issues about where to begin.

As soon as she slid her fingers through his, he pulled her toward him and into his lap until she straddled it.

"The first thing I'm going to do is undress you," Liam said, his voice deep and husky, whispering over her skin like the most glorious of caresses. "But I wouldn't deprive Noah of the pleasure, so we'll split the duty."

She shivered with anticipation.

He ran his fingers underneath the thin straps of her top and slid them upward until they perched atop her shoulders. Slowly, he pulled them downward and then leaned his dark head over to kiss the curve of her neck.

"So beautiful," he murmured.

As if changing his mind about the way he wanted to undress her, he reached for the hem of her cami and carefully began to lift it, uncovering her bare skin as the material slid upward.

"Raise your arms," he said huskily.

She lifted her arms, and he pulled the top upward until it skimmed over her face and finally came free of her head. She lowered her arms so he could pull the straps away, and then he dropped the shirt to the floor.

She was bare. Starkly vulnerable. His gaze feasted on her, and then he leaned in to kiss the side of her neck. His teeth grazed lightly, and then he nipped with a little more force until she moaned and swayed in his lap.

Then his hands covered her belly and slowly moved upward to cup her breasts. She sucked in her breath, overwhelmed by her body's response to his hands covering her flesh.

Her nipples hardened painfully and when he brushed his thumbs over them in tandem, she let out a breathy sigh and arched toward him, her head going back.

And then Noah was there, his hands gathered in her hair as he leaned in to kiss her neck on the opposite side of where Liam's mouth had just been.

He nuzzled up to her ear and then licked the lobe before sucking it into his mouth. A full-body shiver erupted, and then Liam's mouth found one of her nipples.

Electric. Oh God, her body was supersensitive to their every touch. Anticipation heightened her senses. She could smell them, their rich masculinity. She could hear and feel every breath that passed their lips. Hot on her skin.

Noah slid his hands underneath her armpits and gently lifted upward just as Liam curled his hands around her legs to propel her upward.

She was on her feet, in front of them both. Noah turned her to face him, and he reached for the tie of her pajama bottoms, unlacing it slowly. So slowly it was driving her insane.

When it was undone, he paused, found her gaze and stared intently into her eyes.

"Before we go any further, Lauren, I want you to promise me that if we do anything you're uncomfortable with, you'll tell us immediately. It's not going to piss us off. We want this to be perfect for you. We don't want to frighten or overwhelm you."

Her heart ached at the sincerity in his voice. She trembled in front of him, overwhelmed—yes, overwhelmed—by the moment.

But she wouldn't tell them that, because it was the best kind of being overwhelmed.

"I promise," she said, not recognizing her voice.

It was hoarse and husky, the sound of a satisfied woman confident in her lovers' ability to pleasure her.

Noah pulled at the bottoms and eased them down her legs, leaving her in just a lacy pair of panties. Then he pulled her to him, his arms encircling her as his mouth found her breast.

He sucked gently at one taut nipple and it hardened even further. Then he moved to the other and drew a lazy circle around it with his tongue before sucking it into his mouth as he'd done the other.

His hands slid down the small of her back, delving underneath the band of her underwear. And then lower, dragging the silky material downward. He let it drop to her feet, and she was completely bare to both men's gazes.

"Get onto the bed, honey," Noah said in a low voice.

Even as he spoke, he guided her to where he wanted her. Right between where he and Liam still sat on the edge of the bed.

He got up then as she sat, and Liam loomed over her, easing her down to her back.

"Spread your legs," Noah whispered. "I want to taste you so bad, I ache."

She hesitated a moment, suddenly self-conscious at the idea of being laid out and spread wide. Liam's hand glided down her belly and she tensed when it brushed softly over the apex of her legs and then between them, gently parting her thighs.

"Relax, baby," Liam encouraged. "Let us make you feel good."

She let her thighs fall open, aided by Liam. When she looked down, Noah had gone to his knees between her splayed legs.

Liam shifted farther up her body, and his hand left her thigh and smoothed up her belly to cup one breast and then the other. He caressed and toyed with her nipples, teasing them to rigid points.

And then Noah's fingers gently parted her folds, opening her further to him. He brushed over her clit, down to her entrance and then back up again.

Liam leaned over her, his dark head obscuring her view of Noah as he licked at her nipple. Her body tightened, bowed. She flexed and arched. It seemed she was going in a dozen different directions and had no control over her body.

The moment Noah's mouth touched her, she cried out. Her hand flew to Liam's head, twisting in his hair. Soft and silky, the wild mane of hair flowed over her fingers.

Liam sucked and nipped, alternating between her breasts. Noah's tongue glided over her clit, teasing and bringing her closer to the edge.

He moved lower, bestowing tiny kisses to every part of her pussy, and when he reached her opening, he licked delicately at first and then grew bolder, plunging his tongue inside, sucking and tasting her intimately.

"Noah!" she cried.

Even as she called out his name, she pulled at Liam's hair in a silent beg for him to stop. She was already on the brink of her orgasm and she didn't want it to end. Not this soon!

Liam and Noah both halted simultaneously.

"Did I hurt you?" Noah demanded.

She could barely pull together her thoughts. She was so painfully on edge that if he so much as touched her again, she was going to come. She sucked in steadying breaths, her hand still tightly fisted in Liam's hair.

"No," she said hoarsely. "God no. I'm about to come. It's too soon!"

Noah laughed softly. "We've got all night, sweetheart. Let yourself come. Then we'll start all over again."

Liam lifted his head and she loosened her hold. He moved

upward, capturing her mouth in a heated kiss that told her just how aroused he was. For several long moments, he ravaged her mouth, tasting every inch of her lips, delving deep with his tongue until she was breathless.

"I promise there'll be another," Liam said as he dragged his mouth away. "Because I want a taste of what Noah's getting right now."

She went limp, helpless against the seduction of their words.

"I like your hand in my hair," Liam said as he lowered his head back to her breast.

She was only too willing to thrust her fingers back into the silken mass as his mouth closed around her nipple. Noah slid one finger inside her and she arched into it, wanting more, wanting deeper.

Then his mouth returned to her clit and he rolled his tongue in a lazy circle around the rigid bud.

Her free hand curled into the sheets, digging into the mattress as she fisted the material. Her breathing sped up, and the hand in Liam's hair tightened until she knew she had to be causing him pain.

He only sucked harder.

Noah added a second finger, sliding deep. But he was so gentle. There was no roughness to his penetration.

Her breath caught and held. The dual sensation of their mouths on her most sensitive pleasure points was devastating and exquisite. The most wonderful kind of torture.

Tension built. Every muscle tightened. Pleasure radiated through her body. Hot. Swelling. Building. Higher and higher.

Noah increased the pressure of his tongue, withdrew his fingers and plunged again. Liam nipped more sharply at her nipples.

"Don't stop!" she begged.

"Never," Liam growled.

Her hips rolled and she bowed painfully upward to meet Noah's mouth, wanting more. Her body was begging for release, and they were determined to give her all she could take.

Just when she didn't think she could take any more, her orgasm flashed, swelling and rushing through her like a windstorm.

She knew she cried out. She was thinking their names. It was all that was in her mind except for pleasure so sweet she thought she could die of it.

She arched one last time and then fell back to the bed, her strength gone, her body so limp and sated that it was impossible to move.

She moaned softly when Noah withdrew his fingers and then replaced them with his mouth. He slid his tongue inward, working her slowly down from the explosion of her release. He continued to lick and kiss her softly until she sighed and quivered.

So boneless she thought she might never move again, she stroked her fingers through Liam's hair before letting her arm fall limply to the bed.

Liam drew away, propped on his elbow and then looked down at her as he rubbed his hand over her belly. Noah crawled onto the bed on the other side of her and positioned himself similarly to Liam, his hand joining Liam's to caress her.

"How was that?" Noah asked in a husky voice.

"Mmm," she managed to get out.

Liam chuckled. "That good, huh?"

"Mmm hmm."

Noah leaned over to kiss her, his lips curved into a smile. She could taste herself on him, an odd experience, but she found she didn't mind.

"That's only the beginning," he whispered against her mouth.

CHAPTER 14

LAUREN lay back atop the mattress, Noah and Liam on either side of her, caressing her with gentle motions.

After a moment, Liam shifted, pushed himself upward and then off the bed. Her eyes widened when he lifted her feet to prop her heels on the metal bedframe for leverage. The position allowed her thighs to spread wider and then he knelt, as Noah had done so that her pussy was right on level with his mouth.

She moaned, a sound that started more vocal and ended in a long, breathy sigh. She was still sensitive from the first mind-bending orgasm and at the first touch of his tongue, her muscles jerked and locked, stiffening her legs.

She reached blindly upward and came into contact with Noah's shoulder. He lowered himself over her upper body and slid his palm over her rib cage toward her breasts.

"Beautiful," he whispered just as he closed his lips around one nipple.

The room grew hazy around her. She floated in a sea of pleasure, her body tightening as she began the long, slow climb to release once more.

The sounds of satisfaction that Liam made heightened her arousal. His mouth vibrated against her most intimate flesh while his tongue danced wickedly over her clit and then down to slide inside her opening.

It was odd that she could tell the two men apart and how different their styles of making love were. She wouldn't have imagined there being such a difference and yet she could tell instantly by the way they touched her or kissed who was who, and yet both were deliciously talented at making her respond.

Liam rocked upward, his mouth pressing to her belly, and he kissed a line toward her chin. Noah pulled away and Liam captured her mouth, his tongue delving deeply.

"I want to be inside you, baby," he growled in a low whisper. "You make me crazy."

She smiled faintly. After one orgasm, and she was precariously close to another, she could safely say that they made her crazy. She couldn't even think. Only feel. And she loved the way they made her feel.

Protected. Cherished. Cared for.

They silenced the ghosts of her past when they were near. They put themselves between her and those painful memories, a buffer to anything that would hurt her.

"Let me get a condom," Liam whispered against her mouth.

She touched his face, kissed him back and then slowly let him go, his gaze burning into her as he withdrew. He hastily pulled his shirt over his head, leaving her to admire his ink again. He was just as quick to peel his jeans down and take off the remainder of his clothing. A moment later he was between her thighs again, his fingers testing her readiness.

He teased the line from her opening to her clit and then back down again, feathering around her entrance.

Noah drew one nipple into his mouth, sucking firmly until it was a rigid peak. Then he gave the other equal treatment until her breasts were plump and swollen, her nipples erect and puckered. Then he kissed the valley between her breasts and gently worked his mouth up to her neck as Liam positioned himself between her legs.

The head of Liam's cock breached her entrance and for a moment he remained still, allowing her to adjust to his size.

She hadn't gotten a look at him from her position on the bed. All she'd been able to see was his chest and the intricate tattoos on his upper body. She had no idea of his size, but he felt enormous as he pushed in farther, stretching her with every movement.

She wiggled, angling her lower body so she could take him deeper. It was instinctive to wrap her legs around his waist even though it wasn't something Joel ever allowed. He preferred that she lay motionless while he did as he liked.

She shook off the fleeting memory, determined not to let it intrude here where it didn't belong.

"How does it feel, Lauren?" Noah asked in a husky voice.

Her eyelids flickered and she looked up to meet his gaze, overwhelmed by the moment. The sheer magnitude of having these two men . . . worship her. They treated her like she was . . . precious.

"Why?" she whispered.

His brow crinkled in confusion. "Why what, honey?"

"Why me?"

He smoothed his fingers over her brow, easing the lines. Then he kissed her, long and sweet, until she knew nothing but the sensation of Liam deep inside her body and Noah deep inside her mouth.

"Because there can't be anyone else for us," Noah said as he pulled from her lips.

Liam's hands slid underneath her ass, lifting as he pushed even deeper. He leaned over her, holding her close to his body before finally releasing her to plant his hands on the mattress on either side of her hips.

He thrust harder, and she closed her eyes, reaching for Noah again. Just wanting to touch him. With her other hand, she slid her fingers over the top of Liam's hand where it rested on the bed. And she held on to them both while Liam continued to power into her body.

She knew he was holding back. There were stress lines on his face. His jaw was tight and his thrusts became more measured.

She smiled and reached up to touch his face.

"Don't hold back, Liam. I want to see you when you come."

He groaned and let out a long breath. "Oh God, baby, I wanted to make you come again. I didn't want it to be over so soon. But you feel so damn good and I've waited so long for this."

She put a finger to his mouth. "We have all night. Isn't that what Noah said? We'll do it all over again."

He smiled when she turned the words back on him. Then he lowered himself even further as Noah pulled back, allowing him the room. Liam gathered her tightly in his arms and then flexed his hips, driving deep.

Faster and harder. He picked up speed and thrust more forcefully. He hugged her tighter, holding her so close she could barely breathe, but she'd never felt safer or more . . . loved.

Then he buried himself deep and remained there, his entire body quivering, his hips jerking spasmodically. He nuzzled into her neck and his breath exploded against her skin as he lay there panting softly.

Even as Liam covered her, completely possessing her, Noah's hand found hers where it was sprawled away from Liam. And he curled his fingers around hers, stroking over her palm. Letting her know that he was there. With her. Just as Liam was.

She was touched beyond measure at the gesture. It was symbolic. A silent promise. Tears gathered in her eyes. Had she finally found what she'd searched for for so long?

Liam kissed her cheek and then the corner of her mouth before finally pushing himself upward so she no longer bore his weight. Then he carefully withdrew and stepped aside to discard the condom.

Her gaze immediately went to Noah. She wanted to give him that same pleasure. She wanted it for herself. Their gazes connected and he leaned in to kiss her again, almost as if offering her reassurance.

He crawled off the bed. She watched as he undressed, determined to get a better view of him than she had Liam. She propped herself up on her elbows so she was able to see.

The ripple of muscles was impressive. He wasn't as thick or as large as Liam, but he was every bit as muscled and toned. Just different body structure and build. Damn but he was so very nice to look at.

When he got his pants off and tore off his boxers, she took his erection, mentally comparing him to Liam. Liam had certainly felt . . . huge. But Noah? *Looked* huge.

The two men stood at the edge of the bed, Liam's gaze soft and satisfied while Noah's glittered with hunger. She shivered, licking her lips in anticipation.

To her surprise, Noah reached for her, turning her over onto her belly. Her cheek brushed over the sheet and for a moment she was too stunned to react.

This wasn't what she'd expected.

Unease stole over her. For a moment she was too muddled to even realize why she was gripped by such discomfort.

It was instinctive for her to be wary, and to fight. Her first instinct was to fight?

Noah's hands slid up the backs of her legs and he kissed the cheek of her ass, and then the other, nipping playfully.

She tried to reason with herself. Tried to be calm. This was Noah. Noah would never hurt her.

But the position was a symbol of helplessness to her. And she hated that feeling above all others. She didn't want to be scared when Noah made love to her.

Then he spread her thighs, and all reason fled. There was no fighting the surge of panic. Her throat swelled with it until she nearly choked.

His grip tightened and in her disoriented state, all she could process was that she was being held down. Pinned. Helpless.

"No!" she choked out around a sob.

Even as the word exploded into the quiet, she was already kicking. The hands left her and she rolled away, against the wall. She put her back to it and curled her knees protectively against her chest.

She put her head down until her forehead touched her knees. All her most vulnerable parts were covered. Her stomach and ribs. Her face was hidden.

Because she knew what happened when she said no. There was always *instant* retaliation. It was a testament to just how afraid she'd been that the word had even escaped her lips.

CHAPTER 15

NOAH stared down in horror—and shock—as Lauren curled herself into a protective ball and huddled as far away from him as she could on the bed.

Her back was to the wall. It was a practiced move. It gutted him that this was something she'd obviously had to do before.

He honest to God wanted to puke.

Liam started forward but Noah put his hand out. When Liam turned to glare at him, Noah shook his head.

"I did this," Noah said in a low voice he doubted Lauren even heard.

"Goddamn it, Noah," Liam bit out. "You heard what he did to her that last time. He put her on her belly so she couldn't fight him off, and then he held her down and raped her. She *told* us she hated that position. What were you thinking?"

Noah closed his eyes. He understood Liam's anger. Noah was furious with himself. But this wasn't the time to hash it out with his friend. Not when Lauren was in a protective ball because she was afraid of being hurt.

He held up his finger to Liam and shook his head once more. Then he crawled onto the bed, his gut in knots.

He hesitated, his hand hovering over her shoulder, afraid to touch her. He couldn't bear for her to flinch away. The idea that she was expecting pain and humiliation instead of the pleasure he'd so wanted to give her made him sick to his soul.

"Lauren," he whispered. "Honey, look at me please. I'm not going to hurt you. I'd never hurt you."

Gingerly, he let his hand rest on her shoulder. She tensed but she didn't flinch away or recoil. Her hair completely hid what little of her face that would have been visible, and he pushed it back, trying anything to calm her panic.

Liam sat on the bed and scooted until he was opposite Noah. His hand shook when he lifted it to Lauren's dark head. He rested it on the back of her head and let it glide down to her nape.

"Lauren?" Noah prompted again. "Will you please look at me?"

Gradually, she lifted her head from her knees. Liam smoothed her hair back with both hands. He pulled it away from her face and made gentle, repetitive motions as if he were forming a ponytail, but Noah knew he was soothing her much like he would a wounded animal.

When she lifted her gaze to meet his, her eyes were dull with embarrassment and the remnants of fear. It made his chest ache.

"I'm sorry," she whispered hoarsely. "I just panicked. I couldn't make it go away. I'm so sorry."

Noah swallowed back the rage that threatened to explode out of him. Now wasn't the time. He had to handle this just right or he'd never get her back. She'd never trust him. He couldn't afford to fuck this up.

"Will you let me hold you?" he asked softly.

She hesitated a moment—the longest moment of Noah's life—before she finally made a move toward him.

It was shaky and hesitant, but with Liam's help, she uncurled herself and then got to her knees. But she didn't launch herself into Noah's arms. She simply knelt there, glancing anxiously at him.

"Come here, sweetheart," he said, pulling her into his arms.

He gathered her naked body against his and wrapped as much of himself around her as he could get. He held her tightly against his heart, rocking back and forth as he kissed every inch of her face.

"You will not apologize to me for this," he said fiercely. "It's my goddamn fault and it's me who needs to be on my knees in front of you begging you to forgive me and give me another chance. I'm so sorry, Lauren. I wouldn't frighten you for the world. I'd do anything at all for you to never be afraid again."

He kissed the top of her head, her hair. He couldn't get enough of her. He wanted to absorb her right into his soul.

"Please look at me. Say something. Just as long as it's not an apology."

She lifted her head again and stared back at him, tears swimming in her eyes. His stomach plummeted. It felt like someone kicked him right in the balls. He certainly deserved it.

"Lauren, I'm sorry. Me. I ruined what was the most beautiful moment I've ever experienced. I ruined it for you. I ruined it for Liam. And I damn sure ruined it for me."

"I was the one who let him back in," she said painfully. "I was so determined to keep him out, to keep the past in the past and not let it intrude on tonight. I knew you wouldn't hurt me, Noah. Please believe that. I never once thought that you would do anything I didn't want. But even knowing that, panic took over and I couldn't control what I did. My heart screamed that you would never hurt me and my mind just took over and shut me down."

Noah positioned her so that she straddled his lap and he could look her in the eyes. He cupped her face, stroking her soft, sweet skin as he searched for just the right thing to say.

Fuck it all, but he didn't know what to say. He could only be honest. He screwed up.

"Honey, you can not blame yourself for this. I did a stupid thing. It would be one thing if I hadn't known what happened, but you told us. I just didn't think. I wanted you so badly and I wanted to touch every inch of you. I wanted my hands and mouth on you and I wanted my dick inside you. And maybe in the back of my mind I thought I could replace those bad memories with good ones, that I could show you how it could be with someone who cares about you. It was arrogant and stupid of me. I was too caught up in the moment and I didn't stop to think how it was affecting you. I'm sorry. I should have made damn sure you were with me every second of the way."

She swallowed and her gaze went all shiny and wet again.

"I wanted all of that too."

"I know you did," he said gently. "I fucked up. Not you."

She leaned until her forehead met his. Her mouth was tantalizingly close, but he reined himself in, refusing to make a single move until she issued the invitation.

Then she wrapped her arms loosely around his neck. He put his own around her waist, resisting the urge to haul her up against him until neither of them could breathe.

"Guess we have a lot to learn about this threesome thing," she breathed.

He smiled. "Yeah, honey, I guess we do. But you know what? We'll figure it out. Together."

She turned then, her gaze seeking Liam out. He was perched on the edge of the bed, his gaze intently focused on what was going on between Noah and Lauren.

She extended her hand to him and he readily took it.

Then she glanced back to Noah. "Are you both sure this is what you want? Me? Us? Together?"

"Damn straight," Liam growled before Noah could respond.

Noah took more time, gauging the expression on Lauren's face. He searched for reluctance or regret. Second thoughts. Anything to hint that she was looking for a way out.

He touched her cheek, rubbing his knuckle down to her jaw.

"I think the more important question is whether *you're* sure this is what *you* want."

She nodded solemnly. "It is. I am. Just be patient with me. I can't promise not to freak out again. I don't want to. I don't want to give that bastard any power over me, but it doesn't appear that I have a choice."

The sadness in her voice was Noah's undoing. He gathered her in his arms, forcing her to break contact with Liam. He held her so tightly he was probably hurting her, but he wanted to tell her with more than just words what he felt.

"I promise we have all the time in the world," he said gruffly. "One day at a time. There's no hurry, honey. We'll get that bastard out of your head. Just give it time. And give us time. You talk about us being patient with you, but sweetheart, I'm the one fucking up over here. Promise that you'll be patient with me, and I'll do my damnedest to make you happy."

She lay her head against his shoulder and buried her face in his neck.

"I think we'll both make our share of mistakes. I just have to recondition myself not to expect violence as a result of a mistake I make."

Noah closed his eyes, his teeth clenched so tightly that his jaw hurt. When he reopened them, he saw the same rage in Liam's expression.

How could anyone hurt such a beautiful, sweet woman? Any

woman? What kind of an asshole got off on controlling someone weaker than himself?

More than ever, Noah wanted to hunt that little bastard down and make him suffer for all the women he'd ever hurt. He doubted Lauren was the first or that she'd be the last.

"You'll never receive violence from either of us," Noah said in a low voice. "I may get mad as hell. Liam's got a black temper and he can be a moody son of a bitch."

Liam scowled at Noah in response.

Noah chuckled. "My point is we can fight and argue and I'm sure we will. But you don't ever have to worry about either of us physically retaliating. I'm more of an air-my-grievance-and-get-over-it guy."

Lauren nodded, and he gently pried her away from his neck so that she could once more see him and Liam.

Liam reached forward to claim the hand he'd held before, and Noah slid his hand up her arm to squeeze her shoulder.

"Don't you understand, sweetheart? You're going to have us both so wrapped around your little finger, that I doubt there'll ever be that much disagreement."

"We plan to spoil you rotten and give you everything you could possibly ever want or need," Liam added gruffly.

Lauren smiled, chasing away the shadows in her eyes. Her gaze sparkled once more. No ghosts haunting from the past. No remnants of pain or shame.

"Is it wrong that I love the idea of having both of you wrapped around my finger?" she asked, her voice so sweet that it made Noah want to groan.

Liam lifted her hand to kiss each finger in turn.

"Not a damn thing wrong with that," Liam said, his tone resolute. "It's good you like the idea, because that is one thing you aren't going to have a single say in. We're going to spoil you rotten and we're going to enjoy every damn minute."

CHAPTER 16

❦

TO Lauren's surprise, when she got out of the shower the next morning, both men were up, dressed and waiting in the living room for her.

Dawn hadn't even broken yet and the apartment was cloaked in darkness except for the lamp one of the men had turned on in the living room.

"Still have half an hour before you have to show up for work. Want some breakfast here? Thought you might be tired of the same ole stuff at the diner," Noah said when she walked out of her bedroom.

She smiled. "Honestly I don't normally eat the food there. I did at first, but you're right, it got old fast. It's good, don't get me wrong. But different is definitely better."

"I make a mean breakfast taco," Noah said with a grin. "I don't figure you have that on the diner menu."

Lauren laughed. "No, can't say we do. A breakfast taco sounds . . . intriguing."

"Come on then. Come sit at the table while I make it. Then Liam and I will take you to work. We're going to have a look around town today. We'll be checking in on you periodically. I also programmed both our cell numbers into your phone while you were in the shower. If you have any trouble, if you even *think* something's off or wrong, you call one of us immediately. Okay?"

She nodded.

Noah headed for the kitchen and Liam followed behind, taking Lauren's hand on his way by. She settled at the table with Liam while Noah banged around in her tiny kitchen for the stuff he needed.

Ten minutes later, he presented her and Liam with a flour tortilla shell he'd fried brown in butter, filled with scrambled eggs, seared ham, and cheese with jalapenos and salsa.

Knowing it would be afternoon before she'd get the opportunity to really talk with them, she spoke up while they were eating.

"I handled last night all wrong," she said firmly.

They were going to argue. She could see it in their eyes. Especially Noah's. He got this fierce look on his face and his eyes filled with self-condemnation all over again.

She sighed and held up her hand to stop the flow before it began.

"You guys did everything right. I overreacted. I did. You were very honest and up front with me. You told me explicitly that if you did anything I wasn't comfortable with to tell you and that you'd stop immediately. It should have been that simple. All I had to do was tell you I didn't like what was happening."

Noah shook his head, but she held up her hand again.

"I don't want to turn it into another huge ordeal. I just thought that I owed you that at least. I got scared. I overreacted in the moment. That doesn't mean that you did anything wrong. It just means that we hit a bump in the road. And as you said, we'll get past it. I promise not to beat myself up about it, if you promise not to beat yourself up over it," she said pointedly, staring Noah down as she spoke.

Liam's lips twitched and he stuffed a bite of taco in his mouth, probably to stanch his laughter.

Noah opened his mouth, then promptly shut it. Then he nodded. "Deal."

She smiled. "Okay, I need to get to work now."

Noah rose, quickly clearing the plates away while Liam headed into the living room. He had his back to her when she came in on his heels, and when he turned, he was putting on a shoulder harness with a pistol. He reached for his leather jacket draped over the back of the armchair and pulled it on to cover the gun.

It was a sharp jolt of reality. She may be immersed in the fantasy of having two hot guys in her bed and in her life, but the reality was that they were here to protect her from a man who had no compunction about hurting her.

It was a sobering thought, and some of her good mood evaporated.

"Don't look like that, baby," Liam said. "It's only here for your protection. So Joel Knight can never touch you again."

"I know," she said quietly. "I guess I just want to be able to forget about him for a while, and every time I think I can, I'm reminded in some way of why I'm here and why you're here."

He pushed into her space and pulled her into his arms.

"I hate the circumstances that put us together, but baby? I don't regret the result for one minute. I wish we could have met under other conditions, but I'll take you however I can get you. And if it means having to keep a close watch over you, I'll just count that as a bonus."

She hugged him to her, her mood lightening once more. Liam had a way of reaching in and wiping away the darkness that occupied certain portions of her mind.

"Ready?" Noah asked from the doorway to the kitchen.

Lauren pulled away and turned in his direction. "Ready."

IT was a busy morning in the diner. Mondays typically were. It was as if everyone wanted to get out to see what the weekend gossip was. Tuesday mornings were always dead. Definitely her worst tip day of her schedule for sure.

The Colters and even her own brother usually made it in on her shift at least once a week, and they always left ridiculously large tips. After the first couple of times of arguing with them, she finally had saved her breath.

They loved her and they used any opportunity they found to take care of her. It was nice to have that kind of unconditional support.

Liam and Noah had garnered much attention. The townspeople hadn't even bothered trying to be subtle. They stared while Noah and Liam had a cup of coffee at the start of Lauren's shift. They stared when the two men left and returned a couple of hours later.

And when Seth ambled in close to eleven for a cup of coffee, two people made a beeline for him to warn him about the big strangers lurking at the diner. Lauren had stifled her laughter as Seth had patiently explained that Noah and Liam were good men and that Seth knew them personally.

"Everything going okay, Lauren?" Seth asked as she set his coffee down at his table.

She smiled. "Just fine. Typical Monday."

Seth rolled his eyes. "You're telling me. Your protectors have made quite a stir in town. They've been spotted all over Clyde and now the good denizens are convinced that they're hit men. Believe me when I say, our receptionist has been fielding calls all morning and I've been stopped on the street, been flagged down in my patrol car and have even gotten calls on my cell."

"Oh I'm sorry, Seth," Lauren said. "This has to be a giant pain in your butt."

"I'm not complaining, honey. I want you safe. It's just life in a small town, and it should make you feel better that so many people are concerned about you. It should also make you feel better to know that if some stranger shows his face here, we'll definitely know about it."

She gave him a rueful smile. "That's true. Joel would arrive in his flashy sports car and before he got out, the entire town would know about it."

Seth laughed. "You're so right there. There are drawbacks to living in such a small community, but the plusses far outweigh the minuses. We have good people here," he said seriously. "I've known them all my life. I wouldn't want to live anywhere else."

"I love it here too," she said wistfully.

She looked up when the bell over the front door jangled, and then she lit up. "Oh look! Callie and Lily are here!"

Before Seth could respond, Lauren hurried to greet the other two women.

They hugged her as soon as she got close.

"Are you here for lunch?" Lauren asked her friends.

"I see my husband is here," Lily murmured. "Figures when I make an escape with Callie, he has to be here instead of at work."

"Don't look now, but here he comes," Callie said with a snicker. "He has a frown. You know, one of those concerned husbandly frowns."

Lily sighed. "Seat us, Lauren. Far, far away from wherever Seth is sitting, please."

Lauren giggled and pulled the two women in the opposite direction as Seth. She settled the two women in a booth that only accommodated two people and overlooked the street. It was a beautiful, sunny spring day and the sun was shining against a brilliant blue sky.

The town square and Main Street truly were beautiful in the spring. Flowers lined the square and the street, and there was a quaintness that spoke to Lauren's longing for a place to call home.

"Ladies," Seth said as he approached.

He leaned down to kiss his wife, and then he brushed his lips across Callie's cheek.

"How are you feeling, baby?" he asked Lily softly.

She smiled up at her husband. For all her exasperation, it was obvious she adored him, and well, Seth always looked at Lily like the sun rose and set at her feet.

"I'm fine. Dillon cooked breakfast but I knew I was eating with Callie, so I didn't eat much. I left him at the house grumbling because I wouldn't take him along, so he went into the office to do some stuff for work. I'll ride back home with him when I'm done."

Seth nodded approvingly. "Good. You shouldn't be driving up and down the mountain alone. You're not that far from your delivery date."

Lily snorted. "Two months, Seth. Believe me when I say two months is an eternity when you're as big as a house."

Callie and Lauren laughed.

"Have you taken a break yet, Lauren?" Lily asked. "Can you sit with us a few minutes?"

Lauren checked her watch, then scanned the crowd. It was starting to quiet just a bit. The people of Clyde liked their lunch early, and so there was always an initial rush at eleven when lunch was starting to be served, but things usually quieted down by eleven thirty.

"Let me check with Clark and Evie and make sure there's someone to cover my tables. I'll be right back."

Seth leaned over to kiss Lily again. "I've got to get back to the station. I'll see you later."

Lily and Callie waved Seth off as Lauren hurried to the back. She nearly ran into Evie as she walked into the kitchen.

"How are things looking back here?" she asked Clark.

"Getting the last two dinners up. Why?"

"Was going to take my break if we're caught up."

Evie shooed her away. "Go on and take it. I'll hit your tables for any refills. You're caught up on your deliveries. As soon as I take my two out, I'll be caught up and I'll take any newcomers that walk in."

Lauren flashed a grin. "Thanks, Evie. You're the best."

Clark gave them both indulgent smiles. "You two are the best waitresses I've ever had. Can't begrudge you a break. You've earned it. We've been busting ass since opening time this morning."

"Typical Monday," Evie said with a shrug.

Lauren turned and hurried back to where Lily and Callie sat. She snagged a chair from a nearby empty table and parked it at the end of the two-person booth.

"So what are you two up to today? Just doing lunch? And where is Mama C?"

"She's baby shopping. In Denver," Callie added. "Which means the dads went with her because they still won't let her drive pretty much anywhere by herself. She's decided she needs to outfit an entire nursery at her house for when the baby stays over."

Lauren chuckled. "I can only imagine."

Lily smiled. "She's been so wonderful to me. She's already explained that she's coming to stay with me for the entire week after the baby is born and that I won't have to lift a single finger. She's barked orders at the men. Dillon is on cooking duty. Michael and Seth are sharing diaper changing and bottle-feeding when I need a break from breast-feeding."

Lily grew misty eyed. "I don't know what I'd do without her.

Or the entire Colter family. Even the dads have volunteered to come over so Seth, Dillon and Michael can get some rest. I can't even explain how much just knowing that they'll be right there, for however we need them, means to me. It's like a huge weight off my shoulders."

Callie reached over to squeeze her hand. "And you forget me and Max. We'll be right here whenever you need us."

"And me," Lauren piped up.

Lily smiled. "Yes of course. You'll be right here in the middle of all of us. It's a pretty wonderful place to be, you know."

Callie turned a purposeful stare in Lauren's direction. "Okay, so, I'll fully admit, Lily and I came here with a purpose, and we also waited until Noah and Liam left before we came in because we wanted to corner you and interrogate you mercilessly."

"Uh-oh," Lauren muttered."

Lily laughed. "You have to tell us what's going on with those two. And don't give us the cock-and-bull story about how they're just protecting you until things are resolved with Joel. Because the way they look at you? Makes me shiver. There's definitely more to this story than you're letting on."

Lauren blushed, her face warming under their scrutiny.

"I knew it!" Callie crowed. "Look at her face! Totally busted."

Lauren sighed. "Okay, okay. Yes, there's something more than just a professional relationship."

"Which one?" Lily said, pouncing on the subject. "My money is on Liam. He's so dark and broody and delicious. And those tattoos. Yum. He totally reminds me of Dillon."

Callie shook her head. "I'm betting Noah. His gaze never leaves her. He's constantly watching her. Always looking for any kind of threat to her. But when he looks directly at her, I swear that man's eyes just smolder. If you could bottle that look? We could make millions. He is sex in a can, I'm telling you."

Lauren burst out laughing. "Oh my God, you two are killing me!"

"So which is it?" Lily demanded.

"Uhm, well . . . both," she said, dropping her voice so there was no chance of being overheard.

"What?" Callie squeaked. "Oh my God, you lucky bitch."

Lily's eyes widened. "Really?

Lauren nodded.

"Wow," Callie breathed. "I swear I'm the only one who took on one man."

"Yeah, well, can you imagine two of Max?" Lily pointed out.

Callie rolled her eyes. "No kidding. I'd never survive. Max is like having three men. Still, there are times when I look at you and I look at mom and I think, wow, that must be so awesome to have three men who absolutely worship and adore you. And now you, Lauren. You have two drop-dead gorgeous, stacked guys who want to spend every waking moment cherishing and protecting you? Jealousy is going to eat me alive."

Lauren blushed again. "We're still working through some stuff. I mean this is completely brand new to all three of us. None of us have experience in this and we're having to feel our way around."

"None of us had experience with it either," Lily said in a serious tone. "I know it sounds crazy because of the way Seth, Michael and Dillon grew up, but they never considered for a moment that they'd have the same kind of relationship their parents had. So when they met me, they had things they had to work out and we definitely had to be careful in the beginning. We're still working at it."

"Is it hard and stressful?" Lauren asked.

Lily smiled. "At times it can be, but the good times far outweigh the bad, and I can't tell you how wonderful it is to have the love and devotion of three of the most terrific men I've ever met. I feel like I'm the luckiest woman in the world."

"I feel that way too," Lauren said quietly. "It scares me to death and yet it's thrilling all at the same time. I don't want to mess this up and for it not to work out."

Callie and Lily both reached for her hands.

"You'll do just fine," Callie said, her expression fierce. "They're lucky to have you."

Lauren grinned. "That's what I love most about you guys. Even when I'm wrong, you still take my side."

Callie sniffed. "Colters are never wrong. Just ask my mother."

They all laughed. Evie brought out Lily's and Callie's plates, and the two women began eating.

After a moment, Lauren reluctantly rose, knowing she needed to get back to her tables so Evie wasn't stuck covering the whole diner.

"I'll see you two later, okay?"

Callie and Lily both waved a fork at her, and Lauren headed back to her section of tables.

CHAPTER 17

❧

LAUREN knew something was wrong the moment Liam and Noah entered the diner at the end of her shift. She met them just a few feet inside the doorway, anxious as she surveyed their expressions.

"What's wrong?" she asked.

Liam touched her elbow. "Are you finished?"

She hesitated. "I just need to go in back, put my apron up, collect tips and clock out."

"Go on and get done," Noah said. "We'll wait for you here."

She hurried away, dread tightening her chest. She hated the flutter of anxiety that bubbled in her stomach. What could possibly have happened in the short time they'd been gone?

She hastily untied her apron and threw it on the hook behind the kitchen door. Evie was already in the back counting out the totals, when Lauren hurried up.

"It was a good day, Lauren!" Evie exclaimed.

Lauren tried to smile. "I'm going to clock out, okay? Think you'll be done by then?"

Evie frowned. "Is everything okay, hon?"

Lauren nodded. "Yeah, just need to go. I, uh, have plans. That's all."

Evie's expression eased and her eyes gleamed. "Anything to do with those two hunky men who've been hanging around all day?"

Lauren pretended she didn't hear as she went to do her time card. She called out a good-bye to Clark and hoped that Evie would be done with the tips when she got back.

Evie pushed a stack of bills across the small counter when Lauren returned.

"There you go. Have fun and I'll see you tomorrow!"

Lauren smiled brightly and pocketed the bills, not even bothering to count as she usually would.

"See you tomorrow," she said and headed out of the kitchen.

Liam and Noah were where she'd left them. She didn't even worry over the scene they were causing. Every single person in the diner was staring hard at the two men, and even more so when they directed Lauren out the door to the street.

"What's going on?" she asked.

"We'll talk in your apartment," Noah said grimly.

They flanked her as they crossed the street and she noted that their gazes were scanning the sidewalks in both directions as they hustled her toward the steps to her apartment.

Only when she unlocked her door and they were inside did they seem to relax. But even then she could feel the tension radiating off them in waves.

Noah paced a circle in the tiny living room. Liam just stood to the side, his face so tight she could bounce a brick off it.

"You're scaring me," she said.

Noah immediately stopped his pacing and then pulled her into a fierce hug.

"I'm sorry. Sit down and we'll talk."

He guided her toward the couch and then took the seat next to her. Liam hunkered down into the armchair, but his expression hadn't eased.

Noah ran a hand through his hair. "We made some calls today. Just trying to discreetly get some information. We have to be careful with who we trust because of what you've said about Joel having people on his payroll."

She nodded.

"The thing is, the whole reason we found out about Joel and that you'd . . . misled us in the beginning was because we talked to a woman who I'm guessing is one of his girls."

"She knew about me?" Lauren whispered.

"She knew enough that you and Joel were an item. She ID'd your photo and told us who Joel was. But she clammed up after that. Didn't want anything to do with us. That's when we came here to confront you with what we'd learned."

"So what's wrong now?" she asked with a frown. "I don't understand. Does he know where I am?"

"She's dead," Liam said bluntly.

All the blood drained from Lauren's face, and she swayed. Beside her, Noah cursed and wrapped his arm around her to steady her.

"Damn it, Liam," Noah growled.

"What happened to her?" Lauren whispered.

"I spoke to a buddy of ours who's a detective at NYPD. We took a risk, but we feel he's trustworthy. In the course of our conversation, he informed us that this woman was found dead in her apartment. Someone beat her to death. It wasn't pretty. Time of death puts it a day after we spoke to her in her apartment."

"Oh God," Lauren moaned. She put her face in her hands, Noah's words echoing over and over in her mind.

"It doesn't mean he knows where you are," Liam said. "What

it means, though, is that he likely knows we were asking questions about you and Joel Knight."

"She died because of me," Lauren said bleakly.

"Bullshit," Liam bit out.

She shook her head. "You don't understand. I could have prevented this. It should have never happened."

Noah took her shoulders in his hands and turned her to face him. His expression was hard and focused. "How was it your fault, Lauren? Is there something you're not telling us? Now is *not* the time to be holding back anything. If you have information, then we need to goddamn well know about it."

She shook away his hands and stood. "Please. Just leave me alone for a minute. God, I need to think."

Without waiting for a response, she bolted from the living room into her bedroom. She closed the door and leaned heavily against it, her heart beating like the roar of a freight train.

Then she flew to the bed and lifted the mattress, reaching her hand frantically underneath it, reaching for the small memory card she'd taped to the underside.

She tore at it, the tape finally giving away. The plastic chip fell into her hand and she shakily peeled the tape away, staring at it in her palm.

Oh God. This was her fault. That woman had died because Lauren hadn't had the courage to do what she should have done. How many other women had suffered because Lauren had only wanted to escape and to forget Joel Knight ever existed? And how selfish did it make her that she'd been so wrapped up in her own survival that she hadn't given a single thought to women she could have protected and saved?

Poor little Lauren. So helpless and naïve. So damn stupid. This time she wouldn't shake off the blame and tell herself that she'd made mistakes and that everyone made them. She couldn't say that everything would be all right if she'd only had a fresh start and could forget her past.

Her past was there. Unchangeable. No matter how much she might wish differently. And it was affecting the lives of others. Her own. The women Joel used and abused. Murdered.

Revulsion gripped her.

She could have prevented this if she'd only been willing to stand up and do the right thing.

How ashamed would her family be? The Colters were *all* about doing the right thing. Standing up against injustice. They'd offered her unconditional support, but what had she offered them except lies and deception? What had she offered the women left to Joel's abuse and mistreatment?

How could she ever look them in the eye again?

She looked down again at the disk in her hand and she closed her fingers, gripping the plastic card until it cut into her palm.

It was time to get her damn head out of the sand. Joel wasn't going away. He wasn't going to stop what he was doing until someone stood up and took him down.

No matter how terrified she was or how ashamed, it was time for her to be willing to bring him to justice. Even if it meant risking her own life to do it.

How could she move on with Liam and Noah, or immerse herself in the Colter family and surround herself with their support and her brother's support if she knew it was at the expense of so many other women?

There was no future for her until she laid her past to rest. And there was no way to put her past behind her until she faced her demons and had the courage to do what it was she needed to do. What she *had* to do.

CHAPTER 18

LIAM stared at Lauren's closed door, worry gnawing a hole in his gut. He glanced at Noah to see his friend's expression wasn't any better.

"What the fuck was that?" Liam asked in a low voice.

Noah blew out his breath. "She's holding back something. She hasn't told us everything."

"Goddamn." He took a steadying breath. "She doesn't trust us yet."

Noah shot him a disgruntled look. "Do you expect her to this quickly? It may not be so much an issue of her trusting as it may be something big. Something that terrifies her. Look at it from her perspective. We barge back into her life, bust her for lying to us, and 'oh by the way, we want a relationship with you.' It's a lot to take in such a short period of time."

"Yeah, I get it," Liam muttered. "What the fuck do we do now?"

Before Noah could respond, the bedroom door opened and Lauren stepped out, her face drawn and blotchy. There was a look in her eyes that Liam didn't like. He couldn't even put his finger on what it was exactly, but the woman who'd bolted into her bedroom was not the woman walking out right now. And that scared the shit out of him.

"Lauren?" he began hesitantly. Hell, he was at a loss for words. Not an affliction he usually suffered.

Her gaze skittered to him, and he was taken aback by the pain in her eyes. Worse than the pain was the fear that reflected in those soft brown eyes.

She was scared to death.

"I have to go back to New York," she said, in a flat, emotionless voice.

Noah's complete *what the fuck?* look mirrored Liam's own reaction.

"Whoa, wait a minute here," Liam said. "We need to talk, baby. Tell us what's going on."

She took a deep breath, squared her shoulders and then glanced to Noah, then back at Liam again.

"I have to go back. Immediately."

Noah finally found his tongue.

"Tell us why," he said bluntly.

Her lips trembled, and it was evident that she was clinging to her composure by the barest thread. One hand was fisted into a tight ball at her side and the other was shaking, her fingers quivering even when she tried to press it to her leg.

"I have to go to the police," she said quietly. "I know he has cops on his payroll, but I have to try. I can no longer stand here and do nothing. Someone has to stop him."

Liam could stand it no longer. He crossed the room and gently grasped Lauren's shoulders. "Come sit down. Please? We'll talk it out. You tell us why you need to go to the police and we'll figure it out together, okay?"

For a moment he thought she'd argue, but then she sighed and let him walk her to the couch. Noah still stood by the coffee table, his brows drawn together in confusion—and worry—as Liam seated Lauren and then sat next to her.

"What the hell is going on, Lauren?" Noah asked.

Her balled fist was now in her lap, and slowly, she opened it until Liam could see a computer memory disk in her hand.

"I took this from him," she said in a near whisper. "Or rather, I copied information from his laptop before I left."

Oh shit. Liam glanced up at Noah to see the same grim fear in his friend's eyes. This didn't sound good. Not good at all.

Noah shoved the coffee table out of the way and knelt in front of Lauren. He didn't try to take the disk from her hand, but he took her other one and rubbed it between his palms.

"What kind of information?" Noah asked.

"Contacts. Records. Business and financial records. Entries detailing his client lists. When and where they met with what girls. Remember the whole hoopla over the high-profile madam case several years ago? This is basically the same thing, only it proves Joel for the pimp he is. And he has some big-name clients. Politicians. Doctors. Lawyers. Famous people. He runs a very big business peddling . . . women."

She nearly choked on the last word and it ended in a quiet sob.

"Women like the one he killed for talking to you about me."

"Now, baby, we can't prove that," Liam began.

She shook her head. "You and I both know that's exactly why she died. It's not a coincidence that the day after she talks to you she gets beat to death. You know it and I know it. Let's not try to make it what it isn't. The simple fact is, if I'd gone to the police with this information instead of running like a scared rabbit, that woman would be alive."

Liam swallowed hard. This was going south fast, and he had no idea how to get things back on track.

"Why didn't you tell us about this before?" Noah asked. "I get why you didn't when we were in New York. But why didn't you tell us when we got here? When we found out the truth about Joel?"

She raised her head, her gaze so dull and filled with self-condemnation that it made Liam hurt.

"Because I was afraid that you'd want to do the right thing, and I was too self-absorbed and afraid to do it myself. I had this hope that I could just move on with my life, pretend Joel never existed and continue to live in denial. If I didn't think about what he did or the other women he's hurt, then it wasn't real."

"Then why did you take the time and the risk to copy this information if you never intended to do anything with it?" Liam asked. "If he found out—hell, if he knows you took something from him like that—you have to know he'll come after you."

"Because I wasn't thinking!" she burst out. "I was in complete panic. I wanted to get as far away from him as possible but at the same time I wanted an insurance policy. It sounds so stupid now, but at the time I was only thinking that if he tried to come after me, if he tried to find me, I could pull out my trump card and blackmail him into getting out of my life forever."

Noah sighed. "It doesn't work that way, sweetheart. Men like Joel don't just go away when they know someone has incriminating evidence. If what you say is on that disk, it could topple his entire network and put him behind bars for a very long time. Not to mention the people implicated in his prostitution ring. I don't think you realize how far reaching the ramifications are for this. If he killed a woman for talking to someone, what do you think he'd do to someone who threatened everything he's worked to build?"

She went completely pale. Liam couldn't even reprimand Noah

for being so blunt, because it was what Lauren needed to hear. He hated to see the fear in her eyes, but he *needed* her to be afraid and to be aware of just what she'd stepped in.

"I can't pretend anymore," she said hoarsely. "I can't pretend I never had this information. If I had done the right thing, that woman would still be alive. Who knows who else might still be alive. Who's to say he hasn't killed other women? Or that he hasn't done to other women what he did to me?"

She turned to include Liam in her passionate speech.

"I can't look at myself in the mirror any longer knowing the mistakes I've made and the chances I've had to rectify them. I don't like that person. I don't like who I've become. I'm someone who has lied to her family and to the men hired to protect her. I'm someone who has information that could bring down a man who deserves to be behind bars, but was too cowardly to hand it over to the police. I'm someone I don't even recognize anymore," she said painfully. "And if I don't like myself, how can I expect either of you to ever love me?"

Liam reached for her, pulling her into his arms. "You made mistakes, baby. You were desperate, scared and alone."

She pulled away, her expression fierce. "But I'm not alone anymore. I have family who loves me. I have you and Noah, if you can still stand to be around me. It's time that I do something besides hide and act like a helpless victim."

Noah's expression grew fierce. "That's bullshit. You damn well do have us and you're stuck there. We aren't going anywhere, and we sure as hell aren't angry with you for doing what you thought was necessary to ensure your safety and well-being."

"Then you'll help me?"

Her eyes were hopeful as she looked pleadingly at them.

"Help you do what, baby?" Liam asked softly.

"Go with me to New York to turn the disk over to the police."

Liam and Noah both went silent. Liam's mind was buzzing like a chainsaw. This was huge. Not to mention dangerous. Lauren's life wouldn't be worth a shit the minute it got out that she'd turned evidence on Joel Knight.

"It's not quite that simple," Noah began.

She frowned. "Why not? If I give them the disk, there'll be no question as to what Joel's involved in. They'll arrest him and bring him to trial."

"You have to remember that he has people on his payroll," Liam said carefully. "We can't just waltz into the precinct and announce we have evidence implicating Joel Knight and various other people of distinction."

"Then what *can* we do?" she asked in frustration. "I can't turn my back again. He has to be stopped."

"The first thing we need to do is have a look at what's on the disk," Liam said. "We need to make a list of all the people mentioned. Figure out what we're dealing with. You have to understand that anyone listed as a client would go a long way to make sure that information never comes to light. Once we see what's there, then we have to decide who we think we can trust. There is no way in hell I'm allowing you to trot off to New York and put your welfare into the hands of just anyone."

"But you'll help me?" she asked hopefully.

Noah touched her face. "You don't seriously think we're going to let you do this alone, do you?"

She didn't answer, and Noah let out a curse.

Liam took her hand and squeezed. "What he's trying to say is that you belong to us, Lauren. And we're not going to do anything that puts you in danger. We'll take a look at the disk and then we'll go from there. We'll find a way to do this with the least amount of risk to you."

A tear rolled down her cheek followed by another and then

another. She hastily wiped them away only for more to come. It was as if the last secret she'd so desperately guarded had finally broken free, and a huge weight had been lifted.

"Do you have a computer?" Noah asked.

She shook her head.

"What about Seth? They live the closest to town, right?"

She nodded, still wiping at the tears rolling down her cheeks.

"Can you call him and ask if we can come over to use his computer?" Liam asked.

"Yeah," she said in a quivery voice. "I'm sure he wouldn't mind."

"Seth needs to know anyway," Noah said grimly. "He'll be able to offer some ideas from a law enforcement perspective."

Lauren lowered her head, closing her eyes.

"They're your family, baby," Liam said. "You've always told us how wonderful the Colters are. They're not going to judge you. They're just going to want you safe."

"I let them down," she said quietly. "I let myself down."

Noah reached for her hand, squeezing it as Liam had done. "Then it's time to make it up to yourself."

CHAPTER 19

❦

THE drive to the house Seth shared with his two brothers and Lily was silent except for Lauren giving them directions where to turn off once they got out of town.

Dusk had already descended when they pulled in next to the parked vehicles in front of the house. The porch lights were on, and Seth appeared in the doorway as they got out of the vehicle.

Concern reflected on his face as he watched them approach. Dread pitted deep in Lauren's stomach because she knew that before it was over with, everyone would have to know. Max. The Colters. And they would all know what a selfish coward she'd been.

She couldn't meet Seth's gaze when they stopped on the porch.

"What's going on?" Seth asked quietly.

"We need access to a computer," Noah said. "And depending on what we find on the disk we brought, we'll need to discuss our options with you."

Seth turned to Lauren. "Why don't you go in and visit with Lily. I don't want her upset. I'd rather her believe this is a social visit and that Noah and Liam need the computer for work."

"I won't say anything to her," Lauren said in a low voice.

She started by Seth, but he caught her arm.

"I never thought you'd do anything to intentionally upset her, honey. But the look on your face speaks volumes right now. She'll take one look at you and know something's wrong right away."

Lauren nodded her understanding. It was hard to pretend nothing was wrong when she knew she was responsible for a woman's death. More than anything, she wanted Holly Colter. She was the closest thing Lauren had to a mother since her own had passed on. And right now, she really needed a mom.

Seth let her go and she walked into the living room, very nearly colliding with Michael Colter.

"Whoa there," Michael said with a laugh.

Lauren forced a smile and willed herself not to outwardly show her internal devastation. "Where's Lily?"

"She'll be right out. Everything okay?"

Lauren nodded. "Yeah. Noah and Liam had some work stuff and I didn't have a computer so Seth offered to let them borrow yours."

On cue, the men walked into the living room. Dillon walked out of the kitchen and immediately dropped a kiss on the top of Lauren's head.

"Hey kiddo. How you doing?"

She kept the smile on until her face ached. "I'm good."

"When you going to dump the diner and come to work for me?"

It was a running joke between her and Dillon. He'd been mortally offended that she hadn't come to him for a job, but she'd wanted to find work on her own and she liked the diner. While Dillon operated a great bar and grill, the bar scene wasn't really her thing. She liked the quietness of the diner and getting to know the locals who came in regularly.

"When you buy the diner," she said with a genuine grin.

He laughed. "You never know. I may yet add it to my growing list of real estate."

Dillon Colter owned several businesses in Clyde, including the sporting goods store that was previously owned by a man Lauren only knew as Riley. He'd retired some time ago and had sold the business to Dillon.

Lily came into the living room, her belly looking tight as a beach ball. She smiled when she saw Lauren and came over to hug her.

"Have you eaten?" Lily asked.

Lauren blinked. She hadn't. Hadn't even thought about it.

"No, she hasn't," Liam said bluntly. "She's probably starving."

Lauren nearly groaned. So much for subtlety.

Lily grabbed Lauren's hand and dragged her toward the kitchen. "Dillon made the most awesome pasta dish. I already ate, but I swear I'm hungry again. I'll make us both a plate."

Then she looked over her shoulder to where Noah and Liam stood. "Would you like something to eat too?"

Both men shook their heads.

Lily shrugged. "More for us," she said with a grin in Lauren's direction.

Noah watched as the women disappeared into the kitchen, and then he was immediately cornered by three large men who obviously had questions.

"Is Lauren in danger?" Dillon asked bluntly.

"Most likely, yes," Liam said just as bluntly.

Seth swore. "What happened? Has that bastard shown his face here?"

Noah held up his hand. "Look. I really need that computer. Lauren has a disk with information she says she copied from Joel

Knight's computer. If what she says is on this disk is actually on it, we've opened one big-ass can of worms. But first I need to see exactly what's on here, and then we can discuss what the hell we do with it."

"Shit," Michael muttered. "That doesn't sound good at all."

"I'll get the laptop," Dillon said as he turned to walk away.

"How serious is this looking?" Seth asked in a low voice after Dillon had left the room.

"Very," Liam said shortly. "Lauren is devastated. The woman Noah and I questioned, who led us to Joel Knight and then eventually here to confront Lauren with what we'd found out, was found dead in her apartment. She was beaten to death the day after we spoke to her. Lauren's taking it very hard. She blames herself."

"Son of a bitch," Seth bit out.

"Yeah," Noah said. "We didn't know about the disk. Another surprise, and not a good one. She's determined to go back to New York with the evidence she has so she can put Joel away, and she blames herself for not having the courage to do it before. She feels guilty for running away and hiding behind her brother and your family. She feels like she's let you all down."

"That's bullshit," Michael said, his face drawn in anger.

"I want to shake her," Liam said. "I'm pissed that she kept something this heavy from us. Or even you. Someone needed to know. I'm pissed that she blames herself. I'm pissed that she's taking responsibility for everything that bastard has done."

Dillon had returned for the tail end of the conversation and he scowled openly at Liam. "You didn't hurt her, did you?"

Liam's brows drew together in an angry cloud. "What the fuck? You think I'd hurt her? You think I'd do anything to make her *afraid* of me?"

Seth held up his hands. "Enough. I don't want Lily or Lauren to overhear us. Dillon, you didn't hear the whole story and we don't have time to repeat it. Noah and Liam are protecting Lauren's best interests."

"She *is* our best interest," Noah said flatly. Let them make what they wanted of that statement. He was staking a claim now so that when the shit hit the fan, there was no way the Colters or her brother were stepping in and taking over. Over his dead body would he and Liam simply step aside.

Michael's eyebrow went up as he stared between the two men. "I suppose coming from me, surprise would be hypocritical."

Liam snorted. "Yeah, you could say that."

Dillon wasn't quite ready to back down, though.

"Either of you do anything to take advantage of her or hurt her, and I'll make you both very sorry."

"I'm not fighting with you over Lauren unless you do something to interfere in our relationship or her safety," Noah said calmly. "We both want the same thing. What's best for Lauren. And we want her out of danger."

Dillon relaxed. "Sounds like we're on the same page then. We care about her a lot. She's like a little sister to us. When she came here from New York, she . . . Well, she was a different woman."

"We know," Liam said quietly. "We were there just a few days after that bastard worked her over. We had to bully her to get her to eat, and she couldn't stand the sight of us for a long time."

"Let's go into the office," Seth said when Dillon held up the laptop. "I don't know how long the girls will be, but I'd rather not hash this out in front of them. Besides the upset it's obviously causing Lauren, Lily will worry, and we're trying to make sure she has absolutely no stress during this pregnancy."

"I understand," Noah said. "I'm sorry we had to bother you. If it wasn't so important, we would have waited, but this is potentially explosive and I don't want to be caught unprepared when it comes to Lauren's safety."

"I'd be pissed if you *hadn't* come to me," Seth said.

He motioned them into an office just off the living room. The room smelled strongly of cedar. Fresh cedar. The room had a new-ness to it that the rest of the house lacked.

"Is this an addition?" Noah asked.

Dillon nodded. "We've added on quite a bit since Lily came to us." His expression softened as he spoke of his wife. Noah doubted he even realized it. "Extra bedrooms. We gave Lily space for her painting and we added this office that we all use. Michael runs a veterinary clinic, I run several businesses, and Seth needs space at home to work as well."

Seth motioned for Noah to take the seat behind the desk. He put the laptop down and opened it up as Noah maneuvered his way behind the desk.

When he put the disk in, Liam pushed his way in to look over Noah's shoulder.

Once he opened the drive for the disk, he clicked on the file that was only labeled by a date. The date Lauren had left Joel and called her brother for help.

Once inside, there were several different files, and he clicked on the first, which was a spreadsheet. He quickly scanned over it, not-ing the categories. It was remarkably detailed with the name of the client, his sexual preferences, everything down to specific kinks. Deal breakers were listed for each client. Prices were different depending on which client it was, and the charges ranged from hourly to entire weekends.

There was a list of his "girls," but they didn't look like real names. Each client had a detailed list of past girls with notes rating each woman on her performance.

Disgust boiled in Noah's gut. The bastard had basically done a follow-up every time one of the women serviced a client. There were marks of the times one of the girls was "disciplined" for not satisfying the client properly, and Noah could only imagine what that punishment entailed.

Once he got past the initial astonishment of how detailed the information was, he focused in on the client names.

"Holy fuck," he murmured.

"What?" Seth demanded.

"Are you seeing what I'm seeing?" Liam asked in disbelief.

"What?" Dillon and Michael both bit out.

"I doubt the names would mean anything to you," Noah explained. "Well, some of them would. There are quite a few celebrities listed. Movie stars, pro athletes, entertainers."

"Where?" Dillon asked, shoving in so he could see the screen.

Noah pointed to several well-known names.

"I'll be damned," Dillon murmured. "These are the asshole's clients? Men who used women for sex?"

"Women they paid for sex," Liam said grimly. "Though I doubt the women pocketed nearly what Knight charged. His fees are exorbitant."

"I'm more interested in these names," Noah said, tapping the top of the screen.

"That one's a judge." He dropped his finger down two lines. "That one's an aide to the mayor. This one is a state senator from New York. And this one is the one who most concerns me. This one is the police commissioner. Lauren said he had several cops on his payroll. It's more likely he has blackmail material, and they make damn sure nothing touches Knight because if he goes down, he brings them all with him."

"Fuck."

The expletive exploded from Liam as he stood bristling with anger next to Noah.

"This sounds big," Michael muttered.

"Yeah, it's huge," Seth said grimly.

Noah opened another of the files, and there was a list of the women on Knight's payroll. Real names, social security numbers, addresses, phone numbers and background information.

What drew Noah's alarm was that there was a list of family members, friends, even neighbors. Detailed information on the women's personal lives, where they liked to vacation, hang out, the salons they used. It was clear that Knight kept his women firmly under his thumb and that once they went to work for him, there was no escaping.

As he studied it closer, his mouth dropped open. There were notations out to the side of some of the women's names that sounded ominous.

Situation taken care of.

No longer poses a problem for the organization.

Went to police. Threat eliminated.

Noah turned to Seth. "Is there any way you can discreetly run these names and details of the women with these notations and see if they're still alive? And if they aren't, find out date of death and circumstances? Because it sure as hell looks to me like he made notes on the women he killed or had killed."

Seth's expression was grim. "Yeah, print it off for me. I'll do what I can."

Dillon perched on the edge of the desk, angled so he could see Noah and Liam.

"What does this do for Lauren's safety?"

"It damn sure doesn't help," Liam growled.

"She wants to go to New York and turn in the disk. She wants to nail Joel Knight's ass to the wall," Noah said.

"Shit," Seth swore.

"She took Suki's death very hard," Noah continued.

"Suki?" Michael asked.

"She's the woman Liam and I talked to and who was beaten to

death the day after," Noah replied. "Lauren blames herself. Said that if she'd gone to the police when she left Joel instead of running here to hide that Suki would be alive."

"That's crazy," Dillon bit out. "She'd probably be dead herself. He would have gotten to her before Max ever got there."

"Exactly," Liam said. "But she has it in her head that she's to blame and she wants to rectify the situation by going to New York and handing over the disk to the authorities."

Seth rubbed a hand over his hair. "Does Max know about any of this?"

Noah shook his head. "We came straight here. I wanted to see what was on the disk before I made any decisions with regard to Lauren."

"He's going to flip out," Michael said.

Liam leveled a stare at Seth. "What do you think, Seth? What are our options here? We have to be careful who we trust. We can't just ignore the issue. It's not going to go away. And the minute we relax our guard, that's when that bastard will show up. For all we know he has someone looking for Lauren now. It's obvious by looking at his records that he doesn't take kindly to women leaving the fold. I can only imagine how personally he took it that a woman he considered his possession walked out on him."

Seth nodded his lips drawn into a grim line. "I agree. From everything you've told me about him and from what Max has said, I'm inclined to agree that he's not going to just forget about Lauren and move on. Which means you'll always have to be looking over your shoulder unless something is done to stop him."

"I think we should contact the district attorney and set up a meeting," Noah said. "On our terms. We name the place and we prepare for the worst-case scenario, which is that the D.A. is dirty and the meeting is a setup to take Lauren out. We make damn sure she's protected and that he's on the up-and-up before we let him talk to her. And at no time do we give him any details about where Lauren is now or give him any of her family's names."

"Max wouldn't be hard to track down," Dillon pointed out. "If someone does any digging, they'll discover Max and they'll come here looking for her."

Seth shook his head. "No, that's not true. Max is a cagey bastard. I did some checking up on him when all that shit was going down between him and Callie. All I was able to discover about him was his connection to the business he owned. Apparently he's always been big on privacy, because the only link was to the corporation, and the headquarters lists an address in New York City. I highly doubt that changed after he hooked up with Callie. He's very protective of her, and he's a wealthy son of a bitch. He wouldn't want any risk to her whatsoever and she's a free spirit, so putting her under lock and key wouldn't exactly work."

"Okay, well, that's a good thing," Liam said. "No one but Max and your family knows that she's here or that she came from New York. I assume the locals only know she's Max's sister and not much else."

Seth nodded. "Exactly. I don't think you should take her anywhere near New York."

Noah frowned. "Hell no. If the D.A.'s interested in talking to her, he'll have to meet us someplace that isn't connected to here or New York."

"I'm sure Max would fly you out on his jet," Seth said. "No paper trail that way. No IDs. No way to trace you back here. Have Lauren either dye her hair or wear a wig. Alter her appearance as much as possible for the meeting."

"I like the way you think," Liam said.

"And I don't think you should go alone," Seth added quietly.

Noah lifted his brow again. "Meaning what?"

"I think some of us should go with you as backup."

Liam sent Noah a worried glance. The last thing they wanted was to involve the Colters. But he also recognized that he and Noah were only two people, and while they'd risk their lives to protect Lauren, if they went down, who would be left to protect her?

"I don't know . . ." Noah hedged.

"Seth and I can go," Dillon said firmly. "Michael can stay with Lily. We can talk to the dads. Max is going to have to know. We really need to let everyone in on what's going on so we can plan Lauren's meeting with the D.A. but also make sure that mom, Callie and Lily aren't left unprotected here."

"This is going to devastate Lauren even more," Liam said. "She looks at you and your parents as her family. She loves all of you and she feels like she's let you down and that she's not worthy of the unconditional support you've offered her. She's going to hate that it's all going to come out this way."

"Mom will nip that in the bud," Michael said confidently. "The important thing is that we get the family together and decide what's best for Lauren."

Seth nodded his agreement. "Lauren is family. There's no way in hell we're just going to stand by on this. No offense to you and Noah. I'm sure you're damn good at your job, and it's obvious you care a lot about her."

"No offense taken. We could use the help," Noah said bluntly. "We need people we can trust, and I feel like we can trust you and your family absolutely."

Seth checked his watch. "It's late and I hate to drag everybody out tonight for a family meeting. But I think we should do it first thing in the morning so we can get rolling on what needs to be done. You take Lauren back home and try to get her to rest. Michael, can you call Doc Burton and ask him to call in something for Lauren to take to help her sleep tonight?"

Noah shook his head. "Don't worry about Lauren. Liam and I

will handle things with her. Just tell us when and where to meet you tomorrow. I'll make sure she calls into work. There are things we need to get worked out between us before we bring in the rest of her family."

Seth nodded his understanding. "We'll meet at Mom and the dads' place first thing in the morning at eight. I'll go into work early and see what I can find out on those women on the printout. I'll call Dad and let him know we're coming. And then I'll call Max."

Noah rose from the chair he was seated in and extended his hand in Seth's direction. "Appreciate the help. I know Lauren will too once she's gotten over her fear and upset."

Seth took his hand, shaking it. "You just watch out for our girl. She's one of us even if her last name isn't Colter."

"What about Lily?" Michael said in a low voice. "For that matter, what about Mom and Callie? This is going to upset them."

"Lauren is going to need their support," Dillon said. "Lily would be pissed if we tried to keep this from her. Mom would kick all our asses. We've been through tough times before. Our women can handle it. We can't protect them from everything. Besides, they need to know what we're dealing with so they aren't blindsided. They need to know to be on the lookout and to be careful until things are resolved."

"I agree," Seth said. "We can't *not* tell them. They need to stick together and make sure they don't go anywhere alone."

"Okay then. We'll take Lauren home and we'll meet you at your parents' place tomorrow at eight," Noah said.

"Let's go get *our* girl," Liam said gruffly.

CHAPTER 20

⚜

LAUREN was doing her best to do justice to the wonderful-tasting pasta Lily had plated for her, but every bite felt like a rock in her stomach.

In the other room, the guys were talking. Deciding her fate. As if she had absolutely no control over her own choices.

But then could she blame them when she'd done nothing but make bad decisions? Over and over, at every turn, she'd chosen wrong.

This time she knew what she needed to do. It was clear in her mind and heart. Yes, it scared the holy hell out of her. She wasn't so stupid that she thought it would be a simple matter of turning over the evidence to the police, and then Joel would spend many years behind bars and cease to be a threat to her.

Doing the right thing wasn't easy. It wasn't supposed to be easy. If it were, then everyone would always go that route and the world would be a much better place.

But it wasn't, because men like Joel Knight continued to grow and prosper at the expense of the women he owned and controlled, threatened and intimidated.

That was no longer going to be her, and if she could help it, it would no longer be the women he peddled to men willing to pay Joel's price to use their bodies.

"Is everything all right, Lauren?"

Lily's anxious voice cut through Lauren's thoughts. Her smile was automatic as she stared back at the other woman. But the longer she stared at Lily, the more she knew she couldn't lie to her friend's face.

There'd been too many lies as it was.

"I don't know yet," Lauren said in a low voice. "Liam and Noah are talking to Seth about it."

Lily put her hand over Lauren's and squeezed. "You know that we're here for you. All of us."

This time Lauren's smile was genuine. "I do know that and thank you. You can't possibly know what your support means to me."

"Oh but I do know," Lily said. "It wasn't so long ago that I was in a terrible situation. The Colters were wonderful to me. I'll never forget what that felt like after living with so much pain and regret. You'll get there, Lauren. You just have to give yourself time to heal."

They were interrupted when the group of men walked into the kitchen. Lauren immediately pushed her plate away, relieved to have an excuse to be done with it.

Liam came to stand beside her and slipped his hand over her shoulder. "You ready to go? It's getting late."

She nodded, examining each of the men's faces in turn, looking for some sign of . . . condemnation. But all she saw was steady resolve. Determination.

She slid from her chair and rubbed her hands down her pants in a nervous gesture. Noah reached for one of her hands and laced his fingers through hers. His hold was comforting and strong. He tucked her into his side and ushered her toward the door amid good-byes from the Colters.

The cool night air was a much-needed balm for her senses. She breathed it in deeply, savoring the crispness. For a moment she hesitated, staring up to the blue-black sky. Stars cascaded across the expanse, like glitter tossed carelessly from the hand of a child.

The mountain loomed over them, silhouetted against the sky, and the moon was just visible between two peaks. Around her, the pines, furs and aspens swayed with the gentle breeze, bringing to her the spicy scent of pine.

What was most remarkable was the quiet. Silence had settled over the land with the blanket of night. Only the occasional rustle wrought by the wind stirred any sound.

It was a peaceful place. The most beautiful place Lauren had ever experienced. She wanted it to be her home. Her haven.

A lifetime away from the hustle and bustle of her former life in the city. The shopping, lattes, delis, busy streets, honking horns, every other business a different restaurant, cell phones, traffic lights, constantly going, going, going and never pausing to simply breathe.

Here she could walk down the sidewalk in Clyde and never bump into another person. There wasn't a single traffic light in the town, and only one stop sign, at the intersection of Main and Maplewood.

People smiled when she made eye contact. The citizens here were always willing to lend a helping hand.

On the day she'd moved into her apartment, though she'd had the help of Max and the entire Colter clan, they'd had no less than a half a dozen offers from passersby to get her furniture up the stairs.

And Margery, one of the regulars at the diner, had fried chicken and made potato salad and homemade rolls along with a pitcher of fresh-squeezed lemonade, and she'd brought it all to Lauren's apartment so everyone could eat.

She felt . . . relevant . . . here. Like she mattered. She wasn't just another number in a massive population. Here, she was one in a small crowd.

"Lauren?"

Liam's voice drifted to her and she realized that she was still staring up at the sky, a dreamy expression on her face. And maybe she was dreaming. Or wishing on the scattering of stars glowing brightly in the distance.

"You ready, baby? We need to get you home."

Reluctantly she tore herself away from the beauty surrounding her and climbed into the SUV.

"What did they say?" she asked softly as they drove back toward town. "And did you look at the disk?"

"We did," Noah said grimly. "You're right. There's definitely enough information to put him—and several others—away for a long time."

"They'll cut a deal and roll on him," Liam said.

"As for what the Colters said, they only voiced their unconditional support for you. They're concerned for your safety, and they threatened to kick mine and Liam's asses if we ever hurt you."

Warmth traveled through her chest, squeezing her heart.

"We're going out to their parents' tomorrow morning first thing," Liam said.

He angled in the front seat so he could see her where she sat in the back.

"Seth's doing some checking for us, and we're going to meet so that in essence as a family we can put our heads together and come up with the best plan of attack."

Lauren blew out her breath. "Okay."

Noah glanced in the rearview mirror and met her gaze. "You going to be all right with it?"

She nodded. "It's me who has the problem. I do them a great

disservice by thinking they'll be disappointed in me. The truth is I'm disappointed in myself, and so I'm projecting that viewpoint on everyone else. They've been nothing but wonderful to me."

A moment later, Noah pulled onto the side street of her building and then into the small parking lot in the back that was mostly used for the clinic. At the end, there was a designated spot for her use, but most of the time, if the clinic got busy, someone always took it anyway.

Liam opened her door, helped her out and immediately pulled her into his side, wrapping his arm protectively around her as they walked around to the side facing the street. They mounted the steps, Noah following closely behind and Liam waiting as she unlocked the door.

She flipped the wall switch, flooding the living room with light. Liam left her long enough to turn on the lamp in the corner and then he returned, turning the main light back off again.

"I like it better this way," he murmured as he pulled her into his arms.

His mouth found hers in what was at first a tender kiss. But he grew more forceful, more demanding, taking her breath as he deepened the kiss.

He cupped her jaw in his hands as he stared intently down at her.

"Tonight, you tell us how you want it, Lauren. We'll only do what you want. How you want. Show us."

It required a lot of courage to be so bold. She was suddenly shy and self-conscious. Images flashed through her mind, tempting, tantalizing her. Was it possible? Was any of it possible?

Noah came up behind her, his hands closing over her shoulders. He leaned in to kiss her neck, moving her hair out of the way as his lips nuzzled her skin.

"This is what I want," she whispered. "Both of you. Touching me. At the same time." She turned into Noah, the warmth of his body wrapping around her slow and sensual. "I want you inside me."

He let out a low groan. "I want to be there, honey. More than you can possibly know."

Liam maneuvered her toward the bedroom. She was reaching for the fly of her jeans, when the three of them crowded in. Before courage deserted her, before she could overthink this, she began undressing, determined to take an active part in their lovemaking.

She pushed down her pants, and when she stood again, Noah was there, his hands sliding underneath her shirt, his palms warm and erotic on her skin.

Emboldened by desire flooding her veins, she began to undo his pants. One particular fantasy had taken hold, and she wanted it to come true. They'd given her the power. All she had to do was speak up.

Her movements were clumsy, not at all practiced. It frustrated her that she couldn't be elegantly smooth and composed.

As she struggled with Noah's pants, her frustration got the best of her.

"I feel like such a damn amateur," she muttered.

Noah captured her wrists and pulled her abruptly against him, his eyes fiery.

"I like that you want me so much that your hands shake. Honey, I don't give a damn how much finesse it's done with. All I care is that the end result is me and you naked."

She smiled. "Then would you please get the rest of your clothing off?"

"Happy to accommodate," Noah growled.

She turned to Liam and held up her arms. Needing no further encouragement, he pulled her shirt over her head and then immediately turned her so he could unfasten her bra.

Left in only her panties, she took a quick peek at Noah, who was down to his underwear, and then she glanced back at Liam, who was still fully dressed.

"This won't do at all," she murmured in a husky, seductive tone she didn't recognize.

"We can't have that," Liam said. "We can't have you not pleased. By all means, tell me how you want me, baby."

"Naked," she said bluntly. "I want to feel you. Touch you. Kiss you. *Taste* you."

It was a heady sensation to be so bold and seductive. She loved the reaction in Liam's eyes. Loved the way he began stripping away his clothing with no finesse or patience.

He yanked down his jeans along with his underwear, freeing his cock from constriction. It bobbed free, long and already hard.

It was instinctive to drop to her knees in front of him, her hands circling his length. He moaned and slid his hand roughly through her hair, fisting the strands in his fingers.

Even as she lowered her mouth, she reached for Noah, wanting him close. He stepped forward so that she could grasp him in her free hand. Her fingers curled around the thick erection, and she rolled upward and then back down again, satisfied when he hardened even further in her hold.

She licked around the broad tip of Liam's dick and then turned her head to give Noah equal treatment. She teased him a moment, bestowing tiny licks and kisses before taking him deep inside her mouth.

He let out a strangled sound and his hands joined Liam's in her hair. She let her mouth slide back again, until the head popped free of her lips, and then she turned to Liam and sucked him in just as deeply.

"Goddamn," Liam bit out.

She smiled and pulled away, turning back to Noah as she rose. He reached out to help her, grasping her arms for support. She put both hands on his chest and pushed back until he came in contact with the bed.

"Condom?" she whispered.

"In my pocket," he said hoarsely.

She reached down to fumble with his pants and then retrieved one of the packets. Before returning, she hastily shoved her panties down, kicking them away when they tangled at her feet.

"Lie back," she directed, when she returned to Noah.

He settled back on the bed, his legs hanging over the edge, feet planted on the floor. She rolled the condom carefully down his length, and then she motioned for Liam.

"I want you here, beside Noah," she said. "You'll have to get up on the bed so you'll reach my mouth."

Lust flared in Liam's eyes. He didn't need to be told anything further. He obviously got where she was going with this.

She'd honestly never been on top before. Joel would have never allowed it, and the very few sexual partners she'd had before Joel had been more of a quick, awkward experience. But she was determined to rock Noah's—and Liam's—world tonight. They'd certainly rocked hers the night before.

She eased on top of Noah, straddling his muscular thighs. He reached for her waist, helping her as she positioned herself over him.

"Make sure you're ready, honey," Noah said. "I don't want to hurt you. I'll be deep this way."

She wanted him inside her so badly that it was a physical ache.

Curling her hand around his latex-encased erection, she dug her knees into the mattress on either side of his hips and carefully positioned him at her opening.

They both gasped at the first touch.

She let go of his cock so she could brace her palms on his firm, flat belly, and she slowly began to lower herself, taking more and more of him inside her.

Noah's hands flew to her hips, his fingers digging into her flesh.

His eyes were closed, head thrown back, and his expression was one of intense pleasure.

That look fascinated her. She was glued to his every reaction. She loved that she had this kind of power over him. He wanted her. He desired her. There was no disputing that.

He was thick inside her. It was different taking him this way than when Liam had pushed inside her the night before. Noah was right. He was deeper this way. He just felt bigger.

She hesitated, a little worried that he was *too* big.

"Liam, help her," Noah rasped out. "She needs to be wetter to take me. She wasn't ready."

The bed dipped, taking Liam's weight. And then he was pressed against her upper body, his lips finding hers. But then his mouth slid downward to her breasts, and as he took one rigid peak between his lips, his hand slid down her belly, between her and Noah, his fingers finding her clit.

It was a shock to her senses. The two men were in a precariously intimate position. Liam's fingers were right there! His hand had to be touching Noah in order to touch her the way he was.

Her gaze flew to Noah, to see his reaction, but his eyes were hooded and focused solely on her. It was as if he wasn't even aware of the proximity of Liam's hand to his own body. He only seemed concerned about her. Her pleasure.

Her physical reaction to the sheer eroticism of being astride one man while another pleasured her in other ways was explosive. It was suddenly a lot easier to move around Noah's rigid cock. She'd gotten wetter, but she didn't want Liam to move his hand away, so she held herself upward, still not fully taking Noah as deeply as she could.

She loved having Liam at her breasts, his fingers between her and Noah. It somehow fit. It just came together for her. That they'd be comfortable enough in their own sexuality to focus only on her pleasure, without worry that they were somehow making contact, touched her deeply.

With a last sigh as Liam sucked strongly at her nipples and his fingers stroked over her clit, she put her hand on his shoulder and squeezed to get his attention.

"I want you up on the bed," she whispered. "I want you in my mouth while Noah's inside me."

"Oh hell yes," Liam breathed.

He pushed further up on the bed, his hand pulled away from her and Noah. In the end, he had to almost stand on the bed and duck to keep from hitting the ceiling, but he threaded a hand through her hair and helped guide himself to her waiting mouth.

Noah's hands tightened around her hips. She needed his help and he seemed to realize it. Between the two men, they worked in a gentle, steady rhythm, enabling her to ride atop Noah while working her mouth around Liam's cock.

It was the most exciting, crazy, hot, lusty experience she'd ever imagined. No, she couldn't even say she'd imagined it. Nothing could have prepared her for the reality of having these two powerful men for all purposes at her mercy.

She reached one hand for Liam, curling her fingers around the base of his erection while she pressed her other hand against Noah's hip to keep her balance.

"I want to taste you," she said as she pulled her mouth away for a brief moment. "I want you to come inside my mouth."

"I'll take care of you, baby," Liam said, his voice hoarse and strained. "Concentrate on Noah. Keep your hands down. I'll take care of what you want."

Noah reached for her hand as she lowered it, twining his fingers with hers. He was so deep and huge inside her. Each time she moved forward, the pressure of his pelvis against her clit sent streaks of sharp pleasure through her body.

She wanted more.

She found her rhythm just as Liam framed her face and took control, sliding his cock deep inside her mouth and then withdrawing. She rocked and rolled over Noah, finally finding just the perfect amount of pressure for her to orgasm.

Never before had she been able to orgasm without clitoral stimulation. Joel simply hadn't cared, and he'd refused to allow her to use her fingers to satisfy herself during the act. With the men she'd been with before Joel, she'd simply taken it upon herself to take care of her own orgasm.

Who gave a shit what Joel allowed? This was here and now. She was with two men who seemed determined to give her the world. They weren't so insecure in their sexual prowess that her pleasuring herself would be seen as an insult.

She slipped her free hand down, arching up just a bit so she could slide her fingers between her and Noah to find her clit.

"That's it, honey," Noah encouraged. "I want you to come too."

Even as he spoke, he lifted his hands to her breasts, toying with her nipples.

"Do you like that?" Noah asked. "Does it make you feel good?"

She moaned around Liam's cock, her body tightening all over as she began to stroke her clit while Noah applied gentle pressure to her nipples.

She began to move faster and harder. Her breathing sped up and she knew she was close.

Liam thrust deep and then performed several more shallow thrusts to allow her to catch her breath. But she was beyond simple coherency. She no longer was aware of what she was doing or what they were doing. She could only feel their hands, their cocks.

"You first," Liam said gruffly. "Come for us, baby."

With a sharp cry, she gave in to the rising tide. Her orgasm billowed over her, cracking like ice under pressure. It was sharp and unrelenting. It was the most oh-my-God pleasure she'd ever felt in her life.

She sagged and then realized they were now holding her up. She was limp and boneless, so sated that all she wanted to do was curl up on Noah's chest and sleep.

But first, she wanted them to feel as good as she did.

Liam tilted her head back, allowing his cock to slide from her mouth. Then with his hand, he began pumping, the pace wild and frantic. He angled the tip of his cock to where it lined up with her mouth and a split second later, she felt the first hot burst of semen hit the inside of her cheek.

She remained completely still as he directed more into her mouth. His fist pulled to the end, and then the tip of his cock brushed over her lips, leaving a warm, wet trail.

She stuck her tongue out, licking around the head and removing the remnants of his orgasm from his skin. He moaned softly and then pulled away. He lowered himself and brushed a kiss across her forehead.

"Finish Noah," he whispered. "I'll go get something to clean you up with."

She righted herself and then leaned forward, planting her hands on Noah's broad chest. His face was tight, his jaw bulging. She realized then what it must have been like to watch the scene between her and Liam play out right in front of Noah.

"I'm close, honey," he bit out. "I'm feeling a little crazy right now. I don't want to hurt you."

She smiled and then began to ride him hard. Fast. Furious. She wanted to take him to the very edge and then let him plummet over the side.

His breath hissed from his lips. He gripped her hips and began to power upward to meet her downward movements. After a moment, she let him take over. Her attempts at maintaining the pace were fruitless. He was much stronger, and he seemed to have lost what little control he had left.

The sound of flesh smacking flesh was loud and filled the small room. Each upward thrust jolted her clit, sending an aftershock of pleasure through her groin. She was hypersensitive after the roaring orgasm she'd experienced, and each time his pelvis slapped against hers, she moaned, nearly undone by the sensation.

And then he tensed, bowed under her, arched in a supremely uncomfortable-looking position as he pulsed inside her. Finally he collapsed onto the bed, and he wrapped his arms around her, taking her down with him.

They both lay panting, trying desperately to catch their breaths as Noah caressed her back with both palms. He moved lower, cupping her buttocks, squeezing them possessively.

The gesture made her tighten around his cock, which was still buried deep inside her, and she moaned softly again.

"You okay?" he murmured close to her ear.

She turned her lips to the side, turning just enough that she could kiss his chest.

"Perfect," she said on a sigh.

She closed her eyes in utter contentment. It was true. The moment was absolutely perfect.

No matter what happened tomorrow, tonight she was at peace. Noah and Liam made her feel cherished and protected. They made her feel like she mattered.

Tomorrow—and the future—would work itself out. She had to believe that. All she could do was take it one day at a time and going forward make intelligent decisions she hadn't made in the past.

The important thing was that she wouldn't be alone. Noah and Liam would be with her every step of the way.

CHAPTER 21

LAUREN slept with Liam that night while Noah slept in the living room. She woke the next morning, curled into his embrace, him tightly wrapped around her. She was spooned against him, her back molded to his chest. One of his legs was thrown over hers and his palm was flat against her belly.

She smiled, sighing in utter contentment. It was a nice way to wake up. It was a nice way to sleep. So far they'd alternated nights, but what would happen when they had better sleeping arrangements? If she were in a place that could actually accommodate a king-sized bed, then it would be possible for them both to sleep with her and one wouldn't always have to take a separate room or bed.

She wiggled slightly, working free of Liam's embrace so that she could look at him. He was beautiful. Not many would say so. He'd probably always been judged because of the hair and the tattoos. Most people likely cut a wide path around him.

But his heart was gold. He was so loving and so protective. There wasn't a mean bone in his body. Not when it came to her.

She let her palm glide over the intricate artwork on his arm, taking in the bright colors and the patterns. There wasn't a set rhythm. It wasn't a specific scene or even a recognizable symbol. It was quite simply a work of art. Eclectic. Vibrant. It made him stand out in a crowd, but then he was the kind of man who would with or without the colorful tats.

He was a man impossible to overlook.

While she was staring, his eyelids opened and he gave her a sleepy look, his blue eyes cloudy.

"Good morning," she murmured.

Without a word, he wrapped his arm around her waist and hauled her to him, kissing her lightly on the lips. He didn't seem to care about issues like morning breath. She could only imagine what hers was like.

"You look . . ." His eyes narrowed as he studied her.

"I look what?"

"Content," he finally said.

She smiled. "I am. Maybe I'm making peace with things. Finally. Or maybe you and Noah just make me so happy and confident that I don't care about anything else."

"I'm glad," he said softly. "I love you, Lauren. I want you to be happy. I want you to fly. Whatever makes you happy, I want it for you."

She swallowed, her features frozen. Her heart fluttered in her chest like an injured butterfly.

He loved her.

Oh, she knew he cared about her. But love?

He sounded so very serious that she knew this wasn't an instance where he got carried away in the moment and tossed out careless words that had no meaning.

And she realized something else too. She loved *him*. Completely. Without reservation.

She touched his face, wanting the words to be taken as seriously as she'd taken them from him.

"I love you too, Liam."

The relief in his eyes was crushing. It was as if his entire body had been locked in tension and had suddenly been set free. He wrapped both arms around her and pulled her to him in a fierce embrace.

"Do you mean it?" he asked gruffly against her ear.

She withdrew immediately, propping up on her elbow so they could see eye to eye.

"I love you," she said. "I mean every word. You aren't some passing fancy for me. I don't have the whole damsel-in-distress thing going on where the weak woman falls for her protector. If you want me to explain it, I'm afraid I can't. I just do."

"I don't want you to explain it," Liam said. "I just want to hear it again and know you mean it. I never thought . . ."

"Never thought what?" she asked gently.

His mouth twisted and discomfort registered in his eyes.

"I never thought a girl like you would give a guy like me a second look."

She blinked, completely at a loss for words. "Girl like me? Guy like you? What on earth do you mean? Liam, you're beautiful," she blurted. "You're successful. Confident. You have a heart of gold. You're striking to look at. Any woman would count herself lucky that you'd give her a second glance. On the other hand, I'm a cowardly nitwit. I've trusted the wrong people. I've made bad decision after bad decision. I've lied to you," she said painfully. "I'm weak. I gave up my identity and all I was to a man I never should have looked at twice. And you actually think that you somehow don't deserve my love? Good God. I'm the lucky one here. I not only have you but also Noah, and you *both* care about me. I can't wrap my head around it, but I'm not questioning it, because I don't want anything to persuade you differently."

He smiled and twisted his fingers in her long, dark hair. "Striking to look at, huh."

"You're gorgeous," she murmured as she leaned in to kiss him. "You're also mine. Any woman looking at you better keep her distance. I'm very possessive with my man."

His grin broadened. "Your man. I like that. And I am, you know."

"Yes, I do. Now I really need to get up and brush my teeth before we start kissing again."

He laughed and rolled out of bed, taking a moment to stretch before relaxing his broad shoulders again.

She was struck by how magnificent his body was. He was standing naked in front of her, and she hadn't lied. He was simply beautiful. She'd never grow tired of watching him.

He was semihard with his morning erection and it made her want to coax it to further rigidity.

Was she bold enough to make an overture? What if he turned her down? She hated the anxiety that crept up her neck at the thought of propositioning him.

She closed her eyes. She was being an idiot.

She stretched languidly, giving him a good view of her naked body. His eyes darkened and his cock twitched, going from semi-erect to three-quarters in two seconds flat.

"Think you could find a condom in the time it takes me to brush my teeth?" she murmured.

"How fast can you brush your teeth?" he growled.

She smiled and rolled to the edge. She got up and brushed against him, her hand sliding down to cup his balls. She fondled the heavy sac for a long moment before allowing her fingers to dance up his erection to the tip.

"I'll be right back."

She ducked into the bathroom, grinning the entire time. Hurriedly she brushed her teeth and then worked some of the wildness out of her hair so she didn't look quite the hag.

Three minutes later, she was out of the bathroom, and Liam was standing where she left him, only he was already sheathed in a condom and he was enormously aroused.

Worked for her.

While she loved the attentive foreplay they always gave her, what she really wanted was a down-and-dirty quickie. And she told him as much.

"I'll give you whatever you want, baby," he said.

Sucking in a deep breath and gathering her courage to face her fears, she got on the bed, positioning herself on her hands and knees.

"Lauren?"

Liam's voice was unsure and concerned. She turned so she could look at him over her shoulder.

"I want to try," she said firmly. "Besides, it's not the same. I'm not flat on my belly pinned by a body so I'm powerless. And . . ."

"And what, baby?" Liam prompted.

"I want to get over this fear," she said. "I don't want to ever make Noah feel badly about the other night. Help me get through this, Liam. I want it quick and dirty."

He moved in behind her, his palms gliding softly over her behind. He parted her thighs further, his fingers caressing the sensitive flesh of her pussy.

"I can promise you quick," he said. "But not dirty, baby. Never dirty. You're too beautiful for that."

Her heart melted. Her fingers curled into the sheets until her hands were tightly fisted balls. She closed her eyes and pictured Liam behind her. Liam pushing into her.

And then he did.

*   *   *

NOAH pushed himself up from the floor and glanced at his watch. Damn but they were going to be late. He listened for any noise coming from the bedroom, the sound of a shower, anything to let him know Liam and Lauren were awake and moving.

He was going to have to wake them up so they could get moving if they were going to make it out to the Colters' by eight.

He opened the door to her bedroom and was greeted by the sight of Lauren on her hands and knees and Liam pounding into her from behind. Lauren's head was thrown back and Liam's big hands gripped her hips as his cock disappeared into her pussy over and over.

Noah's own cock hardened painfully. It was an erotic sight to behold and an unwanted stab of jealousy pierced his chest. She trusted Liam enough to let him fuck her from behind.

Liam looked up, his gaze locking with Noah's. Then he lowered his big body over Lauren's much smaller one and said close to her ear, "Noah's going to take you now, baby. You wanted quick and hot. How about two men taking turns fucking you from behind?"

Lauren's eyes flew open and she found Noah, her eyes glowing with lust and desire. Noah's initial jealousy disappeared, leaving him faintly ashamed. It was clear she wanted both and that she was working hard to overcome her fears.

Liam withdrew, his cock heavy and stiff and he looked expectantly at Noah. All thoughts of time and being late fled. He moved toward her, his hand fumbling with the fly of his jeans. Liam tossed him a condom and Noah rolled it on, leaving his jeans pushed down to his hips.

Lauren's pussy was swollen from Liam's hard fucking, and Noah twitched with impatience to drive just as deep inside her as Liam had been. He leaned down to press a gentle kiss to the small of her back, just so she'd know he was here and what was about to happen.

Then he positioned himself between her slim thighs, fit his cock to her small opening and pushed inward, forcing her to accommodate his width and length.

"Harder," she whispered.

He pushed down his own fears of hurting her or frightening her and let himself go, doing what he'd wanted to do from the moment he'd met her. Mark her. Make her his own. Possess her and own her.

He pounded into her, his need for her all consuming. His orgasm rose, edgy and sharp. It took everything he had to pull out, but he didn't want it to end this quickly and he was a second from exploding.

Liam pushed in, taking Noah's place. Lauren moaned and dropped her head a little as Liam thrust inside her again. She angled her upper body downward until her cheek rested against the mattress, but the entire time, she was pushing herself back to meet Liam's thrusts.

"I'm coming, baby," Liam ground out. "You wanna do yours now or wait for Noah?"

"I'll wait," she said.

Liam let out a roar and thrust into her so hard that it shook her and the entire bed. Then for a long moment, he rested against her, buried deep inside her, his eyes closed, his hands resting possessively on her body.

Finally he withdrew, leaving her opened, her pussy a darker pink and still swollen.

Noah couldn't resist running his fingers over the puffy lips. So soft and silken. She moaned and twisted restlessly as he fingered her clit.

"Use your hand, honey," he whispered huskily. "I'm not going to last long and I want you with me."

Her hand slid through her tight curls, bumping against his, as she found the sensitive nub he'd fondled. Satisfied that she was prepared, he positioned himself against her damp opening and pushed in, relishing the feel of her snug heat surrounding him, enveloping and swallowing him whole.

Remembering her request before, he thrust harder and faster. He closed his eyes as sweet pleasure worked over every inch of his body. His balls drew up, tightening until he thought they might explode. Tension built.

She cried out and went liquid around him. She was slick and hot as her orgasm made it easier to get deeper inside her.

His mind went blank. He had no awareness of anything but the overwhelming ecstasy of being inside her. And then finally, finally the building tension released.

He shuddered with mind-numbing pleasure. He strained into her, wanting deeper, not wanting the moment to end. Only the knowledge that she'd be extremely sensitive after her orgasm kept him from continuing to push into her over and over until he was incapable of doing so.

Reluctantly he withdrew from her quivering body. He was so sensitive that he couldn't bear the condom on for another second. He stripped it off, tossed it into the trash can beside her bed, and then he and Liam helped her into a sitting position.

"Quick enough for you, baby?" Liam drawled.

Her lips curled with amusement. "That was amazing. Thank you."

She turned to face Noah, her fingers going to his jaw in the lightest of touches. "I wanted to try again. I won't allow him to control my mind when I'm with you and Liam. You both mean too much to me to allow anyone else to intrude on our time together."

He captured her fingers and kissed the tip of each one. "And to think I was on my way in here to hurry you two up."

She laughed softly. "Are we late?"

"Yeah, we are," Noah said. "But for that, I'll be late every damn day from now on."

CHAPTER 22

I T was nearly eight thirty when Lauren, Noah and Liam pulled up to the Colters' home. Max and Callie as well as Lily, Seth, Michael and Dillon were already there.

Butterflies stumbled around her stomach as she sat in the front seat, staring through the windshield to the front porch. Liam reached across the seat and squeezed her hand.

"Ready for this? It's not too late to back out. No phone calls have been made."

It shamed her that for a brief moment, she considered doing just that. It was instinctive to want to run and hide, but then that's what she'd been doing for far too long.

Taking a calming breath, she shook her head. "No, I need to do this. Not just for the women he's brutalized and murdered, but I need to do it for me."

Noah shifted forward from the backseat. "Just remember that Liam and I are behind you. Always. No matter what goes on in here, no matter if emotions run high. We support you one hundred percent, no matter what you choose to do."

She turned, allowing her love for both men to shine in her eyes. She only hoped he could see it. That he knew it and felt it. The words had come easily with Liam because he'd given them first. She needed to give them to Noah. And she would, as soon as they got through the meeting with her family.

"Thank you," she choked out.

"Ready?" Liam said as he opened his door.

Taking one more deep breath, she opened her door and stepped into the sunlight, allowing it to remove the chill deep inside her chest.

Noah and Liam flanked her as they walked toward the porch. The door was opened by Holly, who immediately pulled Lauren into her firm embrace.

"How are you, baby?" Holly asked in her sweet, motherly voice that always made Lauren feel as though she'd come home.

"I'm fine, Mama C. Or I will be," she amended.

Holly pulled away, her eyes worried and dark. "Max is upset. I thought you should know so you don't get blindsided."

Lauren's stomach somersaulted, and she glanced anxiously up at Noah and Liam.

"It'll be fine, honey," Noah soothed. "We'll get through this together."

Holly took her hand and pulled her into the house, leaving the men to follow.

"They're right," Holly said. "We'll get through this together. Just like we always do. Max was just caught off guard and he's not taking it well."

As they entered the living room, everyone turned to look in Lauren's direction. Max, who'd been sitting beside Callie on the couch, shot to his feet, his expression dark.

Callie put her hand up to his arm and murmured something to him, but he shook her off and advanced toward Lauren. But it wasn't her he was intent on questioning. He stopped a short distance away, his angry gaze finding Noah and Liam.

"Do one of you want to explain why I'm getting information from Seth and not either of you? Last time I checked, I was signing your checks. Your job is to protect my sister and report to me. I didn't know of any of this and I should have been the first to know," he seethed.

Even as he spoke, he pulled Lauren into his side, wrapping a protective arm around her. She could feel the anger—and the tension—vibrating from him.

Noah's eyes narrowed and Liam's lip curled into a snarl.

"When have you received a bill from us ever?" Noah snapped. "Better check your records, Wilder, because we haven't asked you for a cent. Lauren isn't a damn job to us. Our priority is keeping her safe, not keeping you posted on every detail we have before we even know if it's an issue. We spoke to Seth last night and then set up this morning's meeting so we could plan accordingly."

Max stiffened even further, apparently not appeased by Noah's explanation.

"What the hell are you saying?" Max asked softly. "Just what is the nature of your relationship with my sister? I damn sure didn't hire you to take advantage of her."

Lauren jerked away from Max's hold. "Max, stop it. Please."

"I'd say that's none of your damn business," Liam said in an equally soft, dangerous tone.

"The hell it's not!" Max burst out.

"Max, enough, son," Adam Colter said firmly as he inserted himself between Max and where Noah and Liam stood. "We aren't going to get anywhere with you and Noah and Liam snarling at each other like a bunch of pit bulls."

Holly put her arm around Lauren and led her beyond Max and farther into the living room where the others sat.

Dillon and Michael were both perched on the hearth, while Lily sat next to Callie on one of the sofas. Seth, Ryan and Ethan occupied the other couch, and two armchairs were vacant. Chairs from the dining room had been brought into the living room to accommodate more people and were staggered between the couches and armchairs.

Holly led Lauren to the couch to sit with Lily and Callie. Lauren settled next to Callie, who immediately took her hand, holding tightly in support. Holly took position on Lauren's other side and wrapped an arm around Lauren's shoulders.

Lauren couldn't help but smile. The Colter women had closed ranks around her. Not even Max would dare to take on Mama C, much less her *and* Callie and Lily.

"Have a seat," Adam instructed Noah and Liam. "According to Seth, we have a lot to discuss."

Noah and Liam walked past Max, who was still standing and seething with anger. Max's jaw was drawn tight when he turned to follow the others into the living room. He glanced toward the couch where the women sat, clearly not happy that he was being blocked by both his wife and his mother-in-law.

"He'll get over it," Callie murmured. "He's just worried about you."

"I know," Lauren whispered back.

When Max had settled onto one of the dining room tables— across from where Noah and Liam had taken their seats in armchairs—Adam turned one of the wooden chairs around and straddled it so he could take in everyone.

Seth leaned forward, his hands clasped together as his elbows pressed into his knees. "I took the liberty of bringing everyone up to date on what we discussed last night. I figured it would save time so that we could move forward once you all arrived."

Noah and Liam both nodded their agreement.

"I waited for you to arrive to give you the rundown on the women you wanted me to run through the system." Seth's lips thinned as he continued. "It's not good."

Lauren's heart plummeted. "Are they dead?" she choked out.

Seth grimaced. "Yes, honey, I'm sorry."

All the blood drained from her face. Noah and Liam swore.

"What women?" Ryan Colter demanded. "What are we talking about here?"

"The disk that has the information Lauren copied from Knight's computer has a list of the women who work or worked for him. Some had notations by their names that sounded ominous," Noah said. "We had Seth check to see if he could find any information about them. Mainly whether they were still alive."

"How did they die?" Liam asked bluntly.

Seth merely shook his head. His silence spoke volumes, and it was obvious he didn't want to go into details in front of Lauren and the other women.

Callie's hold on Lauren's hand tightened, and Holly hugged her closer to her side.

"Something has to be done about this bastard," Max said grimly. "I won't allow a threat to my family to exist."

"I *am* doing something," Lauren said softly, drawing the attention of every occupant of the room.

She was done having Seth or even Noah and Liam do her talking for her. This was on her. She was the only person who could stand up and take Joel Knight down. Not Liam. Not Noah. Not her brother. Not Seth or any of the other Colters.

Max's stare hardened, and he paled as he took in the determination in Lauren's voice.

"What do you mean by that, Lauren?" Max asked, alarm clear in his voice.

The older Colter men frowned. Ryan and Ethan sat forward, casting worried glances in her direction. Callie had a death grip on Lauren's hand, and she could feel the same worried gazes from the women on either side of her.

Her nostrils flared as she inhaled sharply. She glanced at Noah and Liam, bolstered by the support in their eyes.

"I'm going to turn in the evidence I have and testify if necessary, which I'm sure it will be."

The explosive responses were immediate.

"The hell you are!" Max shouted, bolting to his feet.

"Lauren, I'm not sure you should make that decision so quickly," Adam said, a frown marring his face.

"Do you think that's best?" Ryan asked, his expression a mirror of Adam's.

There were more questions. Exclamations of worry. A volley of conversation between the dads and Seth, and then Max and Noah and Liam. It was all a dull roar that made her head ache.

Only the women remained quiet. Callie gripped Lauren's hand so tightly that her fingers were starting to tingle. Holly had gone completely still next to Lauren, and Lily leaned forward, her worried gaze seeking out Lauren's.

"I'm scared for you, Lauren," Callie whispered.

"So am I," Lily said just as quietly.

Holly reached across Lauren's lap, holding out her hand to both Lily and Callie until all four women were connected. Lauren allowed the quiet strength of these women—survivors—bleed into her soul.

"I'm scared too," Lauren admitted. "But the one thing you've all taught me is that I have to do the right thing. A woman— *women*—are dead because of me."

She shook her head when they would have refuted her statement.

"Not because of me. I know that I'm not responsible for Joel's actions. But I could have prevented at least some of their deaths.

Maybe I could have only prevented one. But how many more will die or be abused or degraded because I'm afraid? I don't want to spend the rest of my life hiding. I don't want to forever be looking over my shoulder. I just want . . . peace."

It was only at the end of her impassioned speech that she realized her voice had carried beyond the scope of the other women, and that everyone else had quieted to listen to what she was saying.

As she glanced up, every single one of the Colters—and Max— were staring at her with gentle understanding, worry, fear and . . . pride.

She swallowed, and then again as the knot swelled in her throat and tears burned her eyelids.

"I want to be somebody you can all be proud of," she choked out. "And right now I'm not proud of myself, so how can I expect anyone else to be?"

"Oh honey," Holly said, emotion clouding her voice.

She hugged Lauren to her and rocked back and forth, stroking her hair.

"Listen to me, baby. I want you to look at me."

Lauren reluctantly lifted her gaze to the older woman and was taken aback at the pride and consternation in her eyes.

"We *are* proud of you. So very proud. Now it's time to forgive *yourself* for the mistakes you've made. You can't continue to beat yourself up over choices you've made. You have to be willing to let go and forgive yourself. No one else blames you. Only you. I look at you and see a beautiful, kind young lady with a heart as big as these mountains. I couldn't be more proud of you even if I'd given birth to you. You're one of mine. Never doubt that. And as anyone will tell you, what's mine is mine, and I love what's mine fiercely and without reserve or condition."

Tears slid down Lauren's cheeks and a sob hiccupped from her throat. "I love you too," she whispered. "All of you."

Holly hugged her again, squeezing her until she was breathless. After a moment, she gently separated herself from Lauren and stroked the hair from Lauren's face. Then she turned to Noah and Liam, all business.

"What is your plan for this?" she demanded.

CHAPTER 23

IT was hard for Liam not to charge over and take Lauren in his arms. It damn near broke his heart to listen to her break down in front of the people she loved most. He wanted to shield her from any hurt or stress, but her decision meant that hurt—and stress— were inevitable.

When Holly Colter turned her determined stare on him and Noah, and demanded to know what the plan was, he glanced at Noah and then at Seth.

Seth spoke first.

"We don't have one yet, Mom," he said gently. "It's why I called the family together, so we plot out the best course and make damn sure Lauren is protected."

"She's our first and only priority, ma'am," Noah said in a serious tone.

"I still want to know what that means exactly," Max growled. "I'm having serious issues with the fact that you took advantage of

Lauren during a time she was emotionally and physically at a disadvantage."

"It means that I love her and I'm not going to stand by while someone is a threat to her," Liam all but roared. He was pissed and growing more pissed by the minute. Now wasn't the time to bring this shit up. "Furthermore, you don't call the shots. Noah and I don't work for you. We haven't accepted one goddamn cent from you and it's going to stay that way. Lauren is ours and what that *means* is that we don't take orders from anyone when it comes to her safety and well-being. Is *that* clear enough for you?"

Holly rounded on Max, her mouth tight and her eyes shooting holes through Lauren's brother. "That's enough out of you, young man. This isn't the time or the place to bring up a personal matter that is none of your concern. What's important here is what we do going forward to make sure Lauren is protected."

Liam wanted to give Holly Colter a high five. She was a little scary when she got pissed off. She was like a mama lion protecting her cubs, and look out if anyone messed with them.

When Liam glanced back at Lauren, she was staring at him, her eyes filled with love and gratitude. Warmth traveled through his body as surely as if she were in his arms.

She sent the same expression of love in Noah's direction, and Liam saw that his friend was just as affected as Liam had been.

"My wife has a very good point," Ethan said, speaking up for the first time. "What's important here is what we do to ensure Lauren's safety. Seth? Do you have ideas, son?"

Dillon scowled. "Other than making a trip to New York City and ensuring the asshole takes a fall down a long flight of stairs. Twice?"

Michael smothered a smile. Liam had to cover his own smile when Holly Colter nodded her agreement vigorously.

"Our first step has to be to decide on a meeting place and conditions," Noah said.

"I agree," Seth said.

"We make contact, but we have to make it clear we call the shots," Liam interjected. "That includes the meeting place but we also have to be prepared that the D.A. may not follow our set of rules, so we have to be in place well ahead of him, monitor his arrival and not put Lauren in front of him until we've determined it's safe to do so."

Adam nodded at that.

"And we need to decide who goes," Seth said as he surveyed the room.

"I'm going," Max said flatly.

"No, you aren't," Ryan Colter said just as flatly.

Everyone turned in surprise that the older man had shut him down so quickly.

"Why the hell not?" Max demanded. "Lauren is my sister. I'm not going to sit here while someone else is charged with protecting her."

Liam remained quiet as he waited for Ryan to speak again. He'd been about to tell Max there was no way in hell he was going, when Ryan had beat him to it.

"You're too much of a hothead and you're too pissed off," Ryan said. "That's the very last thing we need in an already volatile situation."

Seth nodded his agreement. "At the risk of pissing you off, man, I agree with Dad."

Noah stepped in, his tone placating. "We don't want any possible way to trace Lauren back here. You're a visible guy, Mr. Wilder. The very last thing you want is to bring trouble back to where your family lives. If they can connect Lauren to you, they'll find her through you."

Max looked as though he'd been ready to argue, but he conceded to Noah's logic.

"You're right," he said in a low voice. "The very last thing I want is to put her in further danger or for anything to threaten the rest of my family."

"Dillon and I will go," Seth said. "Michael stays here with Lily. At least one of the dads will need to stay as well. I don't want any of the women to be alone."

Liam and Noah both nodded at that.

"They'll want to put her in protective custody," Adam said in a grim voice.

Lauren looked up in alarm.

Adam cast an apologetic look in her direction. "I'm not trying to scare you, sweetheart. The fact of the matter is, you're a key witness, and this case has far-reaching implications and involves some very high-profile people. They're going to want to keep you close and put you in the witness protection program until you testify."

"Noah? Liam?" Lauren asked in a shaky voice.

"We've considered that possibility," Noah said soothingly. "We're only going to allow you to do this if it's on our terms. We want certain things in writing or the D.A. doesn't get to talk to you. Period. It might get our asses thrown in jail, but you'll be on your way back here with Seth and the others where you'll be protected."

Her face went white and her eyes widened in alarm.

"It won't happen, baby," Liam said calmly. "We'll work it out. Trust us."

She sucked in her breath and slowly relaxed.

"We'll need use of your jet, Mr. Wilder," Noah said. "We don't want a paper trail, anything with Lauren's name on it. We don't want her showing ID, using a credit card. Nothing. We're going to alter her appearance for her meeting with the D.A. so that if something does go wrong, they won't have an accurate description of her."

"We were unable to locate any photographs of Joel Knight and Lauren together," Liam interjected. "Nor could we find any people who knew of Lauren. The only people who are likely to know what she looks like are Joel Knight and the people who worked closest with him. One of the women who worked for him ID'd Lauren, but she's dead now."

"He kept me isolated," Lauren said in a low voice. "We didn't make many public appearances together and it was always very low key. And I was expected to be the consummate companion. Well dressed, perfectly submissive. In other words a pretty ornament to compliment him. He tried to keep me separate from his 'business' and anyone associated with it. I was basically a plaything he pulled out when it was convenient."

The bitterness and self-loathing in her voice ate at Liam. He wanted nothing more than for her to be able to forget the bastard ever existed. They were in for a rough road in the next months. Hell, this thing could stretch out for years.

"I brought up the witness protection issue because I wanted to advise you to keep her close," Adam broke in. "Don't let them separate you. Make sure that if that's what has to happen, you're able to stay with her." He glanced at Holly as he spoke, pain darkening his eyes. "My wife was once in the same position, and she stayed away from me and my brothers to protect us. That separation was hell for us. If you love her, then make damn sure she stays with you."

There was instant agreement from both Ethan and Ryan. Holly's gaze softened as she stared at her husbands.

"We aren't letting her go, sir," Noah said, resolve hardening his voice.

"I don't think so many of you should go," Holly spoke up.

Seth's eyebrow rose.

"Don't give me that look, young man," she said in exasperation. "Have you looked at the men in this room? There's no way a whole horde of you are going to go unnoticed when you roll into town. I realize that more is good when it comes to protecting Lauren, but if you're trying not to gain notice, you're going to fail miserably if two of my husbands go and two of Lily's."

Michael's eyes gleamed with amusement. "She's got you there."

"Not all of us will be visible," Seth said patiently. "In fact, the whole point is to stay out of sight. We'll fly in at night. Have one person check into a hotel. It means we'll all have to stay in the same room, but I'd rather not broadcast how many are in our party and as Mom so eloquently put it, if we're out in broad daylight, we're not going to go unnoticed. One person goes to the meeting with the D.A., however, we place two of us in the same location in case the situation goes south or it's a setup. The other three will remain with Lauren with strict instructions that if they aren't contacted at a prearranged time, they're to cut and run with Lauren and get the hell out."

Lauren lowered her face to her hands and rubbed tiredly. "I can't allow you all to risk this. It's starting to scare the hell out of me. All the what-ifs and the possibilities are making me crazy."

"You aren't allowing us to do anything," Dillon said mildly. "You're a part of this family. That means we go with you. End of story."

Holly nodded approvingly. "That's my boy."

Seth snorted. "Until the next time you disown him."

Holly silenced him with a quick glare.

"Okay so we're agreed on who goes and who stays," Noah said, sharply bringing the subject back on target. "The next step is to make contact with the D.A. and see if he bites."

Liam sought Lauren's gaze, waiting until she felt his stare and looked back at him.

"You ready to do this?" he asked softly, giving her one last opportunity to back out.

She slowly lifted her chin and straightened her shoulders. Callie tightened her grip on Lauren's hand and Lily reached across Callie's lap to add her own. Holly wrapped her arm around Lauren's shoulders, lending her strength as the other women had done.

There in the tight hold of her family, Lauren nodded. Her voice was firm and full of resolve.

"Yes. I'm ready. Make the call."

CHAPTER 24

S WEETIE, you've got to stop pacing," Holly soothed from her perch at the bar. "You're going to wear a hole in my floor."

Lauren paused and sighed. "I'm sorry. This is making me crazy. How long can it possibly take to make a phone call?"

"Not just any phone call," Callie pointed out.

"Come sit," Lily urged. "All this anxiety can't be good for you. I know it's not good for me."

Lauren plopped onto the stool next to Holly, wanting the comfort and guidance of the older woman.

"What made you decide to stand up to your ex-husband? I can't imagine the strength it took to separate yourself from the Colter men and be alone through that whole process."

Holly sighed. "It's not as courageous as you make it sound. The truth was, I was terrified. I had just been horribly attacked by a man hired by my ex-husband to kill me. Ryan had been shot trying to protect me. I thought he was dead."

Her voice quivered and pain filled her eyes.

"All I could think was that Ryan had been hurt because of me, and I didn't want to lose the men I loved more than anything. I also knew that they'd never agree to let me go, so I made the decision for them. I contacted the D.A. in San Francisco. I arranged for him to come to the hospital to talk to me, and then I left the hospital in protective custody and remained so for several months. It was during that time that I learned I was pregnant."

Her lips turned up into a rueful smile.

"The best and worst time of my life. I was overjoyed at the thought of having their child and devastated because I was isolated from them with no definitive timeline. Thank God my ex-husband pled out, which meant I didn't have to testify. I was only gone for a little over five months, but I swear it felt like an eternity."

"I don't want to be separated from Liam and Noah," Lauren said in a low voice. She glanced over at the women sitting at the bar. "I don't want to be separated from any of *you* either."

"We don't want you to go either," Callie said fiercely. "This will work out, Lauren. It has to. You'll be safer here with us than in any witness protection program. There's no way the dads or my brothers or Max and Liam and Noah are going to let someone come into our home and hurt you."

Lauren sighed again. "That's a nice thought and it sounds good to say, and I have no doubt that the intention is certainly sincere. But how realistic is it to say that I'm untouchable? We have no way of knowing what Joel will do. As afraid as I am, I could not bear the thought of something happening to one of the dads or to one of Lily's husbands or my brother."

"Or the men I love," she added quietly.

"Oh honey," Holly said, squeezing her hand tightly. "You've got to stop taking on so much. You aren't to blame if something hap-

pens to one of our men. That blame lies squarely on the shoulders
of Joel Knight."

"And is that what you thought when you decided to go away
from the dads?" Lauren asked pointedly.

Holly flushed, her cheeks going pink. "The point is, I wasn't
thinking at the time. I was scared out of my mind. I'd gone through
a traumatic experience and I was acting on instinct. My instinct
was to protect them."

"My instinct is to protect the people I love," Lauren said.

"We understand," Lily said. "Really, we do, Lauren. But let them
help you. Our strength is in our family. Not one individual."

Holly beamed at her daughter-in-law. "My daughters are
extremely smart women. And Lily is exactly right. Our strength
doesn't come from one person. It's from our bond. Our willingness
to go to bat for one another."

They immediately went quiet when Liam entered the kitchen,
his expression grim. Lauren's heart dropped to her toes and she
reached blindly for Holly's hand, needing her support more than
ever.

Holly grabbed her hand and gripped it with bruising force.

"What happened, what did he say?" Lauren blurted.

"He wants to talk to you," Liam said.

Her eyes widened. "Why?"

"He just wants to make sure we're not jerking him around. I don't
think it's anything to worry about. Just don't tip your hand in the phone
call. No names. He can say what he wants, but keep your responses
to the minimum. Yes or no answers are best. If there's anything you're
unsure of, you put him on hold and run it by us. Okay?"

She swallowed and nodded. "Okay."

He held out his hand to her. Holly disentangled her hand from
Lauren's and urged her forward. Liam wrapped his arm around

her, squeezing her briefly before guiding her into the living room, where the others sat.

Noah was sitting on the couch, his hand curled around a cordless phone. When he saw Lauren, he put the phone back on the base and hit the button for the speaker. He held up one finger to his lips to signal to Lauren not to mention that everyone was listening in. Then he pointed at her to begin the conversation.

"H-hello?" Lauren began hesitantly.

"With whom am I speaking to?"

The man's voice was sharp and distinct, and it made Lauren instantly nervous.

She glanced up at Liam, who nodded that she should answer.

"Lauren Wilder," she responded.

"And, Ms. Wilder, would you be so kind as to provide a few simple pieces of information to verify your identity?"

She frowned, her brow furrowing tightly. Noah held up a hand and nodded and then motioned for her to answer.

"Okay," she reluctantly agreed.

"Can you give us your last known address?"

She frowned harder. Technically her last address was her apartment here in Clyde and no way in hell she was giving this man that information. And before that, there was the apartment that Max had moved her into after she'd left Joel. Again, no way she was giving that out either. But neither of those addresses were ones the police would have any knowledge of, so they wouldn't expect either.

Liam was furiously scribbling something on a piece of paper and then he held up a notebook that said, *give him the address of the residence you lived with Joel.*

In a halting voice, she gave the man on the phone the address of the penthouse where she and Joel had spent a year.

"Thank you," the man said. "Can you also verify your date of birth and the town you were born in?"

All the questions were making her uncomfortable, but Noah and Liam were telling her to answer, so she provided the requested information, wishing they could just get on with it.

"Thank you, Ms. Wilder. I can't tell you how glad we are to hear from you. My office has been looking for you for quite some time."

The relief was obvious in his voice, but his words sent alarm shrieking through her system. She yanked her head upward, fearfully seeking out Noah and Liam once more.

Noah reached over and squeezed her knee in a gesture meant to soothe her, but the fact that there were even more people looking for her freaked her out.

"Now that her identity has been established, you'll speak to me about the arrangements," Noah inserted bluntly.

"Yes, of course Mr. . . . What did you say your name was again?"

"I didn't."

There was a lengthy pause, and then Noah motioned for Liam to take Lauren away again. She frowned, wanting to hear what was said, but Noah punched the speakerphone off and picked up the phone again.

"Come on, baby," Liam murmured.

"Why can't I hear?" she asked as they walked back to the kitchen.

"Because we'd rather whatever is decided on to come from me and Noah," Liam said frankly. "Hearing suggestions or bits and pieces is just going to cause you unnecessary stress. Noah won't agree to anything that isn't in your best interest, and he damn sure won't put you in a position we feel is unsafe."

She went into his arms, wanting and needing his hug. She looped her arms around his waist and rubbed her cheek against his chest.

"I know you won't. I'm just scared, Liam. Not just for me. I'm scared for all of us."

"What's going on, Liam?" Holly demanded. "We're all dying to know here. If someone doesn't tell me soon, I'm going to hurt someone."

Liam grinned. "Sorry, Mrs. C. As soon as I know, you'll know. I promise. Noah is shoring up the details now. The D.A. was leery about proceeding without knowing whether he was actually talking to Lauren or not. Apparently they've been searching for her, which means they've wanted to question her for a while. If that's the case, he's going to want to talk to her immediately. He'll be beside himself over the evidence that Lauren has."

"You just take care of my baby," Holly said.

"I'll do my best to make sure nothing ever hurts her again," Liam said in a somber voice.

"Lily, are you okay?" Lauren asked, alarmed at Lily's paleness.

Holly and Callie both jerked around, their worried gazes locking immediately onto the heavily pregnant woman. Holly hurried toward the bar, putting her arm around Lily's shoulders.

"I'm fine," Lily protested.

"If my boys see you looking as pale as you are right now, it's all over but the cryin'," Holly said grimly. "They'll have you home and in bed, worrying their fool heads off. Talk to me. Are you feeling okay? Is it the baby?"

Lily shook her head. "I didn't sleep well last night. I'm worried about Lauren. Nothing else. Honest. Baby is sleeping right now and not trying to two-step on my ribs."

Lauren's lips turned down in unhappiness. Everyone in the Colter family was affected by her situation. She wished now that it was just her, Noah and Liam going and the others didn't have to be involved.

Lily was about to have a baby, and she had to worry herself over the fact that two of her three husbands were off with Lauren going blind into a situation where the worst could happen.

"If you say one word about what I think you're thinking, I'm going to hurt you," Lily said menacingly.

Lauren's eyebrows went up as she realized Lily was talking to her.

Lily got clumsily off the bar stool and walked over to where Lauren stood. She took Lauren's hand and held it between them.

"Seth is the sheriff. Protecting people is what he does. He's called out at all times of the night. There's never one of them I don't worry about him. There's no way he'd ever allow a threat against his family to go unresolved. It's just who he is."

She smiled softly and glanced at Holly. "I think he has a lot of his fathers in him. They all do."

Love for her husbands and her sons shone like a beacon in Holly's eyes. She turned that loving gaze on Lauren and her daughter-in-law.

"Seth has the very best of his fathers," Holly said, her voice rich with emotion. "My boys have never once disappointed me."

"That's my job," Callie said dryly.

Holly chuckled. "I'll admit, I like it that for the most part your days of wanderlust and restless spirit are in the past. I like having you here, at home where you belong. You and Max both. But baby, you've *never* disappointed me." Her tone was firm even as love and pride shone in her gaze. "None of my babies, whether biological or not, have ever disappointed me. I can be disappointed in the fact that you aren't home where you belong and still be as proud of you as I can be."

She pulled Lauren into a fierce embrace. "And now maybe you'll be home where you belong too. Having you all right here where I can fuss over you and mother you endlessly would make me the happiest woman in the world."

Lauren didn't dare peek at Liam, because this was still a painful subject for her and one she tried not to broach with Noah and Liam too often.

They may have strong feelings for each other. They may have made a sincere commitment. But at the end of the day, Clyde, Colorado, was a long way—a lifetime away—from New York City and the life she'd once led there.

A life she no longer wanted.

CHAPTER 25

NOAH hung up the phone and eyed the other men gathered in the room. "Okay, well you heard the details. Anyone have something I didn't cover in the conversation?"

Seth shook his head. "I think we should get to Raleigh at least a day ahead of Castanetti, if not two. I want to be there when he checks into the hotel, and I want to monitor his movements, phone calls, whatever we can get a lead on."

Noah had wanted the D.A. to think that Lauren had fled further down the East Coast. A logical place for someone in the New York City area to go. He'd purposely dropped several innuendos to make Castanetti think that Lauren was even now along the Eastern Seaboard.

"I can have the jet ready whenever you need it," Max said. "I'll file it as a golfing trip for executives of my company. The flight will originate officially from New York City, so I'll have it moved immediately."

"We'll travel to Denver together," Noah continued. "I don't want Lauren alone or unattended for any length of time, no matter how short. I don't even want her going to the bathroom alone. Once we arrive in Raleigh, I'll meet with Castanetti, but Liam and Seth will be in the same restaurant a few tables away."

He turned to the older Colters and Dillon. "I'll want the three of you to remain with Lauren at the hotel we choose. We'll have a set time to report in and if you don't hear from us, if we're so much as a minute late, you're to cut and run with her. Get her to the airport as fast as possible and get the hell out of there. The only priority is her safety. If something happens to me and Liam, I'll want you to take her home and take whatever steps are necessary to ensure her protection."

The others nodded their understanding.

"Okay then, I'd like to take Lauren back home so Liam and I can talk to her privately," Noah said. "We'll check back in before we take out for Raleigh. If we leave in three days, that gives us plenty of time to arrive ahead of the D.A. and set up."

Adam, Ryan, Dillon and Seth nodded their agreement.

To Ethan, Michael and Max, Noah grew more serious. "You'll need to be on guard while we're gone. We have no idea how far reaching this is or what Joel Knight will do in order to keep Lauren quiet. You'll need to watch Holly, Callie and Lily like a hawk. Don't let them go anywhere alone, and make sure one of you is always with them."

The other men scowled and crossed their arms over their broad chests. Their body language said all they didn't.

"We'll keep in touch," Noah said quietly. "Right now I want to take Lauren home. She's upset and shook up. I want a chance to explain what's happening to her privately so she's not considering the potential danger to her family. She's very reluctant to do anything that causes any of you harm."

"She's ours," Adam said simply. "It's what we do for family." He paused a long moment and then looked to both Liam and Noah, taking them both into his intent gaze.

"You're family now too. That protection extends to you."

Noah swallowed, blindsided by the surge of emotion he felt at the older man's words. Noah knew he had family. Liam's parents. They were as much his parents as if he'd been born to them.

But as soon as he'd walked into the Colter home, as soon as he'd met Seth and Seth's brothers and knew how fiercely protective of Lauren they were and of their own women, there'd been a part of him that had selfishly wanted that connection himself.

Since he was a teenager, Liam and Liam's parents had been Noah's only support. The only people he had to turn to. And now, through Lauren, an amazing, beautiful woman, he had even more extended family. Good people. The kind he'd always wished for.

"That means a lot to me, sir," Noah said, his voice cracking.

Adam smiled, his eyes full of understanding as if he knew every part of Noah's past.

"And you can stop calling me sir, son. I'm proud Lauren has men who know the meaning of respect, but you're family now, so you can either call me Dad like everyone else, or you can call me Adam. And if I know my wife, if you call her Mrs. Colter, she'll have a kitten. She has a lot of names but all of them are said with love. You can call her Mom, Mama C, Mrs. C, but not Mrs. Colter. She gets persnickety about that."

The knot grew bigger in Noah's throat and he glanced automatically to Ethan and Ryan Colter to see if they shared Adam's opinion.

Ryan Colter stuck out his hand and merely said, "Welcome to the family. I expect you to take good care of our little girl. She's the baby now. We care a lot about her. She's been through a rough time."

"We will," Liam spoke up from a few feet away as Noah shook Ryan's hand. "This isn't some passing fling for us, sir. I love Lauren. She's been it for me since the moment I set eyes on her. I didn't want to let her go when Mr. Wilder came to get her, but I knew she needed time with her family and that she needed time to heal. But there was never a question of me coming for her."

"Same goes," Ryan said gruffly. "You can call me Ryan or Dad. I'll answer to either. Mr. Colter just makes me sound old and stuffy."

Max cleared his throat and rose. "I need a moment alone with Liam and Noah if the rest of you don't mind."

Ethan glanced sharply at Max, speaking up for the first time. "That depends on what you plan to say. I don't want any trouble, and the last thing your sister needs is more turmoil. You upset her and it's not us you'll have to worry about, because you'll have one very pissed-off Holly Colter to contend with."

Max shook his head. "There are some things we need to get aired out. That's all."

"Then we'll be in the kitchen," Adam said. "You boys come get Lauren when you're done. I'm sure you have a lot you need to work out between you when you get back to her apartment. But before we go, I do want to extend an invitation for you three to come stay out here. It's a hell of a lot more isolated. It's private. And it would be a lot safer than being in town. Those locks on Lauren's apartment aren't worth a damn. I'd planned to get in there and fix them once she got moved in, but with everything that's been going on, there hasn't been time."

Liam and Noah exchanged glances. Liam lifted his eyebrow and nodded.

Noah turned back to Adam. "It's not a bad idea, sir—Adam."

"We'll talk to Lauren about it and get back with you," Liam added. "I like the idea of having her out of the diner where anyone can see her."

"Just give me a call. We have plenty of room," Adam said.

The older Colters filed out of the living room toward the kitchen, leaving their sons to follow. Max remained and Noah braced himself for the confrontation.

When they were alone, Max glanced sharply at the other two men.

"I don't like the speed in which this 'relationship' has progressed," he said with a frown. "Lauren is extremely vulnerable right now."

Liam's lips twitched and he glared at Max. "Just because you had your head up your ass where Callie was concerned doesn't mean the rest of us do when it comes to our woman."

Max's face flushed a dull red, and then he sighed. "Sit down, both of you. I'm not going to try to kick your ass. I just want some answers."

Noah took his seat in one of the armchairs. Liam was more reluctant to sit down but perched on the edge of the other armchair.

"You're right. I made my share of mistakes with Callie. I fought the inevitable. I'm damn lucky I didn't lose her and that she has such a loving, generous, forgiving nature."

"Then perhaps you understand why we're not willing to do anything to risk Lauren. Physically or emotionally," Noah said in a low voice. "We aren't fighting anything. We want her. No matter how long it takes."

"Look, it's hard for me to wrap my head around the kind of relationship you're wanting with my sister," Max said painfully. "There are so many reasons why, it makes my head spin. I realize the Colters have a very atypical relationship and family. No one blinks an eye over them. It's just part of the Colter package. You don't even really question it because you look at them and it's who they are. And it's so apparent that those men love their wives and that the women love each man equally. But it's also like looking at a fantasy. Something that isn't real. Lauren is my sister. I love her dearly and she's been hurt far too much in her young life. I want to protect her and I want her to be happy. And while a relationship like the Colters have is just fine for them, the idea of Lauren being involved with both of you concerns the hell out of me."

Liam cleared his throat, but Max held up his hand.

"Let me finish. Let me get it out so that we can clear the air."

Noah nodded and gave Liam a quick glance to make him stand down.

"The Colters live here. In Clyde. A town they've been a fixture in forever. Their son is the sheriff. The dads have friends dating back over thirty years. They live a very isolated existence in a very small population that accepts their unusual arrangement. This isn't the rest of the world, though. Have you given any thought to where you'll live with Lauren? Have you considered if you'll ever have children and what kind of life they'll have?"

Max's words didn't come out in an angry torrent. He was passionate and obviously concerned for his sister, something Noah could well understand.

"What about your families?" Max added quietly. "Are they going to accept and understand the relationship you and Lauren have?"

Noah glanced to Liam because it had been the same question he'd had in the beginning.

"Noah doesn't have family," Liam said quietly. "My family is his family. They'll love Lauren and as long as Noah and I are happy, they'll be happy for us."

"My point is you can't protect her from everything," Max said. "There'll always be someone who questions or doesn't understand or openly reviles you and Lauren because of who you love."

"We understand that," Liam said gruffly. "And we don't have all the answers right now. The only thing that occupies our mind is getting Lauren through this thing with Joel Knight safely. Once she's free of that threat, then the choice will be hers to make as to whether she wants a life with us. From there we'll take it one day at a time, but she'll never be alone. She'll always have us. And she'll always have you and the Colters."

Max nodded. "I understand and I appreciate your devotion to her safety. I apologize for some of my earlier remarks. Lauren is very dear to me. After our mom passed, it was just the two of us, and I feel like I failed her because I wasn't around to see the kind of man Joel Knight was. I was too locked in my own private hell over Callie."

"Apology accepted," Noah said.

Max stared hard at Noah, as if trying to see deeply inside Noah's head. "Do you love her?" he asked bluntly. "Liam's been very adamant about his feelings, but you haven't had anything to say."

Noah didn't need any time to think about his response. He just wasn't as comfortable about throwing the words around publicly. To him they were intimate, private words and if used too much, they lost their meaning. He coveted them, never having heard them growing up. To him, they were the most precious gift to give to another person.

"Those words are for Lauren only," Noah said in a soft voice. "She means more to me than any other person has ever meant to me. I wouldn't be here if she didn't."

Apparently satisfied with Noah's response, Max rose and extended his hand to shake Noah's. Noah shook it and then Max turned to Liam to do the same.

"If you need anything, anything at all, don't hesitate to contact me," Max said. "Give me a go date and I'll make sure the jet is ready."

Noah nodded, then he turned to Liam. "Let's go get Lauren. We have a lot to go over with her."

CHAPTER 26

WHAT did he say?" Lauren asked anxiously as they pulled away from the Colter house.

"He's very eager to talk to you," Noah said. "Apparently they've been looking for you for some time. They were worried that you'd met a similar fate as some of the other women of Knight's association."

"They thought I was dead?" Lauren gasped.

"They weren't sure what to think. Only that you'd disappeared and they were very interested in talking to you. They've been investigating Knight for over a year, but he's squeaky clean and no one inside his organization will talk. They've been looking for any way in they can find."

"So he believed you? I mean about the information we have?"

"We didn't go into that kind of detail," Liam said grimly

She frowned. "I don't understand. What did you tell him then?"

"Just that we had incriminating evidence, detailed evidence, that he would be interested in," Noah said. "I didn't want to tip our hand this soon. He jumped on the opportunity. I could practically hear him drooling through the phone."

Lauren went quiet, Holly Colter's words echoing through her head.

"This could take a long time," she finally murmured, her gaze sliding sideways so she could take in Noah's and Liam's expressions. "I was talking to Holly about when she was in protective custody. It was months before she saw Adam, Ethan and Ryan again, and it could have been much longer except her ex-husband pled out at the last minute instead of going to trial."

Liam's hand slid over her shoulder and squeezed reassuringly. "No matter how long it takes, we're going to be right there with you."

"What about your family, though?" she asked anxiously. "This seems like an awful lot to spring on them. Not only are you and Noah involved with the same woman . . . me . . . but now you may have to disappear for months or longer because of what I'm doing."

"I'll call them before we go meet Castanetti," Liam said. "I'll explain everything to them then."

Lauren twisted her hands in agitation. "I don't want them to hate me before they ever even meet me."

Noah smiled. "I can't imagine the Prescotts hating anyone, and certainly not someone as sweet and beautiful as you are. They're going to love you, Lauren. I admit, I was worried at first, but I was doing them a huge disservice. They're some of the most loving, giving people I've ever met. I was fortunate enough to be able to call them my family."

"We're very lucky," Liam said in a low voice. "We have your family solidly behind us and they're obviously hugely loyal, and we have my family who I expect nothing less from. With families like ours, we can't possibly lose."

"I'd like to meet them," she said wistfully.

Noah pulled her hand up to kiss it. "As soon as we can arrange it, we'll absolutely take you to meet Liam's parents. But you come first."

When they reached town, Noah parked in front of the clinic in one of the on-street parking slots. He left the SUV running and Liam got out and opened Lauren's door for her.

She frowned. "What's going on? Where are you going?"

"It's where we're going," Liam said, taking her hand. "You and I are going to run up to your apartment so you can pack a bag. We'll tell you all about it and the plan. I promise."

The blood drained from her face. "Do you think we're in danger here?"

"We just don't want to take any chances, honey," Noah said gently. "Now that we've made the call to the D.A., we have to prepare for any eventuality. Now go on. I'll wait here. Liam will go up with you."

She turned and numbly allowed Liam to lead her up the stairs to her apartment door. Once there, he took the key from her hand and inserted it into the lock.

"Stay glued to my back," he ordered tersely.

She pressed herself to his back as he pushed open the door. He drew his pistol and did a quick sweep of the room.

"Shut the door but don't lock it," Liam ordered. "Not yet. You stay here by the door and don't make a move, while I check the other rooms. If I yell at you to get out or if you hear anything that sounds off, you hightail it back to Noah. Understand?"

She nodded.

He disappeared into her bedroom and returned mere seconds later, his gun down by his side.

"Okay, go in and get your bag packed. I'll have mine and Noah's stuff ready in just a few seconds."

It was hard deciding what to pack and what to leave. What if she never came back to this apartment again? It was a hysterical thought, but it wasn't out of the realm of possibility.

Her decision had the power to alter the course of her entire life. Not only hers but Noah's and Liam's too. Her family's as well.

She closed her eyes. Oh God, please let her have made the right decision. The right choice. Just once.

"Lauren?"

Liam's call from the living room galvanized her to action. She hurriedly went through her closet and pulled several outfits from the hangers. She only had one suitcase, but she had a duffel bag that could carry quite a bit, so she used that for shoes, underwear and socks, and all her toiletries.

In the suitcase, she piled jeans, slacks, two skirts and all the tops she'd chosen. Her stomach churned when she realized that she would most certainly be expected to make a court appearance.

She went back to her closet and took three dresses from the end, and then made sure she had the matching shoes. How ironic would it be for her to wear one of the dresses Joel had bought for her to testify in the trial to convict him?

In the end, she couldn't get her suitcase to zip. Frustrated, she leaned and pushed but couldn't budge it. Knowing she needed help, she called for Liam.

"I can't get it closed," she said, flipping her hand impatiently at the open suitcase on her bed.

Liam's eyebrow went up. "I can see why."

"I wasn't sure what to pack," she said defensively. "I mean packing for an indeterminate amount of time is kind of daunting, you know?"

"Shhh, baby," he soothed. "It's fine. We'll take what you've packed and if you need something later or if you figure out you've forgotten something, Noah and I will get it for you. Don't let this stress you out."

She took a deep breath. "I know, I know. I'm sorry. I am kind of freaked out right now."

He tugged her into his arms and kissed her brow. After a quick, fierce hug, he gently pulled himself away and went to close her suitcase.

His muscles bulging, he pushed down on it enough to get it zipped, and then he hefted it upward so he could get it off the bed and onto the floor so it could be rolled.

"All ready?" he asked.

She glanced around the room one last time and then nodded.

"Get your bag. I'll take the suitcase. Once I get you into the car with Noah, I'll come back up for mine and Noah's bags."

She grabbed the oversized duffel and hoisted the strap over her shoulder, and then followed Liam back through the living room and down the stairs to the street.

Noah got out to help put her bags in the back, and then he guided Lauren to the passenger seat while Liam sprinted back up the stairs for the other bags.

"Where are we going?" Lauren asked as they waited for Noah.

"We're going to stay tonight in a hotel so we can talk about everything that's going to go on and so you're comfortable with the plan. Tomorrow we'll drive back out to the Colters', where we'll stay until we fly out to Raleigh."

Liam opened the door to the backseat and slid inside. "All set. Let's roll."

"You two don't mind staying at the Colters'," she asked as Noah pulled out of the parking spot.

Noah shook his head. "It's isolated. It's private. It comes with a hell of a lot of built-in protection. And they're your family. That's good enough for me."

She smiled.

"But for tonight, we wanted you to ourselves," Liam said from the backseat. "We have a lot to talk about, yes, but we also want a night with you where we aren't concerned with what your family can or can't hear or who's right down the hall."

Her cheeks grew warm, but she couldn't control the shiver of delight at the veiled promise in his voice.

Noah reached for her hand and laced his fingers through hers.

"We wanted one night—*this* night—to show you just what you mean to us before we have to deal with what's coming down the road."

CHAPTER 27

NOAH went inside the hotel to check them in while Liam waited in the car with Lauren.

"I hope you and Noah aren't expecting much with this hotel," Lauren hedged. "Clyde doesn't have much in the way of fine hotels or lodging. Those are all over in the ski resort towns to the north."

"We aren't concerned with how nice the room is," Liam said. "As long as you're in it, we're fine."

"I love you," she said quietly, testing the newness of the words on her lips.

He looked surprised, but then his eyes burned with heat, leaving her no doubt as to the satisfaction she'd brought him.

"I love you too, baby."

"I've never told anyone that before," she blurted. "I mean except Max and family."

He reached up to touch her hair, stroking his fingers through the strands. "Then I'm glad that Noah and I get to be the first."

"You're the first in a lot of ways," she admitted. "You're the first men I've ever actually made love with. I haven't been with that many, but love certainly wasn't a factor in the sex."

"You understand that we intend to be the last," Liam said with a low growl. "This isn't something we take lightly. As far as I'm concerned, this is *forever*."

She smiled ruefully at the irony. "Joel used to say that he and I were forever, and God, I hated that word. He would tell me that I'd never get away from him. But when you say it, it sounds . . . wonderful."

"Noah and I will always put you first, baby. Your wants, your needs, whatever it is that makes you happy."

"I used to believe that the Colters and my brother were the only good men, and that they were some kind of aberration. I was so jealous of Holly and Lily that I ached with it. I never thought I would find someone to love me like their husbands love them."

She turned her smile up to Liam, allowing her love to openly shine.

"I was wrong. You and Noah are my white knights."

"I wouldn't go that damn far," Liam grumbled. "We're pretty tarnished knights. We aren't perfect, Lauren, and I don't want you going into this thinking we are. We've made mistakes. We're rough around the edges. And we'll screw up. I guarantee we'll screw things up. Just promise me—and us—that you'll be patient and stick it out because I guarantee you, no one will ever love you more than me and Noah."

Her heart melted, and she wanted to reach over the seat and grab him into a huge hug.

"Well, just in case you and Noah ever have any doubts, there is no one who will ever love you more than me," she said fiercely. "Don't even think about browsing anywhere else."

Liam grinned and then leaned forward to kiss the tip of her nose.

"You sound mighty possessive, Miss Wilder. I like it. You can be possessive of me anytime. I guarantee I won't mind a bit."

Noah slid into the car and handed Lauren and Liam each a keycard. "All set," he said. "I'll drive around to the parking spot outside our room."

Liam dug in the bag on the seat next to him and pulled out a zip-up hoodie. He thrust it over the seat to Lauren.

"Put this on, baby. Hood up. Cover up as much of you as possible. I'd rather not broadcast the fact that you're staying here."

As Noah pulled into one of the back parking spaces, Lauren thrust her arms into the sweatshirt and pulled the hood securely over her head, making sure her hair was hidden from view.

"Go on inside," Noah instructed. "Liam and I will get the bags."

Lauren got out of the car and hurried to the door. She inserted her keycard and then pushed inside.

She took in a deep breath, gratified that it didn't smell smoky or musty. It smelled clean and the furnishings weren't threadbare.

She blushed when she took in the fact that there was only one bed. It was plenty big for the three of them, but it was obvious they had no intention of her sleeping away from them.

A few moments later, Liam and Noah came through the doorway, their arms full of her luggage and their own bags. They dropped them inside the door and then shut it behind them.

"First order of business is what you'd like to eat for dinner," Noah said as he pulled Lauren into his side.

He kissed her temple, brushing his lips over her skin.

"Dillon has offered to do delivery service for us from the pub. Anything he has on the menu, he's said he'll deliver personally."

"I'd love a club sandwich," Lauren said.

"I can handle that," Noah said with a smile. "Why don't you go get changed and relax. Put on some comfy pajamas and I'll order our food. We can eat and talk when the food gets here."

That sounded perfect to her. She was ready to wilt after the emotional twists and turns of the day.

She hurried in the bathroom, wanting to get back to her guys. There was nothing she wanted more than to curl up against them and just . . . be.

They had a lot to plan. Her entire life was going to change. But they'd sworn to stay with her every step of the way. If she'd had any doubt about their love, she couldn't possibly doubt it or them now. They were making huge sacrifices and putting their own lives on hold. For her.

When she was dressed in pajamas and hastily ran a brush through her hair, she ventured out of the bathroom to see Liam sprawled in one of the chairs in the living section of the hotel suite. His cell phone was to his ear and he seemed relaxed. Noah was seated by the window, occasionally sticking his fingers behind the blinds to pull them out enough to see the parking lot.

When Liam saw her, he slipped his hand over the end of the phone and mouthed, *my parents*.

Lauren's eyes widened and she went to sit in the armchair directly across from Liam so she could listen in on the conversation.

"She's amazing," Liam said softly, his gaze riveted to Lauren as he spoke. "You'll both love her."

Lauren blushed and squirmed under his tight scrutiny. It was odd to hear herself being talked about in such glowing terms.

"There's something else you should know, Mom and Dad," Liam said, his voice growing serious.

Even Noah turned from his perch by the window. When he saw Lauren, he got up and crossed the room. He extended his hand down to Lauren to pull her up, and then he sat and tugged her down into his lap.

"Now comes the fun part," Noah murmured.

Lauren fought the smile. Yes, she was nervous about how Liam's parents were going to take the explanation of their relationship, but she wasn't so uptight that she couldn't appreciate the humor in such an unexpected and somewhat awkward conversation with his parents.

Liam looked nervous. He wiped his free hand down his jeans repeatedly.

"Our relationship is not exactly . . . traditional," Liam said, unease apparent in his voice.

Then he blanched, his eyes widening and he immediately began to sputter. "Mom, no, I'm not gay and Lauren isn't a cover name for a man. Yes, I know you'd understand and that you aren't judging me, but that's not what it is."

Lauren started giggling and Noah shook with laughter against her. Liam sighed and closed his eyes as he listened to what apparently was a long stream of conversation from his mother.

"Mom, I appreciate that you're so understanding, but will you listen to me please? I'm not coming out of the closet here. I'm trying to tell you that Noah and I both are involved with Lauren."

There was a long period of silence on Liam's end, and there must have been on his parents' end too because Liam said, "Mom? Dad? Are you still there?"

He gripped the phone a little tighter and then took a deep breath. "It's really not that complicated when you look at it. We met her because her brother hired us to protect her, and we both fell in love with her. It's really that simple. She makes us happy and we're going to do our damn best to make her happy."

He glanced toward Noah and Lauren. "Yes, Noah's here. He and Lauren both are. Uh okay, hang on a minute."

He held the phone toward Noah. "Mom wants to talk to you."

"Ah hell," Noah muttered.

Lauren got up so Noah could lean forward and get the phone from Liam, and Liam pulled Lauren back toward him so she could switch spots from Noah to him.

"Hi, Mom," Noah said.

Even though Lauren knew he was nervous, he seemed to relax the moment he spoke to Liam's mother.

"Your family really is Noah's family, aren't they?" Lauren murmured to Liam.

"Yeah," Liam said quietly. "Noah didn't have an easy childhood. He was a burden to his parents. He was an oops baby to extremely selfish, self-absorbed people who didn't have time for a child nor the desire for one. He spent more time at my house than he did at home. I can remember times when they'd literally drop him off at my parents with a note saying they were going to be gone for two weeks. Sometimes longer. They'd send one change of clothes in a plastic grocery sack. It pissed my parents off to no end, but they knew if they interfered they'd likely never see Noah again, and by then they considered him their son as much as I was."

"That can't have been easy for Noah," Lauren said sadly. "No one wants to feel like they're unwanted."

"I think it was hard for him when he was younger, but by the time he hit his teen years he just seemed to accept it. He loved my parents and they loved him. One day he came to our house with everything he owned in a duffel bag. My dad went outside to talk to him and when they came back in, my dad simply announced that Noah would be moving in with us and would become a permanent member of our family. I never saw or heard from his parents after that day, and I don't know that he has either."

"Wow, just wow," Lauren said in shock. "I can't fathom that kind of emotional disconnect between parents and their child. That couldn't have been easy for your parents to take in another child."

Liam shook his head. "It wasn't. My dad did shiftwork at the local paper mill, and my mom worked in the school cafeteria. They didn't make a lot of money and it was a struggle to make ends meet with just the three of us. We lived in a two-bedroom wood-frame house, and Noah and I had to share a bedroom. But they always seemed to manage. They had a lot of pride too. I'll never forget when Noah and I were seniors in high school, we came home one day. It was a Friday, Dad's off day from work, and he and Mom were pissed. Not upset. Just extremely angry."

Lauren's brow furrowed. "Why?"

"Apparently Noah's parents had a brief moment of guilt, but not a big enough one that they actually tried to see Noah or come to visit him. They sent my mom and dad a check to cover his expenses. My dad hit the roof. And you'd have to understand. Not much makes my dad angry. He's a very laid-back, mild-mannered man. But that day, he was livid."

"I can imagine," Lauren murmured.

"He gave the check to Noah and told him it was rightfully his to do what he wanted, but that he and my mom wouldn't accept a dime for doing what was right. My dad told Noah that he loved him like a son and he didn't take him in to get some check in the mail."

"Did Noah take it?" Lauren asked.

Liam shook his head. "He told my dad to tear it up and return it to sender. Then he told my mom and dad that they were his parents, and that they'd given him something way more valuable than a check with a lot of zeroes. They'd given him love and acceptance."

"That's a beautiful story," Lauren said with a sniff.

"My parents are pretty special folks," Liam said seriously.

"And what did they say when you told them about us?"

Liam smiled. "They were surprised, of course. And they wanted to talk to Noah. I'm their son, but to them so is Noah, and they want to make sure he's happy with the arrangement and isn't settling."

Lauren glanced back toward Noah, who was smiling as he spoke into the phone.

"We'll bring her to meet you as soon as it's possible. It may be a while before you hear from us again, and I don't want that to worry you. We have some things to take care of and it's very likely Lauren is going to have to testify in a criminal trial. Once we're sure that the threat to her has been eliminated, then we can lead a normal life together. You'll like her family. They remind me a lot of you and Dad."

He paused a moment and found Lauren's gaze, his eyes warming as he stroked over her features.

"Yes, they're fine with it. It's not exactly an unusual arrangement in her family. But we'll explain it all to you when we bring her to meet you. Promise."

Noah smiled again. "Love you both. I'll give you back to Liam now."

He handed the phone back to Liam, and Liam put it to his ear.

"We'll talk soon," Liam promised. "Love you both."

Liam hugged Lauren to him a little tighter as he said his good-byes. Then he punched the Off button and set the phone down on the little end table set up between the two armchairs.

"So it went well?" Lauren asked tentatively.

"Yes," both Noah and Liam said at the same time.

"They're very eager to meet you," Noah said. "They're pretty mystified over the kind of woman it would take to get mine and Liam's attention so fiercely. They've despaired of us ever settling down and providing them grandchildren."

Lauren flushed but she was taken with the image of her round with child, like Lily, and the two men fussing endlessly over her. And of having a tiny baby and the expressions on Noah's and Liam's faces the first time they saw their child.

She wanted it so much that she ached. She wanted them. Wanted a life with them, full of love and companionship.

A knock on the door interrupted her fantasy.

"That'll be Dillon with food," Noah said, as he rose from his chair. "Get comfortable, honey, and we'll dig in."

CHAPTER 28

❧

AFTER the three ate dinner, Lauren excused herself to go shower in the small bathroom. She'd closed her eyes and stuck her head under the hot spray, when a warm body pressed to her naked back.

Noah.

She smiled, her eyes still closed. She didn't need to look to know which of the two it was. She loved that she could tell them apart merely by touch. Smell. The sensation each of them caused against her skin.

His mouth nuzzled up the side of her neck, inciting a full-body shiver even under the heat of the shower.

"Hope you don't mind me joining you," he said huskily. "Liam and I thought you would enjoy a little pampering. I get to wash, and he gets to dry."

"Mmmm."

It came out as a soft moan, and she leaned further back into him, molding her wet body to his. His hands slid around her waist to her belly and then upward to cup her breasts. He thumbed her nipples until they were puckered ridges.

She gave a whispery sigh when his hands left her to pick up the shampoo bottle. After squeezing the liquid into his hand, he began to lather her hair, taking his time and working his fingers over every part of her head.

She was nearly in a coma from the bliss of the massage. Her shoulders relaxed and the coiled tension in her muscles fled under Noah's soothing touch.

"Feel good?"

"Oh yes," she breathed.

He kissed the spot just below her left ear. "Good. Tonight is for you."

He turned her so he could rinse her hair, and when he'd made sure all the soap was gone, he set about washing the rest of her body with slow, methodical strokes that had her crazy with desire.

She was so boneless by the time he reached up to turn the shower off, that she wasn't sure she'd be awake for whatever came next.

When the shower curtain was swept aside, she saw that Liam waited, a large towel in his hands. He opened it to her as she stepped out of the tub and immediately enfolded her in the warm softness.

Noah dried himself off in the shower while Liam toweled Lauren completely dry. Afterward, he wrapped her in a thick robe and nudged her out of the bathroom toward the bed.

Collecting a brush from her suitcase, he followed her to the bed and directed her to sit between his spread legs. To her surprise and utter delight, he began to comb out her damp hair.

"You two are so spoiling me," she said with absolutely no real regret.

Liam paused a moment and then leaned forward to brush his mouth over her ear.

"That's the plan. We have to do what we can to ensure you want to keep us around for the long run."

There was a teasing note to his voice but she responded in all seriousness.

"I'll never grow tired of being with you."

It was a statement that sounded new. At the beginning of a relationship when emotions are high and optimism is in abundance. When no one thinks of the potential pitfalls in a relationship. And yet, she believed it with all her heart. How could she possibly ever grow weary of two men who put her above all else?

Noah came from the bathroom, just a towel wrapped low around his hips. He was the sexiest thing she'd ever seen in just that towel. His chest glistened with moisture and the whorl of hair in the hollow of his chest curled damply against his skin.

All it would take was the slightest nudge to bring that towel down . . .

Noah paused, seemingly aware of her avid gaze. He cocked one eyebrow and stared back. "You want something?" he drawled.

She licked her lips and Noah's eyes darkened until they smoldered.

"I want you," she whispered.

Noah slowly pulled at the towel until it slid down his muscular legs to hit the floor. She caught her breath and her pulse ratcheted up, hammering through her veins.

He was . . . beautiful.

All masculine. Muscled. Lean.

As Noah stalked closer to the bed, Liam pulled at the towel wrapped around Lauren until she too was nude.

"Lean back against me," Liam murmured next to her ear.

He pulled her back even as she leaned into him, her back molding to his chest. He angled them both so that they lay on the bed, her between his legs and her body nestled into his.

As Noah crawled onto the end of the bed and between her legs, Liam's hands wandered up and down her upper body, caressing, petting, cupping and molding her breasts in his palms.

On his knees, Noah lowered his head between her splayed thighs and she caught her breath and held it in anticipation of the first touch of his mouth.

Using his fingers to part the delicate folds of her pussy, Noah gently pressed his mouth to her clit.

The contact sent an electric current arcing up her body, nearly short-circuiting every nerve ending. Her legs shook spasmodically and her belly heaved as she tried to catch her breath.

Liam nuzzled her neck, his teeth grazing the sensitive skin. Marking her. Teasing. Sending shivers of delight to collide with the wave of electricity wrought by Noah's ministrations.

Her entire body was an out-of-control tidal wave that was on a collision course with a mountain.

Noah's tongue delved deep, licking and sliding inward, tasting her. She made insensible sounds, completely victim to the pleasure the two men gave her.

Liam's hands were cupped over her breasts, his mouth on her skin. Noah's hands gripped her hips as he used his mouth and tongue to drive her beyond her limits.

Erotic images flashed in her mind, heightened by her burgeoning arousal. Things that she'd never before imagined were now succinct in her mind. Both men, entering her at the same time. Stroking deep. Her securely positioned between them.

Her breathing sped up and her vision swayed drunkenly. She was high on passion. Drugged on their caresses. Intoxicated by their kisses.

Oh, but she wanted it, and she wasn't even sure how it could be done, but she wanted them both inside her. She wanted it as she'd wanted nothing else.

"Noah, Liam!" she cried.

"I'm here, baby. I'm right here," Liam soothed.

"Want you both so much," she gasped out.

Noah raised his head to seek out her gaze. "Tell us how you want us, honey. You know we'll do anything you need."

"Both inside me," she said, taking the plunge. "I want you both. Together."

"Are you sure?" Liam asked hoarsely.

"Oh God yes. Please."

Liam lifted her off him and maneuvered from underneath her. Then he caught her face in his hands and stared earnestly into her eyes.

"Stop us if it's too much."

She nodded. "Promise."

But she knew it wouldn't be too much. It would never be enough. She wanted them too badly. Need consumed her. They consumed her.

Noah positioned himself on the bed so he was lying flat on his back with his legs over the edge, feet planted on the floor. Liam helped Lauren climb astride Noah, and after Noah rolled on a condom, Lauren lowered herself, taking him deeply inside her.

They both let out a low moan when she took his full length.

Then Noah reached for her, pulling her forward so she was angled in a way that Liam could penetrate her. She swallowed nervously, but she was riding so high on anticipation that it didn't even cross her mind to back out.

A moment later, Liam cupped her backside and boldly massaged and caressed the cheeks before spreading them. The movement drew her tighter around Noah's cock, and she closed her eyes, allowing the sensation to wash over her.

Butterflies danced and fluttered in her belly when Liam fit himself to her tight opening. He seemed enormous. No way for him to fit, especially with Noah already stretching her so tight.

Liam pushed forward, and she felt the slickness of the lubricated condom as she opened around him. He was thick and broad. He seemed to go on forever as he eased more of his length into her.

"Okay?" Liam rasped.

"Yesss. Please don't stop."

"Baby, I have no intention of stopping. Give me one more thrust and I'll be all the way inside you."

His words incited her to greater arousal. The burn of his entry eased and a warm haze surrounded her, immersing her in a dream-like fog. His pelvis met her ass and pressed even harder against her, flattening her cheeks against his body.

Oh God, they were both completely inside her.

She began to shake, tremors quaking over and through her body at supersonic speed. She was never going to be able to hold on. She was beginning to unravel and had no way to control her release.

Liam began to thrust. Withdrawing and then surging forward. Noah gripped her hips, and when Liam would ease back, Noah slid deep, filling her, until all she was cognizant of was being stretched and filled by two men. Owned. Possessed. Branded.

"I can't . . . Oh God . . ."

She couldn't even collect her thoughts. Had no idea what she was saying or what she needed.

Hands glided up and down her waist, soothing and calming even as her body spasmed and contorted with the force of their thrusts.

Then Noah's hands left her hips and cupped her breasts, rolling the points between his fingers. He pinched lightly, just enough to exert delicious pressure. A tiny bite of pain that sent her spiraling into the abyss.

She yelled their names, reached for Noah, something to hold on to while Liam drove relentlessly into her from behind. Noah caught her against him, holding her tightly while Liam surrounded her.

Caught between both men. Loved. Cherished. Protected and

pleasured. She sagged against Noah, eyes closed, her breaths coming in tiny puffs as the room swirled crazily around her.

He kissed the top of her head as Liam carefully withdrew from her body, leaving her still connected intimately with Noah.

A moment later, Liam returned with a warm washcloth and he gently soothed the tender, swollen flesh. When he was done, Noah carefully rolled, holding on to Lauren so she went with him. They landed on their sides, and Noah slid from her body.

He rolled away a quick moment to discard the condom, and then he was back, pulling her into his arms. Liam climbed onto the bed on her other side and pressed his body to her back, his legs twining with hers.

She let out a huge sigh of utter contentment. Had she ever been as happy or secure as she was right at this very moment? Snuggled between two strong men who'd do anything to make her happy. If only she could stop time and savor this night forever.

"I love you."

Liam's whisper against her ear was faint but unmistakable. She turned so that his lip met her cheek, and she closed her eyes, basking in those wonderful words.

CHAPTER 29

LAUREN lay sprawled over Noah's chest, her legs tangled with Liam's. Noah idly ran his hand up and down her back, gliding lower to cup her behind before smoothing back up her body again.

"You okay?" Noah murmured.

"If I was any better, I don't know what I'd do with myself."

"Ditto," Liam said in a sleepy, contented growl.

"It was new for us too, Lauren," Noah said softly. "I've never done anything like that before, and I'm a little surprised that it came so naturally. And that it was so powerful. I'm at a loss as to how to even describe it. I've never experienced anything like it."

Lauren pushed herself upward so she could see Noah's eyes. They were utterly serious, warm and glowing with so much else he'd left unsaid. Like her, he hadn't said the words yet, but she didn't doubt for a moment that he loved her every bit as much as Liam did.

The words would come in time, when they weren't forced. When they were as natural as breathing and completely sincere. She looked

forward to that day when they could be so comfortable with each
other. When there was no threat from Joel or any other quarter.

"We—I—didn't hurt you, did we?" Liam asked gruffly.

She went soft at the concern in his voice and pushed herself
upward more so that she was sitting cross-legged between them.
She leaned over to kiss his firm mouth and let her lips linger over
his, enjoying the simple act of affection between two lovers.

"You both were wonderful," she said huskily. "Perfect. I never
imagined something so . . . powerful."

He touched her cheek, stroking his fingers down her jaw as he
kissed her again.

"How much time do we have?" she asked.

Already the curtains were illuminated with the pale shade of
dawn, and though they were going to a place where Lauren felt
completely at home, she also knew that it would bring to a temporary end the intimacy between her and Liam and Noah. She felt its
loss already and they hadn't even left the warmth of their bed yet.

Noah slid his hand up her back, letting it rest at the small, just
above the curve of her buttocks.

"We have time yet. A few hours more."

Liam pulled one of the pillows up to prop behind her back and
the headboard so she'd be more comfortable while the two men
continued to rest on their sides.

Lauren wanted the quiet, comfortable time between them to
discuss the future. It was all still so new and exciting in her mind
that she could speak of little else for the next weeks.

"Can I ask you two something?"

"Anything," Liam said firmly.

"Of course," Noah said at the same time.

"What do you see in our future?" she asked. "Do you see us
together long term?"

"I don't have a crystal ball," Noah said in a serious tone. "I can't predict what will happen a year or five years down the road. But if you ask me what I *want*? I want forever. With you. And I'm going to do everything in my power to see that forever is what we share."

"I see you with us for as long as either of us is breathing," Liam said, his lips set into a determined line.

"And children?" she asked hesitantly. "What are your thoughts on children and a family?"

Both men were angled so they could see her face and she could see theirs. Light warmed Noah's eyes. He looked . . . hopeful. And happy.

"I'd love a family one day," Noah said.

She could hear the yearning in his tone.

"I'd want everything that I was denied as a child. And I'd never do to our children what my parents did to me," he said fiercely.

"You'd make a great father," she said in just as fierce a tone.

Liam smiled, warmth traveling to the very depths of his blue eyes. "I could see a few rug rats."

Her breath caught in her throat as she was struck by a longing so powerful that she simply couldn't breathe.

"Do you want children, Lauren?" Noah asked.

"Oh yes," she breathed. "My own family. It's all I've ever wanted."

She touched both men, letting her hands creep over their arms so she had contact with them both.

"How would we do it?" she asked hesitantly. "I mean if we were trying to have a baby—down the road of course—would it matter to you if we didn't know which of you fathered the child? Or would you want to make sure you each had a son or a daughter?"

Anxiety had crept into her voice and she glanced between them nervously.

"I can only speak for me," Liam began in a low tone. "But for this kind of relationship to work, we'd both have to accept and love *any* child we bring into the world. Whether it's my biological child or Noah's. Honestly I wouldn't care, because either way I'd consider that baby mine. I'd never treat a child differently because it was Noah's biological child and not mine."

"Amen," Noah said. "I completely agree. If you're asking if we want to ensure that a child you bear is ours biologically, then no. I say when the time comes, we both try as hard as possible to knock you up and let the seed fall where it may."

Liam chuckled. "You certainly have a way with words. But I agree completely. Not knowing allows us both to believe that the child is ours. And it will be ours no matter who fathers it. You're their mother and for me that's enough."

"What did the Colters do, do you know?" Noah asked curiously. "Holly had four children."

Lauren laughed. "It's a running joke in the family that no one knows where Dillon came from. Holly swears he was switched at birth. But no. She doesn't know—or care—who the biological fathers were for her children. Neither do any of her kids."

"I think that's the best way," Liam said softly.

"Do you know how overwhelming it is for me to be sitting here between you two contemplating a normal life, a normal relationship and things like family and children?" Lauren asked, her voice choked with emotion.

Noah grinned. "Well, I'm not sure you could consider our relationship *normal*, but I get what you're saying."

"I don't care what anyone else thinks," Lauren said in a determined voice. "All I care about is what you two think and what you want and that I'm able to make you happy."

Liam reached up to pull her down into a kiss. "You make me very happy, baby. Never doubt that for a minute."

She melted into him, kissing him back with the same fervor.

Against her back, Noah's lips pressed into her flesh as he kissed a trail down her spine.

"Do we have time before we go out to the Colters'?" she asked in a husky voice.

Liam's eyes gleamed with purpose just as Noah's hands slid to her hips. "We'll make time."

CHAPTER 30

LIAM and Noah packed the back of the SUV with their bags and then went back to the hotel room to get Lauren. Both men were wearing shoulder harnesses with pistols holstered and light leather jackets to cover both holster and gun.

"You ready?" Noah asked in a low voice.

She took a deep breath and nodded. Though they were just going up to the Colters'—a place she felt very much at home—the knowledge that in just two days she'd leave that shelter and make a trip into the unknown was playing havoc with her nerves.

Liam offered her a quick hug and a kiss, and then ushered her out the door and to the SUV. He put her in the front seat and then climbed in behind her while Noah walked around to the driver's side.

As they pulled out of the hotel parking lot, she glanced down Main Street with the quaint shops, the bustling diner, her old apartment and the Mountain Pass Bar and Grill that Dillon Colter owned.

It was hard to leave behind everything that was familiar and achingly comforting. Thank goodness for Liam and Noah. How could she possibly face doing this alone? But then if it weren't for Noah and Liam, she wouldn't have the knowledge she now possessed, nor would she have had the courage to stand up and face the devil.

They turned out of town and she stared out the window, absorbing the beauty of the mountains. The Colters didn't live very far, distance wise, but it was a drive up the mountain that had several switchbacks, and the going was slow.

But it was a drive she didn't mind, because it had views that were breathtaking. Views she couldn't see anywhere else in the world.

"We've got company," Noah said tersely.

Liam immediately swiveled to stare out the back. Lauren's heart did a flip in her chest and she yanked her gaze to the side-view mirror to see a truck bearing down on them.

"Moving too fast just to be another person on the same road," Liam said grimly. "Lauren, does anyone else live on this road?"

She shook her head, her horrified gaze still glued to the mirror. "Only the Colters and Max and Callie. The doctor in town makes house calls and sometimes they have groceries delivered, but mostly they go into town for what they need because they don't like their privacy intruded on."

Just then the truck rammed them and Lauren was thrown forward, her seat belt cinching tight around her to prevent her from crashing into the dash.

"Son of a bitch!" Noah cursed.

He hit the accelerator, lurching forward, but the road turned into gravel less than a quarter mile ahead, and there was no way to have a race up the mountain without killing themselves in the process.

"Hold on," Noah ordered grimly as he sped up.

They hit the dirt road, fishtailed slightly before Noah corrected and hit the first switchback going as fast as he dared.

As soon as they rounded the bend, putting a little distance between them and the car pursuing them, Noah barked back to Liam, "Get on Lauren's phone and call the Colters. Tell them we're coming in hot. We have no choice but to go up because we sure as hell can't get back down."

Lauren hastily fumbled with her phone, shoving it over the seat toward Liam.

They got to the second switchback, and Noah spun out as he rounded the sharp curve. Liam was punching the button to connect the call to the Colters, when Noah swore a blistering streak that singed Lauren's ears.

When she stared ahead and realized what Noah was reacting to, cold fear paralyzed her.

"Noah, look out!" Liam yelled, dropping Lauren's phone.

Hurtling down the mountain road on a direct collision with them was a Hummer with a reinforced steel grille.

Lauren recognized the direness of the situation. She knew they were going to be pulverized between the two vehicles. Neither had any intention of avoiding the inevitable collision.

"Hold on," Noah said tightly. "There's only one way to avoid this, and I have to hope to hell we survive it."

When she realized his intention, her pulse exploded in her veins. She squeezed her eyes shut just as he turned the SUV and dove right over the edge of the mountain.

For less than a second, but what seemed like an eternity, they were airborne, and then they landed with a jolt that shook Lauren to her bones. She heard shattering glass, the crunch and groan of metal giving way.

And then they were rolling. Over and over until the world was a crazy Tilt-A-Whirl flashing before her eyes. They bounced and slid and then rolled some more, until finally the SUV landed hard on its wheels and the front smashed into a huge pine.

It was instinctive to throw her arms in front of her face to shield her from the air bag, but it never deployed. Glass sprayed her, and she screamed when a branch shot through the windshield and drove itself into the seat a mere inch from where her shoulder rested.

Oh God, just a few inches over and it would have impaled her.

She took mental stock, trying to determine if she had any injuries. But she felt no pain. She couldn't feel *anything*. She was numb from head to toe. For all she knew she'd broken every bone in her body, but she had no way of knowing.

She looked down and then over at Noah. Her cry of horror was muffled by her hand as it flew to cover her mouth. The dash had caved in, pinning him in his seat.

Liam. She had to see about Liam. Her hands fumbled with her seat belt, but it wouldn't come lose. She yanked and pulled, nearly screaming with frustration. Finally it came free and she awkwardly tried to maneuver in the much smaller space.

She managed to hoist herself high enough to see that Liam was sprawled in his seat, his head resting against a shattered window. Blood streamed down his cheek and he wasn't conscious.

Then she heard a sound from Noah.

Her gaze flew to him and she pulled herself above the limb that was embedded in her seat.

"Noah? Noah? Can you hear me? Please talk to me. Oh God, I'm so scared. Liam's unconscious. I don't know how badly he's hurt."

"Listen to me," Noah said hoarsely. "Can you reach Liam's gun?"

She froze, staring at Noah in confusion.

"Get the gun, Lauren. We only have a few minutes before they arrive. They'll drive back down the mountain and they'll come looking for us. They'll kill us. Do you understand? They're after you."

"Can you move?" Lauren asked anxiously. "Can you get out on your side? We could take Liam with us. We have the time."

"Listen to me, honey," Noah said, his voice calm, a direct contradiction to the screams echoing inside Lauren's head. "I can't move. I don't think I'm badly injured, but I can't tell. I'm probably in shock and can't feel pain. But my legs are trapped. There's no way I can get out."

"They want me," she whispered.

"Yes," he said bluntly.

The haze lifted and suddenly she was sharply focused on the matter at hand. These assholes were after her, and if they found her with Noah and Liam, they'd kill them. But if they thought Noah and Liam were already dead and she was nowhere in the vicinity . . .

They'd come looking for her and not waste the time on Noah and Liam.

She hauled herself over the seat and fumbled with Liam's jacket. She grasped the stock of the gun and yanked it out of the holster.

"Good girl," Noah praised. "Now listen to me—"

"No, you listen to *me*," she said fiercely. "I've got a lot to say and not much time. I love you. I love you and Liam so damn much and I'm not giving either of you up without a fight. I'm sorry I haven't told you before now. It just never seemed like the right time. Not saying now is either, but I'm not going to die without you knowing how much I love you."

"I love you too, honey," Noah said. "Now please, listen to me."

She shook her head. "This is what's going to happen, Noah, and I swear to God if you argue with me or if you don't do exactly as I say and you end up dead, I'll kill you all over again."

His eyes widened in surprise.

"Can you reach your gun?" she asked.

He nodded.

"Okay take it out and keep it hidden. Don't use it unless you absolutely have to. I'm taking Liam's gun and I'm taking off. These assholes want me. If you pretend to be dead and Liam is unconscious and seems dead and I'm not here, they're not going to waste a lot of time with either of you because neither of you are any good to them. It's me they want."

"Whoa, what the *fuck*? No fucking way, Lauren."

"There's not a damn thing you can do to stop me," she said calmly. "It's a good plan and you know it."

"It's the dumbest plan I've ever heard!" he roared. "I *love* you, goddamn it. I'm not letting you take off on your own with no protection."

"And I love you!" she roared back. "I love both of you, which is why I'm going to protect both of you by getting the hell out of here. Liam still has my phone. You can call for help once the dickheads figure out I'm gone and go after me. I'm going to try to make it to the Colters."

"Goddamn it, Lauren, *please* don't do this."

Noah was begging her, his eyes glossy with unshed tears. There was stark terror reflected in those shiny pools. Terror for *her*.

"I love you," she whispered. "If I stay here, they'll kill us all. We'll be sitting ducks. You're pinned, Liam's unconscious, and there's just me with Liam's gun. I have to give us a fighting chance, Noah. If we make it out of this alive, you can yell at me all you want."

Before he could argue further, she turned to try to open her door. She could barely budge it, and the metal creaked and groaned as she attempted to push it far enough open to get out.

"Use the butt of the gun and break out the glass," Noah said. "And hurry. You don't have much time. I want you as far away from those bastards as possible when they get here."

Bolstered by his grudging support, she broke out the glass with Liam's pistol and pulled away enough of the shards that she could get through without cutting herself.

Still holding tight to the gun, she hoisted herself out of the window and prayed that she didn't have injuries that would prevent her from running like hell.

When her feet hit the ground, she very nearly went down in a heap. Her knees shook horribly and reaction was setting in. Her hands shook. Her entire body quivered.

She had to get it together. Not only for herself but for Liam and Noah too. She needed to put as much distance between her and them for their safety. If her pursuers thought she was escaping, they would lose all interest in Noah and Liam and come after her.

She turned and ran.

CHAPTER 31

NOAH held his breath when he heard the sound of a vehicle nearby. Liam hadn't stirred, which concerned Noah. But what scared the hell out of him the most was the fact that Lauren hadn't gotten that big of a head start.

She was alone on the mountain with only Liam's gun for protection, and Noah was trapped in the goddamn car, unable to move his legs.

Sitting duck was right. Lauren had certainly been accurate on that count. He and Liam were completely defenseless and as much as he hated to admit it, Lauren's plan was a sound one for drawing attention away from him and Liam. But Noah couldn't live with the results if her life were to be sacrificed for his.

The engine stopped, and then Noah heard voices as they drew closer. He leaned against the door and slid the hand holding the gun between the seat and the door so it was out of sight. He closed his eyes to narrow slits so it would appear he was unconscious. He tried to make his breathing as shallow as possible and to calm the fear and adrenaline churning like a tornado inside him.

"Here it is!"

The shout went up, and Noah heard at least two responses, which meant there were at least three men. His heart sank. Three men who'd shortly turn their attention on hunting Lauren down. He had no idea what their orders were. Shoot her on sight? Take her into custody? Who knew what Joel Knight wanted? He was a twisted son of a bitch who got off on having absolute control over a woman.

It took every ounce of discipline he had not to betray himself. He wanted a shot at the sons of bitches. If he could take them out here and now, they wouldn't pose a threat to Lauren.

"What do you see?" one of the men asked.

They were still a short distance away and they were obviously being careful to avoid an ambush. Too bad they had to be smart.

"The woman's not with them. Looks like they're dead or nearly so. One of them's pinned in the driver's seat. Doesn't look good. The other cracked his head open on the window in the backseat and he's either dead or unconscious. The passenger window has been busted out. Looks like she took off."

There was a round of swearing, and then the next words sent a chill snaking down Noah's spine.

"Come on, you two. How hard can this be? We're talking one defenseless woman running around the mountain like a chicken with her head cut off. This'll be the easiest job we've ever had. Spread out and let's go find her. The sooner we find her and dump her on Knight, the quicker we get paid."

Noah heard Liam stir in the backseat. The fact that his friend was alive sent a surge of relief through him that weakened him momentarily. The problem was, the last thing he needed was Liam coming around right now and making a scene that would get them both killed.

"Liam, if you can hear me, stay completely still and keep your eyes closed," Noah said in a low voice. "I'll let you know when it's okay to move."

The sound immediately quieted and Noah knew Liam had heard and understood.

Another good sign.

The sound of the vehicle starting made Noah open his eyes to mere slits, and he surveyed the area around the crash site. In the distance, two men were disappearing into the trees in opposite directions, while the other had apparently taken the vehicle to move it.

"Liam, can you get to Lauren's phone?" Noah asked.

"What the hell is going on?" Liam asked in a foggy voice laced with confusion and pain.

"I don't have time to explain right this moment. If you can move and reach Lauren's phone, I need you to hand it up to me. Lauren's life—and ours—depends on it."

Liam let out a low groan and then a moment later, Liam leaned forward to hand Noah the phone.

"Where the hell is Lauren?" Liam demanded.

"Give me a minute, okay?"

He pulled up the address book on the phone and his first call went to the older Colter men. They were closest, and he needed people out to help Lauren and for someone to get out to free him from this damn vehicle.

His second call would be to Seth to pull out all the stops and have every available man on this mountain to hunt these bastards down and make sure they didn't get their hands on Lauren.

CHAPTER 32

LAUREN stopped and bent over, holding her side and gasping for breath. Each expulsion of breath was painful and she didn't know if it was because of her desperate flight through the woods or if it was the result of the crash.

Her head hurt. Her side hurt. Every muscle in her body ached.

A sound to her right had her jerking around, pistol up. A squirrel scurried up a tree and the gun wobbled precariously in her grasp.

She was losing her mind and she was rapidly losing any strength she had remaining. The brief adrenaline burst she'd experienced directly after the crash had long since fled, and she was barely existing on fumes.

She had no idea if she was heading in the right direction or not. The crash had completely rattled her and she hadn't logically thought about direction when she'd fled the crumpled SUV.

What bolstered her spirits was that she hadn't heard any shots fired. She hoped that her supposition would be correct in that they would come after her and not bother with Liam and Noah. She just prayed that neither were seriously injured in the crash.

After catching her breath, she took off in a jog again, determined to keep on the move and her attackers at a distance. After one particularly steep climb up a rocky incline, she realized that she was back on the road.

Jubilation filled her and she set off in a dead sprint. When she heard an approaching vehicle, she turned, relief making her weak-kneed. Her relief turned to paralyzing fear when she recognized the Hummer that had forced them off the road. The Hummer skidded to a stop, kicking up a cloud of dust. The driver was out and rushing toward her before it had fully stopped.

It was time for payback. She raised the hand holding the pistol and took aim. It was a peculiar moment of disconnect for her. The person wasn't real. The situation wasn't real. The gun wasn't real and neither were the bullets.

It took her back to some of the dreams she had when she was being pursued and she would point the gun and it either wouldn't fire, or it would be out of bullets. She'd awakened, frightened and frustrated by her inability to shoot her attacker.

It would indeed be over her dead body if she wasn't able to pull the trigger this time.

And evidently, the man charging her didn't think she had the balls to do it either because he never let up. She waited until he was only six feet away, and then she calmly pulled the trigger.

The explosion was deafening. The gun jerked in her hand, the recoil so much that she feared she'd missed her target all together.

But then she saw the bloom of red on his chest. The faint shock that registered on his face. He staggered, barely keeping himself up right.

She shot him again, this time right through the forehead.

He went down like a rock.

Before she could register any relief or satisfaction, pain exploded in her head and she went sprawling to the ground. The gun flew from her hand and through the foggy haze of her semiconscious state, she heard the rapid exclamations from other men.

"Holy shit, the bitch shot Mark! We should kill her and be done with it," he said, his voice full of shock and rage.

"Don't be stupid," the other man said, in a voice that suggested he thought his accomplice was just that. "It's one less person to share the bounty we're being paid to bring the bitch in to Knight. We split two ways now instead of three and the boss is happy. Now let's get the hell out of here before the cops start showing up."

Her stomach twisted into a vicious knot. She'd been so focused on the threat in front of her that she hadn't heard the two men behind her.

Realization of her circumstances sent terror through her veins. Joel Knight wanted her back.

He'd hired these men to do whatever was necessary to bring her to Joel.

They hadn't blinked an eye over their fallen accomplice. It was a financial transaction for them and nothing else.

She was so fucked if they got her off this mountain and back in Joel's world where he made the rules and nothing could touch him.

But at the same time, they hadn't been ordered to kill her. Joel wanted her back. Alive. At least for the short term. Could he not know of what she'd done? Was this all about the blow to his ego because she'd dared to walk out on him?

If he didn't know that she'd stolen incriminating evidence from his computer or that she'd spoken to the district attorney, she might manage to stay alive long enough for Liam and Noah to find her.

Most important she'd led these bastards away from Noah and Liam. She clung tenaciously to that thought. They were alive. They would come for her.

She was barely clinging to consciousness when the two men yanked her to her feet and dragged her toward the truck driven by the man she'd shot.

They merely left him on the road, lying in a pool of his own blood.

At least Noah and Liam and the Colters would find the body, and they would know what had happened to her.

It was her only hope.

They took a roll of duct tape and roughly wound tape around her head and over her mouth. Then one taped her hands together, winding the tape around and around her wrists. Once that was accomplished, they tossed her into the back of the Hummer and grabbed her ankles, bruising her skin with the force of their grip.

After securing her legs with the same tape, they tossed the roll over their shoulder and slammed the back door shut. Without sparing another glance in her direction, they got into the cab of the Hummer.

The driver began the awkward task of turning around on the narrow road and several times sent rocks tumbling over the edge of the sharp incline.

After a moment, he had them turned in the way they'd come, and he floored the accelerator. She bumped painfully all over the backseat, the seat belt buckles digging into her skin and hitting her ribs.

They were bringing her to Joel and what he planned for her she had no idea. She could no longer deny the sort of man he was. The blinders had been off for a very long time now.

She knew what he was capable of. She knew what he'd already done to numerous women.

What was one more woman's blood on his hands?

CHAPTER 33

WHEN Noah heard a shout in the distance, he breathed a
huge sigh of relief. Liam had left, taking Noah's gun with
him, as soon as he'd learned that Lauren had struck out on her own.

He hadn't wanted to let Liam go. Liam was obviously injured
and fighting his hold on consciousness. He was bleeding steadily
from his head wound.

But what choice had either of them had? How could Noah hold
him back when Liam was all the help Lauren could expect so soon?

Liam had been terrified the moment Noah had told him what
she'd done. And it was obvious that he was torn between leaving
Noah in such a horrible situation and going after Lauren.

Noah had quietly pointed out that there was nothing Liam could
do for him. Noah was stuck until help arrived. But Liam could go
in search of Lauren and hopefully reach her in time.

Noah had never felt so helpless in his life than he did now, pinned in the SUV while Lauren was out there fighting for her life and Liam was somewhere in between.

Relief made him temporarily weak, and it took a second for him to muster the strength to shout back upon hearing Adam Colter's call. A moment later, the older Colter brothers appeared at the vehicle, their expressions worried and grim as they took in the wreckage.

"Are you hurt, son?" Adam asked. "Where are Lauren and Liam?"

"No, sir, I don't think I'm injured that badly. Just can't move my legs but I can feel them."

Then he quickly related the events that occurred right after the wreck, and Liam's departure to go after Lauren.

"I'll call Seth and give him the update," Ryan said grimly.

"I did," Noah said. "He was on his way out. I told him to get everyone in the damn town out if that's what it takes."

"Okay then. We just need to concentrate on getting you out of there," Ethan said. "I have some tools in the truck. I'm calling for a wrecker just in case we can't get you out of this. I know you don't want to be stuck here when Lauren is out there and her fate has yet to be determined. We'll do our best, son."

"Thank you," Noah said, his fingers flexing and then curling in agitation. It was killing him to have to sit there, unable to move, while others searched for Lauren.

Ethan and Ryan turned and ran in the direction of their vehicle while Adam stayed with Noah. Adam put his hand on Noah's shoulder and squeezed.

"I don't want you to panic. I know you're worried. I won't tell you *not* to worry because in your shoes, I'd be pissing my pants and freaking out. But I want you to know that not one of us will rest until we get Lauren back."

Noah nodded, not trusting himself to speak. The more time that passed, the sicker at heart he became. Liam hadn't returned and neither had Lauren.

He yanked his head back up to stare at Adam. "Lauren said she was going to try to make it to your place. Did you leave Holly there alone? They could both be in trouble."

"I called Max and Callie to go stay with Holly. He was fit to be tied but we told him we didn't have any details and that we needed him there. I can understand his anger. Lauren is his sister and by rights he should be right here with us, but he doesn't know this mountain like we do and the last thing we need is for someone to get lost while our focus is on Lauren."

"You did the right thing," Noah said. "We need level heads right now."

Even as he spoke, his fingers formed tight fists and he pounded the caved-in dashboard in frustration.

"Seth and the others are nearly here," Ryan said when he returned. "They've set up a roadblock at the bottom of the road, and they're coming up the mountain balls to the wall."

"Can you get me out?" Noah demanded.

"We're sure as hell going to try," Ethan said as he held up a crowbar.

Ryan held a sledgehammer and an axe.

"Stand back, Adam," Ethan said. "Cover your head as best you can, Noah."

The entire vehicle shook as the two men tore into the door and the frame. Several times, the pressure on his legs made him wince, but he was just grateful to be able to feel anything at all. He was damn lucky he hadn't crushed both legs.

Using the crowbar to pry the dashboard up off Noah's legs, Ryan strained, muscles bulging.

"As soon as I loosen this enough, pull him out," Ryan said through gritted teeth.

Ethan and Adam scrambled to get into place. As Ryan pulled back away from Noah, Adam and Ethan grabbed for his shoulders and they hauled upward.

Noah bit back a bellow of pain when he came free.

The Colters lowered him to the ground when in the distance they heard, "Dad! Dad! Damn it, where are you?"

"Over here!" Adam yelled.

Then he knelt back down by Noah.

"Okay, talk to me, son. You hurt anywhere?"

"Help me up," Noah said, extending his hands to Adam and Ryan. "There's only one way to find out."

They grasped his hands and hauled him to his feet. For a moment, the two men pressed close to Noah's side, offering him support until they were certain he could stand on his own.

"I'm okay," Noah said. "Nothing feels broken. Just bruised and cut."

Ethan nodded. "Yeah, you're bleeding in half a dozen different places."

All four men looked up when Seth barged onto the scene, two of his deputies on his heels.

"Why aren't you looking for Lauren?" Noah demanded.

Seth gave him a look that sent a shock of fear hurtling down his spine. "We came to get you. Liam tracked Lauren's route back to the road where he found one of the men dead. Two gunshot wounds. Looks like Lauren shot one of the assholes and then got hit from behind. There was a depressed area of grass with a small amount of blood. A good distance from the other body, so it wasn't his. We also found a roll of duct tape with several hairs that match Lauren's. Half the roll had been used. There are fresh tire tracks that aren't a match to one of ours leading away. If I had to guess, judging by the pattern and the disturbance to the area off the road, the truck was coming up the mountain when Lauren came into view. I think the guy she shot was driving. The other two were tracking her on foot and came in behind her while she was distracted by the first guy. They knocked her down, subdued her and then tossed her in the truck, turned around and hauled ass off the mountain, getting away before we arrived with the roadblock."

Noah went numb. His mouth went dry. His pulse pounded painfully in his head.

He'd failed her. He and Liam both had failed her in a huge way.

They'd planned in detail. They'd taken into account so much. They'd made a plan of action. None of it did a damn bit of good, because those bastards had gotten to Lauren faster than Noah could have ever imagined.

How?

He put a hand to the back of his neck and rubbed, trying to alleviate the knotted tension coiled in his muscles.

"How in the hell could they have put this kind of plan into motion that damn fast?" Noah demanded. "We only called the D.A. yesterday."

"Can you make it on your own or do we need to carry you out?" Seth asked. "We can talk on our way back up. Liam is with my brothers and volunteers and first responders. They were combing the area where the body was found to make sure we weren't missing anything."

"I can make it," Noah said in a determined voice.

He took a step forward, falling into stride with Seth as Seth's fathers followed behind. Seth's deputies went ahead of the men, one of them talking into the radio.

"How did they manage this, Seth?" Noah asked again.

"I think Joel Knight had already made her," Seth said grimly. "He may not even know about the meeting with the D.A. If he's had people looking for her all these months, it's possible they were finally able to locate her and were just waiting for an opportunity to make their move."

Noah swore long and hard. "And the very thing we thought we were doing right—taking her to a more isolated area—proved to be their golden opportunity. They couldn't make this kind of attack in town, even one as small as Clyde. But on a lonely mountain road that's only traveled by the people who live on the mountain? Son of a bitch. We may as well have just gift wrapped her and delivered her to the bastard, complete with a bow."

Seth put a hand to Noah's shoulder as they completed the climb back to the road, where a string of police cars and SUVs were parked.

"Beating yourself up over the what-ifs and maybes doesn't do you or Lauren any good right now," he said quietly. "What we have to focus on is getting her back."

Noah nodded, his jaw tight, and determination so fierce that he wouldn't entertain any other option took firm grip of his insides.

"I heard them talking," Noah said as they continued to walk toward Seth's SUV. "They came looking for her and thought Liam and I were dead. They didn't waste any time going after her, but they didn't say a word about killing her. They specifically talked about dumping her on Knight and getting paid. Knight wants her alive, and so if we find Knight, we'll find Lauren."

CHAPTER 34

✴

THE entire Colter family along with Max, Noah and Liam, plus most of Seth's police force and assorted first responders, were crowded into Clyde's small police station.

Holly was fussing over Liam and attempting to bandage the wound on his head. She was exasperated because every time something was said, Liam raised his head, upsetting her hold on the dressing.

Max was pacing back and forth, agony in his eyes and lines of worry etched deep in his forehead. Callie and Lily's faces were blotchy and tear-stained and they were huddled together on one of the benches, arms wrapped around one another.

Noah had just put a call into the New York City D.A. and was waiting impatiently to be put into contact with the other man. Seth was standing next to him, murmuring in a low voice for Noah to remain calm and not to accuse the district attorney of anything until they could be sure of what was going on.

Noah figured they'd know soon enough if the D.A. was involved. It would be evident by how much help he was willing to give them now that Lauren had been abducted.

"Mr. Sullivan, my secretary said it was urgent. What can I do for you?" Richard Castanetti said, his voice tense.

"Joel Knight got to Lauren," Noah said bluntly.

Noah's eyebrows rose at the string of curses that blew through the phone.

"How? When?" Castanetti demanded.

"When is a short time ago. The how is what we're wanting to know."

There was a long pause. "You think I had something to do with it? You think I'm dirty?"

There was more incredulity than anger in the other man's voice.

"I don't know what to think," Noah said quietly. "We have reason to believe that he's been searching for her ever since she left him. If that's the case then the timing could have just been a huge coincidence. It's possible they've been watching her, waiting for the right opportunity to present itself and today was that day."

"What do you know? Do you have any leads? What about the local law enforcement? I have a few contacts in Raleigh. I can make some phone calls for you."

"We aren't in Raleigh," Noah bit out. "We're in Colorado. But if you want to help, you can help us and Lauren and your eventual case by turning over whatever information you have on Knight. His residences, the places he frequents. Any hidey-holes he has. We need to run a fine-tooth comb over his entire life and we need it done yesterday."

"You think he has her? Alive?" Castanetti asked skeptically.

"We think it's likely that Knight doesn't yet know about the deal she struck with you. He's an obsessed, controlling bastard whose ego took a blow when Lauren walked out on him and didn't return.

I overheard the assholes who took her talking about delivering her to Knight, so if we can find him, there's a good chance we'll find her, and then you can add kidnapping and attempted murder to his charges when you file."

"There's nothing I'd like more," Castanetti said in a tone that made Noah believe the man was sincere. "Give me an hour and I'll pull every piece of information I have on Knight plus put in a few calls to contacts I have with the state attorney general and the FBI. They're all going to want Miss Wilder to make it out alive. Right now she's the one person who can take him down. I will tell you this. He rarely leaves the Northeast. It might save you and yours a hell of a lot of time if you get on a plane and start this way while I work out things on my end."

"I'll keep that in mind," Noah said. "In the meantime, let me give you a couple of numbers so that one of us can be reached at all times."

He gave the D.A. his own cell number, Liam's and Seth's before ringing off.

As he lowered the phone, he met the expectant stares of everyone gathered in the room.

"I don't think he did it," Noah said honestly. "Aside from the fact that it just wasn't feasible for Knight to act on information that Castanetti just received less than twenty-four hours ago, he seems as anxious as we are to nail Knight's ass to the wall."

"I hope to hell you're right," Liam said grimly. "Once Knight discovers that Lauren copied information from his computer and planned to turn it over to the district attorney, her life isn't going to be worth two cents. The only thing working in our favor right now is that he desperately wants to save face with the people who surround him, and he wants Lauren back under his control. That may buy us enough time to go in and take him down."

"So who's going and who's staying?" Dillon Colter asked. "It's one thing when we're talking about something local. We tend to do things our own way here on the mountain. New York City is a whole different story, and we could all end up getting our asses hauled to jail if we don't handle this just right."

Seth nodded, his lips tight and turned down into a frown. He glanced over at Max. "Have you ever had any face-to-face dealings with Knight?"

Max's lips curled in disgust. "Hell no."

"That could work in our favor. You fit in well with the posh, business crowd. You wouldn't stick out like a sore thumb. We could use you for this."

Relief was stark in Max's eyes. "I'll go," he said with no hesitation.

Seth turned to his brother and one of his dads. "Michael, I still think you and Ethan should stay here with the women. Preferably in one place so you aren't spread out. You'll have Mom, Lily and Callie to look after."

Holly crossed her arms over her chest, her glare as ferocious as her frown. "Why can't we go? My baby is going to need me when we get her back from that asshole. A girl always needs her mother at a time like that."

Liam's gaze softened and he impulsively gathered Holly Colter into his huge embrace. She seemed delighted with the spontaneous hug and gave him one of her own that rivaled his in ferocity.

"I appreciate you being willing to be there for Lauren, and there's no doubt she'll need you. But we want you safe, Mrs. C. All of you. Lauren loves you all so much and she'd be devastated if something happened to you. I promise to bring Lauren home to you where she belongs just as soon as we have her back."

Holly patted Liam on the cheek and then leaned up on tiptoe to kiss the spot she'd patted. "See that you do. Home is important when you're hurt and scared. I know from personal experience," she added quietly.

"How soon can you have the jet ready to go, Max?" Seth asked. Even before Max could respond, Seth turned to one of the younger deputies and slapped him on the shoulder. "You're in charge while I'm gone. Don't let me down."

The deputy looked befuddled but didn't argue. He stammered out a "yes sir" and then promptly took a seat to contemplate his temporary promotion.

"By the time we drive to Denver, Castanetti should have had plenty of time to dig up the info he promised us," Noah said. "I vote we roll out now and work it out on the way to New York City."

The others readily agreed and there was an instant exodus from the sheriff's station as everyone began to file out. Noah hung back, motioning Liam over.

"Are you okay, man?" Noah asked in concern.

His friend had been mostly quiet throughout the entire process and planning session. It was obvious that he was in pain and that he'd suffered a pretty severe head wound.

"I'm fine," Liam said firmly. "Nothing a few painkillers won't solve. I've had far worse and still got the job done. This time, it's not a job, though. It's personal. I'm going to get her back, Noah, or I'll die trying. I can't stand the thought of her having to spend a single minute in his presence, of his hands on her. Of him touching her. Frightening her. Making her doubt even for a moment what a wonderful, sweet, loving woman she is."

He stared at Noah for a long moment, pain burning brightly in his eyes. He lowered his voice even more. "We have to get her back, Noah. I can't live without her."

CHAPTER 35

❧

I T was dark when the harrowing ride in the back of the Hummer came to an end. Lauren ached from head to toe from the accident, and being thrown in the backseat without care hadn't helped her screaming muscles.

The back door opened, and she tensed when the two men dragged her roughly from the seat. Tears burned her eyelids when her ribs were jostled. Pain shot through her chest and abdomen, and for a moment she felt as though she couldn't breathe.

It took a minute for her to realize where she was. Forced to stand on shaking legs between her two abductors, she tried to make sense of her surroundings. As they shoved her forward and her feet came into contact with hard pavement, lights turned on a short distance away, and then came the explosive sound of a jet engine starting.

They were at a regional airport, though it looked more like a privately owned airstrip, but it was clearly designed for commercial jets to land and take off.

The cabin door opened, sliding downward to reveal four steps leading into the plane. A figure loomed at the top of the steps, and through the haze of pain and fear, recognition seared through her mind.

Her stomach balled into a painful knot and her already tense muscles tightened automatically. A defensive gesture associated with the person standing and staring down at her as she was hauled to the bottom step.

Joel Knight met her in front of the open doorway, his eyes glittering dangerously. She recognized that look. He was furious and high on a power trip. It was a mood where he felt challenged and forced to prove himself to those around him. She'd learned to avoid him at all costs when he got this way.

He backhanded her without a single word. Her head flew sideways and agony flashed through her face. If the two men hadn't been holding her arms, she would have tumbled to the ground. Tears leaked from her eyes and slid down over the duct tape still wrapped around her head and mouth.

She sagged precariously and Joel looked at her in disgust. Then he dug into his pocket, pulling out two ten-thousand-dollar wraps. He handed one each to the two men and then called over his shoulder into the plane.

"Come get the bitch." Then to the two men he'd just paid, "Get lost."

The two men didn't waste any time. They dropped their hold on Lauren and she staggered to keep her footing as they took off for the Hummer.

A second later, Ron appeared behind Joel. She recoiled when Ron moved past Joel and put his hands on her. This wasn't happening. She wouldn't go back to her old life. Not that her current reality would bear any resemblance to the past. Joel had never treated her well, but he wouldn't show *any* restraint now. He felt betrayed by her and he'd want revenge. He'd want to save face. Losing her had been a blow to his ego.

She'd walked out on him. She'd refused to recognize her *good fortune* in landing a man like him. He'd never forgive her for that transgression.

Ron hoisted her up and tossed her over his shoulder. As soon as his body made contact with her ribs, she screamed in agony. The sound was horrible, muffled by the tape over her mouth, but it was the sound of agony that couldn't be disguised.

"What the hell did you do to her?" Joel demanded as Ron climbed the steps into the plane.

"Not a damn thing," Ron defended.

Ron tossed her down onto the couch in the back of the plane, and she let out another garbled sound, nearly passing out. She couldn't get enough air in through her nose.

"Be careful damn it," Joel barked. "I don't know what those dumbasses did to her. Swear to God if they touched what is mine, I'll cut their dicks off and force-feed them to each other."

"You're not going to find out much until you get the tape off her mouth," Ron said dryly.

"Give the order to take off," Joel said tersely. "Then find me something to cut the damn tape off."

Hysterical laughter bubbled in Lauren's throat. He'd just nearly knocked her teeth out and he was pissed because the assholes he'd hired may have hurt her. Apparently only *he* was allowed to abuse her.

She rolled back against the couch when the plane started forward. Ron returned a second later, holding a knife out to Joel.

Joel pulled her over onto her belly and panic blew up. It was worse because she had no way to fight. She hated being pinned down this way. Hated it!

He sawed at the tape around her wrists and finally worked it free. Her arm flopped forward, falling over the edge of the couch, and her shoulders protested the sudden change in position. She moaned against the tape over her mouth and tried valiantly to keep the tears at bay.

Next he freed her ankles, and then he began working on extracting the sticky tape from her hair. She was surprised he didn't grow impatient and just hack her hair off, but then her hair has always been something he liked and hadn't wanted to change about her.

She braced herself to have half her skin and lips taken off when he ripped the tape from her flesh, but he was surprisingly gentle, working it a little at a time until finally it came free.

She automatically licked her cracked, dry lips. Then she pushed herself upward, refusing to remain in so vulnerable a position.

Joel assisted her, nothing forceful in his touch. It only made her fear him more, because she knew how quickly the pain could come. It was almost as if he liked to keep her aware at all times that he could do as he chose. He liked to follow tenderness with brutality, and then he'd always follow up pain with a caress.

"Would you like some water?" he asked, frowning at her appearance.

She nodded, not trusting her voice not to crack, and the last thing she wanted was to demonstrate her terror. She wouldn't give him that satisfaction.

Ron appeared with bottled water, and Joel took it from him and carefully held it to her lips, refusing to let her hold it.

She drank greedily, closing her eyes as the cool liquid soothed the rawness of her throat.

When Joel took it away, she lifted her gaze warily, waiting for whatever came next.

Joel frowned. "What happened to you? What did those idiots do to you?"

Since he seemed concerned, at least on the level that someone had possibly damaged something he viewed as a possession, and he was exceedingly possessive of things that belonged to him, Lauren didn't provoke him and instead played his game.

"They forced my vehicle off the side of a mountain," she said in a low voice.

Joel's frown turned to an all-out scowl. "They caused you to wreck?"

She nodded.

"Fucking morons," Joel exploded. "They had explicit orders to deliver you to me. Alive. How the hell could they possibly be certain you'd survive a plunge over the side of a mountain?"

She lowered her gaze as questions bit at her lips. She wanted to ask him if *he* was the idiot since he didn't seem to get that she wanted nothing to do with him. But she was hurt and the last thing she wanted was to enrage him to the point he got violent. At the moment, he seemed genuinely concerned—or at least inconvenienced—over her injuries.

"Where are you hurt? I heard you cry out when Ron carried you onto the plane."

"My ribs," she said slowly. "Hurts to move. Hurts to breathe. I'm worried they're broken."

Joel swore and then bellowed for Ron to return. When the man appeared in the sitting area, Joel said, "Call ahead and have my personal physician waiting for us when we arrive. Give him the rundown on Lauren's condition and tell him she needs pain medication and X-rays."

Ron nodded and disappeared once more.

"I'm not happy with you, Lauren," Joel said coldly. "Look at me when I'm talking to you!"

Swallowing back the rage building in the pit of her belly, she slowly lifted her gaze to meet the eyes of a demon.

"You wouldn't be in your present condition if you hadn't been stupid and tried to walk away from me. No one walks away from me. Do you understand that? There is not a place on this earth you can hide from me. I will find you. I'll never stop looking. And I'll kill anyone who helps you, who is with you, who interferes in any way. Do you understand?"

"Yes," she whispered.

"You're mine, Lauren. You belong to me. You're my property. I make all the decisions regarding your well-being, your life, your very existence. The sooner you accept that, the more peaceful your life will become."

Oh God. She couldn't bear it. She wanted to scream Noah's and Liam's names and keep screaming until they came for her. They had to find her.

"Now get down on your knees and prepare to apologize," he ordered.

Her eyes widened and she stared at him in horror. His face reddened with rage at her reaction and before she could defend herself, his hand was in her hair, twisting the strands in his fist. He yanked her from the couch and she landed on the floor, the jolt sending pain racing through her midsection.

"You don't learn," he ground out. "Your defiance will bring you nothing but misery. I guarantee it, Lauren. Now get up on your knees."

He let go of her hair, his hand going to the fly of his pants. Tears sliding endlessly down her cheeks, she pushed herself upward until he cupped her chin in his merciless grip.

She closed her eyes and forced herself out of her body, to a place where Joel couldn't hurt or humiliate her. She focused on Noah and Liam and their love for her.

Joel might control her body, but he'd never control her heart or her mind.

For the men she loved, she could and would endure anything Joel forced on her. She just had to hold on and do whatever it took to survive until they came for her.

CHAPTER 36

NOAH'S cell rang as he and the others were boarding Max's jet. Recognizing the number as an NYC area code, he hastily answered.

"Noah, this is Rick Castanetti. I have something for you. We just got a huge break."

"You found him? Did you find Lauren?" Noah demanded. "Is she okay?"

Around him, everyone went completely silent. Liam pushed in next to Noah and put his ear close to Noah's head so he could hear the conversation.

Noah punched the button to put Castanetti on speaker and then held the phone in front of him so everyone could listen.

"We just got a tip from an informant that Knight's personal physician got a call to meet Knight at his lake house in upstate New York to treat Miss Wilder's injuries."

"What injuries?" Liam demanded. "What the hell did that bastard do to her?"

Noah held up his hand to silence Liam before he blew completely up. "We don't know if she was hurt in the accident or not. Let's not assume the worst. He can't have had her in his possession that long yet."

"They're flying to a private airstrip owned by Knight. He typically takes his helicopter and lands it on the property, but this is where you catch a break. The airstrip he owns is a good forty-five minutes from his house. There's a commercial field ten minutes away you could land at, and it will even the odds on time. With the head start he got on you leaving Denver, there's a good chance you'll get there not long after he does."

"Where is this lake house?" Noah bit out.

"You have to know that you can't be the first in," Castanetti said in a low voice. "I have to go through the channels on this one."

Noah sucked in his breath and hoped like hell he wasn't trusting the wrong man. "You can't call this in."

There was a long silence over the line.

"What the hell?" Castanetti demanded. "You don't want me to ensure that the police get there to prevent any harm coming to Miss Wilder? Are you crazy?"

"You can't call it in because Knight would know about it and then we'd lose Lauren. Right now we know where he's going. That gives us the edge. If you arrange a sting, he's going to disappear, taking Lauren with him, and we'll have lost our one chance to get to her and take Knight down."

"I don't like what you're insinuating," Castanetti said in an angry, pissed-off tone.

"I'm not insinuating anything. I *know* damn well that he has some dirty cops on his payroll. I've seen the information on the disk Lauren copied from Knight's computer. And this goes all the way to the top. I'm taking a huge fucking risk even talking to you."

There was another long silence, and then a string of curses from Castanetti.

"I want what's on that disk, especially if what you're saying is true."

"And if we get Lauren back, you'll have it," Noah said smoothly. "She's our top and *only* priority right now."

There was a sigh, and then Castanetti mumbled his agreement and provided specific addresses and locations as well as the airport for them to land.

Noah motioned for one of the others to copy down the details as Castanetti gave them.

"He better not be dead when this is all over with," Castanetti said when he finished supplying the location.

"I can't guarantee you anything," Noah said in a low voice.

If Lauren was threatened in any way, Noah wouldn't think twice about taking out the bastard.

"Just don't get yourselves killed," Castanetti said in a somber voice. "Knight's been responsible for too many lost lives as it is. I hope Miss Wilder makes it out of this okay, and I'm not just saying that because I want her on the witness stand."

"Thanks. We'll keep in touch," Noah said.

"See that you do."

Noah hung up as the plane lifted into the air, and grimly surveyed the group of men who'd listened in on the call.

"We've got some time to make up. Knight got a head start, and Lauren's life depends on us getting to that lake house as quickly as possible."

LAUREN huddled on the sofa of the plane and moaned softly when she was jostled by the aircraft touching down. Fear was immediate, because she had no idea where they were or how Noah and Liam would ever be able to find her.

It was time to be real and not solely rely on someone else to rescue her. She'd escaped Joel once. She'd just have to do it again.

Only, the first time he hadn't been expecting it. Now he'd watch her constantly, keep her more firmly under his thumb than he had ever before.

Despair settled heavy and bleak. Then she grew angry at the defeat that nagged at her. She'd survived Joel once and she was stronger now. She'd survive again.

"Lift her and be careful with her," Joel ordered. "If you hurt her, it'll be your ass."

Rough hands slid underneath her, lifting her in one motion as Ron settled her roughly against his chest. It made her furious that Joel was such a nauseating hypocrite. That he acted like he gave a flying fuck about whether she was hurt or not. She thought it more likely that he was so insanely controlling that in his mind she was his to torment, much like a favorite toy a child jealously guards from use by other children.

She was still numb from the violent episode of earlier. He'd used her. Not for sexual release, but to humiliate and degrade her. He was proving a point and chipping away at her rebellion.

He was trying to break her.

He had no way of knowing that unlike before, she was infused with purpose. Resolve. She knew her worth. Knew she was loved for who she was. She knew the difference between love and control.

If he thought he was getting back the same naïvely stupid Lauren Wilder, he was wrong. Dead wrong.

She was placed in the back of a waiting car and then Joel slid onto the seat next to her, his hand going immediately to her head. It wasn't a tender gesture. It was a warning. An expression of his dominance and control.

She curled herself into a tighter ball and closed her eyes, shutting out his presence. The car pulled away, the seat vibrating against her cheek. She didn't try to rise. She didn't move a single muscle.

Her face was bruised and throbbing from when he'd struck her and then from his rough handling of her later. And her entire mid-section ached fiercely. Though she'd played up her injuries to try to get Joel to lay off her, more and more she thought that she may well *have* broken her ribs in the wreck. It scared her, this faux concern from Joel. He was like a bubbling cauldron just waiting to explode, and she waited for it at any moment.

The drive took forever, and she was desperately tired but afraid to let herself fall asleep even for a minute. She didn't want to be put in a position where she was vulnerable and not on her guard.

When the car finally ground to a halt, she automatically tensed. Joel's hand tightened on her head.

"You *should* be wary," he murmured.

His voice was calm, but the threat was there. She'd have to be an idiot not to sense the thinly veiled violence that radiated from him.

"Do as you're told, Lauren. Don't make me angry. I'll have a doctor look at your injuries and determine whether you're able to accommodate me. If you defy me, I'll hold you down and fuck you whether you have broken ribs or not."

Her stomach lurched and her pulse accelerated. Her hands grew clammy and her forehead was dotted with cold sweat.

She had no doubt that he'd carry out his threat. When she lifted her head to glance warily at him, she saw that the idea of raping her, knowing she had injuries, *excited* him.

As much as she wanted to defy him, to tell him to fuck off and go to hell, she knew she had to be smart and wait for her oppor-tunity.

He cupped her jaw, holding it painfully tight, his fingers pressing into the bruise he'd put on her earlier.

"You're mine, Lauren. You belong to me. You don't walk away. You don't make the decision that it's over. Only I make that decision, and I'm not finished with you *yet*."

When she didn't respond, he squeezed harder until a whimper escaped her lips.

"Do you understand?" he demanded. "Say it. Say the words. You belong to me."

"I'm yours," she croaked.

His hold lessened and tears stung her eyelids. She inhaled sharply, determined not to give him the satisfaction of seeing how much he'd hurt her.

"Take her into the house," he ordered Ron.

Then Joel got out of the car and strode toward the walkway to the front door, leaving Ron to deal with Lauren.

As Ron pulled her from the backseat, she quickly surveyed the terrain and considered whether now was the time to try to make her escape. It would take her being able to get free of Ron, but where would she go? They were in a heavily wooded area, and she couldn't see any highway or lights from other residences.

Panic scurried up her spine, and she had to work hard to keep herself calm and focused. Ron obviously didn't like being saddled with the responsibility of packing Lauren around. His brows were drawn together in a disgruntled expression as he carried her up the walkway.

"Told him he should have just gotten rid of you a long time ago," Ron muttered.

At first she thought she hadn't heard him correctly.

"Told him you were a silly bitch. Too easy and too dumb. And now you're just a pain in the ass. He has a business to run and shouldn't be wasting time chasing you all over the damn place."

"I'll be sure to let him know you think so," she said through her teeth.

"You'll keep your mouth shut or I'll come at you," he said coldly. "Joel likes to watch when I fuck a woman. He says it inspires him. Because I don't give a shit if I break them. I'll shove my dick up that tight ass of yours and I'll enjoy making you scream. If you think Joel will protect you, then you're wrong. He'll get off watching me work you over and then he'll fuck you while you lay there and cry."

He strode through the open door while she lay rigid in his arms, his words echoing over and over in her horrified mind. It was a threat, yes, but he sounded so certain. There was knowledge in his tone, as if he'd done just as he'd described to other women Joel had been with.

They were both twisted, fucked-up psychopaths whose hatred for women ran soul deep.

He entered the living room and dumped her onto the couch, earning him a frown from Joel, but Joel didn't reprimand him.

When Lauren straightened herself, she saw another man about Joel's age standing beside Joel, arms crossed over his chest.

This must be the physician Joel had summoned to meet them.

"See to her," Joel said. "She was in an accident. She may have broken her ribs."

"I can't be sure without X-rays," the doctor began.

"I only want to know if she's okay to fuck," Joel said coldly.

Lauren was utterly appalled, humiliation sucking her into its dark embrace. The doctor hesitated but then made his way over to Lauren.

He went to one knee on the couch in front of her.

"Lie down, please," he said in a stiff voice that told her he was uncomfortable with the situation.

Slowly she lowered herself until her head met the cushions. She went tense when his hands lifted the hem of her shirt and started to pull it up over her breasts.

"I won't hurt you," he said in a low voice. "I'll do my best to be gentle."

He splayed his hands over her rib cage and then began to press in a series of areas with his fingertips.

"Tell me if at any point you feel more pain when I apply pressure," he said.

When he reached the lower part, she winced and let out a gasp. He paused there and then worked his fingers into the area around the tender spot.

"I'm sorry," he said when she let out another cry.

He probed another few moments and then lifted his gaze to meet hers. "Can you tell me what happened? Did anything hit you in this area? Have you had any difficulty breathing?"

She recounted the events of the accident in a halting voice.

"But I don't remember hitting anything," she said. "It was all a blur. We rolled several times and it was just so fast. And afterward, it didn't hurt because . . ."

She broke off, refusing to say she hadn't felt pain because of the adrenaline of running for her life away from the men pursuing her. Joel's men. It would only piss him off more.

But Joel had stepped to the side and was having a rather animated conversation with Ron. She used that moment of distraction to whisper her plea to the doctor.

"Please, help me," she begged. "He did this to me. And you heard what he wants to do. He wants to rape me. I'm not here willingly. Can you at least call the police when you leave?"

His face remained expressionless, but his eyes were heavy with regret and he could no longer hold her gaze. He dropped his eyes and continued his examination.

Finally he rose and turned in Joel's direction.

"She most assuredly has broken ribs. It's important you take care with her. I can bind them until you can take her to the hospital. They'll need to do X-rays, give her proper pain medication and supervise her medical treatment."

"That's what I pay you to do," Joel snapped. "I thought you said there was no way to tell if her ribs were broken without an X-ray. And now you're so sure they are?"

"There is bruising in the lower rib cage. Tenderness to touch and at least one feels displaced. If there are breaks higher, she risks puncturing a lung if she isn't careful."

Joel scowled. "You write her the script for painkillers. I'll see how things are in the morning before I worry over X-rays."

The doctor sighed and turned, casting an apologetic look in Lauren's direction. He'd tried and she knew he was afraid to do more. She didn't know what hold Joel had on him, but it was obvious the doctor was captive to Joel's demands.

The doctor spent a few seconds scribbling out a prescription from his pad, and then he pulled the top page off and held it out to Joel, who shoved it at Ron.

"Go have this filled."

Then he focused his attention on the doctor and told him to get out. The doctor was only too eager to disappear. He nearly stumbled in his haste to get to the front door.

When both Ron and the doctor were gone, Joel walked to the couch where Lauren still lay, and he stared down at her, a malicious gleam in his eyes.

"Here's how this will go, Lauren. Cooperate and please me and I won't touch your ribs. Piss me off and be difficult and I'll make you wish you were never born."

CHAPTER 37

LAUREN lay there frozen, so terrified that she couldn't think of what she should do. She had no doubt that he would indeed make her very sorry if she fought him, but how could she not? How could she lie there and allow him to use her body as he'd already used her mouth?

What if she became pregnant? Joel hadn't ever used condoms with her. He refused. And after she'd left him, she'd gone off birth control because she couldn't imagine wanting to become involved in a sexual relationship with anyone. She hadn't counted on Noah and Liam.

How could she force herself to have sex with him for the sake of survival? It was rape. Even if she didn't fight him, because her mind and heart was screaming no. She didn't want this!

And how could she ever face Noah and Liam if Joel raped her and she'd done nothing to prevent it? Would they even want her anymore? Could they look at her without disgust in their eyes, and could she ever look at them without shame in hers?

Joel stopped next to the couch, unzipped his fly and shoved his pants just to his hips so that his erect cock came free. It disgusted her that he was so turned on after hearing how injured she was, that he'd actually get off on the idea of forcing her to endure the humiliation of his possession in addition to the pain forced on her because she wasn't ready or willing. And he knew she wasn't willing and that she had no desire for him.

He stroked his erection, the action menacing. He reached with his free hand to knock her thighs apart but then he backed away, his gaze hard.

"Get up and take your pants off," he ordered. "I want you completely nude. Be quick about it."

Oh dear God. She was out of time. What could she do except obey?

She pushed herself up before he could find fault and take her hesitancy for disobedience. When her feet hit the floor, she rose shakily, her hands going clumsily to the button of her pants. All the while, she kept her gaze glued to Joel, hoping desperately for an opportunity.

And then it presented itself.

Apparently impatient over the time it was taking her, he advanced, releasing his grip on his cock, his hands outstretched as if he'd tear her clothing from her himself.

Instinct took over. Before she even realized what she was doing, she lunged forward, her hand reaching for his dick and twisting with all her strength.

Joel's howl of pain was instantaneous, and he struck out at her face to ward her off. Pain exploded in her jaw, but she hung on tenaciously, determined to do as much damage as she could. She doubled her other fist and struck him repeatedly in the jaw.

She released him and then drove her knee right into his balls, ignoring the pain in her ribs.

Joel dropped like a stone onto the floor and she wasted no time turning and running toward the back patio door. She couldn't go out the front because Ron was suddenly there. She had no access to a vehicle now, but she'd take her chances in the woods, because anything was better than the fate Joel had planned for her.

She heard Joel's roar of anger and his instant call for Ron. She flung open the door and bolted into the night, running as fast as her legs would carry her toward the tree line in the distance.

Almost there. Almost there.

It was a chant in her mind, a never-ending litany that made her push on even though agony ran like a river through her body.

Oh God, she was going to make it. She was almost there.

She was hit from behind with the force of a train. She went sprawling, screaming in agony when she hit the ground, a heavy body atop her.

Ron.

He'd caught her.

Tears of frustration coursed down her cheeks. She'd nearly made it into the cover of the woods. She could have hidden.

"Stupid bitch. You really do have a death wish," Ron snarled in her ear.

His groin was pushed into her behind and she could feel his enormous erection. The sick bastard was getting off on her helplessness and the chase.

He pumped his hips forward, mimicking the motion of fucking her from behind.

"Now I get you," he said with savage satisfaction. "You should have let Joel fuck you. He's much easier to take than I am, but now you've pissed him off and he's going to let me punish you, and I assure you, I'm going to enjoy every minute of making you cry."

He pushed himself off her and then dragged her upward. One

hand curled tightly into her hair and the other gripped her arm with bruising force as he propelled her forward.

Moments later, he pushed her back into the house where Joel was waiting in the living room, his face nearly purple with rage. His eyes were so black that she shivered.

As soon as they appeared, he stalked over and backhanded her across the face. If Ron hadn't been holding her so tightly, she would have instantly gone down.

Then Joel looked up at Ron. "She's yours. Bend her over the couch and tie her there. Use her for as long as you want. I don't care what you do with the bitch, but make sure she suffers."

Ron's eyes gleamed in satisfaction. "She might be a little loose by the time you get to her."

Joel shrugged. "I don't plan to keep her long anyway."

A chill blew over her body at the finality in his tone. He meant to kill her. He wanted to punish her and then he'd kill her for her rebellion.

Ron tore at her clothes while she stood there, numb, so scared that she couldn't even think. And then she was naked and he was shoving her toward the couch, his hands mauling her and making her cry out in pain.

She couldn't do this. She couldn't face what was about to happen. She just wanted to die.

Her mind went blank and she blocked out her reality, retreating to a place where no one could hurt her. She didn't feel the pain when Ron shoved her over the end of the couch and wrenched her arms back to tie them in place. She closed her eyes and withdrew, blanking everything until she was floating in a soothing sea of nothingness.

CHAPTER 38

LIAM was about to come out of his skin as they raced down the winding drive of Joel Knight's lake home. Every beat of his heart was magnified ten times until it felt like his chest would explode with the pressure.

He was terrified. Lauren had been in Knight's hands for hours. If Knight hadn't already killed her, Liam could only *imagine* what he'd done to her.

The tension inside the SUV was tangible. Noah's hands gripped the steering wheel while Seth and Dillon were in the second row, stiff and ready to bolt into action. In the back, Adam and Ryan looked worried, their brows creased with anxiety as they imagined Lauren's fate.

Max was on the floor in between Seth and Dillon, his hands knotted together, his knuckles white. Liam wasn't sure if he was praying or plotting vengeance. Probably a little of both.

Noah turned off the headlights as they made the last turn and the house came into view. He slammed on the brakes and turned off the engine a good distance from the house and then motioned everyone out.

There was a car parked in the front. A sleek black Mercedes. Only one light burned from within the house, a beacon for Noah and Liam.

Seth drew his weapon while Noah and Liam both pulled their guns as well. Then Seth turned to his brother, his dads and Max.

"You stay behind us. This isn't time to play hero and get yourself killed. Let us go in first and take care of any threat. We don't want this to get bloody unless it's necessary."

They nodded their agreement, but Noah and Liam were already starting across the gravel drive to the house. Liam broke into a run, not willing to wait a second longer to get to Lauren. Noah caught up to him and they charged toward the front door.

It was the view from the picture window that stopped them in their tracks. There were no curtains or blinds on the large window looking into the living room, and what they saw made Liam's blood run cold and then instantly molten with rage.

Lauren was bent over a couch—naked—and the welts on her back were visible even from a distance. The son of a bitch had beaten her! It looked as if someone had taken a belt to her back. Joel Knight stood to one side, his face set with satisfaction as another man roughly parted Lauren's legs as he prepared to rape her.

Liam hurtled to the front door, throwing it open. He barreled into the living room, gun raised.

"Get away from her!" he roared. "Hands up, asshole!"

"Liam, look out!"

He heard Noah's shout and then several things happened at once. One gunshot. Then two. Pain bloomed in his left shoulder. The man who'd been abusing Lauren dropped and rolled, and Liam could see he was going for the gun lying beside his discarded pants.

Liam tried to move to cut off the man's access, but his reaction time was ridiculously slow and part of his body felt encased with lead.

Seth stopped in between Liam and the man on the floor and all Liam could get out was, "No!" He didn't want Seth Colter to go down for him.

Seth dove low, tackling the man while Max surged forward and kicked the pistol away from the man's grasp.

Knowing that threat had been eliminated, Liam turned his attention to Lauren. Noah was also rushing toward Lauren, and they reached her at the same time.

Noah worked furiously at the ropes around her wrists, while Liam knelt by the couch and gently turned her head in his direction. Her eyes were closed and his heart nearly stopped in his chest.

"Lauren?" he asked softly. "Lauren, baby, it's okay now. Noah and I are here."

Even as he spoke, he put his trembling fingers to her neck, feeling for a pulse. His left arm hung uselessly at his side, but he shut out everything but the woman in front of him.

As Noah got the ropes free, Max pushed in with a blanket to cover Lauren's naked body. Noah pulled her upward, wrapping her in the blanket, ignoring Max's demands that *he* see to his sister's well-being.

Ryan and Dillon tried to pull Liam back, their questions urgent about his wound. They tried to get him to sit down, but he shook them off, only wanting to get to Lauren. He pushed Max aside, uncaring of his own injuries or that Max was her brother and by all rights should be the one seeing to her. Lauren was Liam's. His and Noah's, and Liam wasn't leaving her side.

Noah eased onto the couch, holding Lauren in his arms. Liam knelt in front of Noah, his shaking hand going to Lauren's bruised and bloodied face.

Behind them Seth was on the phone, his voice low and urgent. Liam had no idea what happened to Joel or how he himself had been shot, or if Seth had the other man under control, but he wouldn't allow himself to do anything but focus on Lauren.

"Lauren, honey, you're safe now," Noah said in a choked voice. "Open your eyes. You're safe, I swear it."

Her eyelids fluttered sluggishly and then opened. She stared sightlessly at Liam, almost as if she didn't recognize him.

"Lauren?" Liam whispered. "It's me, baby. It's Liam."

Her eyes were dull and she didn't react to his voice. It was apparent that she'd retreated to somewhere far away from where she was.

Noah lowered his head to kiss her brow, but she didn't stir. She continued to stare lifelessly at Liam, but it was as if she looked beyond him. Into nothing.

Tears burned Liam's eyelids. His fingers curled into tight balls. Helpless rage fired through his body. He'd allowed this to happen. She'd been taken by this bastard because she'd protected him and Noah.

As he lifted his gaze to his friend's, he saw the same answering grief and rage in Noah's eyes.

Liam leaned into Lauren, resting his forehead against hers. "Fight this, baby. Don't let that bastard win. Come back to us. Come back to me and Noah where you belong."

He turned, searching out Knight with fury in his heart. He wanted to kill the son of a bitch with his bare hands. But Knight was lying on the floor in a pool of blood, his eyes glassy and fixed in death. He glanced back to Noah, question in his gaze.

"He shot you," Noah said in a low voice. "You barged in, intent on saving Lauren, and you never even saw him pull his gun. I had to put him down."

"Good," Liam said savagely.

Then he put his forehead to Lauren's once more.

"He can't hurt you anymore, baby. He'll never hurt you again."

She didn't stir, and fear gripped Liam's throat. He glanced up at Noah again, grief so thick he had to swallow back the knot in his throat.

"What did he *do* to her?" he asked in an agonized voice.

He touched her bruised face again in a whisper soft touch. He was afraid of causing her more pain. He had no idea what Knight had done to her before he and the others had arrived.

Noah's mouth tightened and his throat worked up and down as though he were fighting the same overwhelming grief that consumed Liam.

"We were too late," Noah whispered. "He hurt her. The son of a bitch put his hands on her. Did you see the marks on her back? The bruises on her face? Not to mention the bruises and marks we *can't* see."

"Noah, Liam."

Seth's grim voice broke into their conversation. Liam turned to see the other men standing right behind them, worry reflected in their gazes. To the side, the man who'd been about to rape Lauren when they arrived was bound hand and foot, forced to sit upright against the wall.

"The ambulance just pulled up," Seth continued. Then he looked at Liam. "You and Lauren both need to go to the hospital. You've been shot and you're still losing blood."

"I'm not leaving her," Liam said fiercely.

Adam held up his hand. "No one said you had to, son. We'll all be there. She won't be alone. Let's get you patched up so you can be with her that much sooner. The quicker you let them take a look at that arm, the quicker you can be back with her. She needs to be in the hospital."

Noah nodded his agreement. A moment later, the paramedics entered the living room, followed closely by the local police. It was a madhouse of endless questions. To Liam's frustration he was separated from Lauren as one medic tended her and the other bandaged his arm.

When they began to wheel her away on a stretcher, Noah walking beside it holding Lauren's hand, Liam bolted up from the couch and strode after them. Over his dead body were they leaving without him.

Max was about to climb into the back with Noah and Lauren when Liam shoved him out of the way and hauled himself up to sit beside Noah on the bench next to the stretcher. When Max would have protested, Adam put his hand on his shoulder.

"Think what you would do if it was Callie and her brothers were trying to be at her side. They love her. Just like you love Callie. You'd never allow yourself to be parted from her, just like Noah and Liam won't allow themselves to be away from her. Let them go. We'll follow behind and you can see her at the hospital."

Max sighed, but Liam could see that Adam's words had hit the mark. Liam sent Adam a grateful look. The last thing Liam wanted was a confrontation with Max Wilder when the priority had to be on getting Lauren the care she needed.

The other medic closed the doors and then hurried to get into the cab. Liam reached down for Lauren's hand, pulling it up so he could twine their fingers together.

"We're with you, baby," he whispered. "We won't leave you.

He leaned down to brush his mouth across her delicate hand.

"I love you. Don't leave me, Lauren. Hang in there and be strong. We'll guide you back home."

CHAPTER 39

DOES it make me a complete bastard that I'm not sorry you had to shoot that asshole?" Liam muttered in a low voice as he waited for the nurse to return so he could get out of this goddamn room.

"No," Noah said simply. "It simplifies matters. Lauren won't have to testify against him now that he's dead. We turn over the disk to the D.A. and let him do the clean up."

Liam nodded and glanced impatiently toward the door. Max was with Lauren, a concession he and Noah had been willing to make only because she currently slept, and they'd been assured by the doctor that she would remain so for a few hours yet. When she awoke, Liam and Noah would be by her side, and Max would just have to deal.

But first he had to get the hell out of this damn exam room.

"Where the fuck is she?"

Noah sighed. "Chill, man. You took a bullet. It's a wonder they haven't tied your ass to the bed. You should be lying down and taking it easy, not running all over the damn place."

"You saw her," Liam said in a quiet voice. "Would you have her wake up and us not be right there? She was out of it, Noah. She'd retreated to God knows where, and at this point I'm worried we're not going to get her back."

"We'll get her back," Noah said firmly.

His arms were folded tightly over his chest and his jaw was set in a tight line. There was a hard glint to his eyes and his face was set in determination.

Then Noah's gaze settled on Liam's bandaged arm.

"You know that's going to hurt like a son of a bitch when the adrenaline wears off."

"It already hurts like a son of a bitch," Liam muttered.

Noah shook his head. "Then take the goddamn pain medication."

Liam's lips twisted into a mutinous line. "I don't want to be fucking fuzzy-headed when we see Lauren. There'll be plenty of time to take that shit later. She's what's important."

He turned his head toward the door again.

"Where the fuck is the nurse? What could possibly be taking so long?"

He would have slid from the exam table and stalked out, but Noah stepped in front of him and shoved him back. Hard.

"Sit your ass down. She's only been gone a few minutes. Adam and Ryan are outside Lauren's room, and they promised to let us know the minute she begins to come around."

Liam bit out a string of expletives but settled back on the exam table, his injured arm tight against his body. He wouldn't admit it, but it was killing him. Nausea coiled low in his belly and sweat beaded his forehead. But he wouldn't admit it, because he didn't want to chance any delay in getting to Lauren.

He was still haunted by the scene he and Noah had witnessed. He was tortured by what had happened before they arrived. He'd seen the marks and bruises from Knight's abuse, but how many more were inside Lauren where no one could see?

A heavy ache settled into his chest, more pressing than even the pain in his arm. Lauren had withdrawn. A self-defense mechanism to protect her from her terrible reality. Liam just wanted her back. In his arms. But he'd failed her in a big way. He'd sworn that he'd do everything possible to keep her safe, but had he?

He bolted more upright when the nurse came back into the room. She glanced warily at him and he supposed he couldn't blame her after the way he'd acted. He'd threatened all sorts of things if he wasn't released soon.

Feeling regretful, he tried to ease his expression and relax while she went over his discharge instructions with Noah. She gave everything to him and not Liam, as if she didn't want to get close enough to Liam to risk potential harm.

That put a knot in his stomach. Yeah, he wanted to get back to Lauren, but intimidating women was something *Knight* got off on, and it didn't make Liam feel good to be in the same vein.

"Thanks," Liam said gruffly.

The nurse looked startled, and then she offered a tentative smile, her face softening.

"I know you're worried about her," the nurse said in a quiet voice. "She hasn't awakened yet from the sedative and she's resting comfortably, in no pain, I promise."

Noah let out a whoosh of air in relief and Liam nodded, murmuring his thanks again.

"Take care of yourself," the nurse said. "No way you should be leaving this soon. I gave your scripts to your friend, and you need to make sure you take them or you could end up very sick and in the hospital, and I'm sure you don't want that."

"No ma'am, I don't," he said meekly. "Thank you. I appreciate your help. And your understanding."

She offered a bigger smile and then said, "You're free to go. Miss Wilder is in room eight just down the hall."

Liam slid from the exam table and winced when he bumped his arm. He'd refused even a sling or for them to immobilize it against his body. He needed his arm to be free just in case. He could hardly protect Lauren tied up and one-handed.

He followed eagerly behind Noah, simmering with impatience as they strode down the hall. When they got to Lauren's room, they saw the Colters outside the doorway, leaning against the door frame and across the hall against the wall.

Adam frowned when he got a look at Liam.

"Should you be up, son?"

Ryan held up his hand to Adam. "I know how he feels. And for that matter, if it were Holly and you were the one shot, would you stay away from her?"

Adam's lips tightened but he remained silent. Liam sent Ryan a grateful look.

Ryan put his hand down over Liam's uninjured shoulder. "She's still resting and Max is sitting with her now."

Liam nodded and then found Seth's gaze. "What happened with the police?"

"Nothing yet," Seth said. "They've been by of course. Surprised they hadn't made it down to you yet, but their primary focus is Lauren of course. Castanetti is on his way. He wants that disk badly. They're going to want statements from everyone involved. They've already questioned us and we'll have to go down to make official statements, but we told them we weren't going anywhere until we knew for certain how you and Lauren were doing."

Noah sighed. "Damn it, I don't want to have to deal with this mess right now. I just want to take Lauren home."

Dillon cleared his throat. "And where is home?"

Liam and Noah exchanged looks and then glanced back at the Colter men, whose eyes all mirrored the question in Dillon's.

"She's family," Dillon continued. "She's come to mean a lot to us. She's like a sister to me and my siblings. She's like a daughter to our mom and dads. She was . . . happy . . . in Clyde, or at least she was beginning to be. She'd come a long way from the frightened, vulnerable young woman who arrived before Christmas. We just don't want to see her unhappy again."

"We haven't discussed it," Noah said in a quiet voice. "We have a *lot* we still have to discuss. All we care about right now is that she's okay. Not just physically. Everything else can wait."

"You're right about that, son," Adam said in a serious tone. "Everything will work itself out. Just focus on Lauren and making sure she has what she needs. Be there for her. She's going to need you now more than ever."

"She'll need us all," Liam said.

Even as he spoke the words, he knew them to be true. No matter what may have been in the back of his and Noah's minds about where they would make their home with Lauren, Liam realized that Lauren would need time. She hadn't fully healed from her relationship with Knight, much less her abduction and abuse at his hands. It wasn't something that would be resolved in days or even weeks.

There was no way he and Noah could take her from a place she felt safe and a family who loved her and offered her invaluable support.

A sudden commotion from down the hall made them all jerk around, alert and wary.

"Where are my sons?" an imperious tone demanded.

It was a voice that instantly warmed Liam and terrified him all at the same time, because if there was one person he toed the line with, it was his mother.

CHAPTER 40

LIAM'S eyes widened and then narrowed as he swung back around to pin Noah with his glare.

Noah shrugged. "She needed to know and I wasn't about to get my ass in a sling by not telling her you got shot."

"Hell," Liam muttered.

It was at that moment that Lisa Prescott stalked down the hall, her husband close on her heels.

"Liam!" she cried when she saw him.

He braced for impact and in the next moment was enfolded in her fierce embrace. It was automatic to smile, because how could he not?

She let go of Liam and then pushed by him to drag Noah into her arms.

"Are you all right, son?" his father asked in a serious tone.

Liam's mom, who by now had finished making sure that Noah was unharmed, tuned back just in time for Liam's dad's question.

"Why are you up?" she demanded. "Shouldn't you be in a hospital bed? What kind of hospital are they running here?"

Liam held up his hand. "Mom, I'm fine. Just a flesh wound. It's been taken care of. I'm more worried about Lauren."

Lisa Prescott's eyebrow went up. "Lauren was hurt? What happened?"

Dillon Colter coughed discreetly and then said, "We're just going to go down and get something to drink. We'll be back in a little while to check in on Lauren."

Before introductions could be made—and really, they could certainly wait—the Colters walked by Liam, Noah, and their parents and disappeared around the next corner.

"What is going on, Liam?" his mom asked. "Noah scared the life out of me when he called to say you'd been shot. I know your job isn't the safest job in the world, but someone *shot* you?"

Liam sighed and then sent Noah a look to say that he wasn't going to do this alone.

"Why don't we walk down to the waiting area," Noah suggested. "We can talk more privately there."

Liam hesitated, not wanting to leave Lauren, even for a short length of time. He still hadn't even been able to get in to see her!

"Give me just a minute," Liam finally said.

He pushed Lauren's door open, and Max swung around to see who entered.

"How is she?" Liam asked in a whisper as he approached the bed.

"Resting," Max said.

He didn't offer more and Liam didn't press. He simply stood at the bed, staring down at Lauren's bruised face. A harsh growl echoed through the room, and for a moment, Liam thought he'd made the sound, but then he realized it came from Noah, who'd followed him into the room.

"My parents are here," Liam said to Max. "We'll be down the

hall with them. Lot to explain. We'll be back soon. Please let us know if she awakens. I don't want . . . I don't want her to wake up and for us not to be here."

"I understand," Max said. "I'll let you know."

Liam leaned down and pressed a gentle kiss to her forehead. "Come back, baby," he whispered. "It's safe now and we love you."

He stepped away and let Noah have a moment with Lauren before he walked from the room to meet his parents back in the hallway.

They were both staring at him with concern in their eyes, but there was also curiosity as they watched Noah come out behind Liam.

Liam's mother hugged him again and whispered against his chest. "You scared me. Never do that again!"

Then she turned to Noah. "And you! Don't think you're off scot-free. Thank God you weren't hurt too."

Noah hugged her again, a broad smile on his face.

"Let's go sit down," Liam's dad said. "Liam doesn't need to be standing."

They walked down the hall to a small waiting area, and Liam sank onto one of the chairs. He'd never admit it in a million years, but sitting down felt pretty damn good at the moment.

"So what's going on?" Lisa Prescott asked bluntly. "You explained about Lauren on the phone, but I thought it was a matter of her testifying and that there would be lots of protection. I never imagined that either of you would be taking such a huge risk."

"The man who abused Lauren found her in Colorado," Noah said in a quiet voice. "They forced our vehicle off the road and took Lauren. I don't even know what all has been done to her yet. When we found her, it didn't look good."

Lisa's expression turned to one of sympathy, her eyes darkening. "And do the both of you still feel . . . the same? I mean that you *both* want to be with her?"

"Absolutely," Liam said with no hesitation.

"Have you thought this through?" Carl Prescott asked in a somber voice. "I mean *really* thought it through your initial attraction and feelings? Is this something you really believe is going to work out long term?"

"I don't want a woman to come between you," Lisa cut in, her expression pained. "That's my only concern with your . . . arrangement. I don't want this to put a wedge in our family. You boys are too important to me."

Liam reached over and squeezed his mother's hand. "I understand your concern, Mom. I do. I can't even explain it, but this is . . . right. For all of us. We love her. She loves us."

"I hope for your sake she does," she said softly. "I *want* you to be happy." She looked to Noah, including him in her gaze. "I want you *both* to be happy. I always imagined a slightly different future, though."

Her face twisted into a rueful smile as she said the last. But there was also acceptance in her gaze, and it warmed Liam's heart. His mom was the best. Always looking out for her boys. She wanted the best for them. And Lauren *was* the best thing that ever happened to either him or Noah.

Carl just shook his head, obviously puzzled by the whole situation.

"You'll love her," Noah said. "Just as much as we do. I'm sure of it. No one can be around Lauren without falling in love."

"Mom?" Liam queried.

She'd gone silent, and he wasn't entirely certain what she was thinking. The last thing he wanted was to cause either his mother or his father worry or pain, but he couldn't give Lauren up. He loved her. Lauren was his future.

She gave him a genuine smile. "I'm sure we'll adore her. How could we not when she's shown such good judgment in loving not one but both of my sons? You'll just have to give me—us—time to understand. This isn't something you come across every day. It's going to take some adjustment in my thinking."

"That means a lot to all three of us," Liam said.

She reached over to pat his leg. "Will you at least promise me you'll rest and take it easy until you're healed?"

"I'll try," he conceded.

"Noah, Liam, she's coming around," Seth said from the doorway.

Both men's heads came up, and then they surged upward from their chairs.

Ignoring the pain in his arm, Liam hurried to the door. His mom caught his other arm, causing him to turn back momentarily.

"Liam," she said, her brows drawn together. "Your father and I want to meet her, but we realize this isn't the time. We'll try to understand, but what you have to understand is that this is hard for me. A mother wants so much for her children, and this arrangement scares me because you or Noah could so easily be hurt."

Liam's heart went soft as he stared back at his mom. He pulled her against his chest with his good arm and squeezed tightly.

"Thanks, Mom. But please don't worry. Noah and I have given this a lot of thought. This is what we want."

"And is it what *she* wants?" Lisa asked quietly.

"God I hope so," Liam breathed.

She patted his face and then reached over to give Noah's hand a quick squeeze. "Go on. I know you two are anxious to see her. We can talk later."

Liam needed no further urging. He strode down the hall to Lauren's room and saw the Colters congregated outside her door. They looked up as Liam and Noah approached.

"How is she?" Liam asked anxiously.

Seth gave him a look that sent Liam's hopes plummeting.

"She's awake. Max is trying to get her to talk. She still seems like she's in shock or at least unaware."

Noah cursed and then, without another word, pushed past the Colter men and walked into Lauren's room. Liam hurried behind him.

Max looked up when they walked in, his gaze hopeful. He got up, leaving Lauren's bedside, and strode over to intercept them.

"Maybe she'll respond to you," Max said in a low voice. "I've been talking to her but it's like I'm not even here."

Noah and Liam glanced toward the bed and then left Max. They took either side, both reaching for her hands. Liam brought her fingers to his lips. They were so cold.

He blew his breath over the tips to warm them and then captured her hand between his palms, rubbing to generate heat. Then he lowered himself to put him in the path of her sight.

"Lauren, baby, can you hear me?"

He waited a moment, and when she didn't so much as blink, he brushed his hand across her forehead and trailed his fingers down the curve of her cheek. He followed his hand with his mouth and inhaled her scent as he pressed his lips to her temple.

"We're here, honey," Noah said, his voice cracking under the weight of his emotion. "You're safe now. That bastard can't ever hurt you again."

Her eyes flickered and slowly she turned her head so she focused on Noah.

"Is he dead?" she whispered.

Joy and hope exploded in Liam's mind. He gripped her hand tighter, his urge to pull her into his arms overwhelming.

"Yes," Liam said with savagery.

"Good."

The simple word conveyed a wealth of relief.

"How are you?" Noah asked. "Are you hurting? Did he . . ."

He didn't finish because Lauren flinched and looked away, her body immediately tense. Liam wanted to put his fist through the wall. He and Noah exchanged fierce glances even as they tried to maintain their composure.

"My ribs," she said faintly. "I think I must have broken some in the accident. Hurts."

Noah turned toward the door where the others were standing. "Get the doctor in here. Or a nurse. Someone who can tell us what her condition is."

"On it," Dillon said before disappearing.

"Listen to me," Liam said in a low voice, his head close to hers. "I want you to rest and focus on feeling better and the fact that Noah and I love you. Joel Knight can never hurt you again. You're free."

Her eyes filled with tears and it nearly broke his heart right in two. They tracked down her cheeks in silver streams as she stared sightlessly toward the ceiling.

"I want to go home," she choked out.

"We'll take you home," Noah promised. "As soon as the doctor says it's safe for you to travel, we'll take you back home."

Even as Noah made the quiet vow, Liam knew that it was the right thing to say. Whatever sacrifices he and Noah had to make to ensure Lauren's happiness was worth it. She belonged in Colorado with her family and the two men who loved her surrounding her. She needed them *all*. Now, more than ever.

Somehow he and Noah would have to make it work. Love was about sacrifices, and Liam would sacrifice anything and everything to be with Lauren and to see her smile again.

CHAPTER 41

❧

W HEN the nurse came in, Liam told her that Lauren was in
pain, and as the nurse administered the pain medication,
Lauren drifted off, her eyelids fluttering closed.

Her lashes were dark against her cheeks and bruises shadowed
her beautiful face. As Noah stood there staring down at her, he was
struck by the enormity of what she'd survived and escaped.

He knew there was more. He knew she'd endured the worst, but
he was so goddamn relieved to have her back that he was weak
with it.

"The doctor will meet you outside," the nurse said in a quiet
tone. "He'll be able to give you the X-ray results as well as tell you
how long she needs to remain in the hospital."

"Thank you," Noah said.

He leaned down to press his lips against her forehead and closed
his eyes for a long moment.

"I love you," he said against her skin. "I love you so goddamn much. We'll get through this, sweetheart. I swear there's nothing we can't beat together."

She sighed and turned her face upward as if seeking the comfort of his voice. He ran his fingertips over the delicate lines of her face before finally retreating.

Liam waited at the door and when the two men stepped out, the doctor walked down the hall toward them. His step was brisk, and he stopped in front of the group of men, his gaze sweeping over them.

"Which of you are Miss Wilder's family?" the doctor asked.

Every single man spoke up.

The doctor cleared his throat and glanced skeptically at the assembled group.

"We're her family," Adam said in a grave tone. "We're her fathers and brothers."

Max nodded his agreement.

"How is she?" Noah blurted, no longer able to be patient. "When can she go home? She's been asking."

The doctor sighed. "I see all manner of things through this emergency room. Some you wouldn't believe. One would think as often as I see the results of violence that I would be immune to it. And yet it still pisses me off every single time a woman comes through these doors because some bastard used her for a punching bag."

The others simmered and seethed, their anger a tangible thing that hovered over them like a cloud.

"She fractured two lower ribs and has extensive bruising in that area, whether from the car accident or from abuse. It's hard to say, and it's likely that it's from both."

He paused a moment before continuing.

"Considering what she's been through, her physical condition is better than I would have expected. Quite frankly, it's her mental state that has me the most concerned and why I'm hesitant to release her from the hospital."

"She needs to be home where she feels safe and surrounded by the people who love her," Liam said.

"I agree," Max interjected. "I think the sooner we get her back home, the sooner she'll come around."

Noah faced the doctor, his chest tightening with dread. "Besides the fractured ribs, did she sustain any other injury?"

The doctor folded his arms over his chest, trapping his clipboard against his body. "It's my opinion that she wasn't sexually assaulted. She's bruised and she'll be sore for several days, but given the circumstances, she fared far better than one might expect. She's a tough young woman."

Noah let out his breath, nearly light-headed from holding it. "So can we bring her home? How long will you want her to stay?"

The doctor seemed to consider the request for a moment. "If you are indeed going to take her home and see that she gets the proper rest and care, then I'll discharge her as early as tomorrow morning. I want her to stay at least one night for observation."

"She'll have the best care possible," Max said in a terse voice. "And she won't so much as lift a finger."

Noah and Liam both nodded their agreement with Max's statement.

Movement behind Adam and Ryan made Noah's gaze veer in that direction. Liam's parents had come to stand just behind the assembled group and were listening as the others spoke.

"Then I'll have her moved to a private room so she can rest overnight. If all looks well in the morning, the on-call doctor will see her when he makes rounds and he'll discharge her."

Noah extended his hand. "Thank you."

The doctor shook Noah's hand and nodded at the others. "We'll get her up to a room as soon as possible."

When the doctor turned to leave, Noah motioned for Lisa and Carl Prescott to move forward. He introduced them to Max and the Colters and saw Lisa's eyes widen when the Colter familial situation was explained.

"Is Lauren all right?" Lisa asked after pleasantries were exchanged.

Liam sighed. "No. Not really. But then she shouldn't be expected to be all right. She was kidnapped by a monster and subjected to God knows what."

"She will be, though," Noah said with determination. "Liam and I are going to take her back to Colorado. Home."

Noah saw the knowledge in Liam's mother's eyes. To her credit she didn't argue or try to persuade them differently. Her face softened, as only the love of a mother can soften a woman's face.

"I know you'll both take good care of her."

Carl stepped forward. "If you need anything, don't hesitate to let us know. And, Liam, don't forget in all of this to take care of yourself as well. Your mother worries about both of you. A bullet wound is no small thing so don't treat it as such."

"I will, Dad," Liam said as he was pulled into his mom's arms.

Lisa pulled Noah closer until she stood between the two men she called her sons. The Colters and Max had discreetly moved farther down the hall, affording Liam and his parents privacy.

"When she's better, I'd like you to bring her to visit and to meet us," Lisa said in a low voice. "I don't want to burden her right now and I think it better if we leave. I just wanted to be sure you were okay, Liam."

"We'd like that," Noah said. "I think Lauren would like it too."

Liam nodded his agreement. "As soon as she's up to it, we'll bring her for a visit. Promise."

"Good enough," Carl said.

Liam's father pulled Liam into a bone-crushing hug and then

did the same to Noah. Noah winced. Liam got his size and build from his father. Carl Prescott was no slouch at sixty years old. He was a former mixed martial arts fighter and had served in the Marines before going to work in the paper mill he'd retired from. Even so, it was amusing to see that Lisa Prescott had the big man in the palm of her hand.

This was what Noah wanted. He wanted what Liam's parents had. He wanted what the Colters had. He wanted Lauren and her love, and wanted to shower her with his love and devotion so that one day their children could look at them and think that they wanted the same.

"We'll let you two get back to her," Carl said in a gruff tone. "Call us when you get back to Colorado and let us know how things are going. Your mother will worry if she doesn't hear from you."

"Will do, Dad. Love you," Liam said.

"Love you too, son. Both of you."

Lisa kissed them both and gave them one last hug before she and Carl headed down the hallway toward the exit.

Liam turned to Noah, blowing out his breath. "Well. That went a little better than I thought it might."

CHAPTER 42

LAUREN laid her head back against the seat and closed her eyes
as the plane lifted into the air. On either side of her were Liam
and Noah, both touching her in some way whether it was a leg
against hers or a hand on her arm. It was a silent reminder that they
were there. Just as they'd been every minute since they'd burst into
the lake house where Joel had died.

The last day had been a blur. Constant flow of people in and out
of her hospital room. Noah and Liam had been determined that
they were taking her back to Colorado at the very first opportunity,
despite requests for them to remain in the area for further questioning.

She'd been questioned at length by the investigator assigned to
the case as well as the district attorney whom Noah had turned the
disk over to. In truth, she'd paused briefly, considering whether she
should give the information now that Joel was dead. It shamed her

that she feared reprisal from other quarters once the investigation was launched.

But Castanetti had guaranteed her anonymity and that she wouldn't even have to testify since all she'd done was collect information from Joel's computer. They'd have to launch their own investigation based on the information she'd provided. She'd given the disk to the D.A. and had immediately felt a weight lifted from her shoulders.

It was something she should have done from the start. It was hard to come to terms with the fact that, had she not done so much wrong, she wouldn't have been abducted and subjected to Joel's abuse, and Liam wouldn't have been shot rescuing her.

She shivered and her stomach coiled into a knot. Just being on a plane brought back the memory of what Joel had done to her. What he'd forced her to do. Tears burned her eyelids and she bit into her lip to maintain control.

"Are you all right, baby?"

Liam's concerned voice reached her from what seemed a huge distance. She tried to respond, but she couldn't even suck in a breath.

Panic clawed at her throat, squeezing and knotting. Her chest burned. She was paralyzed with fear.

There were muffled curses, the sound of seat belts clicking as they were thrown off. Then she was lifted from her seat and carried toward the back where the lounging area was.

A cold cloth was pressed to her face and strong arms surrounded her.

"Breathe, honey," Noah said gently. "Take a breath for me. Can you do that? Look at me. Like this."

He inhaled deep and slow through his nose and then let it out through his lips. His gaze bore into hers, willing her to follow his lead.

She reacted sluggishly, the effort taking every bit of strength she had. Noah framed her face with his hands, forcing her to look only at him and the way he breathed. Liam's hand smoothed up and down her back, offering comfort, and gradually her chest loosened and the choking sensation was gone.

Tears streamed down her face, bathing Noah's hands. She tried to lower her head, to shrink away from his and Liam's scrutiny, but Noah held firm and then pulled her into his warm embrace.

"I've got you now," Noah murmured as he rocked back and forth, his arm securely around her.

She clutched at his shoulders as she buried her face in his neck. He kissed her hair, her forehead, stroked his fingers through the strands and rubbed up and down her back. His voice was pitched low in a soothing, nonsensical rhythm almost as if he were calming a child.

Eventually the sobs faded and she lay limply against him, exhausted by the panic attack and emotional breakdown.

"Tell me he's dead," she whispered. "Tell me again."

Noah kissed her forehead and Liam reached for her hands, enfolding them in his much larger ones.

"He's dead, baby," Liam said. "He can't hurt you again. You're free now."

Tears clouded her eyes and she felt the warm trickle down her face but was too exhausted to call them back.

"He forced me . . . on the plane . . ."

She could hear her voice rise with hysteria, could feel the panic returning even as Noah's hold on her tightened.

"Oh God," she choked out. "He pushed me to my knees and he forced himself into my m-mouth."

Even as she spoke, she wiped at her lips with the back of her hand, over and over as if she could remove the memory.

"He used me," she sobbed. "I'm dirty. I *feel* so dirty. How could you possibly want to be with me knowing the things he made me do?"

Liam went to his knee in front of Noah so that she was trapped between them, touching them both. His expression was so fierce that her eyes widened. He tipped her chin with his fingertip and then slid his fingers down her jaw to make sure she was looking at him.

"I won't say it doesn't matter what he did to you," Liam bit out. "It would be bullshit and I'm not going to say shit I don't mean to try to make you feel better. Of *course* it matters. He hurt you. He violated you. He took your choices away from you and he forced himself on you. But if you think what *he* did changes one goddamn thing about the way we look at you or feel about you, then you're wrong."

She stared back into his eyes, seeing the burning sincerity in his gaze. Noah rumbled his agreement, his body so tense against her it was like resting against brick.

"But it changes the way *I* feel," she said, her voice cracking.

Liam's expression went soft, his eyes full of love and understanding.

"Give yourself some time, baby," he said gently. "We'll get through this together. One day at a time. Noah and I will be with you every step of the way."

"I love you," she said, injecting as much conviction into her voice as she could.

Liam's eyes went even softer and he stroked her face with his hand. "I love you too, baby. So much."

She turned so she could slide her hand up over Noah's shoulder, and she hugged him to her. Her face was buried in his neck, his scent surrounding her, filling her. She breathed deep, content here in his arms.

The panic that had so firmly gripped her just moments earlier had receded, and calm had wrapped her in its soothing embrace.

"I love you," she said against Noah's neck.

He put his hand to the back of her head and stroked through

her hair. "Oh honey, I love you so damn much I ache with it. We're going to get through this together. You, me and Liam. No hurry. We have all the time in the world."

The words slid sweetly over her ears and loosened the tension in her chest.

"We do, don't we?" she said in wonder.

Noah pulled her away from his chest, his smile tender and warm. "We have nothing but time."

She reached for Liam, wanting that contact with him. Noah slid his hand possessively up her back as she curled into Liam, laying her head on his shoulder.

"I love you both so much and I was so afraid to let myself. But fighting it didn't feel right. I was afraid to trust myself again after I made so many terrible mistakes, but this time I'm right. I *know* it."

"In time you won't question yourself or your decision," Liam said in a solemn voice. "I plan to convince you on all points that you've absolutely made the right decision this time."

She kissed him, wanting the deeper intimacy, wanting to show him that she had no doubts. That she loved him. That she wanted a life with him and Noah no matter how difficult the road.

She slowly retreated from the warmth of his mouth and his touch to turn her face up to Noah. His lips came down in a heated rush to meet hers, and she sighed in contentment.

Noah pulled back, his hand going to her face in a gentle caress. "We're taking you home . . . to stay."

Hope soared through her chest, lighting up every part of her soul that was still steeped in darkness. But then just as quickly, reality crept in, her euphoria deteriorating.

"Baby, don't look like that," Liam said, his voice filled with tenderness.

"What will you and Noah do in Clyde?" she asked. "It's not fair for you both to have to rearrange your entire lives . . . for me."

Noah smiled and leaned his forehead in until it touched hers. "That's what you do for the person you love. And it'll be worth every single change if it means that you'll be happy, feel safe, and that we'll be with you every single day for the rest of our lives."

Her eyes widened and Liam scowled. It was a gruff look of annoyance that made him look . . . adorable.

"Did you honestly think we weren't in this for the long haul?" Liam demanded. "You're it for us, Lauren, and I hope to hell we're it for you because if not, you're going to have two surly-ass, love-sick men following you around like damn puppies."

She laughed softly, joy filling her heart.

"We want forever," Noah said. "To be honest, I wanted our proposal to be romantic and in the perfect setting, but fuck it. I just want your promise. Marry us, Lauren. We'll figure it out. The Colters can give us advice. They've made it work for over thirty years."

"We'll make it work too," Liam said, his voice full of conviction.

There was no doubt in their expressions or their eyes. No hesitancy. They were offering her all she could ever hope for.

Love.

Forever.

Happily ever after.

All the things she thought she'd never have because she'd made all the wrong choices.

Laughter bubbled up through the tears burning her eyelids.

"What's so funny?" Noah asked, his brows drawn together.

"I was just thinking about all the bad decisions I made, but then it occurred to me that if I hadn't made those exact choices, I would have never found the two of you. I guess in a way I have to be grateful for Joel because he was what led me to you."

"Fuck him," Liam growled. "I like to think we would have found you anyway, and I'm damn sure not going to thank him for anything."

"Do you have an answer for us?" Noah gently prompted.

It was then that she could see their nervousness. They were worried over her answer. Her heart melted and her chest ached from the overwhelming surge of love.

"Oh yes," she breathed. "I'll be with you, marry you, try my best to make you happy for the rest of our lives."

Triumph flashed hot and vibrant in Liam's eyes. Relief was stark in Noah's gaze. They converged on her, surrounding her as they enfolded her in their embrace.

Their lips were on hers, taking turns at her mouth, sliding down her cheek. Kisses pressed to her forehead, her temple. Whispers of love in her ear.

She closed her eyes, savoring every moment. Forgotten was the past, and even the present to an extent. Before her lay the promise of tomorrow, precious and beautiful. Noah and Liam were her future and she was theirs.

As the plane descended over the Colorado mountains, she was gripped by the rightness of being back . . . *home*. In a place where she'd first learned the importance of family and unconditional support.

She was returning. Much stronger this time. Ready to reach forward instead of looking back.

The Colters were her family, and she very much belonged to them, but now she belonged to Noah and Liam as well. They belonged to her. All that she could ever want was right here in her hands and in her heart.

KEEP READING
FOR MAYA BANKS'S NOVELLA

COLTERS' LEGACY

THE CONCLUSION TO
THE COLTERS' LEGACY SERIES

CHAPTER 1

"T HIS is killing me," Noah said in a grim voice.

Liam sighed and rubbed a weary hand through his hair as he stared back at his friend. "It's killing me too," he admitted. "She's not sleeping, and when she does, she has nightmares. I don't know what to do. I feel so fucking helpless!"

Noah sipped at the steaming mug of coffee and stared out the glass patio doors leading onto the small deck of the cabin he, Liam and Lauren now shared. When they'd returned to Clyde six weeks ago, they'd known they had to address the issue of housing. There was no way they could continue to stay in Lauren's tiny efficiency apartment above the clinic in town.

Adam had called in a favor from an old friend who had a cabin just out of town. It was halfway between Clyde and where the older Colters lived up the mountain. The man hadn't lived in it for some time and only used it as a vacation home once or twice a year. He'd been happy for them to move into it. It wasn't perfect, but it would

do until they could figure out what they wanted as far as a permanent place to live.

There was no question that they'd remain here. Surrounded by
Lauren's family. People who loved her and were a constant source
of comfort and solace. But they had a lot to work out. Mainly what
the hell he and Liam were going to do in order to support the woman
they both loved.

They had money saved. They could definitely make that money
last for a long period of time, but it wasn't infinite. And the last
thing Noah wanted was for Lauren to ever want for anything. He'd
give her the fucking moon if that's what she wanted.

"We just have to give her time," Noah said quietly. "She went
through hell. I can still see the fucking shame in her eyes at times,
and it pisses me off that we let that son of a bitch get to her. That
she spent enough time with him that he abused her. *Again.*"

Liam nodded, but his eyes were stormy at the reminder of what
Joel Knight had done to Lauren.

They hadn't made love to Lauren since returning home six weeks
ago. They hadn't even made an attempt. With her sleep wracked by
nightmares, and the shadows in her eyes present during the waking
hours, they hadn't wanted to push. They'd wait forever if that's
what it took. They weren't going anywhere. Lauren was it for them.

"He died too quickly," Liam said savagely.

Noah nodded in agreement.

Both men looked up and went quiet when Lauren walked into
the living room. She was wearing a pair of faded flannel pajama
bottoms and one of Noah's T-shirts. He softened as he took in the
fatigue in her eyes. He liked seeing his shirt on her. Like he was
wrapped around her every minute.

"Morning," she said in a low voice.

She even managed a smile, but Noah knew she had to be
exhausted. She'd woken him and Liam up just after midnight with

soft whimpering. She had been greatly distressed, and when they'd finally managed to wake her, she'd been shaky and distraught.

In a voice that still made Noah's gut tighten, she'd lashed out, asking why? Why was she still plagued by Joel Knight? Why couldn't she just forget and move on? He was dead. Could never hurt her again. She resented the hold he had on her even from the grave.

Liam rose and strode toward where Lauren stood. He pulled her into his arms, hugging her tightly. Then he leaned down to brush a kiss across her mouth.

"Good morning, baby. How are you today?"

At least he hadn't asked her a really dumbass question like, *How did you sleep?*

"Better," she whispered.

She must have seen the doubt in Noah's face, because she smiled and then pulled away from Liam to cross over to where Noah sat. He reached for her, pulling her down into his lap, his arms wrapped securely around her.

"I really am," she said.

He kissed her temple and squeezed. "Glad to hear it."

"Aren't Dillon and Seth coming this morning?" she asked.

Noah nodded. The two men had called the night before and asked to come out this morning.

"Is anything wrong?" she asked, her expression troubled.

Noah squeezed her again. "Not at all. They said they had something they wanted to discuss with me and Liam. Didn't expound. But I'm sure it's nothing."

She didn't look convinced. "It just seems odd that they'd both come all the way out here with Lily being so close to her delivery. With her on bed rest until she goes into labor, her husbands haven't so much as left her side."

Noah hadn't considered that, and now that Lauren brought it up, he too wondered what the two men wanted. Lily had been placed on bed rest three weeks earlier when she'd begun having contractions. Her husbands had wanted to move her to Denver immediately so she'd be close to a large hospital, but she'd been adamant that she wanted to be here. Surrounded by her family. Her husbands hadn't liked it, but they couldn't refuse her anything. And Noah was sure they wanted their family with them when the first Colter grandchild was born as well.

A knock sounded at the door, and Lauren yanked her head up and then looked down at her pajamas and grimaced.

"I'm going to go jump in the shower while you talk to Seth and Dillon."

Noah kissed her again as Liam headed for the door. "Don't worry, okay? I'm sure nothing is wrong or they would have come out and said so rather than make a deal out of coming out to talk to us."

She nodded and smiled, her eyes brightening. She leaned down after she rose from his lap, and kissed him long and sweet.

"I love you," she whispered against his mouth.

"Love you too, sweetheart."

She hurried toward the bedroom and closed the door just as Liam returned to the living room, Seth and Dillon right behind him.

Noah rose to shake the two men's hands before motioning for them to sit on the couch in the small living room.

"Is something wrong?" Noah asked cautiously.

Seth looked startled but shook his head. "Not at all. Dillon and I had matters to discuss with you and Liam. About your future here. And Lauren."

He said her name last, more pointedly, and despite the fact they said nothing was wrong, Liam tensed at the mention of her name.

Dillon and Seth exchanged looks and then focused their gazes on Noah and Liam.

"Look, we know this is difficult. For all of you," Dillon said grimly. "We also know you're doing the right thing for Lauren, and we appreciate that. Our entire family does. Especially Max. We've all been worried about Lauren, and the thing is, she's worried too. About you two."

Noah and Liam exchanged quick *what the fuck?* looks. Lauren was worried about *them*? Oh *hell* no. She had enough on her plate without them adding to her worries.

"What the hell do you mean by that?" Liam demanded.

"There's no roundabout way to discuss this," Seth said. "So I'm just going to put it out there. I need a deputy. Jim is retiring soon. He already would have if I'd had a ready replacement. A few years ago when I took over the sheriff's position from Lacy England, she said that Jim wanted to work a few more years to secure his retirement. My other deputies are young. They're good, but I need someone with more experience."

He glanced at Liam. "I'd like you to consider that position. It doesn't pay the moon, but it has good benefits and this is a good town. Not too dangerous. Most importantly, it keeps you here, close to Lauren, and keeps Lauren close to her family."

Liam looked poleaxed. His brows drew together and his lips pressed into a firm line.

"The other thing," Dillon said, breaking the silence. "I need someone who can manage my businesses, the pub in particular. I own several in Clyde, and I'm looking to expand to an Internet presence with the retail stores."

He was looking expectantly at Noah as he spoke, and realization crept up Noah's spine. Noah grimaced.

"Look, I appreciate what you're trying to do here, but it's not necessary. We don't want to be a fucking charity case. We can support Lauren on our own until we figure out what we're going to do."

"Don't piss me off," Dillon growled. "I wouldn't be extending this offer if I didn't absolutely need someone. Neither would Seth pony up something as important as a deputy's position. Too much rides on the man he chooses. In order to keep his job as sheriff, he has to make the town happy."

"I don't even know what to say," Noah murmured.

"Here's the deal," Dillon said bluntly. "I'm out. With Lily having our child in a very short time, there is no way in hell I'm going to put in the hours I've been putting in at the pub and the other businesses. She needs someone with her twenty-four seven. Michael will be cutting back on his practice hours, at least for the first while after the baby gets here, and if Seth hires another deputy to fill Jim's position, then he won't have to put in the extra call hours.

"Now, I want someone I can trust and someone I know will do a good job. Callie could do it, but I don't want to lay that on her. She and Max travel frequently and the thing is, she doesn't need the job. Max has more money than his *grandchildren* will spend in a lifetime. Not to mention, I don't want my sister to shoulder that kind of a load."

"Why did you say Lauren was worried about us?" Liam asked softly. "And how would you know this?"

Seth's mouth turned down into a grimace. "She confided in Mom that she's scared that you both gave up too much for her. That you won't be happy here. She's worried that you'll feel too much pressure to support her and her desire to stay here with family. She's mentioned that she wonders if she shouldn't be willing to go back to New York so that you two can resume your lives and careers, but at the same time, it terrifies her."

"Son of a bitch," Noah muttered. "That's a hell of a note."

Liam didn't look any happier with the news.

"Jesus, and here we've thought that she's still dealing with what happened," Liam said. "I never once imagined she had gotten such a crazy thought in her head that we wouldn't be happy here or that for the love of God, we were making this huge sacrifice for her. Fuck that. We're right where we want to be. That's not changing."

Dillon grinned broadly. "So you'll take the jobs?"

"Whoa. Let's not get ahead of ourselves here," Noah said. "That's a lot to lay on us all at once. While I don't doubt for a minute that Liam could do the job as a deputy, I have zero experience in retail."

Dillon shrugged. "You've run your own business for years. Now you'll be running mine. Business is business. If I didn't think you were capable, believe me, I would not hand over my entire livelihood to you. I have a wife and a child to think about. Those businesses are how I support them, how I support my family."

Noah glanced at Liam again to see a thoughtful look on his friend's face.

"Liam?" Noah asked. "What do you think?"

Liam's expression darkened a bit. "What I think is that we have a lot to talk to Lauren about. And a lot of points to reassure her on. She's our fucking life. And our life is here. There's no sacrifice too big to make to have that life with her."

"This could go a long way in reassuring her," Noah said quietly. "If we had jobs here. Worked with people we like. No amount of talking is going to completely convince her that we're happy. But we can *show* her."

Liam looked at Seth, a grimace etched on his forehead. "Have to tell you. I've been my own boss for a lot of years. I appreciate the offer, and I'll do the best job I can, but I'll warn you now. I'm used to doing things my way and not having a boss hanging over my shoulder all the time."

Seth chuckled. "I never imagined you did. Look, I don't micromanage my deputies. Do the job, and you and I will never have an issue. I'd rather you look at this as a partnership. A shared duty to protect this town. And the people we love."

"I think I can handle that," Liam said slowly.

"What about you?" Dillon asked Noah. "Are you in?"

"Hell, I'd be a fool not to, but we need to at least discuss my salary. I don't come cheap you know, and eventually I plan to have children to support as well."

Dillon threw back his head and laughed.

"You up for a trial by fire? I only have a few weeks until Lily delivers, and when that happens, I'm out. I won't leave her. Not even for an hour. This is too important. She's been through hell before, and over my dead body will that ever happen again."

"Liam and I need to discuss this with Lauren. This affects her too, and I want to be sure she's on board. And evidently, Liam and I haven't been seeing what's going on in her head lately. We thought . . ." He ran a hand through his hair in a weary motion. "She hasn't been sleeping. She still has nightmares. And the fact that she's been stressing about us . . . Goddamn. That guts me. I wish to fuck we'd known. We purposely haven't addressed the issue of what we'll do, because we haven't wanted to spend even one minute away from her. She needs us. We had plenty of time to work it all out, and I wish to fuck she hadn't worked herself in knots over it."

"She's a sweet woman with a heart of gold," Seth said. "She wants what's best for everyone around her. She never thinks of herself."

"That shit's got to stop," Liam said bluntly. "Starting now."

Noah nodded his agreement.

"How about you come into town this afternoon and fill out an application at the sheriff's office?" Seth said to Liam. "There will be a town council meeting in a few days to announce Jim's retirement. He'll be happy that I found a replacement so soon, because he promised to stay on until I hired someone else, but he wants out now. And the council will listen to my recommendation. As long as you don't have any skeletons in your closet, you'll be a shoo-in. With your military background and your experience in personal security, the town will feel safe in your hands."

"I don't know what to say," Liam said. "Noah and I appreciate this. More than you could possibly know."

"You're family," Dillon said with a grin. "One of us now. Which means you'll have the dads breathing down your neck, making sure you stay on your toes. Mom will smother you with hugs and take over your lives. And of course babysitting the new niece or nephew will keep you occupied from time to time."

"That goes both ways," Liam said, a gleam in his eyes. "I'm planning to have a few munchkins myself, and I can't think of a better place to leave them than with their aunt and *three* uncles."

Wonder seeped into Noah's heart. How easily they sat talking about the future. A future with Lauren. And their children. The families spending time together and babysitting.

But first . . . First they had to ease Lauren's fears and make sure she knew that there was nothing in the world they wouldn't do to have her with them forever.

CHAPTER 2

❧

LAUREN brushed out her hair and strained her ear toward the door, trying to figure out if Seth and Dillon were still here. She wasn't sure what they'd wanted to discuss with Liam and Noah, but she didn't want to intrude.

Her hand shook slightly as she laid the brush down and stared back at her reflection. She needed no one to point out the fact that she still had shadows in her eyes. She could see that herself. And no matter what she did, she couldn't seem to shake the residual fear, shame and worry from her heart.

She sighed. It was senseless, all of it. Joel couldn't hurt her. His sidekick couldn't hurt her. He was going to rot in jail, of that she had no doubt. And even now, the district attorney in New York was cleaning house. The scandal had already been blasted across the media.

She'd been terrified that somehow her name would be linked to it all. That there was nowhere she could escape her past. She'd watched the news for four straight nights, glued to the television, despite Liam's and Noah's objections. They hadn't wanted her to see it, to dwell on it. They wanted her to put it behind her. But she'd needed to know if she was somehow linked to it all.

But no, the news had been full of the resulting arrests and the splashing about of prominent names on the screens. All involved in a prostitution ring.

She shivered, more grateful than ever that the D.A. hadn't involved her. That he hadn't needed to. She would have likely been a target for a lot of people if it had been known she was the one who turned over the information to the authorities.

"Baby?"

Lauren picked her head up, startled by the soft endearment Liam whispered. He was standing behind her, in the doorway of the bedroom, watching her intently. Concern was bright in his eyes, and she hastily smiled to reassure him. She didn't want them worrying. They worried far too much and had lost as much sleep as she had since they'd come home.

One day . . . One day it would all be behind them. Not so fresh in her memories or in her mind. Until then, all she could do was take it one day at a time, knowing that each day that passed was one day closer to redemption. Forgiveness. *Self-forgiveness*.

Liam walked over and slid his hands over her shoulders, squeezing gently before gathering the strands of hair in his hand and allowing them to slide over his fingers.

"You're so beautiful," he said. "Have I told you today that I love you?"

Her smile grew bigger and her chest tightened.

"Yeah, you have, but that's one thing I'll never grow tired of hearing."

He leaned down, sweeping her hair aside so he could kiss her neck. A shiver overtook her, prickling her skin as chill bumps popped and danced their way across her flesh.

"It's a good thing," he murmured. "Because I'm never going to get tired of telling you."

He kissed her again before righting himself.

"Come into the living room. Noah and I have some things we'd like to talk to you about."

Worry hit her square in the chest. Knotted her throat. Her gaze flew upward, searching his expression for any sign of . . . Of what? Discontent? Unhappiness?

"Don't look like that, baby," he said, his voice calm and reassuring. "You worry far too much, and after we have this talk, I intend to make sure you don't worry again."

Her brow furrowed as she took in his words. Whatever did they want to talk about?

He helped her to her feet, tucked her into his side and then led her out of the bedroom and into the living room, where Noah was pacing back and forth in front of the fireplace.

Noah stopped when he saw her, and love warmed his eyes. There was a softness in his expression that hadn't been there before. He held out his hand to her and she left Liam, moving quickly across the room to stand next to Noah.

He pulled her into his arms and pressed his lips to her forehead.

"Need to talk to you, sweetheart. Me and Liam. We've got a lot to say. And we want you to listen."

She sucked in her breath, ignoring Liam's earlier command not to worry. Something was going on. Dread settled over her. Worry crowded her mind.

Noah cursed softly before pulling her toward the couch. He settled her down, and then he and Liam promptly took seats on either side of her.

"Look at me, Lauren," Noah said.

She glanced between him and Liam, but she wanted to see them both. Wanted to be able to look at them both. So she slid from the couch, onto her knees in front of them, and turned to face them. Needing reassurance, she slipped her hands into theirs, lacing their fingers tightly.

Liam pulled her hand to his mouth and pressed a kiss into her palm. That more than anything soothed her concerns. There was love and warmth in both their eyes. And worry. It struck her that while she was busy being so worried—about many things—that they had been every bit as worried. If not more.

Her heart softened. She was going to get through this difficult time, damn it. She wanted them to be happy. She wanted herself to be happy. And she wanted them all to be happy together.

"We've been offered jobs here," Noah said.

Her eyebrows went up. She hadn't even realized they'd been looking. She'd been scared because they'd shown no sign of making this their permanent home. She'd wondered if they were having second thoughts.

"When? How?" she asked.

Liam smiled. "Seth wants me to replace a retiring deputy."

"And Dillon wants me to take over and run his businesses here. He owns many. Far more than I'd imagined. Hell, he owns almost the whole damn town of Clyde, including the building the city rents as the sheriff's department."

Lauren frowned. "But what will he do?"

"He's going to be with Lily," Noah explained. "They don't want her to ever go through what she did with her first baby. It nearly destroyed her, and they're all determined to be with her every minute of the day. Dillon wants to pull back. Have me run his businesses. He's proposed a partnership. He'll still own everything, but I get a percentage plus a salary."

Hope flared, warm and dizzying. Her breath sped up as she

imagined her life. Here. With the two men she loved more than anything. Them happy. Surrounded by friends and family. It was more than she could bear to dream about.

"And what do you and Liam think about those jobs?" she asked quietly.

"Baby, I'd dig fucking ditches if it meant having a life with you," Liam said.

She turned her troubled gaze on him. "But don't you see? I want you and Noah to be *happy*. I don't want you to sacrifice—"

Noah held up his hand. "I've heard about enough of that word today. Wouldn't care if I never heard it again. There is no sacrifice I wouldn't make for you, Lauren. Nothing I wouldn't do to have a life with you. But honey, this is no sacrifice. Liam will make a great cop, and I'll be a damn good business manager. But even if we were flipping burgers . . . Honey, you don't get it. We'd be happy doing *anything* if it meant being with you."

Her eyes widened and she stared up at them, transfixed by the determination on their faces. "You mean that, don't you?"

Liam sighed. "Baby, I don't know how we can make ourselves any clearer."

She threw an arm around each of them, hugging them to her as she huddled between them.

"Oh God, I've been so scared," she whispered. "So worried and so afraid. I want this so much. But I want you both to be happy. It wasn't fair that you had to make all the sacrifices."

Noah interrupted her with a displeased growl.

She giggled and then said, "Okay. Not sacrifices, but your lives were the ones that changed. You moved away from everything you've worked so hard to achieve, further away from your family. All for me. And what did I give up? Nothing. It wasn't *fair*."

"At the risk of pissing Noah off for using the S word again, love is about sacrifice, Lauren. Love is giving, not taking. Love is what you do for the person you can't live without. And don't tell me you've made no sacrifices. That's bullshit. What about when you sacrificed the most precious thing in the world to us? Your *life*, Lauren. You put yourself in harm's way to keep me and Noah safe. I'll never forget it. I go to sleep at night dreaming about it. That you were taken by that bastard because you saved me and Noah. What the hell are we doing that even comes close to that?"

She didn't have an answer for that.

"Hell, we get to work with people we like. We've been adopted into a huge-ass, wonderful family. And we have *you*. What more could we possibly ask for?"

"This is really going to work," she breathed. "Oh my God. All my dreams. They're coming true."

"Except one, honey. And don't think Liam and I aren't going to deliver that one as well."

Puzzled, she cocked her head to the side, not knowing what he was talking about.

"Your own home," Liam said quietly. "On your own piece of land. Seth and Dillon also informed us that their parents are sectioning off ten acres across the meadow from Max and Callie. It's a wedding gift to us. And then we're going to build your dream home right there in the middle of your family."

Tears swam in her eyes, making everything go glossy and shiny in front of her. Unable to call them back, she wiped at the damp trail marking her cheeks.

"I don't know what to say," she choked out. "I'll live right there by my brother. Callie. And Holly and the dads. I don't know of anything more perfect."

Noah smiled gently at her. "I do."

"What's that?" she asked softly.

"The day you give birth to our first child in that home, on that mountain, surrounded by your family."

"Oh Noah," she said, her voice cracking. "I don't know what I'd do without you and Liam. You are my very heart. My soul. I love you both so much. Do we have to wait a long time to have children? I can't think of anything more terrific than to provide Lily's child with a playmate close in age. And other babies. Oh Liam. Just think of all the fun we'll have with so many children. A whole new generation to grow up free and loved on this mountain."

Both men's eyes softened with love and anticipation. Noah caressed her back, smoothing his hand up and down as she hugged them again.

"And I know Max and Callie are waiting a bit. They both agree that Callie is young and they want to see so much of the world, but I just know that when we have our children, they'll want their own."

Liam chuckled. "You're a year younger than Callie, baby. Are you sure you want children so soon? We have all the time in the world."

She smiled, so big that her cheeks ached from the strain. Joy was bursting from her soul. After so many weeks of worrying, of trying to forget her past, she was getting a glimpse of a future brighter than the sun.

"I've always wanted a big family. And I don't want to be too old to enjoy them nor do I want to be old and gray when they finally leave the nest. But if you two want to wait, until we're more settled that is . . ."

Noah put his finger over her lips. "We want children, Lauren. Just as soon as you're ready for them. But maybe we should wait just a little while. At least until you're more comfortable making love to us."

Heat flushed her cheeks and she dropped her gaze guiltily.

"Don't look like that, baby," Liam said in an aching voice. "We aren't pressuring you. We'd wait forever and that's a fact. It was just a matter-of fact-statement, one that I agree with, that perhaps we need a little time together so you're certain of our love and commitment, and you have time to deal with what you've been through before we take that leap."

"I want to make love to you," she whispered. "I ache at night. I want it more than anything."

Liam brushed a kiss over her forehead. "And we want to make love to you. But only when you're ready. Until then, we're quite content to hold you. To love you. To spend each day with you just as we are."

She smiled again, giddy over the talk of the future. "It's happening. It's really happening. Our life here. A home. Children. Family. Oh I don't even know what to say. I feel like bursting!"

Noah chuckled. "One day at a time, honey. We'll get there."

"Feel like running into town with us?" Liam asked. "Seth wants me to go down and fill out an application so he can expedite my hiring. Thought we'd run you by Lily's while we do our business in town."

"Oh, I'd love that," she said. "It's been a few days since I saw her last, and I know she's going stir-crazy. She texted me all day yesterday. Me and Callie."

"Then what do you say we pack up and head into town. After we're done, we'll buy you dinner," Noah offered.

She kissed them both, letting her lips linger over theirs, tasting them, inhaling their scents. "I can't think of a better way to spend the evening."

CHAPTER 3

L ILY Colter was propped up in her bed, a mound of pillows supporting her back, when Lauren walked into her bedroom. Lily's face immediately lit up, and she held out her arm for a hug when Lauren got closer.

"I'm so glad you came over!" Lily exclaimed. "I'm about to go out of my mind. Bed rest is for the birds."

Lauren laughed and slid onto the edge of the bed to sit next to Lily.

"You've had your husbands to entertain you, surely."

Lily rolled her eyes. "They're driving me crazier than the bed rest is."

But even as she said it, her eyes softened and glowed with so much love.

"They're so determined that I not feel one ounce of worry," Lily said softly. "They've been wonderful. Everyone has been wonderful. Holly and even the dads come over at least once a day to reassure me that I won't lift a finger after the baby comes. I feel guilty, actually."

Lauren lifted an eyebrow. "Guilty?"

Lily sighed. "They're so worried that having the baby will bring back all the memories of when I had—and lost—Rose. And the thing is, I don't have those worries anymore. They've proved to me time and time again that I can count on them. That I'll never be alone. That I don't have to go through it alone. I wish I could make them see that. That I trust them implicitly. That I don't have any worries that what happened with Rose will happen this time."

Lauren squeezed her hand. "They love you."

"And I love them," Lily said softly. "If I hadn't acted like such a freak when I found out I was pregnant, they wouldn't be so stressed over how I'm coping. But the truth is, I'm so excited to meet our child, that I'm wishing away my days, counting down to when he or she will be here. The very last thing on my mind is concern that things will be like they were before."

"You weren't a freak," Lauren said fiercely. "You're human. And it was a shock. When you had time to digest it all, you were wonderful. And Christmas. We'll never have a more wonderful Christmas than we did last year."

"Oh yes, we will," Lily said, her smile blazing across her face. "This year we'll have the first Colter grandchild, and we'll all be together. You and Noah and Liam too! What could be more perfect?"

"Maybe when we have a child as well," Lauren said with a grin.

Lily laughed. "Listen to us. Saying each year will be better than the last when the ones we've had have been pretty darn spectacular."

"But they will be," Lauren said. "Just think. Each year. More surprises. The family growing. Us all so happy."

Lily squeezed her hand. "You're right. We only have it getting better and better to look forward to. That's pretty special."

"So, how are you?" Lauren said, directing the conversation back to Lily.

Lily sighed. "Still having contractions off and on. I try not to say anything to the guys because they'll just worry and try to convince me that we need to move to Denver until the baby is born."

Lauren's brow wrinkled, her troubled gaze finding Lily's. "Maybe that's for the best. We don't exactly have the best medical care here."

Lily smiled, a warm glow overtaking her eyes. "But I want it born here. Right here in this house. Just like Seth and Michael were born in Holly and the dads' cabin. What could be more special than bringing the next generation of Colter children into the world right here in these mountains?"

Lauren looked at her in shock. "Do they know that's what you plan?"

Lily slowly shook her head. "They are adamant that we leave this next weekend. They already worry we're cutting too close to the delivery date in two and a half weeks."

"So what are you going to do? They'll flip!"

Lily smiled. "I'm just taking it one day at a time and hoping the baby decides to come a little early."

She broke off, a grimace tightening her face momentarily. Her body seemed to spasm, and then she relaxed, sinking back into the pillows.

"Lily, was that a contraction?" Lauren asked in concern.

"Yeah," Lily breathed out. "They've become stronger in the last several hours. But still very irregular. I'll be glad when this is over."

"But if they've gotten stronger, isn't that something that should be of concern?"

Lauren couldn't keep the anxiety out of her voice. She wanted to go and get Lily's husbands, or at least one of them, but she didn't want to rat Lily out. Even if Lauren was very concerned over these contractions.

Lily shook her head. "I don't think so. With Rose, I definitely knew when it was time. They were stronger with time and more regular."

"Uhm, Lily, I hate to be the one to point this out to you, but you just said they were getting stronger. If they were Braxton Hicks, they wouldn't be stronger. And you know not every pregnancy and birth is the same. Haven't you listened to Holly's stories of when her children were born? No two were ever the same, which is why of the four, only one was born in a hospital!"

Lily started to speak, but then her eyes widened and they both looked down as moisture seeped into the bed, dampening the sheets.

"Oh no," Lily breathed out. "I think my water just broke."

CHAPTER 4

L AUREN raced from Lily's bedroom and into the living room, where Michael was sitting. Seth and Dillon were both still in town but thankfully, town was only a few minutes away.

Michael looked up with a frown when Lauren screeched to a halt in front of him. "Lauren? What's wrong?"

"It's Lily," she said breathlessly.

Michael was on his feet before she got it all out. She put her hand out to his arm to restrain him. She hated the fear in his eyes. The instant panic. And she wanted to reassure him. She shouldn't have freaked out but oh my God, Lily was in labor. Here. Not in a hospital, but *here*.

"She's in labor, Michael. Probably has been for a while. Her water just broke. But she didn't know. Don't be angry with her."

Michael stared at her in stupefaction. "Angry? Why the hell would I be angry with her?"

His expression softened and he purposely bit back a further

response. She ducked her head because she knew none of the Colters were anything like Joel. They'd never hurt a woman. But her instinct was to protect someone she cared a great deal about. She didn't want any of the Colters angry with Lily over the fact she'd be granted her fondest wish. To give birth to their child in her home.

Michael squeezed her hand and smiled. "It'll be okay, Lauren. Can you do me a favor, please? Can you call Seth and Dillon and then call my mom and the dads? Let them know what's going on, and tell them to hurry. I need to go check Lily and see just how close she is."

Lauren nodded vigorously and was already reaching for her cell phone when Michael strode away toward the bedroom where Lily lay.

Michael entered the bedroom to see Lily struggling to get out of bed. She was prying the wet sheet away with a grimace and then she bent over, holding her stomach, her entire face beaded with strain.

"Baby," Michael said lovingly as he went to her, holding and supporting her as she breathed through a contraction.

She glanced up, her eyes wide with fear. "I wasn't afraid before, Michael. I wasn't! But oh God, it's real. It's here. What do I *do*?"

The panic in her voice hit him right in the chest, and he went absolutely soft with love. For her. For their child.

He hugged her to him, placing his splayed palm over her still-rippling belly.

"We're going to have a baby," he said cheerfully.

She looked at him with such relief in her eyes that it gutted him.

"First thing we need to do is strip these sheets off the bed and get you into something dry and warm. Then I'm going to see just how far along in this process you are."

"Is there anything I can do to help?" Lauren asked from the door.

Michael turned to see a very worried Lauren standing there.

"I called everyone. They're freaking out but they're on their way. All of them."

Michael nodded. "Can you help Lily into a new gown while I strip off the sheets and replace them?"

Lauren rushed forward and took Lily's arm, guiding her toward the chest of drawers where her nightclothes were folded. Michael made quick work of the bed and then positioned the pillows so she'd have plenty of back support. When the others got there, he'd put Dillon and Seth on point to give her all the support she needed.

Right now he was going to do everything in his power to ensure that Lily was calm, even if he was about to lose his fucking mind.

Give him an animal? He could deal. But delivering his own child? Suddenly he wished like hell the dads were already here. They'd delivered three of their children. He could use some reassurance, because all he could think was what if something went wrong? What if he screwed up? He could never face Lily again if he did anything to harm her or their child. And Lily simply couldn't bear another loss.

"Michael?"

His wife's soft, sweet voice filtered through his panicked thoughts. He turned to see her watching him, her eyes shining with love. She put her hand on his arm and then leaned into him, nestling her swollen body close to his.

"It's going to be okay," she whispered.

How like her to be the one comforting him when he should be doing everything in his power to offer her reassurance.

He smiled and squeezed her close just as her body went tense and a low moan slipped from her lips.

"Let's get you comfortable," he said in a husky voice laced with emotion.

"I'll go watch for the others," Lauren said anxiously. "Seth and Dillon seemed . . . stressed."

Lily smiled as Michael guided her toward the bed. "I just bet they did. Poor guys."

Michael kissed her forehead and then helped her settle down. He gently pulled her gown to her waist so he could see if she was crowning. God, he hoped she wasn't. Not yet. He at least wanted the others present before their baby slid into his waiting hands.

She bent her knees and spread them, giving him access. When he got a glimpse, he sucked in his breath. Oh shit. She *was* crowning. Not hugely, but the baby's head was *right there*.

He felt light-headed. His hands shook. Hell, he didn't have anything.

"Lauren, get me my med kit! It's on the counter. And blankets. I need blankets and some water to clean Lily and the baby when we're done."

"Is it time?" Lily asked, her body tensing once more. "Oh God, Michael, I need to push. What's happening? Is the baby coming now?"

He lifted his head so she could see him over her belly. "Yes, honey. It's time. But I don't want you to push yet, okay? I need to get a few things. It's going to be all right. I swear it. Okay? Trust me?"

Her eyes glowed warm as she blew out the rest of her breath in a whoosh. "I do trust you, Michael. You won't let anything happen to our child."

"Or to you," he said softly. "You're my life, Lily. *Our* life. I'll go to hell and back to keep you with me. Never doubt it."

She smiled and nodded. "I love you too, you know."

"Yeah. I do."

Just then a commotion sounded in the living room, and Michael breathed a huge sigh of relief. Reinforcements were here.

Seth and Dillon burst into the bedroom, a crazed look in their eyes.

"What the hell is going on?" Dillon demanded. "Lauren said she's having the baby *now*."

Seth went immediately to Lily's side, his forehead creased in concern.

"That she is," Michael said calmly. "I need you both to not freak out and give me a hand here. There's no way to get her to the hospital in time. The baby will be born right here in our bedroom."

Dillon looked deranged, but then he made a concerted effort to collect himself. His hands were shaking violently, though, as he went to Lily's other side.

Seth took Lily's hand and curled his fingers around it. Then he kissed her temple, fear stark in his eyes.

"What do you need us to do?" Seth asked hoarsely.

"Lauren is getting my med kit. I need a suction, scissors to cut the cord and something to tie it off with. We also need some blankets to wrap the baby in and something to clean up the baby and Lily afterward."

"I can do that," Dillon said. "Don't worry, sweetheart. We'll do this. Okay?"

Despite the contractions wracking her body and her fighting the urge to push, Lily laughed. "I'm fine, guys. Really. I can do this. *We* can do this."

"Where the fuck are the dads?" Seth muttered. "They're the ones with all the childbirth experience."

Lily laughed again. "That's so funny. One would think you'd be looking to your mother at a time like this, and instead you want to know where the hell the dads are."

"Mom didn't deliver three babies at home," Dillon said in a disgruntled voice. "The dads did."

Lily rolled her eyes. "She didn't? What exactly do you call push-ing a kid the size of a small watermelon out of her womb?"

"How can you joke at a time like this?" Seth asked, the panic rising in his voice.

"It's either laugh or cry," Lily said. "I'm scared to death!"

Dillon and Seth immediately looked contrite. They gathered in close to her, kissing her and offering reassurance.

"We're assholes," Seth said. "Sorry, honey. But don't be scared. Between the family we'll get this baby safely here."

She reached up and stroked his cheek. "I know we will."

Another sound came from the living room, and Michael realized that his mom and the dads were here. Relief soared. Hell, he had a medical degree. He'd delivered every kind of animal imaginable, and yet he was relieved that his fathers were here. But they'd always been his rocks. Mom and the dads.

"Need help, son?" Adam said from the bedroom doorway.

Holly Colter shoved Adam aside and hurried for the bed, where Lily sat propped against the pillows. She took Lily's hand from Dillon and squeezed reassuringly.

"It's going to be okay, baby. The dads are here, and they have more experience with childbirth than most women do!"

"That's what I'm counting on," Lily said just before she went silent as another contraction hit.

"I can't hold off any longer," Lily panted. Her face was red with strain and her cheeks puffed outward as her entire body coiled into a knot.

Lauren rushed in with all the things Michael had asked for, and Ryan took them from her and began arranging them on the side of the bed.

"Tell us what you want to do, son," Ethan said. "Though I have a feeling our young lady here planned it this way, and she probably wants you to deliver her child. If she talked to your mother at all, then the idea would have been planted that this baby would be born here."

Holly's lips tightened and Lily flashed a guilty smile.

"Busted," Lily murmured.

"Is that what you really want?" Dillon asked as he wiped her hair from her brow.

Lily glanced up at Dillon and then to Seth and finally at Michael. "Yes," she said quietly. "I want our child to be born here. Delivered by his fathers. I want our children to grow up in this house just like you all did in the house you were born. I can't think of a better way to usher in the next generation of Colters."

Tears gleamed brightly in his mother's eyes. The dads were no less affected. Adam wiped at his face before lowering his hand to touch his wife's shoulder.

"Then that's what we'll do," Seth said, kissing Lily again. Then he looked up at Michael. "What do you need us to do?"

"Stay there and support Lily," Michael said. "Hold her, support her, talk to her. Encourage her. She needs to push now so our child can be born."

In the distance he heard Callie's and Max's voices. Knew they were here. Satisfaction gripped Michael. Lily was right. What better way for their child to be born then right here, surrounded by parents and grandparents. Aunts and uncles.

"Help me," Lily said, breathless as she struggled upward.

Seth and Dillon went into action, propping her forward like she wanted. They each wrapped an arm around her back, anchoring her in place.

Adam quickly went to work sorting through all the things Lauren had brought in. Michael spread a blanket over the mattress and tucked it under Lily's bottom. The baby's head bulged, pressing forward, stretching Lily as it prepared to make its entrance into the world.

"Okay, honey. Bear down with this next contraction okay? I need you to take a deep breath in, hold it and then count to ten."

Her face reddening, she sucked in a breath and then leaned forward, her chin nearly to her chest. Beside her, Dillon began counting.

"Too fast, Dillon. Slow down some," Michael said. "I don't want to rush things and I don't want her pushing too hard. She'll tear. Let's just take things nice and easy and let the baby come in his own time."

He locked gazes with Lily and then his brothers. This was it. The woman they adored beyond reason was gifting them with something more precious than anything in the world. She'd struggled and overcome so much adversity in her young life, and he was determined that she never go down that road again.

When Dillon got to ten, Lily slumped back against Dillon's and Seth's arms, her breath escaping in rapid pants.

"This hurts," she ground out.

Dillon pressed his lips to her temple, his face a wreath of agony on her behalf. Dillon looked as helpless as Michael felt. He'd do anything to spare her this pain.

He'd been so absorbed in monitoring her contraction and the progress of the baby's head, that he hadn't even noticed his mom and the dads had made a discreet exit. Panic nearly overtook him again, and he was tempted to call the dads back. Or at least Adam. Not much rattled him. Except when it came to Holly.

Lily leaned forward, sucked in her breath, and Dillon began to count again.

"That's it!" Michael said excitedly. "It's coming! I've almost got the head. Don't relax until I tell you, honey."

The warm, gooey head slipped into Michael's waiting hands. And then Seth was there, handing Michael the suction and a blanket. Michael suctioned the baby's airway, and then the most wonderful sound he'd ever heard. The baby let out a soft wail that echoed through the room.

"Okay, Lily. Just one more push, honey. Can you do that for me? The baby will be here. Just one more push."

Her body heaved, and then she bore down and the baby slid easily into Michael's grasp. He stared down in befuddlement at the squirming, sticky baby in his palms.

"A son," he said reverently. He glanced up at his brothers and then met Lily's tired gaze. "We have a son!"

Seth quickly helped cut the umbilical cord, and then wrapped his son in a blanket before carrying him very carefully to the head of the bed, where Lily waited.

Her expression was one of awe as Seth laid their son in her arms. Dillon's eyes were bright with unshed tears, but as soon as Lily held their child to her breast, they slid down his cheeks unheeded.

"He's beautiful," she choked out. She lifted her head to stare at her husbands, so much love reflected in her gaze that Michael couldn't breathe.

They'd done it! Mother and baby were fine.

"I need to ensure the placenta is delivered and there is no hemorrhaging," Michael said in a low voice. "Help her nurse him."

No one paid him any attention as he tended to Lily's needs. She barely even registered the placenta being delivered or his carefully cleaning her afterward. He itched to hold his son again. But he was nestled firmly in his mother's arms, sucking at her swollen breast.

He stood at the head, staring down for the longest time until Lily lifted her head and their gazes connected.

"Thank you," she whispered in a voice tight with tears. "Thank you for this. For my son. For another chance. I'll never forget this day. *Never.*"

Michael swallowed back his own tears. "No, thank *you*, honey. For giving us our son. For loving us."

"He's beautiful," Dillon said hoarsely. "The most beautiful baby I've ever seen."

Seth smiled, wiping away his own tears as he gazed down at his wife and child. "You up to letting everyone come in to see the newest Colter? I imagine Mom and the dads are chomping at the bit out there."

"Yeah," Lily whispered. "Let them come. I want them to see their first grandchild."

CHAPTER 5

I'M reminded of when Seth was born," Adam said, his voice aching with memories.

Holly smiled at her three husbands as they sank onto the couch at home. They'd left Lily and the boys just a half hour earlier, and returned home to rest and leave the new parents to fuss over the baby themselves. The boys insisted on bringing Lily and the baby to the hospital the next day so both could be checked out and make sure there weren't any problems. But Holly had a feeling that if Lily got her way, they'd settle for having the doctor come out and tend to mother and child at home.

"Never a more beautiful moment," Ryan said softly.

"I'm reminded of when you came home," Ethan broke in. "That first time I saw you after all those months. Big and swollen with our child. I'll never forget that day. It was the best day of my life."

Adam nodded. "Can't argue there."

Holly sighed and settled between Ryan and Ethan on the couch.

She was just as beautiful, if not more so, as she'd been nearly thirty-five years ago when she'd had Seth. Adam loved her more with every passing day, and he hadn't imagined being able to love her more than when she'd returned to them.

But he had. The day she gave birth to Seth. And then to Michael and Dillon. And finally Callie. The scare she'd given them just last Christmas still lingered in his mind, a shadow that may never fade.

"It's hard to imagine we're grandparents," Holly murmured. Her voice was a little sad, her face drawn, though Adam knew how happy she was to be a grandmother. "The years go by so very fast. I don't know where they've all gone."

"The best are yet to come," Ryan said, pulling her into his side.

"I'm still that young girl falling in love with three men at the same time," she said. "And yet that was a lifetime ago and yesterday all at the same time. I'm not ready to go. I'm not ready for this life to be over. I love it so much. I love you so very much."

Adam's chest clenched, and he read the same dismay on his brothers' faces. They didn't even want to consider a time when they wouldn't be together.

Ethan touched her cheek, his eyes softening in love, the wrinkles at the corners more pronounced than they'd been a decade ago. "Our love is forever, sweetheart. The end of our lives here is only the beginning for us. Not even death can separate us."

"Not to mention we all have a lot of years left," Adam said gruffly. "So don't even think about checking out early. I'll drag you back by your hair if I have to."

Holly laughed and the sound sent sunshine straight to Adam's soul. Her eyes twinkled and the shadows had lifted.

"I have no doubt you'd do just that."

"Count on it," Ryan growled. "Never giving you up, honey. That's a fact."

"They're going to be fine," Holly said with a contented sigh.

"Did you see the boys? I've never seem them that undone. And Lily. There's no more sorrow in her eyes. She positively glowed."

Adam smiled. "Thank you, baby."

She cocked her head, looking at him in puzzlement. "What for?"

Adam leaned over the couch to touch his lips to hers. "For giving me four wonderful children. For giving me a life full of more love than I ever dreamed. For accepting us. For loving us. For coming home to us."

Tears shone brightly in her eyes as she stroked his cheek.

"You know, we never did get around to taking that trip we talked about at Christmas. I distinctly remember discussing a beach, being naked and making love for an entire week."

Ethan chuckled. "That's because you refused to even consider leaving when Lily was pregnant."

"But she's not now," Holly said with a mischievous grin. "I'm thinking after we give them a few weeks to settle into a routine and they don't need as much anymore, that we should pack up and go on that vacation."

"I think that's a very good idea," Ryan murmured as he kissed her again. "I have a distinct need to show my wife how very much I love her."

CHAPTER 6

❧

LAUREN took longer than usual in the bathroom as she prepared for bed. The last several days had been full of activity with the arrival of Caleb James Colter, named for two of his great-grandfathers. The Colters and the Wilders had descended on the younger Colters' home, providing food, childcare, and whatever else was needed to ensure Lily rested and was stress free.

Lauren had delighted in these days. They'd given her a preview of her own future. Her children. Surrounded by family. People who loved her. But mostly of how it would be when she gave Liam and Noah their own child.

They'd been enraptured by Caleb. The entire family was. As if sensing how fragile his mother was, Caleb was the perfect baby. So quiet and sweet. Not fussy at all. He'd been a dream to breast-feed, something that had worn Lily down with her first child. But then true to their word, Lily hadn't lifted so much as a finger.

Holly Colter had gone through like a drill sergeant making a list of duties that covered every need. All Lily had to do was rest and feed the baby.

Lauren let out a happy sigh. She wanted Holly there when she had her own child. She missed her own mother dreadfully. Wished she'd lived to see both Max and Lauren happy and settled. Looking to the arrival of their own children. Holly was that mother figure to her now. And well, the dads were her fathers too. She was one of them. A Colter. Not by name, but in all the ways that mattered.

"Are you okay in there, honey?" Noah called.

She smiled and then slid her hands down the silky lingerie she'd chosen for this occasion. Taking a deep breath, she opened the door and walked out to face the two men who waited for her.

They were sprawled on the bed where she'd told them to wait. As their gazes lifted, sultry heat entered their eyes. They went smoky with desire.

"Where in the hell did you get that?" Liam breathed out. "I definitely would have remembered that."

She grinned and glanced at Noah, whose mouth was open.

But she also saw hope in their eyes. Not that they'd ever push her. They wouldn't even hint or suggest. They simply waited for her to make the first move. And she loved them so dearly for that.

"I want to start practicing for those babies," she said as she crawled onto the end of the bed. "I don't want to use condoms anymore. The timing's not right for me to get pregnant tonight, and well, if it happened, it happens. I'm not going to lose any sleep over it when it's something I want so badly. But I don't want to use anything anymore. If we aren't ready to take the plunge quite yet, then I'll go on birth control. But I want there to be nothing between us. Not anymore."

Liam expelled his breath in a long exhale. "Oh God, baby. We want that too. But are you sure? I mean tonight? We don't mind waiting. We want this to be perfect for you. I'd die before hurting or frightening you."

She ran her hand up his leg to his knee and squeezed. "It *will* be perfect. It couldn't be anything else with you."

Noah leaned up, curled a hand around her nape and brought his mouth to hers. Hungry. He was so hungry. He swallowed up her breaths, his tongue delving deep as though he'd waited years for this moment. And the last six weeks had seemed like years. For her and no doubt for them as they waited so patiently for her to take the next step.

She sighed into his mouth and then sighed again when Liam pushed in on her side, his arm curving around her body. She was right where she belonged. Between the two men she loved and who loved her with everything they had. She didn't doubt that love. Not for a minute. They'd spent every moment of the last six weeks proving to her without words what she meant to them.

"I love you," she whispered. "I love you both so much."

"I love you too, baby," Liam said into her ear.

Noah hauled her forward, falling to his back with her sprawled over him. His eyes glittered over her face, warming her as though it were a tangible touch.

"I love you, honey. Never want you to doubt that for a second. We're going to be together a damn long time. Every day, you'll wake up and Liam and I will be here. Every night when we go to bed, we'll be the last thing you see. And when you wake up, the first thing you see. Us. Our love."

"You're going to make me cry," she said accusingly.

"Don't want you crying," Liam growled. "Screaming our names, yes. Crying, no."

"I like the way you think," she murmured.

"Not that I don't love that lingerie, but think we can dispense with it so we see you naked?" Noah asked, a wicked gleam in his eyes.

"I'm yours to command."

Before she'd even finished, Liam was tugging at her top, sliding it over her head before tossing it aside. Noah pulled at her lacy panties, Liam taking over when he'd worked them over her buttocks.

"Now you," she said, moving off Noah long enough for the two men to take off their underwear.

"Don't have to talk me into it," Liam muttered. "I damn near ripped my underwear the minute you walked out of the bathroom."

She grinned and then swallowed when both men stood by the bed, their erections turgid and straining upward. Liam wrapped his fingers around his length and stroked up and down, coaxing it to further rigidity.

She licked her lips and both men groaned.

"Hell, honey," Noah rasped out. "Don't do that. Not when we want to make this perfect and make love to you like nobody's ever made love to you before. You make me think of nothing but having those sweet lips wrapped around my dick, and that's not what I want to happen tonight."

"Then what *do* you want to happen?" she asked huskily.

"Tonight is all about you," Liam murmured. "Us loving you. Showing you our love."

"Then what are you waiting for?" she teased.

"Not a damn thing," Noah growled.

Liam picked her up, cradled her in his arms and then gently put her down on the bed, laying her out like a feast before the two men.

They caressed her, hands everywhere, coaxing and soothing. They followed with their mouths, licking over her skin, sucking at her most sensitive spots until she was a writhing mess.

Noah's tongue, hot and rough, slid over her clit, eliciting a sharp gasp. Liam licked and sucked at her nipples, taking each in turn, forming rigid peaks that strained and begged for more.

Her thighs began to shake when Noah pushed his tongue inside her, licking from the inside out. He fucked in and out with that wicked tongue until she was crying his name over and over. Then he slipped two fingers inside, moving his mouth upward so he could tease her clit again.

"Noah, please! I don't want to come. Not yet. It's too soon. I want you both inside me!"

He chuckled, the sound vibrating over her sensitive flesh. She could almost come from that alone. She was perched high, precariously close to tumbling right over the edge, and she didn't want to. Not until they were both inside her. Flesh to flesh. Nothing separating them.

She wanted to feel them come inside her. Didn't want their semen trapped in the latex, shielded within. She wanted everything they had to give.

Liam's lips covered hers, hot, wet, his tongue sliding deep inside her mouth. She licked back, tasting him, inhaling his air, savoring it before returning it back to him.

"I love you," he said, the words escaping into her mouth. "So damn much, Lauren."

"I love you too," she whispered back before kissing him into silence once more.

"I want that sweet ass tonight," Noah said, his voice laced with want and need. "Liam had it last time. It's mine tonight."

She closed her eyes as images of that night weeks ago. Before her world went to hell again. The night when they'd pledged so much to one another. When they'd both taken her at the same time. What she'd begged them to do. Tonight would be about reestablishing that connection. Not broken. Merely tested.

"Can you get on top of me, baby?" Liam whispered against her mouth. "And let Noah have that pretty ass?"

She moaned. She could do anything they wanted as long as it meant both of them being inside her.

Noah left his spot between her legs, giving her one last long lick that left her quivering, right on the edge.

Carefully the two men turned her, Liam sliding underneath before reaching for her hips to move her up his body to straddle him.

"We're going to take this nice and slow, baby. I'm going to get inside you first. Make sure you're damn close when Noah takes your ass. We'll make it good. Like before. Trust us, Lauren."

Liam reached to grasp his cock, and with his other hand gripping her hip, he eased her upward, tucking the head of his penis to her opening. She closed her eyes, savoring that first touch. How she stretched to accommodate him. The sinful sensation of him pushing inside her.

They both moaned low in their throats as she took more of him. She braced her palms against his taut belly and lowered herself still more.

When she settled onto his hips, he smoothed his hands over her belly and then up to cup her breasts, caressing her nipples between his fingers until they were hard and puckered.

"Is she ready for me?" Noah asked in a low voice. "I don't want to hurt her."

Lauren smiled at the worry in his voice. He was bigger than Liam, which was probably why Liam had taken her anally the one time before.

"Give me a minute," Liam said.

He continued his gentle assault on her breasts and then slid one hand down between their legs, where they were joined. He stroked over her clit, rubbing slowly in a circular motion until she went wet around his cock.

"She's ready," he said in satisfaction.

"Spread her for me," Noah said, an edge to his voice that made her shiver.

Liam slid his hands around her waist and then over her buttocks before cupping them with his palms. He gently squeezed and then spread her to Noah. Noah's finger rubbed down the seam, spreading slick lubricant in its wake. Then he pushed inward with a finger, easing more inside her.

Where on earth had he gotten lubricant, and how had he done so without her knowing? But then she'd been pretty occupied with Liam for the last moments. And it was likely they'd planned for this. Eventually . . .

She smiled, confident in their desire. That she was never far from their minds and neither was their making love to her.

"Relax, honey. I'm going to push inside you now. Just breathe and try not to fight it," Noah said.

She automatically tensed the moment the blunt head of his penis nudged her entrance. Noah's hands caressed up and down her sides. Over her back, into her hair, petting and relaxing her once more.

She moaned again when he began to breach her opening. Relentless, with just enough steady pressure. She opened around him, greedy for his possession. She wanted both men inside her. Deep. Hard. A part of her. Forever.

"Almost there, honey."

She sighed and closed her eyes.

"Open those pretty eyes, baby. I want to see them," Liam rumbled.

She complied, gazing down at him, allowing all her love to show.

The burn increased and then suddenly her body gave way, taking him all the way inside. He rested a moment, his pelvis pressed flat against her ass. Never had she felt anything to compare to this. Right here. Right now. Like missing pieces to a puzzle. Finally complete. Whole.

Noah pressed a kiss to the middle of her back and then gently eased back. She let out a soft groan, and then he pushed forward again. With more force this time. He rocked her against Liam, and Liam was waiting, his arms surrounding her. Holding her. Supporting her. Never letting her go.

Both men began an alternating rhythm. Thrusting. Withdrawing. Back and forth. Deep and then deeper still.

Her body was taut. Tension coiled in her muscles, becoming tighter with every passing second as her orgasm rose and sharpened.

"Never felt anything so sweet," Noah murmured. "Your love, honey. Never had anything sweeter. Never will."

Bracing herself on Liam's chest, she pushed back, taking a more active part in the lovemaking. They all found a rhythm. Perfect harmony. Moving in unison. With one accord. Like they were meant to be.

"Want you there first," Liam whispered. "I want to see you come apart in our arms. Fall, Lauren. Let go. We'll catch you. We'll always catch you."

His words sent her spinning out of control. The room tilted and blurred. All she could see was Liam's face. His eyes. Beautiful and so full of love.

Her breath caught, knotting in her throat until her chest felt like it would explode.

And then she let go.

And as Liam had promised, he was there to catch her. He gathered her in his arms, holding her close as Noah thrust into her harder, faster.

Liam arched his body upward, his muscles as tight as hers had been. Strain was evident in his face, but his eyes never left her face.

Then Noah lunged forward one last time. With a shout, he thrust deep and then remained there, his body jerking spasmodically against hers. Liam's muffled curse rose and then he groaned harshly, his body bowed, straining under hers and Noah's weight.

Both men were breathing hard, plastered against her. She was sandwiched between them, one heartbeat against her back, the other against her cheek. Never had she felt safer or more loved than she did right now in their arms.

She emitted a dreamy sigh and then let out a sound of protest when Noah began to withdraw.

He kissed her back again, right at the small, before pulling the rest of the way out.

"Need to clean you up, honey," he said gently. "I'll be right back."

She lay there on Liam, his arms wrapped around her body, holding her snugly to his, him still deeply embedded inside her.

"Was that okay?" Liam murmured.

She smiled against his chest. "Oh yeah. Perfect."

He squeezed her. "I'm glad. Welcome home, baby."

Tears blurred her vision. She was home. Right where she belonged. But she couldn't ever truly be at home until the men she loved were with her. Fully. And now they were.

Noah returned, wiping a warm cloth over her skin to clean her. Then Liam gently lifted her, pulling free from her body in a hot rush. They laid her down and finished the job Noah had started.

When they were done, Noah tossed the cloth in the direction of the bathroom and then climbed into bed next to Lauren. He pulled the covers over her while Liam settled on her other side.

"Now, there's something we want to discuss with you," Liam said.

Her eyes widened.

"Don't look like that, honey. It's nothing bad. Well, I hope to fuck it's not."

She laughed at the sudden uncertainty in his voice.

Liam was more serious, though. His expression never faltered as he took her hand, guiding it to his mouth. Then he reached back and into the nightstand to pull out a small box. Putting it between them, he glanced up at Noah as if waiting for his friend to speak.

"I know we discussed it on the flight home. It wasn't the best time, and I regret bringing it up when your world had been upended. But there's not a more perfect time than right now when you're in our arms, soft and sleepy from making love to both of us."

"What is it, Noah?" she asked quietly.

Liam cleared his throat. "We want you to marry us, Lauren."

As he spoke, he opened the box and pulled out a sparkling diamond ring. Her hand shook as he carefully slid it onto her third finger. Then he kissed it.

"I know we discussed it," Noah continued. "But we want to ask you now. Now that you've had time to process it and what our life would be like together."

"We talked to the Colters," Liam said. "Found out how they did their ceremonies. Holly is dying for you to be married right where she married her husbands, and Lily married hers, and where Max and Callie both got married."

"In their garden right there on their mountain," Lauren said in awe. "Oh that would be perfect!"

"Then is that a yes?" Noah asked hesitantly.

She flew into his arms, knocking him over onto his back as she hovered above him. She kissed every inch of his face until he was laughing and begging for mercy. Then she launched herself at Liam and gave him the same treatment.

"Yes!" she exclaimed. "Oh my God, yes I'll marry you!"

"Now, about those babies . . ." Liam said with a grin. "Just how serious were you?"

"Very," she said, returning his grin. "Think you two can help me out on that?"

"We'll sure as hell try," Noah murmured as he rolled her underneath him again.

CHAPTER 7

⁂

LAUREN, Liam and Noah were married under the same arch where Holly Colter had married her husbands nearly thirty-five years before. As had Max and Callie, and Lily, Seth, Michael and Dillon. Gathered was the entire Colter family. Holly. The dads. Seth, Dillon, Michael and Lily with little Caleb. Max and Callie.

They all surrounded Lauren Wilder as she pledged her life and love to Liam and Noah, and it was decided that from that day forth, Lauren would take the name Lauren Sullivan-Prescott to honor both the men who in turn pledged their love and devotion to her for all eternity.

They married when the aspens had turned, their incandescent glitter transforming the landscape into a simmering sea of gold. It was the same month that Holly Colter had returned to her husband all those years ago, pregnant with their first child.

Over the years, many children were born to the Wilders, Colters and Sullivan-Prescotts. They grew up secure in the love of the older

Colter generation, guided by the gentle hand of Holly Colter and her steadfast husbands, who swore to love her into the next life and beyond.

The children ran wild and free over the mountains where the Colters had lived for decades. They grew up with an unshakable purpose, confident and backed by the love of Colters' Legacy.